Shards
of the
Glass Slipper

Queen Cinder

by Roy A. Mauritsen

www.shardsoftheglassslipper.com

Shards Of The Glass Slipper: Queen Cinder
Published by Padwolf Publishing, Inc.
Padwolf Publishing & logo are registered trademarks of Padwolf Publishing, Inc.

Padwolf Publishing Inc.
PO Box 117 Yulan, NY 12719
www.padwolf.com

Cover art & book design by Roy Mauritsen
First Printing, 2012
Printed in the United States of America

ISBN 978-1-890096-48-9

Acknowledgements

It seemed to me in the process of writing this novel that in fact no book is truly written by one person—well, maybe a few literary greats out there, but at best even that is highly suspect. There are many that help to shape a book along the way. From feedback of agents and critique groups to editors and writer conferences, and friends, family and coworkers, the story is influenced by many, but in the end it is the author who must sit alone and forge the work, sifting through ideas, suggestions, and opinions to marry it with the vision that started long ago with a single, crazy idea to write a novel.

I'd like to take a moment to acknowledge some people for their love and support and for their help along the way: My mother, my dad, Diane Mauritsen, Diane Raetz, Patrick Thomas, Stephanie Wardach, Darin Kennedy, Wendy Jacobs, Cindy Rosenfield, Patricia Doty, Tamara Winfrey, Stuart Ott, Chris Bound, Marty Leibolt, Judy Kovaleski, Chris Vega, Tricia Servino, David Wade, Ellen Kaskoun, David B. Schlosser, Kristan Cioffi, Peter Carrolla, David Johansson, and Ken Hulse. Many thanks to the rest of the fans who support me on Facebook. This book simply would not have been possible without the love and support from my wife, Caren.

This book is dedicated to the spirit of accomplishment, of not being someone who only talks about doing something and does nothing, but being someone who steps up and does it—of not giving up and not believing the naysayers who say you can't, but listening instead to the one voice saying go and do it. There is a satisfaction of finishing something you started. It is a significant accomplishment to even start a thing, but it is a greater achievement to see that thing completed. It is far more important to reach the end once you start than to ever begin at all. That is the only way to truly accomplish self-confidence, integrity, and growth as a person.

I've grown and learned a lot through this journey of novel writing. I've learned not just about fairy tales but about myself—what I'm capable of—and about the technical aspects of writing and storytelling. I've learned about friendships, from some that have existed over years and decades, to those that have recently flourished via the Internet. I've learned you cannot spell-check a blank page. I've learned the only way to write a novel is to sit down and start writing one. And lastly, I've learned that happily ever afters are only the beginning of someone else's once upon a time.

-Roy Mauritsen, March 2012

PROLOGUE
LITTLE FOUNDLING

Syrenka had left home when she was fifteen, desiring to travel and see exotic places; however, her legs and a broken heart had turned those dreams to distant memories. She had aspired to tell stories of daring adventures, but now resigned herself to the solitary life she led.

These days, she looked forward to time with her only friend, Goldenhair, who would visit Syrenka's beach cabin on occasion and spend the day with her. Goldenhair would sometimes help her with projects, or bring Syrenka books to teach her to read and write. How Syrenka loved the tales in some of those books. They told of places she longed to see, people she longed to meet. She knew they were only stories, but they were also her escape.

These friendly visits seemed as much a welcome change for Goldenhair as they were for Syrenka. Together they would sit over tea as Goldenhair told piecemealed stories of the troubled times that existed outside of Syrenka's little world. Syrenka listened intently as Goldenhair spoke of heroes and generals, evil queens and witches, and other astonishing news of the kingdom. Syrenka recalled one tale in particular, more so than any other story; it was the tale of how the King of Marchenton and his son led an army up a mountain and into the clouds, never to return. Dark times had befouled the land shortly thereafter, and it seemed a curse had fallen over the kingdom ever since.

Goldenhair was not with Syrenka today, though, and what had begun as an overcast afternoon on the beach had turned into an angry, howling storm by nightfall. Syrenka was happy on such nights to sit in bed and read one of Goldenhair's books. The orange glow from a lantern provided ample light and a sense of warmth and peace. She read her story quite contentedly, interrupted intermittently by the storm when the rain battered the windows or the howl of the wind blew by.

The roof creaked loudly as an especially strong gust struck Syrenka's little cabin. She looked up, her brow furrowed with irritation. *Noisy tonight*, Syrenka thought to herself, annoyed by the disturbance. She turned back to her book, but realized she had already read that page. The wind rose again with another howl that carried the sound of waves crashing on the beach. Syrenka looked up until the noise subsided, and then once again went back to reading.

She flipped the page, sighed, and finally plopped the book on her blanket. Meanwhile, the rain continued to pound on the roof, accented by booms of thunder and bright flashes of distant lightning.

Syrenka debated going to sleep or making a pot of tea. The coals from the fireplace were still warm and the kettle above them was probably hot enough. She looked over at her cold and uninviting wooden wheelchair, and then at her canes. Neither choice appealed to her, nor did she relish the thought of the pain she would incur by walking over to the fireplace.

Syrenka was not elderly; in fact, she was far from it. She was not yet thirty by her measure and had a very athletic build, but her legs had become debilitated and it was quite painful for her to stand and walk. She could if she had to, but doing so felt like a thousand daggers stabbing at her legs and feet. Even worse, if she stood for any length of time, her legs and feet were prone to bleeding.

No, she did not like walking.

Syrenka was warm and comfortable in her bed. It gave her a sense of normalcy and security, and they were these simple feelings that she cherished. She leaned over, lifted the glass of the lantern, and blew the candle out. Darkness enveloped the room except for the dim glow of coals from the fireplace, and Syrenka settled down to sleep as the storm raged outside.

Not more than an hour later, a great gust of wind tore across the beach, howling with terrifying strength. It was an unsettling, unearthly sound, and it rattled the front door, jiggling the latch free. With a loud bang, the door slammed open and the rain and wind stampeded in.

Syrenka's eyes shot open and she drew a startled gasp. In an instant, she threw her blankets aside, grabbed her canes, and rose from the bed. Stabbing pains shot up her body as she hobbled to the wildly swinging door. Each step was agony.

By the time she reached the door, the wind-driven rain had managed to drench everything in the cabin, including Syrenka. She leaned her canes against a table and fought the wind to shut the door. That is when she saw it.

Syrenka's exceptional eyesight quickly adjusted to the dark distance of the beach, and her gaze scanned the waterline for the figure that had caught her attention—a human shape pulling itself from the rough, pounding waves of the storm surge. A white shirt defined the form, so out of place on a night like tonight that she could do nothing but watch for a moment, just to ensure it was not her imagination.

When a bolt of lightning flashed across the sky, she saw the figure again for an instant, but as her eyes refocused, it was gone. Another flash of lightning, and this time the figure was lying motionless on the beach.

Syrenka was certain there was someone there. She could close the door. After all, had the driving wind and rain not blown it open that night, she would have been none the wiser. However, she did not close the door and return to her warm bed. Syrenka's legs may have been weak, but her will was strong, and her heart was kind. She would offer help if help was needed.

As she grabbed a cloak from a nearby hook, her hands paused over her canes, unsure if they would be more hindrance than help. She would not bring them, she decided. Instead, she grabbed a tall staff with a small glass lantern wrapped with cord and dangling from the top. Inside the lantern, she lit a candle wick and quickly closed the glass. She leaned heavily on the staff until the pain in her legs became bearable. Even after so many years of coping with the pain, it could still shock her with its intensity. Nevertheless, the pain once acknowledged, was something she could conquer. She pulled the cloak's deep hood over her blonde hair and, with her head down, stepped into the storm.

The onslaught of the heavy rain and wind railed against her body as she navigated the slippery wood planking across the dunes. Syrenka slowly made her way along the walkway from the relative safety of the higher dunes, down the steps to the beach. She took the stairs slowly, each step punctuated by sharp pain. The candle lantern bounced with every agonized step she took. Looking up from her path, she searched for the strange storm victim with the white shirt, but he was gone from her view.

Syrenka groaned as she navigated the last set of steps. Scanning the beach methodically, she focused on what she was looking for. Near the water's edge lay the crumpled shape of a man. The surf was churning, pounding heavily, and he was so close to it that she feared it would wash him away. She hurried in his direction, hoping she was not too late.

When she reached the prone figure, Syrenka could see in the dim light of her candle that blood stained his white tunic. A large splinter of wood jutted from his shoulder. As if on cue, he rolled onto his back and weakly reached out his hand before letting it fall limply upon the hard, wet sand.

Syrenka stabbed her staff into the sand and knelt down next to him. His eyes slowly opened to the light as she tugged at his shirt. Ripping a piece of cloth from her cloak, Syrenka pulled the chunk of wood from the stranger's shoulder, as the man cried out in pain. She took the cloth and pressed hard against the wound. Then she grabbed the man's hand and pressed hard against the cloth. Though semiconscious, the man understood enough to hold the cloth as Syrenka lifted his body so she could get her arms around him. Syrenka had always been strong, much stronger than she looked. Her dependence on canes and crutches had maintained a constant source of exercise for her arms and upper body as well.

The man moaned as she lifted him up to her waist and planted her feet firmly in the sand, biting through the stabbing pain in her legs. Slowly, she began to drag him away from the water. Each forced step sent searing ripples of shock from her feet to her hips. Her eyes watering, Syrenka forced back her tears as she pulled the man through the tall grass of the dunes, bypassing the stairs and stopping only briefly to rest. Syrenka's body screamed in agony, but outwardly, she was silent. She was of one purpose only, and each breath focused on that purpose.

After what seemed like hours of excruciating effort, she dragged the unconscious, wounded man back to her house, and with great difficulty, she managed to maneuver him onto her bed. Once he was ensconced there, she stumbled backward with pain and exhaustion, and fell into her wheelchair.

The relentless pain finally subsided to a deep ache as Syrenka rested her exhausted body. Looking down, she sighed. The wet sand on her feet and legs was matted with the blood that seeped from her skin and was running down her calves.

Why did I do this? she thought to herself in anguish. Resting her head in her hand, she considered the injured, half-drowned man that lay in her dark room. Syrenka was not altogether surprised at her dramatic rescue. This was not the first time she had come to someone's aid at the expense of her own. She allowed herself to rest in the chair, drained from her efforts and the pain.

How many years had it been?

Syrenka had actually met the Prince of Marchenton once long ago, on a rare trip to the local harbor village for supplies. This man seemed to look like him, but it must have been nearly fifteen years since she last saw him. She concentrated, trying to remember the time more clearly.

The prince had just married and was touring the kingdom with his new bride. Crowds lined the streets, she recalled, and she became caught in the throng of well-wishers. In their eagerness to see the prince, the townspeople had pushed and shoved her as she tried to navigate through them. Suddenly, she found herself face down in the middle of the street, her canes and the supplies she had just purchased spilling in all directions. Worse yet, it had occurred right in front of the royal carriage.

Utterly ashamed, Syrenka had watched the carriage halt before her, and both the prince and princess rushed out to help her. She remembered the beautiful princess in her grand gown helping to gather up the fruits that had spilled in the mud. The prince collected her canes and helped Syrenka, mortified as she was, to her unsteady feet.

The crowd cheered their approval, but Syrenka was terrified. She quickly snatched the canes from the prince's hands, tears of embarrassment and frustration filling her eyes as she hobbled off, too ashamed to express her thanks.

Syrenka stared at the ring on the man's finger for a long moment. *Is this some rogue or pirate who has stolen the prince's ring?* she wondered, *or is this indeed our long lost prince?* The man that now rested in her bed, though older and with more lines on his features, did indeed resemble the prince who had stopped to help her.

With his wounds properly dressed and a special healing salve applied, exhausted sleep settled over her body. Her thoughts drifted to an even earlier part of her life, and she allowed her memories to turn to another prince she had saved.

It seemed like a lifetime ago, and she smiled at the cruel irony of her situation. When she was far younger, she fell in love with a prince who broke her heart when he married another. The old pain of a distant memory ached in her chest. What had the prince called her then? *Little foundling,* she remembered. *That was a long time ago,* Syrenka silently reminded herself.

She blew out the candle, wishing to snuff out those unwelcome thoughts. Leaning back in the large, well-cushioned chair she kept in the bedroom, she stared at the fire and pondered the night's turn of events. Here now she had her own "little foundling." Finally, sleep enveloped her and she dreamed of the ocean.

* * *

Syrenka awoke feeling like she had overslept, but with a quick glance at the window, she realized it was barely dawn. Her legs were quite stiff and ached terribly when she moved them. In the dim grey light of the morning, she could see the man sleeping soundly in her comfortable bed. She felt sure now that he was the prince, but decided to seek a second opinion.

After a yawn and a long stretch, she slowly rose to her feet, the familiar pain returning to her legs. Awkwardly, she walked to her wheelchair, sat down, and then moved toward the main room, quietly shutting the bedroom door behind her. Navigating across the main room to a small desk, she withdrew a pen and a scrap of paper from a drawer to write a quick note. She paused for a second to be sure of her wording. If he was indeed the prince, it would change many things. After taking a moment to reconsider writing anything at all, she closed her eyes, took a deep breath, and committed pen to paper. Then she rolled up the paper and secured it with a bit of string.

Syrenka wheeled herself over to the small kitchen area and broke off a piece of bread. She stuffed most of it into her mouth so that her cheeks bulged. (Syrenka loved bread. It was something she never had growing up.) She placed the rest of the bread on her lap with the note and rolled herself out the front door onto the porch.

Outside there was a cool breeze, and the memory of the evening's terrible storm made the early morning beach seem especially bright and calm. Along the waterline, she could see that the great storm had left evidence of a shipwreck—mostly large pieces of wood planking and some shredded rope and canvas. Syrenka stepped out of the wheelchair and supported herself on the railing of her porch. Swallowing her mouthful of bread, she placed the other piece on the railing. Syrenka closed her eyes as she patted her chest with her hand several times. Then she waited.

Soon, a large, mottled seagull landed on the railing and somewhat cautiously made its way to the bread, quickly scooping it up and swallowing. The bird then turned to Syrenka and quietly stared at her. Syrenka smiled and reached out her hand slowly to gently pet the seagull's head. It was something she had done many times before, and the gull responded by allowing her to tie the note around its neck.

This was a special bird. It would carry Syrenka's words to Goldenhair. How would Goldenhair react when she read what the bird carried? The words of the note echoed in Syrenka's mind as she slowly made her way back to the cabin.

I have found your missing prince. Come quickly.

CHAPTER 1
A GRAVE JOURNEY

"You can't throw away the glass slippers!" the young girl exclaimed to her companion.

"Why not?" the man replied. "They're broken anyway, so what difference does it make?"

"Because," she countered with a sigh, "it wouldn't be right." She shook her head, frustrated at the idea of explaining again. "I'm going back. I need to return them and make sure that they will be taken care of. These broken slippers are the last remaining shreds of a life I would like to leave behind. I need to finish this."

"Take them to a glass blower," the man said with a grin. "Get them resized."

She knew Hamelin was joking, trying to lighten her mood.

"Okay, then," said Hamelin. "Let's give them to the next person we meet. Then the slippers will be their problem, not ours."

"No. They need to be taken to a special place." She paused. "And it needs to be done by me."

"Okay." Hamelin's tone was supportive, but unbelieving.

"It was a last request." Patience wished she could offer a better explanation, but as always, she wanted to avoid discussing too many details with her friend. Finally, she added, "I would be disappointing someone important if I didn't do this myself."

Hamelin shrugged. He dropped the conversation, as he knew it would upset his young traveling companion to continue. Hamelin, a young man himself, found the girl to be rather insightful and mature for her young age. He respected her wishes, especially when she showed interest in returning to Marchenton. The two had grown close as they traveled together over these past few years. Hamelin looked after her, much like an older brother, and since the night they had first met, there had been an unspoken bond. It was something Hamelin could not quite explain, but he never questioned it.

When Patience was a child, she was a servant at the royal castle in the Kingdom of Marchenton. For several generations her family had worked for the royal house, and her widowed mother, a woman by the name of Catherine Brown, had been in service to the castle. Catherine had married Thomas Moufet, another servant from within the ranks of the castle staff. Many remembered the wedding because the king and queen had chosen to attend it, and a princess named Cinderella had joyfully danced with the young Patience after the ceremony.

Those were happier times, Patience recalled. But almost five years ago, a terrible event befell the kingdom, and on that fateful night, she was forced to flee the castle, perhaps never to return to Marchenton, her sole possessions were the remains of Cinderella's glass slippers. The charge of keeping them safe had been thrust upon her under dire circumstances. Now, in recent weeks, Patience felt compelled to return to the kingdom specifically to visit a grave under a particular hazelnut tree. Patience had spent most of her early childhood within the confines of the castle and was never that familiar with the kingdom outside the castle grounds. She came to rely on Hamelin's knowledge of the surrounding lands, as most of the time he was usually correct. However, today, her traveling companion was having problems trying to recall the old routes.

Hamelin was tall and thin, all arms and legs with a short fuzz of reddish hair on his head. His ears were a little too big for his head, and he had sharp, blue eyes, set beneath an angular brow. His mouth was usually set in a roguish, yet sincere smile. He wore a long leather coat with dark, mustard yellow and maroon patchwork stitched haphazardly over the worn areas.

Patience and Hamelin had been traveling companions for many weeks as they made their way back to the kingdom. Hamelin had helped the young girl, as well as many other children, escape from the kingdom that night so long ago. It was a night that Hamelin would never forget, as much as he wished he could. The thought of returning, even years later, made him nervous.

Hamelin rubbed the back of his head and tried to figure out what to do, as it was getting close to nightfall.

"I'm sure there was a connecting road from the path," he said distractedly, looking around in frustration. "The boulder we passed—I told you we'd pass a boulder—that was there, but…"

Days before, they had found the site where the hazelnut tree and grave were supposed to be, but the area was nothing more than a stump and a hole in the ground. It was apparent that someone had made a deliberate attempt to hide the site and relocate the grave of Cinderella's mother. Still, Patience had a mysterious feeling she could find the new site, and they had set off in a new direction. Hamelin was not thrilled at the prospect of wandering around the woods even more. He was happy to try to help his friend, but Hamelin was hoping they would travel to Bremensport before winter.

Patience pulled the pack off her sore shoulder. "It's alright, Hamelin. We will find it in the morning. Let's get settled for the night."

Hamelin squinted as he looked around again. It had been a while, he thought. "It may be overgrown…not used anymore." He had a more nervous demeanor than Patience, and was prone to biting his nails or rapidly rubbing the back of his head as he thought. He was glad to have found a sense of solace in his friendship with this solemn girl.

It did not take them very long to gather firewood and create a makeshift lean-to from fallen branches and evergreen boughs. Soon, with a warm fire and blankets pulled from their packs, they settled in among the trees and moss-covered boulders—far enough from the path to avoid attracting any attention.

"Well," said Hamelin, "we're definitely close." He was eating a piece of dried meat. Pulling off a chunk, he worked the large piece of meat quickly to the side of his mouth so he could finish talking. "I'd say at least another day or two to the coast and then we catch a ship to Bremensport, once we find that tree."

He looked across the fire to the young girl curled up in her blanket who was paying no attention to him at all. Patience held a cloth in her hands that she had unfolded in the firelight.

Hamelin had seen the cloth and its contents only once before. This was the first time Patience had looked at it since they returned to the kingdom. Without looking up, she said somewhat absently, "Do you think we're doing the right thing?"

Hamelin was still chewing—and thinking. The young girl was so stubbornly set about the journey that there were times Hamelin would have bet money she was possessed or enchanted by a witch's spell. Yet there were other times it seemed this journey was an unwanted burden on Patience, a burden that would on some nights drive the young girl to tears.

This time it took a moment until he could shift his food to his cheek to talk. In a somewhat muffled tone, he replied sincerely, "I think so. We're looking for a tree in the forest—it should be easy."

"It should be easy," she agreed. Patience had a strange feeling it was moved to a willow tree by a pond, though she could not explain how she knew, or why it did not puzzle her more than it did. She carefully rolled up the cloth and slipped it into her knapsack. Then, she curled up in her blanket. "Thank you for coming with me, Hamelin. You are a good friend. After this we'll go to Bremensport, I promise." She gave him a smile as she pulled the blanket over her shoulders and settled in for the night.

"You are glad we're doing this, eh girl?" Hamelin nodded, glancing at the knapsack. "It's been a long time since I saw you smile."

"Yes," she replied. "I've had these for too long." She patted her knapsack. "I just can't carry them around anymore. But I want to give them a fitting resting place and keep them from harm. They're too important to simply throw away," she said automatically, reaffirming their conversation earlier in the day. Moments later, her exhaustion from traveling caught up with her and she was fast asleep.

Hamelin watched her for a moment and then stared tiredly at the yellow and orange sparks flickering in the campfire. It was not long before he, too, gave into sleep.

* * *

A chill in the air punctuated the still, cloudy grey of a forest dawn. Hamelin's shuffling awoke Patience. He was disassembling the makeshift camp, scattering the brush to make the area appear undisturbed. Patience sat up stiffly, "You're up early, Hamelin."

Hamelin began rolling up his bedroll—he was trying to appear calm, but was rushing too much to do it quietly. He kept his head down, trying to avoid Patience's confused stare. "Yes, well, I just have a weird feeling this morning. I think we should go," he said curtly.

Patience sat up straighter now, more than a little concerned. She looked around; the forest was the same, though it looked quite different in the morning light from when they had settled in. Hamelin seemed a little spooked, and it was beginning to spook her, as well.

Finished with the bedroll, he stuffed it unceremoniously into his pack. "You must have been dead to the world, girl."

"I was tired," she agreed absently as she stood up and stretched, no longer sleepy. Patience looked at the grey ash of the dead fire. "I guess there's no time for tea?"

Hamelin finished and stood up to throw his pack over his shoulder. Finally, she was able to look at his face. He looked nervous and pale…almost frightened.

"Hamelin, what's going on?" Patience asked with more urgency in her tone.

"Pack up," he replied.

She trusted Hamelin completely, and this situation was making her nervous. Hamelin darted over to her bedding and began to pack it up hurriedly. "I'll tell you more when we get going. We'll take a break further on down the road."

It was the first time Patience could recall packing up a camp that quickly since she started traveling with Hamelin. Usually, there was at least time for tea in the morning.

"Let's find this tree of yours, shall we?" asked Hamelin as he kicked dirt onto the smoldering remains of the fire and handed the somewhat stunned Patience her pack.

They were back on the trail for nearly ten minutes as Patience jogged along, trying to keep up with Hamelin's brisk pace. "Hamelin," she finally said breathlessly, "Stop. What is going on?"

He stopped and spun around sharply, causing Patience to collide into him. The young servant girl was barely chest high and glared up at him with an annoyed expression.

Hamelin sighed. "I'm sorry. I just—" He paused and scratched the back of his head. "Did you hear that wolf howling last night?"

Patience shook her head.

"It was eerie—and very close. And it—I guess it spooked me a bit." The more Hamelin tried to explain, the more foolish he felt. "It seemed as if we were being watched all night and maybe even followed. But it was that strange wolf sound that really bothered me, and it was so close, too. I have never heard anything like it. I was ready to wake you during the night, but…let's just say that I didn't get a lot of sleep," he ended lamely.

On this note, they continued walking, now at a slower pace. Patience was concerned. She had known Hamelin long enough to know that sound must have been something significant to be so unsettling for her friend. She looked at the surrounding woods as they walked. They seemed perfectly normal to her, like much of what they had been traveling through since they returned to the kingdom. She tried to imagine what such a vivid feeling of paranoia would be like, but it did not really make that much sense to her. They had heard wolves howl before; however, if Hamelin wanted to go, then she was glad to be going. At least it was progress, and soon she would be at the one place that she felt would give her closure.

They continued for a little while in silence. Then Patience had an idea—something that might help both her and her traveling companion. "Why don't you play something for us?" she asked.

"Of course!" he replied happily, snapping his fingers, as if he had almost forgotten that he could play a tune at all. Hamelin reached into the inside of his jacket and pulled out a small instrument similar to a set of reed pipes.

"Let the flutes begin!" Patience cheered jokingly.

"They aren't flutes," Hamelin corrected her with a smile. He played a quick, fluttering trill to warm up. "They are my pipes."

Proudly, he began to play a most wonderful, uplifting jig, and as he played, he danced around and hopped to the music. Patience clapped and skipped with easy laughter as the two made their way down the forest trail. She loved that Hamelin could play music, lively or sad, any type of melody that could bring out emotion from her.

They went on for about an hour, racing each other down the path, not considering how the noise might attract attention. He would bow and she would curtsy as they passed each other. The music came fast and his fingers moved in a blur over his pipes. It was a reprieve that gave the two road-weary travellers an opportunity to forget their troubles.

Hamelin finally ended his pipe playing with a laugh as Patience applauded. He pulled a gulp of water from a leather flask, passing it to Patience to share. They walked on farther and began to reminisce about the time they had first met.

Patience could tell that Hamelin was feeling better as he was now starting to talk about breakfast. There was a break in their conversation and Patience scanned the forest around her, seeming to recognize her surroundings. She stopped so abruptly that this time Hamelin almost bumped into her.

"This is it!" she said. "We're here." Amazement grew on Patience's face. How did she even know where "here" was?

Hamelin rolled his head with a look of surprise. He looked around like he wanted to be happy, but was not quite sure he should be. "What's *here*, the road or the tree? How do you know?" he asked, a little amazed.

"I just know it's in this area. I can picture it perfectly in my head," she said. However, it was not any one thing that specifically told her, like a sign or a landmark. There was nothing remarkable about the trail or its surroundings at all.

"I feel like I remember this area. But that can't be possible..." She seemed confused for a moment, puzzled by her own confidence. Then she quickly darted off the trail and down a leaf-covered slope.

"Follow me!" She was already scrambling up the other side of the hollow, grabbing the trunks of saplings to pull herself up.

Hamelin carefully made his way down the slope, catching himself and bracing against tree trunks so that he would not slip and fall.

When he got down to the rocky and leaf-covered gully bottom, hopping across stones of a long-dried riverbed, he looked up to see Patience standing at the top of the hill. She was not so much waiting for him as drinking in the view before her.

"Hamelin!" Patience called out. "You have to see this!"

Hamelin made his way up the other side of the slope, slightly out of breath. On more than one occasion, he threw his hand down to keep himself from sliding on the wet leaves. A few moments later, he made it to the top and stood next to Patience.

"You can't just run off like that! We have to stick together. You should have waited——" he broke off as he motioned to the hill he just climbed. "——or helped a little," he finished, out of breath. Hamelin brushed off his leggings and wiped the dark dirt from his hands onto his long, red and yellow jacket.

"There it is, Hamelin," whispered Patience.

The first thought that struck Hamelin was how out of place it seemed. It was impossible to see from the trail, and the trail was already far removed from any main road. They were overlooking a tree-lined slope that descended rather steeply. Hamelin could see a small, forested valley, at the bottom of which was a tiny bit of meadow and a large pond covered in lily pads and leaves. It felt quite hidden from the world—hidden from time itself.

The two travellers navigated cautiously through the thin trees as they made their way down the steep slope to the pond. From the rise above, Hamelin could now see what he thought at first were boulders. In fact, they were more structured and deliberate; they were stone ruins. Broken remains were scattered about, some rising from the dark pond itself. At the other end of the pond, settled on its quiet shore, was a great willow tree. The willow's tendril-like branches dripped down in a curtain of yellowish leaves, some drooping so low as to brush the surface of the pond.

When Hamelin and Patience reached the flatter ground at the bottom of the hill, they stopped to take in the beautiful sights and sounds before them. The air was calm and still, very unlike the rest of the forest. Sunlight broke through the tree in great beams and danced on the water, and the gentle buzz of dragonflies on the pond could be heard. The pond was like dark glass with the occasional V-like wake of an insect darting on the surface, or a lazy ripple that would break sporadically, indicating a fish had fed on the small, unsuspecting victim. There was a great sense of peace in this secluded area.

"This way," whispered Patience, trying not to disturb the stillness. She grabbed Hamelin's large hand and they walked around the edge of the pond toward the giant willow. Hamelin nodded in silence, for he was quietly awed by what surrounded them.

Patience could smell moss and rich soil, and the sweet scent of the willow leaves as she parted them and moved underneath the canopy of the great tree. Hamelin followed close behind. It seemed that they had entered a kind of sanctuary, almost intruding on it, and he felt the back of his neck get warm at the thought.

"It's so beautiful and peaceful," Patience whispered to herself.

Once through the curtain of leaves, it was as if the outside world had disappeared. The sunlight cast a warm, speckled glow on the roots and moss hidden within. Dragonflies darted about with a whirring hum, and the breeze glided through the leaves of the great tree like a gentle sigh. The warm smell of hazelnut blossoms drifted through the air. There was a small, weathered bench nearby, once elegant and ornately carved, now rotten and stained green with mold and moss.

Patience stepped carefully so as not to disturb the very ground she walked on. The young woman made her way to the tree and raised her hand to the trunk, marveling at its age and strength.

"It feels so warm," she said in amazement.

Hamelin was a little more cautious, looking back to the point where they had come in to make sure they were not followed.

"It seems a little too peaceful, Patience. Don't get me wrong, it's nice. But this whole place seems a little strange."

"Nonsense. How can something be too peaceful?" she replied and gave the warm tree as big a hug as her arms could reach around the wide trunk. For Patience, this marked the end of a long journey. After today, she could finally start to live a new life, free from the constant physical reminder of the past.

Hamelin looked curiously at his friend. "Well, in my experience, if something is too peaceful, it usually means something bad just hasn't shown up there yet."

Patience walked along one side of the tree, rubbing her hand along the trunk as she stepped on the roots like stepping-stones. Hamelin walked around the other side of the tree, away from the water's edge. *Just in case,* he thought. Hamelin imagined a great wolf leaping out of the dark pond to capture him and drag him under the water as a snack. It was an absurd thought, but he would rather be on the safer side of absurdity than be attacked by a pond wolf.

On the opposite side of the massive trunk, a large, smooth rock lay unevenly among the great roots. "I think I found something," he called out to Patience. Hamelin peered closely at the dark, moss-covered rock. "Wait, there's something else," he mumbled to himself, and began to clear the moss covering. It was a simple engraving that read "My beloved wife, Ella." Then below it, obviously chiseled afterwards and almost in a young child's writing, was another word: Mother.

Patience had been watching over Hamelin's shoulder. "This is it. It's her grave," she whispered excitedly.

"This is the grave?" asked Hamelin. Realizing where he was standing in relation to what was obviously a tombstone, he moved respectfully (and quickly) to the side.

Patience pulled her knapsack from her shoulder. "Well, yes." She looked serious and the tone of her voice held a solemn reverence. "This was her mother's grave, Hamelin."

Her tall companion did not seem to comprehend the importance of the ground he was standing on.

"Queen Cinderella—the same queen that presides over the kingdom now—her mother had died when Cinderella was my age." She began to loosen the straps of her knapsack as she spoke, taking a moment to tie back her long brown hair at the nape of her neck. "She was a commoner that the prince fancied, a servant girl to a local family."

"Yes," replied Hamelin. "It was a story all the girls were told, Patience."

She ignored him. "Cinderella's mother was buried near a hazelnut tree. When she became queen, Cinderella must have had her mother's body moved to this place," the young girl guessed correctly. "It's amazing, though." Patience paused to inhale deeply. "You can still smell hazelnut."

"Why wasn't she just buried in the royal catacombs in the castle?" asked Hamelin.

Patience thought for a moment. There had been a reason, she recalled. "It was something about royal lineage...I guess because she was just a commoner."

"How typical; I guess this will work better for us then. I doubt we can even get into the castle," added Hamelin, "with that wall of thorns around it."

"And I don't really want to go back there," replied Patience. "I don't think we would even get an audience with the queen."

"But wouldn't the queen want them back?" Hamelin responded.

"I am not so sure Cinderella would appreciate her glass slippers these days." A touch of sadness accented what Patience said, but it was only for a moment. "I was there that night, Hamelin." Patience patted the pack she had been carrying. "Believe me, the queen would not want these back, not after what happened." She would say nothing further about that horrible night many years ago. "I want to leave them here," she said decisively.

Patience reached into the pack and pulled out the cloth-wrapped objects. The cloth was warm and seemed to pulse under her hands. "They belong here," she said as she began to unwrap the little bundle of cloth.

Then they heard a twig snap.

Patience took a quick breath and looked at Hamelin with panic in her eyes. "Just leave them," Hamelin whispered quickly. "Let's go."

"No, not like this." Quickly she rewrapped the cloth, and fumbling in her haste, let some of the contents drop among the roots. "Oh, no," Patience exclaimed in a loud whisper. She bent down and frantically gathered up as much as she could of the small pieces of crystal. Wrapping them back in the cloth, the frightened girl hastily stuffed the wrapped shards back in her knapsack. Patience had no time to check to see if she had recovered all of the broken pieces of the glass slippers.

The snap had come from outside the willow branches. Hamelin turned to see a long, dark sword part the branches as shadowy, humanoid forms made their way through the curtain of leaves. A rough and gravelly voice broke the peacefulness of the air with the booming resonance of misbegotten authority.

"You there, halt! You are trespassing on the queen's private land!"

Of course, this was after all, the grave of the queen's mother. It had simply never occurred to them that the queen's guard would watch it. Nevertheless, a greater danger was now before them, for the queen's guards were not as Hamelin and Patience remembered. Patience gave a horrified gasp as the guards approached.

They were nothing Hamelin had ever seen before: man-sized and somewhat misshapen brutes that wore grungy, piecemeal armor and clothing. Each one of them wore a shoulder piece of polished silver, stamped with what appeared to be a royal emblem. Most horrifying was their deformity. They all resembled giant rats, much like the ones Hamelin had seen in the villages he had traveled through, making money on the side as a rat catcher. One had patches of matted, grey fur and a tapered, long nose. Another was more human-like in appearance, but with round, thin ears that were more recognizable as rodent than human. The third was an almost complete bipedal, humanoid-looking rat. None of them looked especially hospitable.

These cannot be the queen's guards, thought Hamelin as he sized them up. He grabbed Patience's hand and pulled her behind him. "They're probably some local gang that killed the queen's guards and took their clothes," he said quickly in a low voice. Fear tightened Hamelin's throat as the three rat-looking guards moved toward them.

"We're sorry," Patience stammered. Hamelin was pushing her back slowly.

"We didn't realize…we didn't know." He could hear Patience's voice quavering.

Hamelin's mind was racing. Could they make a run for it? It was doubtful they could outrun these guards, and the climb up the hill surrounding the pond area would surely be too slow to get away. He saw the leader, the most humanlike one with rat-like ears and patches of hair on his otherwise bald and misshapen head, sneering as Patience spoke. Ultimately, Hamelin was more concerned for Patience than himself. He knew they were in real danger. It was the second time in his life that he was forced to face the possibility that he might die. The first time was the reason he left the kingdom in the first place. *Bad mistake to come back*, he thought.

"The punishment for trespassing on royal grounds is death," stated the leader with a confident and gruesome smile.

With a cough-like chuckle, the guards raised their weapons. "We'll start with you," the leader said as he motioned to Hamelin. "And then," the leader paused, looking at Patience, "we'll kill the girl a little bit later."

"Listen," Hamelin spoke up, trying to keep his tone even. "Let's work something out here. Nobody has to die. Why does it always have to be death? Can't we just get a warning this time?" He laughed nervously and then cleared his throat. "I'm sure we can come to some kind of agreement, can't we? We will leave and never come back. You have our sincere and humble apologies. You see, we are not from around here…"

"It don't work like that," the leader interrupted with a growl. Then all three guards laughed.

"Maybe we can reach a price that all parties would be happy with then?" Hamelin offered, knowing it probably was not going to change a thing. That feeling of "I told you so" crept into Hamelin's thoughts.

"We'll take your money after you're dead," the lead guard replied with a rat-toothed grin. "You have been found guilty of trespassing and, by proclamation of the queen, punishment is to be handed out immediately—death." He spoke like he was in fact royal enforcement, but he had the devious and crafty smile of a common street thug.

Hamelin and Patience were about to break into a run when a loud roar bellowed from outside the willow branches. It was immediately followed by squeals and screams of other guards that must have remained outside the curtain of tree leaves. The three guards stopped, confused for a moment by the commotion.

Then the branches erupted as an enormous brown bear broke through the leaves. It stood on its hind legs, towering well above the three guards. Terrified, Hamelin and Patience could only stand and watch. The beast let out another great roar as the three guards stood there, paralyzed in shock and fear. With a powerful swing, the enraged bear sent one guard hurtling over another before slamming hard against the tree. The grungy armor had offered no protection against the animal's deadly claws, and the guard crumbled to the ground, his chest shredded open. In the next moment, the bear crashed down on the other two squealing and panic-stricken guards. Its long, razor sharp claws swatted the guards like flies, and they fell to the ground. In an instant, the ferocious bear dispatched them with crushing fatal bites from its powerful jaws, easily snapping their necks.

Meanwhile, Hamelin and Patience had slowly backed away, almost to the other side of the willow branches, putting the thick trunk of the tree between them and the bear. Hamelin had reached into his jacket pocket and was absently checking his pipes. Patience's heart was beating fast; she felt like the bear could hear it. She thought to climb the tree, but there were no limbs low enough. The huge bear eyed them, and then something curious happened, absolutely nothing at all. The bear watched them, but made no motion to attack. Its mood shifted from ferocious to docile in almost an instant. Instead of attacking, it merely lifted its great furred head and, sniffing the air toward Hamelin and Patience, gave a rather uninterested grunt. Then it turned its attention back to the body of a nearby guard, sniffing and pawing. Finding nothing of interest, the giant bear finally sat upright on the guard, and scratched its brown, furry chest in a lazy fashion.

Hamelin pulled his hand away from his pocket and carefully took Patience's hand. His terror-widened eyes focused on the bear, searching for the slightest movement. "Walk back slowly," he whispered to Patience, who had been squeezing his hand so hard that his fingers were turning purple and white. They backed away, inch by inch, and to their great relief, discovered that the bear did not follow. Cautiously, the two found themselves slowly pushing through the willow tree out to the edge of the pond.

"Let's turn and walk away calmly," Hamelin said in an even more hushed tone.

In mid-turn however, Patience froze. She could see the bodies of several more guardsmen strewn about the shore of the pond. Her main concern, however, was that there were two more bears staring straight at them from the shore, barely twenty feet away. These were similar in color and pattern of fur, obviously brown bears, though not as large as the bear they had just encountered. Patience wanted to scream, but the desire to remain silent narrowly won out. Hamelin, too, had stopped in his tracks. He had noticed something else.

Walking up to them, in total disregard of the nearby bears, was a tall, slender, beautiful woman. She wore patched brown deerskin leggings with criss-crossed lacing along the sides, a simple deerskin tunic, and a bodice adorned with beads and feathers. Her arms were wrapped in brown leather strips, and her skin was deeply tan. She was obviously someone who spent much of her life outdoors.

As she drew closer, Hamelin could see that finely-detailed drawings covered her neck and the right side of her smooth face. The drawings also faintly traced what seemed like hundreds of patterns along her arms and on her hands, and made the woman seem somewhat wild and tribal in appearance. Her deep blue eyes were smart and gentle, and her hair was long, falling in full, lazy curls well below her shoulders; it was the color of the golden, late afternoon sun. She walked toward them with a calm air of total confidence. Hamelin had never seen anyone of such natural beauty. When she spoke, her voice was angelic, both soft and strong, though they did not understand a word of what she said. To Hamelin, it almost did not matter.

"Nikko, deth est offa soo?" Nikko! Dosso, et offa soo!"

It took Hamelin and Patience a moment to realize that she was not talking to them, but rather to someone behind them. The mysterious beauty was staring directly at the willow tree as she spoke. A moment later, from the leaves of the tree emerged the same great brown bear that had just saved Patience and Hamelin. Taking no notice of the two strangers, the giant bear lumbered out and passed them. Its thick furred shoulder was as tall as Patience. With disbelief, Hamelin watched the great bear walk over to the strange woman. Even on all fours, the bear was huge and almost eye level with her, yet she did not seem frightened by it in the least. She put her hands on either side of the bear's huge head, and lifted its head to look into its eyes.

"Nikko. Es dogoo, Nikko bahr." She gave the bear a friendly scratch behind its ears, wrapped her arms around its huge neck, and gave the bear a kiss on his giant snout. When she was done, the bear pulled his head away and shuffled over to the other two bears. The woman then turned and stepped toward the tall man and his young companion.

"Kehvaa es valcor—" she paused, apparently embarrassed. Her brow furrowed for a moment, and then her face brightened.

"Forgive," she said finally, in a language Hamelin and Patience understood. "Speaks many languages—the human one least helpful in most times." It was in some sort of thick accent Hamelin could not place. *At least she speaks our language,* he thought, *sort of.*

Again, the woman searched for the words to continue. She slowly worked out each word of the sentence, trying to recall the equivalent English version. As she did this, she seemed more amused with herself than embarrassed.

"Bahr? Bear. Nikko." She clumsily explained that the large bear's name was Nikko. "Nikko bah—bear upset at life taken." She pointed to the bears. "Nikko, Dosso, and Kerker es—" She gave an apologetic smile. "—is friendly. good Bahrs."

Hamelin nodded in acknowledgement. "Thank you then...for your help." He pointed to himself. "Ham-eh-lin."

The blonde woman smiled at him. "Hallo, Hamelin."

He introduced Patience, who seemed quite confused with the sudden turn of events and kept looking at the bears. She barely managed to squeak out a polite "Hello." The woman nodded knowingly at Patience's introduction, which Hamelin thought was slightly odd.

"You are the guardian of the shards," the woman stated, her speaking ability now much sharper. Patience turned her gaze from the bears, instantly taking notice of what the woman said.

"What did you say? Guardian?" asked Patience with a quizzical look.

The woman smiled. Despite the thick accent, her words were resounding and confident of their truth. "You carry the shards of the glass slipper. We are here to help you."

Hamelin sucked in a deep breath, for both he and Patience thought they were the only ones who knew. They looked at each other. Does one trust a woman who can talk to bears?

"How did you know?" Patience shot back with a somewhat defensive tone.

With a loud screech, a bird announced its presence and flew toward the pond and then quite deliberately to the strange woman. Again, a warm smile covered the woman's face as she recognized the bird. It was a large, grey-mottled seagull.

A seagull is unusual in this area, thought Hamelin, *but most of the day has gone the way of unusual.* The tall man had the feeling that "unusual" was soon to become "normal."

The woman let the seagull alight on her arm, much as a falconer would, and noticed a small bit of parchment tied around its neck. The bird did not seem to mind as the woman took the parchment. She untied it and read the note as the gull remained on her arm, perhaps enjoying a rest from its long flight. The mysterious woman then smiled at Patience.

"It seems the shards are already to bring us good fortune," she announced mysteriously as she placed the note back around the gull's extended neck. Gently, she turned into the breeze, leaned close to the bird, and whispered. The seagull caught the breeze and flew off.

"Are we close to Bremensport?" Hamelin thought to ask as he watched the seagull.

"That is several days south," the woman replied. "We are to head to ocean, yes, but not to that place. We take quicker ways. We have friends to meet," she announced again, just as mysteriously as before. Then she paused abruptly. "I'm sorry to not introduce myself." Her English was better now as she began to recall more of the language, but it was still somewhat awkward and with a heavy accent. "Nikko and the other bears call me…" She paused, trying to translate. "Guldlæx, I guess, would be the closest translation, though that is not entirely correct. You may call me Mavor Goldenhair."

"You speak bear?" Hamelin asked, wanting to be sure he was not dreaming this.

Mavor smiled. "Yes, among other languages of the forest," she said in a polite, matter-of-fact reply. She called to the bears and gave them a wave, and the massive, brown-furred animals proceeded to lumber up ahead of them and toward the opposite side of the pond, in the direction the two travellers had come from. "But we should now be going. More guards to come soon. Not safe." She gestured in the direction of the bears. "More guards to come."

"What does it mean? Guldlæx?" Patience asked sheepishly, trying to pronounce the woman's name correctly.

Mavor thought for a second, trying to figure out how best to explain. Then she noticed a slight breeze that pushed its way through the trees like a whisper, and she paused to focus on it for a moment. Patience thought she had not heard her question.

"We must not to stay here," started Mavor, her tone more serious. She had sensed trouble on the very breeze itself. "We must go to meet more friends. Please do come. I will to explain more on the way, and save the name story for a better time soon." Goldenhair smiled warmly at Patience. "Come," She urged. "Bring your glass slipper shards. They will not be safe here."

Although Mavor Goldenhair was still a stranger, she had saved their lives and seemed to know about them. Somehow, this strange bear woman had knowledge of the glass slipper shards, as well. Perhaps this woman will play a role in the fate of the shards, thought Patience, as she proceeded to walk in the direction that Goldenhair and the bears headed. The young girl nervously clutched her knapsack by the straps and glanced at Hamelin, nodding at him to join them. He shook his head and mouthed, "Bad idea." Nevertheless, in a couple of strides, he caught up to Patience. He had the feeling that to stay would have been far worse than to follow.

CHAPTER 2
A LEGEND

"Can we really trust her? I'm not sure this is a good idea," Hamelin whispered to Patience as the two made their way from the pond and up the steep incline.

"She talks to bears…and they listen. I don't think anything but trust is an option right now," whispered Patience. "Besides I think she is trying to help us."

The climb back up to the path was strenuous. Bracing their feet against the slim tree trunks, the two companions used branches and exposed roots as handholds in the steeper parts. Hamelin and Patience quickly fell behind their new guide.

"But what happened to the queen's guards?" Patience asked as she pulled herself up, catching her breath. "They seemed more like animals! They are not the guards I remember from the castle, Hamelin." She continued in a similar hushed tone. "They looked like…" The young girl thought for a moment. They reminded her most of the huge brown and grey rodents she had seen throughout the castle in her childhood. "They looked like rats."

Hamelin had noticed that his young traveling companion would almost never mention her time in the castle. Any time she did refer to it, it made him somewhat uneasy. Their new guide made him uneasy, as well. He could see that while they were still some distance from the top, Goldenhair and the bears had already climbed to the peak of the ridge.

"Well," Hamelin began as he pulled himself up with a grunt, "I don't trust her; and we should be cautious. We came here to leave your shards at this grave and now we're taking them to show some other people?" His voice quickly turned to hushed tones as he neared the top of the ridge where Goldenhair waited.

Patience finally clambered up to the leveled surface of the ridge that overlooked the pond and the willow tree. She brushed her leggings off as Hamelin appeared from below the ledge. A hand reached out to help Hamelin to his feet. It was slender and intricately detailed with a very fine tattoo that trailed up a muscular forearm and disappeared beneath folds of cloth and leather. After a moment of hesitation, Hamelin took Goldenhair's hand, and was quite surprised at the strength and warmth of her grip.

He gave a slight nod of thanks, but his eyes were already searching for the bears. At any moment, he thought, those bears could wildly turn on Patience and himself, or Goldenhair could order the bears to attack. When he looked at her, though, he found that she was simply staring at him with a disarming smile. The bears lumbered slowly ahead up the path, their heads close to the ground, swaying back and forth, as they checked scents.

"There is much that goes on these days," said Goldenhair, her thick accent adding a touch of mysticism to the words. "The winds of the destinies press many a tree, a branch, and even a single leaf to action. I believe we may cross paths with some bad people on this road, and I suspect we shall find my friend Elizabeth. I had been searching for her as well this day."

She gestured to the travelers as they started to walk down the path, the mysterious bear talker pointing out various fauna and flora, telling stories of the various trees and the woodlands. It was her way of creating small talk to ease her new companions' worries, but more often than not, as she excitedly explained the details of the forest around them, Goldenhair would lapse back into her strange language.

It took Hamelin several moments to recognize his surroundings. "Patience!" he exclaimed. "This was the road we were looking for! We must have been farther south than I thought!"

Now that Hamelin had his bearings again, he thought he might be more direct with their new friend. "Now, one moment. Before we go any further with you…" Hamelin reached out to Mavor and touched her arm.

At the same time, Hamelin noticed that the bears had stopped and lifted their heads to sniff the air. Quickly, he withdrew his hand and softened his tone as Mavor stopped and looked at him in puzzlement.

"Patience and I are very grateful to you for saving us at the willow tree, but we have some questions."

Mavor smiled. "Of course—" she began. Then, in an instant, she turned her head sharply. Simultaneously, the bears let out low growls. "Nikko! Des af nochoo! Ty! Ty!" she shouted to the bears with a quick gesture.

She raised her hand in Hamelin and Patience's direction, motioning to them to be quiet. The pair seemed puzzled as they looked down the road in the direction in which Mavor and the bears had focused, but they saw and heard nothing.

"Something is coming," said Mavor. Her carefree smile and relaxed demeanor had vanished. "Quickly, get to the side. Hide!"

Without question, Patience and Hamelin found themselves running to the other side of the road and crouching behind a nearby section of fallen tree. Fully expecting all of them to remove themselves from the road, Hamelin and Patience were surprised to see Mavor remain exactly where they had left her, the three large bears now standing next to her.

Patience heard the sound first. "Horses," she whispered.

Then they saw it. Rounding a bend farther down the road was an old, rickety-looking wagon pulled by a pair of horses. A large, muscular man drove the wagon, and another horse and rider traveled alongside. They moved briskly at almost full gallop down the road toward Mavor. As they approached, the bears rose on their hind legs and snarled. The horses reared and came to a sudden stop.

"Release your prisoner," Mavor spoke in a sudden authoritative tone, holding her staff defensively. "You have no right to be holding her."

Patience could see that the back of the wagon was more of a short, barred cell on wheels. The rider on the horse, a young woman, pulled back the hood of her cloak, revealing a braid of long brown hair, and replied condescendingly, "We thought we might run into you, Goldenhair. I see you are still letting your pets do your work for you. The winter is coming and I could use a good bear rug...or three."

Crouching well out of sight, Hamelin tugged Patience's tunic and leaned to whisper in her ear. "We should go. We could follow the—"

"No," she interrupted. "Let's wait. It seems like they know each other, but Mavor might need our help."

"I doubt that. I don't think these are the friends she was talking about," replied Hamelin. "I've got a bad feeling about this." He felt the situation becoming tenser by the second.

The cloaked woman turned smartly to control her nervous mount, and her companion worked the reins of the wagon to steady his horses.

Mavor continued, her accent still apparent, but her English was not as broken as it was before. "I know you have a friend of mine captive, and I will ask once more that you free her, Gretel. This is not the first time we have met over this. Get your blood money some other way."

The woman rider was defiant. "I think not. The queen pays well."

"Stand aside!" yelled the man impatiently from the wagon. "Let us be on our way!"

Gretel shot a fiery look at the man on the wagon. "Do shut up, brother. I will handle this."

Now the bears began to approach the wagon, turning their heads to the side and giving low growls at the horses. The largest bear, Nikko, reared up again on its hind legs. Gretel's horse could take no more and it reared up with a panicked whinny, kicking its front legs out at the antagonizing bear. This sent Gretel falling back off her saddle, landing hard on the ground. She sprang expertly to her feet, however, and stumbled back against the wagon while drawing her sword from its scabbard. The other horses kicked their hooves about nervously in the dirt, straining against their reins and throwing their heads back. It was all the man could do to keep the skittish animals from bolting.

Nikko dropped back to all fours and turned slowly toward Gretel. Her brother grabbed a crossbow from his side, stood up, and aimed it at the large bear.

"Let us pass or I'll add another bear pelt to my wall, Mavor!" he threatened angrily.

"Nikko. Doch!" said Mavor and the bear stopped. "You'll just make Nikko very angry, Hansel," said Mavor. "Remember the last time you shot at one of my bears?"

She could see the long scar that went down almost the entire length of Hansel's muscular forearm. Gretel kept her sword pointed resolutely at the bear.

While Patience watched the confrontation at the front end of the wagon, Hamelin's attention turned to the cage in the back. The crude cell in the rear was only about four feet in height and took up most of the body of the wagon. The metal bars were short and straw spilled out from between them. There was a simple lock, but it was a lock nonetheless. A pile of blankets and burlap cloth covered the top of the cage. He could see that the blankets and cloth covered the remains of animals and their furs loosely. The burlap wrappings were wet with blood and dripped into the cage. It looked like a cage for animals, Hamelin thought. Packed haphazardly into nooks and corners around the cage were all manner of animal traps, metal hooks, and tools, all used and worn. They were trappers, Hamelin realized.

"We should leave now. This just got dangerous," he said to Patience, but she was still watching the escalating confrontation between Goldenhair and the riders. Hamelin looked back at the cage more closely now. The interior was dark and shadowed. Something inside stirred slightly. Hamelin strained to see what manner of creature they would be keeping under such conditions. From the shadowy recess of the small cell, a figure moved up against the bars and into the light. To Hamelin's surprise, it was a young woman wrapped in burlap, no doubt from the piles on top of the cage.He had expected to see an animal, not a woman crouched into such a small prison. The woman had a terrified look on her young and dirtied face. Her skin was bloodied, perhaps from the animal carcasses, but it could quite easily have been her own.

Is she the one Goldenhair was talking about? Is that Elizabeth? Why is she in there? he wondered. *Who are these people who have her caged like this?*

The young woman's beauty shone through the dirt and grime of her cell. Her sharp green eyes darted restlessly and then focused in Hamelin's direction. The huge log they were hiding behind was some distance from the road, so Hamelin was shocked when he realized the captured woman had seen him. He froze.

For a moment, the two stared at each other. He felt he was intruding, and turned away, as if to say I cannot help you. Or perhaps, Hamelin thought, he was feeling guilty that he would not help. It would be a selfish indulgence to do nothing but stare at something so beautiful and yet so helpless. He crouched further down behind the log and looked over at Patience, who had slowly crept back to the end of the log, to better hear the exchange between Mavor and the two strangers.

Hamelin peeked back over the mossy log to the cell again. The woman's stare had not broken. She was still looking right at him; sad and pleading. her eyes had never left him. Hamelin could not think to do anything but stare back. His stomach tightened in knots. His heart saddened.

The woman in the cage reached out a slender, pale hand in his direction. She strained, her face pressed against the bars as she mouthed the words "Help me…Please." Hamelin broke from his stare and looked away; he could not bear it anymore. Then he saw something lying in the dust underneath the wagon and, much to his surprise, he had an idea that was very unlike him.

"Not this time, Goldenhair." Gretel repeated. "She's a law breaker and dangerous. The queen's word is law and her bounty is generous. What my brother and I do for a living is completely within reason." Gretel had quickly regained her composure from the fall from her horse and she was now on the offense, if not with her sword than with her words. "We could have you arrested for interfering with us."

"We should be hunting you next!" remarked Hansel from on top of the wagon. "After all, we're witch hunters, and you," he motioned with his crossbow to the bear, "would certainly be suspected of witchcraft with your bears and all the animals that do your bidding."

"Not to mention," added Gretel, "how many times you've spoiled our animal traps. We'd be doing ourselves a big favor by taking you out, with or without the queen's bounty."

Mavor stiffened. "That girl is not an animal," she said, trying to keep the topic focused on her captive friend. This time Mavor sensed that Gretel and her brother Hansel, the kingdom's resident witch hunters and trappers-for-hire were more serious than any time prior in previous encounters. This was not the first time they had crossed paths regarding her friend Elizabeth. The brother and sister team had been growing bolder recently and Mavor did not like the threats she heard now. Though Gretel and her brother were more loyal to the queen's gold than the queen herself, their proximity to the her made them dangerous, as did their skills.

"She is a frightened young girl, like you were, Gretel, when you were imprisoned by the witch." Mavor's thick accent did little to hide the tinge of desperation in her voice.

Gretel stepped up onto the wagon and stood next to her brother. Hansel and Gretel were not stupid. There would be a better time to take on Goldenhair.

"Don't even try, Mavor," hissed Gretel. "Tonight we'll collect our reward for the girl and tomorrow I think we'll be hunting for bear. Now get out of our way!"

A fight was always the last thing Mavor wanted. It was not her way, and she had fought earlier to save Hamelin and Patience, but Mavor could not let Elizabeth fall into the hands of the queen. Elizabeth had unique abilities that Goldenhair hoped to further develop and train as a potential ally against the queen rule, but Elizabeth was in a dangerous and fragile point in the training. Goldenhair needed more time.

When she spoke the language of the bears, she did so with a heavy heart. "I'm sorry to ask this of you my three dear friends. They will listen to nothing but the force of might. Use your great strength against them and be careful."

"Nikko. Dosso. Kerker—Kuratden!" said Mavor softly, but firmly.

The bears charged.

Patience, who had been quietly watching the confrontation, turned to Hamelin to speak to him, but he was gone.

She panicked for a moment and quickly looked around, fearing that he had snuck away and disappeared. Much to her surprise, she saw him crawling on his belly, quickly but very carefully, underneath the wagon. She had known Hamelin long enough to know that he would rarely if ever run *toward* danger, but that is exactly what he just did. At any moment, Patience feared, he could be spotted or crushed underneath the wagon's heavy wheels.

Hamelin had moved as quickly as he could toward a set of keys that lay in the dirt on the far side of the wagon. They had fallen when Gretel came off her horse. While Mavor and the bears distracted Gretel and Hansel, Hamelin snuck over to the wagon and crept his way to the keys. He waited for the right moment, and when Gretel had stepped up on the wagon, he grabbed the keys and then quickly backtracked underneath to the rear of the wagon.

Hamelin did not look at the girl in the cage as he crouched down behind the wagon and fumbled with the keys in the lock. He heard her say "Thank you," and then "Hurry." His heart was pounding in his ears and his hands were shaking.

Hamelin heard the bears attack and hurried to try to find the right key to unlock the cage, knowing he could be caught at any moment.

As the bears charged forward to the wagon, Hansel fired his crossbow at the largest bear, Nikko. The shot went high from its mark but dug into the bear's meaty shoulder behind his head, the small bolt disappearing in the thick fur. The bear did not seem to be the least distracted by the attack and rose up on his hind legs against the side of the wagon. He was eye-level with Gretel and let out the terrifying roar that only an angry bear could make.

Unlike the fight with the queen's guards, little more than rowdy thugs, the bears did not intimidate Hansel and Gretel. They were used to hunting and killing animals, even bears. Gretel pulled her sword back and was about to line up a thrust that would fully pierce the bear's heart when Hansel snapped the reins of the horses, driving the cart forward. Gretel lost her balance with the sudden jolt of the wagon and tumbled into it. She fell hard on top of the piled blankets and animal carcasses.

The two other bears had rushed forward, but could not stop the horse and wagon as it lurched forward in a sudden mad dash. Nikko's great paws came down as the wagon dashed away. His thick claws raked against the wooden side, tearing a plank away and leaving a great gouge.

The wagon sped on with Gretel's horse following, driving past the bears and Goldenhair, who backpedaled out of the way to avoid being run over. Patience sprung from her hiding place behind the log and ran after the wagon. Hamelin was still hanging onto the back of the cage, his feet dangling frantically, dragging a trail of dust. Even Mavor Goldenhair was surprised as the wagon passed by with him hanging onto the back. The wagon moved quickly down the dirt road, yet Hamelin still held on with both hands wrapped tightly around the bars, his long coat flapping about his legs.

"Hamelin!" Patience called out.

The trapped woman fumbled with the set of keys, reaching through the bars, trying to find one that would unlock her cage. A key went in. It did not turn. Hamelin strained to hold on, his hands growing numb and his arms and shoulders burning. The next key went in. It did not turn. Hamelin gritted his teeth and prayed for the captive to find the right key quickly. It was then Hamelin realized the bars he was grasping so tightly were part of the cage door.

Another key went in. This one turned with a loud click. The cage door, with Hamelin hanging on to it, swung open wide. If either Gretel or Hansel had turned to look behind them, they would have seen the door swing far out to the right with a tall, thin, and somewhat terrified man being dragged behind it. Instead, Gretel had fought to regain her balance and had climbed back into the front seat of the wagon.

"Brother! What are you doing?" yelled Gretel angrily.

"We can't risk it, Gretel. The queen's bounty on this one is too great to lose, and we need to get her to the castle before sundown or we'll lose another night."

"Let go!" said the woman in the cage. "Now!"

Hamelin closed his eyes and braced for the impact. He let go of the bars and tumbled upon the road in a spray of dirt and mud. The girl crouched, and then hopped from the small cage, tucking into a roll as she hit the road. The wagon rode on, the cage door in the back swinging wildly and hay spilling out as the wagon disappeared around a bend.

Hamelin lay on his back in the middle of the road, the wind knocked from his lungs. He was dazed for a moment, but amazed at what he had just done. His body ached from scrapes and bruises, but he was not seriously injured. He looked up at the trees overhanging the road and watched them move gently in the wind as Mavor's words came back to him. "The winds of the destinies," he remembered, "press many a tree, a branch, and even a single leaf into action."

Then a shadow fell over him.

"Are you hurt?" asked a woman's voice.

Hamelin looked up at the woman. Although she was covered in burlap cloth and dirty with cuts from jumping from the wagon, she was even more attractive than when he first saw her. Her face was framed by thick, curly, deep auburn hair and her sharp green eyes seemed to dance in front of him. Her voice was soft and confident. Hamelin lay there for a moment and looked at her. *It was worth it,* he thought.

"Are you hurt?" she asked again.

"Just resting," he replied. "I don't do that sort of thing much," Hamelin added, managing a weak grin.

She let out a soft chuckle and patted his shoulder. "Thank you very much for rescuing me," she said, smiling.

"Hamelin!" cried Patience as she ran up to him on the road. "Are you okay?"

Hamelin got up slowly, deliberately, and very carefully. Both the woman and Patience helped him to his feet. "Yes," he winced. "But I will most likely be quite sore tomorrow."

"That was a brave and crazy thing you did. You could have been killed!" exclaimed Patience.

Goldenhair approached, warning, "We must to get off the road before they realize what happened and return."

Everyone gathered themselves and quickly followed Goldenhair into the woods.

Mavor pulled the pack from her shoulder and handed it to Elizabeth. "Here are your things. We'll talk more about it later." Elizabeth pulled from the pack a large, weathered, hooded cloak of deep crimson with which to cover herself. Under the cloak, she quickly changed from the makeshift burlap covering to the clothes that had been in the pack.

They were barely out of sight of the road when Hamelin stopped. "I'm not going any further until somebody explains what's going on," he said. His voice quivered between an assertive tone and a nervous one. "Otherwise Patience and I are leaving—bears or not. You can keep the glass slippers." Even Patience was surprised at her friend's abrupt demand.

Goldenhair turned, looking squarely at Hamelin, as Elizabeth watched warily.

"Did he say glass slippers, Goldenhair?" Asked Elizabeth. "As in *the* glass slippers?"

"You are right," Mavor said to Hamelin. When she continued, her tone was more relaxed and her grasp of the human language was more fluid. "Elizabeth, I would like you to meet some very important new friends." She gestured to the tall man and the young girl. "This is Hamelin, and this is Patience."

Elizabeth had finished dressing into her traveling attire and as she fastened her red cloak, she smiled at Patience first. "It's nice to meet you," she said, nodding to the young girl. She turned to Hamelin. "And we've already met," she said. Then she leaned toward Hamelin and kissed him on the cheek. "It's a pleasure to meet you, Hamelin. Thank you, again."

"Hello," said Hamelin, caught off guard and slightly taken aback at the gesture. Patience looked at him with a smirk.

"What do you mean important?" Hamelin asked.

But Goldenhair was already talking to Elizabeth again while she approached the large bear she called Nikko. In expert fashion, she gently removed Hansel's crossbow quarrel from the bear's shoulder. Looking quickly around, Goldenhair grabbed a few leaves from a nearby plant and some small berries from a bush, and she quickly made a mashed paste. Then she applied it caringly over the bear's wound, and she took a moment to scratch the bear's ear. Leaning close, she whispered something too quietly for the others to hear. The bear growled and huffed playfully, seeming to understand the mysterious woman's language. Then she gave the bear a kiss on the side of its enormous furred head. The bear, in turn gave Goldenhair a lick on her face with its long pink tongue. Goldenhair giggled and wiped the wetness of the bear's tongue away with her hand, playfully scolding the huge grizzly, briefly oblivious to everyone else. Then, like a switch, she was aware of the others and her tone turned serious.

"Elizabeth, Hansel and Gretel are getting bolder and their traps are getting cleverer." Holding up the quarrel, she added sternly, "They shot at Nikko again. You must be more cautious. You have been gone two days in the forest. We will work on keeping awareness next time."

Elizabeth lowered her head for a moment. "I'm sorry. I know things are riskier these days with the...with the queen's guards mobilizing. I will try to keep better control."

"What did you mean, important?" Hamelin asked again loudly, feeling frustrated that his demand was being ignored.

Goldenhair began, "There has been a resistance army against the kingdom's current ruler. Queen Cinderella—she prefers to be called Queen Cendrillon, but most here just call her Queen Cinder."

Elizabeth interrupted, "Goldenhair, I'm not sure General White would approve. She is very strict about revealing too much..."

"General White is not here. And these two would not work for the queen. It is not in their spirits; something the general and her rules are not capable of understanding," Goldenhair reminded Elizabeth. "Besides, this young girl has the shards," Goldenhair continued to explain.

"Please." Patience looked at Mavor and then Elizabeth. "Please explain what is so important about these glass slippers. I don't know if going with you is what I need or want to do. I just wanted to put them someplace without having to throw them away."

Patience looked at Goldenhair and held up the pack. "I think you should take them. And Hamelin and I will head back home."

Goldenhair spoke directly to Patience this time. "Once Queen Cinder took power, everything changed for the worse. Soon, a story began that was told throughout the land. The glass slippers had survived. they were a symbol of hope. If those slippers, born of happier times could survive, then there could be again a better time. Should the slippers be found and returned, then so might the hope they would bring with them. She thought for a second, and then added, "As the years of Cinder's reign have taken their toll on the land, that rumor has become legend. And legends, too, inspire hope. They say that her own glass slippers are the only things that can stop Cinderella's reign."

Hamelin looked at Patience. "She's a legend?" he asked.

Elizabeth added, "The story of the shards is whispered throughout the kingdom."

Goldenhair smiled. "There were many stories of someone who was able to sneak the glass slippers out of the castle." She looked at Patience with a warm measure of fondness and respect. "As it turns out, it was a young servant named Patience Moufet who rescued them."

Patience dropped her eyes from Mavor's gaze. The circumstances were much more brutal than that, Patience thought to herself. The memory of that night once again sent a chill through her.

Elizabeth looked at Patience, then at Mavor. "She has the shards?" she asked with excited realization.

"When I was made aware of their return to the kingdom," Goldenhair explained, "I told the resistance and agreed to help find them and bring them to the general. It is safe," she reassured Hamelin and Patience. "General White hopes to use the shards and their stories to energize the resistance and gain support, and the general does want to meet those who have the shards in their possessions. Despite our past disagreements, General White has noble intentions, and I trust her," said Goldenhair. "She and I both fight against the throne in our own way. Although our means are different, our enemy is the same. General White would not risk compromising an ally."

"General White is a *she*?" asked Hamelin. The question went unacknowledged.

Then Goldenhair spoke directly to the young girl. "There was no way for you to know that you were coming back here into such turmoil. For that, I sympathize. But if nothing else, the shards you carry would help to end the queen's evil rule and free those trapped in the castle, including your mother."

"As for your friend," Goldenhair looked at Hamelin, "I need to know that I can trust you. You are protecting young Patience, so I imagine we are on the same side. Therefore, I cannot do this without you as well."

"Uh," Hamelin stuttered, "Yeah, you can trust me. I've come this far with Patience, haven't I?"

* * *

They followed a small path through the woods, avoiding the road but still heading toward a town called Aishew. From there they would travel to the coast to meet their friends—the resistance, Hamelin guessed. Mavor and Elizabeth walked up ahead, talking quietly to each other. The bears walked behind them and in front of Hamelin and Patience, keeping the two travelers far enough away from Elizabeth and Mavor so as not to hear the two women's discussion.

Hamelin walked slowly, wincing with a slight limp as they continued through the woods. Patience stayed with him. "That was a very brave thing you did with the wagon," she said again with a sweet smile.

Hamelin was slightly embarrassed, but even more so when Patience asked, "You like her, don't you?" She stopped and stared at him. Hamelin laughed a little nervously.

"What? No. I mean she seems nice."

Patience said it again, this time more matter-of-factly and to herself, trying to hide the slightest hint of disappointment. "Yes," she whispered. "You like her."

The group came upon a clearing in the woods where there sat the burnt and rotted ruins of an old house. Vines grew over most of the remaining framework and bits of wall and chimney. Shrubs and tall grass hid most of the decayed flooring.

Goldenhair paused here, and seemed to reflect for a moment at this spot, as if it held old memories for her. And then, like an old memory, it faded. She was in the present again. The bears seemed familiar with the area as well. They sniffed around the clearing and finding a spot in the sunlight, lowered themselves upon the grass. They placed their heads on their massive paws and sighed.

"Now," said Mavor, "we can rest a bit." She sat down and reclined upon the great furred back of Dosso, leaning on the bear like a large fur pillow. The bear did not mind.

Elizabeth leaned against the bear as well. Patience sat next to the smaller bear, Kerker, and hesitantly leaned against the soft warm fur. Hamelin sat upon the ground close to Patience and tentatively reached out to pet the bear Kerker, who all but ignored him. He had never been so close to a real bear before. It made Hamelin nervous, but it was apparent that these bears were more accepting of human interaction; not that they were tame pets, but the bears seemed to have a greater understanding because of Goldenhair's ability to interact with them. They sat in a circle of dappled sun and shadow; a cool breeze took the heat from the sun. The only sounds were those of the bears' heavy breathing, the rustle of treetops in the wind, and the distant buzzing of cicadas.

"We have made good time," Mavor stated, "but we must get to the coast by nightfall."

Elizabeth pulled out a few apples from her pack and began to pass them around. Mavor scowled at her offering and Elizabeth shook her head. "They were the only food I could find yesterday," she said defensively. Mavor took the apple from Elizabeth and handed hers to Patience.

"Eat them here. You know they aren't allowed in the meeting." Goldenhair gave Elizabeth an incredulous look, but Elizabeth ignored it. She smiled at Hamelin and tossed him an apple.

"They are just apples, Goldenhair. Relax." Elizabeth bit into one like a rebellious child defying a parent's wishes.

"How long have you known each other?" asked Hamelin, recognizing the relaxed interaction between the two.

Elizabeth was in mid-bite and answered with a mouthful of apple. "It's been about a year now, this winter, since the resistance destroyed Gruff's Bridge. I met Goldenhair just after that."

"Gruff's Bridge is gone?" Hamelin asked with surprised interest. Everyone in the kingdom used that bridge, he recalled. It was the main crossing to the castle.

"Queen Cinder was not pleased about that," added Elizabeth. "Losing that bridge really hindered the queen's troops. Though I hear they are rebuilding it," Elizabeth added as an aside to Goldenhair.

Patience pulled her pack over and placed it on her lap in a forlorn manner. The young girl seemed sad while the others spoke of the recent news. The weight

41

of caring for the glass slippers now seemed a heavier burden on her shoulders.

With a mouth full of apple, its juice sliding from the crook of her lips, Elizabeth looked over at Mavor, concerned for the young girl.

"So?" Hamelin spoke up. "What does it mean?" He started, "She wanted to return the glass slippers to the only proper place she could think of, which was the grave site. It was just going to be a gesture. No big deal, they were just glass, ornamental leftovers from the big wedding..."

"No, Hamelin," Mavor interjected with frustration in her voice. "They are much more than that. They are the last known source of fairy magic in the kingdom, and those shards are the only things that can stop Queen Cendrillon!"

Goldenhair's explanation seemed to hang heavily in the air. For a moment, she had let her composure slip, just a little.

"Oh—of course, fairy magic," Hamelin remarked sarcastically.

Elizabeth interjected, "We suspect they have fairy magic in them, based mostly on the legends and stories; until you both arrived, it was only a rumor that the glass slippers had survived at all. There has not been a fairy godmother around in years. Anyway, we still do not know what to do with them."

"I have heard that General White's lieutenant, Rapunzel was to try to talk to someone about the magic," replied Goldenhair.

"You know General White is not one to latch on to any ideas about magic either, Goldenhair. At least Queen Cinder does not have them, so I guess that is something good. I just hope Cinder doesn't find out her slippers are still around."

Patience stared at the backpack on her lap. "They have magic?"

Mavor's accent flowed over every word she spoke, as she turned back to Patience to explain. "That night five years ago, when the Bloodthorn Wall went up and surrounded the castle, there were few stories that managed to get out in time before the castle was sealed off. We came across a dying man who spoke of a servant woman still in the castle, who was looking for her daughter, and claimed her daughter had run away with the queen's slippers. The woman was a servant named Brown."

Patience's eyes sparkled for a moment, then her look saddened and softened. That was her mother. *How did her mother know about the glass slippers?* Patience had not heard anyone speak of her mother in years. It brought back feelings of sadness that the girl had buried deeply. She wanted to ask more but was afraid to hear the answer, so she remained silent.

"Afterwards, our group searched the kingdom for any girl whose last name was Brown, but we could not find her." Mavor continued to explain. "It was only years later that we discovered the child's name was to have been Moufet."

"My mother insisted I take my stepfather's name when she remarried," Patience whispered sadly. "The Moufets were of a higher status in the castle. She wanted me to have a better life."

Goldenhair continued to speak in her unusual tone. "We had looked for the wrong child. Thinking she was lost, our attentions turned to more matters of pressing, but your story was to become a local legend. The glass slippers were a symbol of a prosperous time for the kingdom, when Cinderella represented all that was good. The story of the glass slippers surviving gave many in the land hope. But more than that, the resistance might be able to extract the magic from these slippers and use it to counter much of Cinderella's power. When we heard from travellers that a young girl by the name of Moufet had crossed over into the kingdom, I was asked to follow and to look in to see if you were in fact her, the legend."

Hamelin told himself he had been right. He had felt they had been watched the other night and they were, but he had more questions. "Who wanted to know? This general?" he asked.

"Except that it just became more complicated," added Mavor. "I've received word today that the Prince of Marchenton is alive and has returned to the kingdom. Syrenka has found him," she added, talking mainly to Elizabeth. Goldenhair looked at Patience and Hamelin. "That was the message the bird had brought me when we first met," she explained as Hamelin nodded in realization. "And so, in the interest of time, we all will meet at once. General White will be very interested in meeting you both," she added, nodding to Patience and Hamelin. "Much is at risk, but much is to be gained."

This was news that even Elizabeth did not know. "Prince Phillip? Really?" asked Elizabeth excitedly. "He's alive?"

"Time will tell, Elizabeth," said Mavor. She did not convey a sense of confidence with her answer.

Now Patience's head was swimming. She had vague recollections of Prince Phillip from when she was a servant girl in the castle. He had been at her mother's wedding and she had the impression of him as a quiet and sad person, yet happy when required to be. The only other thing Patience recalled was the story everyone else had known also. Prince Phillip and his father, the king, had led the army into the battle from which no one had returned. Everyone thought the prince and the king had died. This was ten years ago, at least, and now he was alive. The news was stunning to Patience.

Hamelin looked at Elizabeth. "What happened to this place since I left?"

"A lot," said Elizabeth, and she rose to her feet, brushing the grass from her pants. She held out her hand to Hamelin and helped him to his feet.

"And why were you in a cage?" he asked pointedly as he stared at her.

She paused for a second, unsure how to answer. To Hamelin, she suddenly seemed uncomfortable, but she quickly recovered.

"We are all wanted by the queen, crimes against the throne and such." Satisfied with her answer, she gave a curt nod and a quick smile to end the discussion. Then, the others rose to their feet, as well.

Mavor added, "Hansel and his sister are not to be trifled with. They are dangerous and very skilled witch hunters."

"Then why did they capture Elizabeth? Is she a witch?" asked Hamelin.

"No! I'm not a witch, thank you!" Elizabeth shot back in an offended tone. "They are witch hunters," Elizabeth explained, "but when Cinderella rose to power, she fell in league with the witches. Her witch name is Cendrillon, it is the only name she goes by these days. She essentially gave control over matters of the throne to the witches. Then hunting witches became illegal, as the witches now work for the queen. Now Hansel and Gretel are essentially bounty hunters, and they are mad as hatters."

It took some rousing by Mavor to convince the bears to get up from their rest. Fed and feeling refreshed, the four travelers and the bears began to head toward the town. As the group started their travels again, Mavor added one last bit of news. "Queen Cendrillon and her General, Dendroba are mobilizing the royal army. She is to be planning something. I hope that General White's troops will be ready in time. I'm sure there is to be a better explanation at the meeting."

Mavor placed a warm hand on Patience's shoulder with a look of sincerity. "Bring the shards, at least to meet with General White. That is all I ask. After that, if you and Hamelin want to leave, we will escort you to Bremensport. Just know that things are much bigger than you realize. And everyone, no matter what their role, still plays a part in saving the kingdom."

CHAPTER 3
LORD DENDROBA

Up at the timberline of the mountains, where the trees stopped and yielded to the rocky peaks, one could look down across the great kingdom of Marchenton. The rivers, forest, and sparkling lakes, the very sea itself, was laid out in a shimmering panorama. Even Castle Marchen, where the queen resided, could be seen as a small dark and distant blemish, rather than the imposing, twisted fortress it truly was. From up here, sweet pine fragranced the air. It was quiet and peaceful; a contrast to the presence of Queen Cendrillon's army.

The excavations took place above the timberline, where the only things that seemed to grow were stone and boulder. There was noise intruding now upon the serene desolation of the upper peaks. A division of the queen's guards was deployed here, quickly, and with a purpose: Find a hidden ruin.

The army division had marched through the mountainous terrain for close to four days, set up camp, and finally had begun to dig. This was the spot, they were told. Start digging. Soon, they found something.

An able runner named Mumpers, a simple soldier, carried an important message. Quickly he navigated the boulder-strewn path that led from the excavation site to the base camp below at the timberline. His orders had been specific. If something unusual was found, he was to report it to base camp immediately. Mumpers quickly scampered through the boulders and down toward the pine trees. He feared the news he was carrying, but he feared Dendroba's wrath even more.

The runner could see the black and gold tents of the base camp, and he began to call out. "Lord Dendroba!" He slowed now, letting his stride relax more as he approached the largest tent, the only one adorned with a banner. Finally, his heart pounding from a mixture of exertion and fear, young Mumpers stopped in front of the closed curtain of Lord Dendroba's tent. He paused for a moment to collect himself. Mumpers had never really seen the general, who had only arrived a day earlier at the base camp. However, there was always talk about his gross deformity. Even the many malformed members of the Queen's "rat army" handled Lord Dendroba's disfigurement with a quiet aversion. Mumpers was about ready to proceed when the very curtain exploded open and Dendroba appeared before him.

"What's this?" he growled in a deep voice, glaring down at the young guard. Mumpers felt himself staring while disjointedly stammering a response, which was forced out by the sheer discipline of a soldier to his superior. He chose to look down at his own feet, avoiding any glance upon the horrific face of his general.

"We've found something, my lord. We were supposed to tell you immediately. It is up on the ridge and it's big. Well, not the part that we found but we could tell it would be big," he stammered nervously.

Mumpers saw that those who spoke of Lord Dendroba's appearance spoke true, down to the large gloved hand of his misshapen right arm. Even the newest recruit knew that the right hand of Dendroba was to be feared.

Lord General Phyllo Dendroba towered over the messenger. His thick, broad shoulders and huge barrel chest seemed to block out the rest of the world. "Get some water," he ordered Mumpers. "I will head to the site myself."

With that, Dendroba walked past the runner, dismissing him. Absently, Mumpers noticed that even the rumor he had heard about the general's odd limp was true.

Phyllo Dendroba, detached and uncaring, kept mostly to himself; he seemed to interact with his army only when he absolutely had to. His reputation as a general was legendary enough to be feared, though his grotesque appearance was almost as frightening. The queen's army feared him for being a well-versed practitioner of the black arts; he was also one of the few warlocks of the queen's coven. He was a skilled warrior as well, a serious and imposing figure. His army was most familiar with this aspect.

There were also the stories that circulated by whispers through the ranks, of how the dark magic he practiced had transformed him into the gross abomination that he was, a spell he cast that had gone horribly awry. At least, that is the story that the queen's army would talk about. Though Dendroba never spoke about it, he let the rumor add more fear to his reputation.

Dendroba was tall and very muscular; his thick leather armor seemed to strain against his huge chest. The left side of his face was typical of a man in his mid-thirties, and would even be considered quite handsome, if not for his almost constant scowl. The right side was a drab brown color speckled with green and yellow blemishes, bumpy and rough textured, and mottled with dark brown markings and blotches. He had no hair on his broad scalp. Dendroba's face seemed to be at odds with itself, as well. His mouth was wide but thin lipped and he had a small, flat nose, not unlike that of a common toad. His right eye was somewhat larger and misshapen with a bronze-specked pattern and a dark oval iris. His left eye was a piercing green and perfectly human. Dendroba's gaze always seemed to glare intently at whatever he was looking at. The mottled pattern followed down his thick, almost non-existent neck, across both his shoulders and arms, diminishing to a more subtle pattern across the rest of his body. In short, his deformity bore an uncanny resemblance to a frog or a toad, though none dared speak of it.

His left arm was strong and muscular, but his right arm was small, withered, and lanky; Dendroba always wore a thick black glove on that hand. The right hand of Dendroba was always to be feared.

Lord Dendroba left the camp directly. In a few moments, away from the company of the soldiers he so despised, his disposition softened. Alone now, his odd limp lessened as he took to bounding across the timberline and into the rocky terrain beyond. Another aspect of his deformity was that his legs and hips were not developed like those of normal men and made standing upright and walking uncomfortable. His hips and legs tended to ache and he would often walk with a noticeable limp and an odd gait. His legs were long and muscular, and on the whole, nothing was visibly different from those of any other man. But when alone, Dendroba would stretch his powerful legs and seemingly jump in great strides. His feet were also disfigured, with longer toes and flatter and wider soles. At night, he would remove his boots and soak his feet in water, careful not to let anyone see them. Dendroba had come to terms with his appearance, but preferred not to draw attention to it. He knew of the rumor of a disfiguring spell cast, and he was content with letting everyone think that it was true.

Phyllo Dendroba preferred that to having to endure the pity and the perception of weakness that befouled anyone born into the world with a disfigurement. He had been this way since birth and always there was pity lavished on him, if not from others then from himself. Most of his lonesome childhood was spent in seclusion. He had been cared for quite well by the coven of witches, in an almost protégé-like existence. They taught him many things, strengthened his mind and body, and developed his skill in fighting and witchcraft. But they could do nothing to reverse his disfigurement. No spell would work any better than a simple cloak, hood, and isolation from the staring world. He preferred that solitude. Even as a child, Phyllo preferred to be alone, without the company of the coven that raised him.

Now he scaled the rocks and boulders easily with comfortable strides, and in far less time than it had taken Mumpers to get from the excavation site to the camp. He walked in his more typical fashion just before he came into view. Almost immediately, he heard the announcement of his arrival by a spotter standing on the rocks above him.

When the general reached the top of the path, two of his chief execrators met him. They babbled in hurried excitement and patted their dirt-stained and dusty robes in a poor effort to become presentable. Dendroba enjoyed the effect he had as he towered over them, but he quickly grew disinterested in their rattling explanations. "Just show me," he grumbled, caring little for descriptions of things he was about to see anyway.

They bowed slightly and then gestured in the direction of a large wall of solid rock. Falling in behind their commander, the two continued to annoy the general with explanation. "This is really a secondary site now. We've moved the main site further along to the other side of this cliff face. That one is making tremendous progress," said one of the excavators. "It appears to be a large temple, though we haven't found an entrance. Despite what looks like some sinking and a collapse covered by a landslide, most of the temple is likely to be intact. It will just take some time to clear the rock slides."

The other chief that accompanied them took over the explanation. "But we had small crews checking out surrounding caves, and we came across this one cave in particular. It is the only one to have any sort of markings. The back of the cave had collapsed, but we were able to clear that and support the ceiling. "What we found was...well, it was extraordinary! But none of the dig crew would continue."

"Too spooked," the first chief added.

"Isn't that always the case?" remarked the second chief, shrugging his shoulders.

"They are simple soldiers," commented Dendroba, "only good for simple things."

They arrived shortly at the cave's entrance and found a small crowd of soldiers and workers hovering near the opening. Tools and buckets were scattered everywhere on the ground. Their hushed chattering stopped as Lord Dendroba rounded the corner.

"Go dig up something!" Dendroba bellowed at them in instant disgust. "Take the whole mountain down if you need something to do!" he barked loudly. Dendroba's army disgusted him, especially when they were not working.

Without a word, they grabbed the tools and buckets and shuffled quickly back around the rock wall, not one of them daring to look directly at Dendroba. One of the chiefs broke away to herd the workers to the temple excavation site, leaving the other excavator chief to stand nervously beside Dendroba.

The chief fetched a torch as he and Dendroba arrived at the dark mouth of the cave. The entrance was large, though taller than it was wide. Dendroba would not have trouble standing upright in it.

"Show me," he ordered sharply.

The two walked inside. Torchlight immediately cast flickering shadows throughout the cave. Dendroba's eyes adjusted quickly from the bright sunlight to the dim light provided by the flame. It was much cooler inside, and it smelled of stagnant dust and rock. Uneven stones were scattered across the dirt floor, and more rocks lay piled in the darker recesses of the cave wall. Dendroba was silent as they continued on. They did not walk long before the chief paused, leaning to inspect the wall more closely. From there, the chief continued on a short way, searching the wall but glancing ahead so as not to trip. He paused.

"Here," said the chief, stopping to motion to a section of the cave wall. "The markings look to be some form of language or glyph at least. We need to make rubbings so we can possibly decipher it when we return to the castle."

The general leaned down to look at the markings carved into the wall. There were ten symbols roughly carved in a straight line about chest level for a man. The markings certainly appeared to be writing.

To the chief's amazement, Lord Dendroba deciphered them with little effort. "An End World," he said matter-of-factly.

Dendroba leaned back to consider the implications of the discovery. He had done a great deal of research in the past few years and knew much about what the queen had ordered him to find. It was his primary duty, even above crushing the resistance army, and the search was to be carried out with the utmost secrecy. Here it was, "An End World." The prospect of what he read raised the hairs on the back of the general's neck, and his stomach turned in knots. If this proved to be true, then it would be quite a significant discovery for his queen. However, Dendroba kept his excitement hidden.

He turned to the chief, who stared at him, and then back at the glyphs. The chief never expected the general, of all people, to be able to interpret such markings. He continued to stare in disbelief. Lord Dendroba did not tolerate staring. To him, disbelief and morbid fascination with his deformities were the same. He shoved the torch angrily at the chief.

"What's 'An End World'?" asked the chief. "What does that mean?"

Dendroba offered little explanation other to say, "It's an anagram. You mentioned a doorway," he said. "Let's go."

The chief blinked. "How did you know how to read that? Are you sure that's what it says?"

Staring back at the chief, Dendroba's jaw muscles flexed for a moment in unspoken annoyance. "Doorway."

"Of course," nodded the chief, unsettled by Dendroba's disposition. They turned and made their way deeper into the cave.

The passage narrowed and angled down a bit. The chief, mostly to quell his unease, began to speak to the uninterested general. Nervously the chief remarked how this was the spot where they began to remove rock, shore up the walls, and support the ceiling with wooden beams. Dendroba barely grunted an acknowledgment.

The cave grew small and tightened into an almost normal-sized hallway, with steps that appeared to have been carved into the rock. Somewhat anxiously, the chief pointed out that the steps were already dug into the slope, long before the collapse. Again, the general gave a disinterested grunt.

After a few steps further down, the chief stopped at a door that was nondescript but certainly old stone. "The workers cleared out the rocks." The chief explained. "But when it came to excavating through it, they became scared and eventually refused. For all we know, there's just more collapsed debris on the other side."

"There's a light coming from the other side," observed Dendroba with keen eyesight. "That's probably what spooked your workers." Dendroba did not elaborate further other than to say cryptically, "It's just as well they went no further."

Pushing the chief aside, Dendroba stood in front of the stone slab door. He could see very well in the darkness, but even so, he had trouble making out the faint glow of green light that peeked through nearly invisible cracks around the tightly sealed stone. The door itself was covered in runes with a similar faint glow. Both the outline of the door and the glowing runes would be impossible for a human to see.

The general studied the door intently for nearly a minute. Then, without looking away, he reached out with his left hand and grabbed the chief's torch, dropping it to the ground and snuffing it out with his boot. The cave went black.

"I...I can't see a thing in this part of the cave, my lord," stammered the frightened chief in the dark.

"Then find your way back outside," Dendroba shot back. "I can see just fine. I have no need of you from here."

"Yes sire, of course." The chief clearly wanted to stay and continue further. He silently vowed to return and continue to explore the passage, with proper lighting, after the general had left. His eyes strained to adjust to the darkness, and he paused to get his bearings before he began to feel his way back up the steps.

Dendroba turned his attention back to the door and briefly studied the runes, but they were unlike those he read earlier, and he did not recognize them. he examined the door structure intently.

"This door slides down from the top," he whispered to himself. He squatted down and dug his fingers into the minuscule crevice where the slab met the floor.

"Wait!" Dendroba wagged his finger with a sudden idea. He called back to the chief, who had barely begun to fumble for the exit. "Grab one of the wooden support beams," he ordered.

Without question, the chief did so. Excited that he might have an opportunity to continue the investigation, he quickly stumbled back up the cave steps in the darkness. More than once, he misjudged a step, sending him hands out to hit the cold stone with stinging pain and bruised knees. The chief clambered around a pile of excavation rubble and found a short piece of solid wooden beam. It was awkward and heavy, but he made his way back with it.

Perhaps it was a sealed entrance to a great tomb, the chief thought to himself. Would there be treasure? Some great secret? Perhaps it was a door leading to the temple they were searching for. Would they be the first inside? Were there traps?

"Got it," said the chief, now standing again with the general at the door.

"If I can lift the door—" the General started.

"A stone door that size?" The chief interrupted, "I don't think it's possible…" Even in the darkness, he could feel Dendroba's annoyance.

"When I lift the door," Dendroba repeated, putting biting emphasis on the word *when*, "you will brace it open with the beam."

"Yes, sir."

Dendroba could see the beam with his excellent night vision and estimated its height. Then, with his powerful arms and even stronger legs, he did something that not even the strongest human could accomplish. He began to lift the huge stone door. His legs strained under the weight as his powerful arms held the slab. He could feel the muscles in his back and shoulders scream as he strained to raise the rune-covered slab to his waist. then shifting his grip, he brought the rock door up to his chest. Hissing through his teeth, he ordered the chief, "Get the beam under it!"

The darkness seemed to ebb a little with the open slab door. Whether it was from his eyes finally adjusting to the darkness, or perhaps the glow was getting brighter, he could see the general's great shape holding the door. Quickly, the chief managed to shove the short beam under to brace the slab.

With the beam in place, Dendroba cautiously released the door onto the beam and moved back. The thick wooden beam was solid under the great weight, and there was now a four-foot opening through which the general could easily slip.

"That door…no man could lift…impossible," muttered the chief in the darkness.

Once Lord Dendroba was sure that the door would stay, he turned to the chief, his chest still heaving with exhaustion. "Do not follow. Leave the cave. Immediately," said the general. His breathing calmed back to a normal rhythm.

"Yes, yes, my lord." There was obvious disappointment in the chief's reply. Without argument, he quickly found his way back up the steps and out, all the while thinking that perhaps there was some hideous trap awaiting whomever crossed through that door, and it was better that it was the general who found it than himself.

Dendroba waited a long moment to ensure the chief was on his way. He walked up the stairs and gazed down the length of the cave, listening to make sure he could hear the slight, panicked breathing of a man stumbling blindly in a dark cave.

Satisfied, he went back to the stone door and quickly slipped underneath to the other side. Pausing a moment to consider whether he should knock the beam out and close the great door behind him, he decided to leave what could be the only exit open.

The genre then headed down into the darkness of a stairway, the mysterious faint glow growing stronger as he descended step by step. The stairway wound downward rather deeply, before opening into a spaciously large, cavern of a room with a vaulted ceiling. The wall at the far end was nothing short of gigantic, well over a hundred feet high. It was intricately carved and over every possible inch of its surface were more runes similar to those on the slab door.

A faint glow of green light glowed throughout the room. There was a crisp chill in the air, even cooler than one would expect from a subterranean cavern. It was cold enough for frost to cover the walls and the floor. The wall on the stairwell side of the room was smaller, more natural looking and rocky with not a single rune on it—far more similar to a normal cavern wall—and about twenty feet up the side of it the vaulted ceiling began to stretch into the darker reaches. This smaller wall had many shelves carved into it, and a simple fireplace mantle protruded from the rock wall above a fire pit. The inside, charred and blackened by many fires, glistened with ice crystals. But there had been no fire in there for quite some time.

General Dendroba stood for a moment and took in the sight before him. Any other man would have been grinning ear-to-ear with excitement at such a discovery, but he was stoic at the sight of it all.

The sound of a voice broke the eerie silence quite unexpectedly and startled the impassive general. It was somewhat matter-of-fact tinged with a hint of annoyance it said, "If you've come for the mirror, you're too late. Someone has already taken it."

CHAPTER 4
AN UNDERGROUND MOVEMENT

Lord Dendroba had expected the temple to be empty. The location of the temple, its very existence, was a lost secret. For years, he had pored over scrolls and records in the royal archives and castle libraries. He had uncovered vague references and the occasional reference that would fill in pieces of the puzzle, moving the work forward until the temple's location was revealed. It was the top priority of Queen Cendrillon and the witch coven. Moreover, it was a welcome challenge for Dendroba. He felt he was groomed for the task as the coven had raised him. He knew many of the secrets of the temple, including what should be in it, though he was not sure what made finding it such a priority for the queen. With all of his research about the temple, he believed it to be long abandoned.

Dendroba was surprised and not pleased that there was someone there. Nor was he happy to hear that someone else, had taken the one artifact that Dendroba himself had come to claim. The general clenched his teeth, flexing his jaw muscles with annoyance. "Doubtful," he mused to himself, "the thief would even know what he has. He's probably at the market trying to sell it." He considered the possibility and grimaced at the thought; but who was the man who now stood before him?

Standing just inside a small and almost nondescript door, perpendicular to the massive rune covered wall, was a strange middle-aged man who was somewhat portly, with a large nose, and a mess of short dark hair that made him look like he had just woken up. A small hat with a flat crown topped his hair. His appearance was a bit unkempt, as he was dressed in a simple, brownish, long tunic that looked more like an apron of sorts. He carried a small wooden tote box of tools—hammers, saws and files—in his chubby hand. Dendroba regarded the stranger as nothing more than a commoner, a carpenter perhaps, who kept a vigil on this temple and kept up its repairs.

The carpenter stood there with a slight frown. "So, if the mirror is your business, your business isn't here." He gestured at the door Dendroba had entered from, "I suggest you leave. This place is going to be very busy in a little while." He pulled a piece of bread from his pocket and shoved it into his mouth.

As he chewed he muttered absently, "I'm going to have to board that door up."

Dendroba furrowed his brow, "What do you mean busy? This was supposed to be an abandoned temple, hundreds of years old."

The carpenter rolled his eyes. "There has been a violation of portal protocols, I'm afraid" he began to explain quickly as he flapped his arms at the general, trying to herd him back through the door as one might shoo a goose into a pen. Meanwhile, Dendroba's eyes widened at the mention of a portal. That was what the queen had charged him to find. He did not move from his spot.

"What sort of violation? Isn't the mirror the portal?" His concern was mainly to find out if the portal was broken or damaged.

The carpenter stopped ushering for a moment and seemed to consider the general's question. When he answered, his tone had changed. "Yes the mirror is a portal, but the main gateway is here in the temple. Perhaps you might be able to help. It would save our world a lot of grief and your world a lot of trouble."

Dendroba pondered what sounded like a threat as the man continued. "The queen is sending a search party to look for a young man who had used this gateway to get back here. He had trespassed into our land and caused many problems. His activation and use of the gateway portal to get here is also a violation. The queen wants him to stand trial. Really, though, she wants his head. At least that is what I have heard. Now..."

Dendroba scowled at the man, but decided to play dumb. "I serve the queen personally. I would know of such things."

The carpenter laughed. "Not your queen, my large friend—my queen. Now if you knew where this man was it would save us a lot of time," the carpenter gave a wiry smirk, "And we wouldn't cause too much trouble while we were here. The lad's name is Jack, and he caused quite a ruckus in our parts."

The portly carpenter with the leather apron again motioned to the door. "He's a young lad, blonde hair, mid-twenties. If you see him on your way out, let us know. We will be here. Now, the time has come—"

The carpenter's attention turned from trying to get his unwanted visitor to leave to the sudden flashing runes on the massive wall behind him.

Dendroba stood silently and watched, trying to take in every little detail he could, his thoughts frenzied with the recent revelations. The runes that flashed seemed to be in no recognizable pattern, but the carpenter understood them, his head darting up and down as he followed the glowing markings around the giant wall.

"Oh dear," the carpenter said, and in a brisk motion scurried to the wall. He dug around in his pockets and produced two small rock-like oyster shells. With shaking hands, he placed them in small notches in the wall. More runes lit up, this time in sequence straight up the wall. The carpenter remarked disapprovingly as he watched the sequence of lights, "You must have brought friends. The guardian is being summoned now."

He turned to face Dendroba, who was now standing close behind him. His startled expression quickly melted into a painful realization that Dendroba had slid a dagger deep into his belly.

"The temple is under attack," said the carpenter, finishing his last sentence as he slowly slid down against the wall, a few remaining oyster shells tumbling from his hands to the floor.

Dendroba stepped back to see the pattern of runes light to the very top of the wall. With a low rumble, the wall itself began to tremble, but the trembling and loud cracking that followed seemed to come from beyond the small nondescript door the carpenter had used.

"Guardian?" he thought to himself. "Interesting."

Then Dendroba heard another voice, one more familiar to him. "General," said the chief, "I'm sorry to interrupt—but you should know that the excavation site is under attack. Dwarves again." The chief looked around the room quickly.

"Thank you chief. I see you've disobeyed orders," said Dendroba dryly. His tone was annoyed mainly at the interruption that would take him away from exploring the temple further. Indeed, his attention was required at the surface now.

There was only one force in all of Marchenton that dared to continue to defy the throne—the dwarven resistance, led by Snow White. This small army, though loosely organized, had proven to be quite a disruption over the past few years. Often, their hit-and-run tactics were as difficult to battle as it was finding any sort of rebel stronghold. The queen's general knew his army outnumbered the resistance fighters, but the resistance was far quicker to mobilize and strike. This attack's timing was very frustrating, and Dendroba who mentally vowed to make a more concerted effort to eradicate Snow White's army after he secured the temple. He quietly turned and walked back up towards the entrance cave, past the chief.

As the general and his chief engineer emerged from the mouth of the cave, the surrounding area seemed serene, quite opposite from what the chief had described. But Dendroba spied something amid the bright boulders that surrounded the mountaintop—a smear of blood against the white rock. As they stepped out into the clearing, the chief was surprised that his general did not follow to where the battle was.

"M-my Lord, the excavation is being attacked. This way, hurry!" He pointed up the ridge.

General Dendroba caught sight of one of his soldiers scurrying among the trees and boulders. He recognized the soldier as Mumpers. "You there!" He shouted. Mumpers ran over, giving him a salute with a bloodied arm. "Find Commander Carabas. He is to take command of the situation. Tell him, on my orders to take down every dwarf he can, and this time try to capture one for questioning. But by all means he is to secure the temple. No matter what."

Mumpers nodded. "Yes, m'lord."

Dendroba added, "I must go and meet with the queen immediately."

The soldier hurried off to relay the general's orders.

"Everyone up at the site, including your workers and the dwarven resistance, will be dead. It's a lost battle at this point." Dendroba remarked coolly to the chief, who quickly paled at the comment.

Had Dendroba realized the strange carpenter had been activating some hidden temple defense, he would have killed the carpenter before he could place the oyster shells. Perhaps then, the battle could have gone differently. On the other hand, had this guardian been summoned by another means? Dendroba admitted only to himself that he had realized too late. "The guardian," the carpenter had said. Whatever the guardian was, thought Dendroba, it was likely big. "I must return to the queen." Dendroba muttered absently.

General Dendroba realized it was now too quiet. With his heightened sense, he heard a rock shift. Dendroba whirled around, startling the excavator chief nearby, and caught sight of a dwarven crossbow aimed at him directly from the rocky outcroppings above. Out in the open, the deadly crossbow had them cold. Dendroba heard the release of the bolt, and in a lightning fast reaction, grabbed the chief, pulling him in front as a shield. The crossbow bolt struck the surprised chief in the back of head with deadly accuracy. Dendroba dropped him quickly and sprang into action. In an instant, he leaped over the dead chief's body with his strong legs and tumbled behind a boulder for cover. Another bolt had fired quickly, but had missed its mark and hit the fallen chief's body again while the general was in midair.

Dendroba knew how fast it took the dwarves to reload a crossbow. He knew now that there were two shooters—one shooting as the other was reloading.

The general cursed himself for letting his thoughts on the temple distract him; cautiously he shot a quick glance out from behind the boulder. There was another dull twang and an instant later the rock beside him chipped with a loud, hard crack as the bolt shattered against the stone. Small bits of rock stung Dendroba's skin, the shot had been too close.

In that instant, he saw exactly where the shot had come from and decided he stood a better chance of shortening the distance than making himself more of a target as he tried to get away. He moved quickly, knowing he was going to force the second crossbowman to fire, but temporarily leaving both dwarves unready for the unexpected move. Quickly, Dendroba used his powerful legs and jumped with as much force as he could toward the dwarves. He felt the burn of a crossbow bolt slice across his left shoulder, but his leap put him against the rock wall underneath the dwarves' position. Squatted down, he leaped straight up, reaching high and grabbing a handhold just underneath their perch. He then found a foothold just as the crossbowman leaned out from the rock, and pointing the crossbow almost point blank as Dendroba stared up at him. The dwarf hesitated for a moment, not expecting to see his target coming directly below him, and within arm's reach.

Dendroba grabbed the stock of the crossbow and pushed it up, forcing the shot to go wide. He shoved the emptied crossbow into the stunned dwarf's face, pushing him backward. Moving incredibly fast, he scaled the rock and was now upon the snipers.

The second dwarf threw his empty crossbow to the ground, and pulled out a long dagger. Dendroba wasted no time. With a powerful kick, his strong leg slammed the dwarf hard against the rock; he could feel the dwarf's ribs give and then crack inward from the blow.

The first dwarf turned and started to scramble through the rocks while holding his bloodied nose.

"Not this time," growled the general. He raced after the escaping dwarf, quickly catching up to the stubby-legged assassin. He then pulled his thick feet out from under him and slammed the dwarf against the rock, knocking him unconscious. "You," he pointed at the unconscious dwarf. "I intend to get answers from."

He took a moment to catch his breath; and began to feel the pain from the wound in his shoulder.

As he collected his thoughts for a second, Dendroba saw a figure standing on a ridge above him.

It was the leader of the dwarven resistance, General Snow White, observing the battle from afar. It was only for a brief moment, as she quickly turned and disappeared behind the ridge. She was unmistakable to him with her white armor and long dark hair. For years now, she had been a thorn in his side. In any other encounter, he would have sent his whole army to capture her, but he could not waste any more time today. There was too much at stake. Snow White proved to be an intriguing foe, and even Dendroba could respect that. She was a challenge to the general, who found her tactics and level of engagement infuriating but also very skilled. Her strategies rivaled his own. The queen's general felt equally matched when their forces clashed and he found this fascinating, despite himself.

"Another day," Dendroba grumbled as he shifted the body of the unconscious dwarf on his shoulder. He had captured one of her dwarves and would make the dwarf talk. He cursed under his breath one last time at the missed opportunity as he watched where Snow White had moved out of sight. He knew it was too dangerous to stay, and that he had to take his prisoner and get back to the camp. But as he began to navigate down the rocks with his stout prisoner on his shoulder, he heard a horrible sound.

It was the roar of the guardian...a deep rumble that echoed through the stone. The sound was unmistakable and unnatural. Even Lord Dendroba gave pause to consider what could make such a terrible bellow. He would regroup his surviving troops and contend with the guardian later, he decided.

Because the general's base camp was further down the mountainside and below the tree line, it had remained undiscovered by the dwarven attack force. The purple skies of dusk began to overtake the mountain. None of the excavation workers had returned to the camp. Large pole mounted braziers gave an orange flickering glow against the deepening shadows and the chilled mountain air. The camp was thrown into high alert when Dendroba arrived, carrying a dwarven prisoner directly to his tent. He summoned two soldiers to stand guard and told them he was not to be disturbed.

A few hours later, Lord Dendroba stepped from his tent as he tugged on the glove of his disfigured right hand. Sliding it over his hand carefully and adjusting it as he spoke to the guards. "Dispose of the body, and then you're dismissed."

With his odd gait, he walked to a water-filled barrel, took a cup from the side, and drank. When the guards had carried out the limp body of the dwarf, one guard nodded with his head at the remains.

"Did you see the glove? It is the right hand, I tell 'ya. That's what killed this dwarf." The other guard mumbled about not wanting to think about it. As one might throw garbage onto a trash pile, they flung the dwarf's body onto a large fire and walked away.

Dendroba took a deep breath, closing his eyes, and smelled the cool, pine-scented wind tainted with the odor of burning flesh. Now it was time to report his findings to the queen.

He took another cup of water from the barrel and brought it with him back into the tent. It was a large tent for a general that did not like to travel with his army, and he kept it rather sparse. There was a folding table with books and maps stuffed in a wooden crate beneath it. Near that was a large cot with a shallow basin of water tucked underneath. Oil lanterns hung from the center pole, casting a warm light into all but the very corners of the tent. Near the bed was a tall empty wooden rack, useful for holding weapons and equipment, but for Dendroba it held his cloak and a couple of leather bags. The general placed the water on the table and carefully took the basin from under the cot. He set it on the table and added the water from the cup, filling the basin. Then he pulled a small gold orb, slightly larger than an apple, from his belt pouch.

Dendroba closed his fist around it and began to chant. These were the chants of the coven, the rhythms of the dark arts that he knew well. In a moment, he finished and quickly placed the orb in the basin. The water steamed and bubbled for a moment, but when it calmed and the steam cleared, the water's surface was smooth as glass, and almost as rigid.

A face appeared, a dark reflection, but it was not Dendroba's disfigured face as he stood above the basin, staring at the water's surface, but that of woman.

"My queen," Dendroba whispered.

The woman's reflection responded sending tiny, uniform ripples across the water's surface.

"Yes, Dendroba," acknowledged the voice coolly; it seemed to come from the very surface of the water itself.

He began his report. "We have the location of An End World. The temple is here. It was covered by a partial landslide and excavators have been clearing the main entrance." Dendroba hesitated; it would be difficult to explain the rest of his discovery.

"I was able to find another smaller entrance..." he started.

The queen's face stared back at him from the water. "Go on."

"It appears the temple may have been looted before our arrival."

The queen responded with a seething, "What?" One brow raised in disapproval. "Is there a portal gate still there? Is it operational? What about the mirror?"

Dendroba continued in a measured voice. "The portal has already been activated from the other side. There was a carpenter there, preparing the temple when I arrived. It seems Wonderland has already begun mobilizing."

The queen's tone was harsh. "How is that possible? How could they have known?" Then she dismissed it. "No matter, the court will contend with that upon arrival." Dendroba knew "the court" referred to the queen and her stepmother, and in that case, he would have preferred to have the temple fully secured. They both were the most powerful witches in the kingdom. Dendroba knew their power to be far greater than his own, and they could better contend with any complications from harnessing the portal's power.

"Yes, my queen." The general continued, "But there are a few other details you should be aware of. The temple has a defense in place...a guardian, a large beast that has already wiped out most of the excavation team."

"I'm sure that is something you can take care of, General. Or would you like me to hire Hansel and his sister to come help you?"

"That won't be necessary," he retorted with mild annoyance. Almost to stress how he had indeed maintained control of the situation, he continued on to an even more important detail. "During the excavation, we were attacked by a small force of General White's dwarves. This temple guardian disrupted their surprise attack, and I managed to capture one of White's dwarves for questioning."

The queen's mood changed instantly. "You have one of General White's dwarves? This is very good, Phyllo. Were you able to hold the temple carpenter you mentioned as well?"

"The temple carpenter didn't survive the dwarves' attack." The general paused at his own lie. "And the dwarf didn't survive the whole interrogation." That part was true. "Then why are you telling me this, General?"

"The dwarf was able to tell us exactly where General White will be. She is traveling with her commanders to the coast to a small meetinghouse on the beach, north of the village of Aishew. She will be meeting there with several others of the underground resistance."

"That is excellent news, Phyllo," praised the queen. "The temple found and now the resistance leaders all but handed to us. Today is a good day. I will send a legion there." The queen paused with a thought. "You shall go there as well. I want to make sure White is dead. You will bring me her heart. Then we shall meet back at the temple."

"What about this temple guardian?" Dendroba asked.

"Do not make it your concern. I have decided I will in fact, send Hansel and Gretel to finish it off. They are due back with the werewolf tonight, and I will throw enough money at them that they will leave immediately to fight whatever is there. It is no real loss if they do not survive. Better they should perish than my trusted Dendroba." Cendrillon's compliments were rare.

"Thank you, my queen. There is one more thing," Dendroba added. "It is about the temple carpenter. A minor detail at best." Dendroba could see the queen tilt her head, puzzled.

"The carpenter said the temple robber came through from their side of the portal, and that the robber took the mirror."

"And?"

"The carpenter referred to the man as Jack." Dendroba stated matter-of-factly, though he knew it had far greater implications.

The queen's face went blank. "Jack?" She was quiet for a moment. "You don't suppose it's him?"

"Well," Dendroba replied, "it could just be the name. After all, it was many years ago."

"No," she responded firmly. "It's him. It could only be him," the queen said with a shallow laugh, amused at the irony and sudden twist of fate. "Only Jack could have survived the Beanstalk War. Only Jack would have come back through that portal." She shook her head in disbelief. "Only Jack would've taken the mirror. Only Jack would be the one to derail my plan." She nodded absently. "Jack is alive."

"But with the portal now activated," Dendroba responded, "is the Looking Glass still needed to serve as the gateway?"

The queen quietly pondered this idea for a long moment. Having Wonderland's Looking Glass brought to her was really a matter of convenience. It would save the queen a trip to the temple. It served the same purpose as the portal, and now with the portal activated, she did not need the mirror. Nevertheless, Cendrillon wanted it. She wanted to be able to study the mirror, to touch it. She looked straight at Dendroba as her image began to fade from the water's surface, and her voice still lingered as the water shifted to a duller, more natural consistency.

"No doubt Jack would be involved with that damned resistance movement, as I am sure that Snow White would be interested in what he has. Find Jack," she ordered. The mere speculation of her lover with another woman, especially General White, was enough to enflame Cendrillon's suspicions. "But bring him back alive," she added with resignation. She had loved Jack very much even before she was queen. Dendroba noted quietly that it seemed her love for him still lingered.

CHAPTER 5
THERE WAS AN OLD WOMAN

Patience had been quiet since the group left the clearing that morning. She did not expect to hear about her mother or the shards, and she was left feeling rather numb to everything. Lost in her own thoughts she walked alongside Dosso, keeping a hand on the bear's fur for comfort and paying little attention to the conversation Hamelin and Elizabeth had struck up to pass the time. She barely noticed that the forest trail had become a well-traveled dirt road, and they were now walking along the outskirts of the forest rather than through it. Patience kept her head down and considered what Goldenhair had said, about the special contents of her pack, that now seemed much heavier than before. She watched her feet shuffle along the road, allowing the bear lead her along.

Absently, she heard Elizabeth ask Hamelin about how he avoided conscription in the army during the beanstalk war. "Well," said Hamelin, "as soon as I heard the prince was conscripting for the army, I thought to myself, hey if there's one thing I'm not, it's a fighter." Then after an embarrassing pause, he added, "I basically hid on my mother's farm."

Elizabeth let out a warm laugh, her eyes sparkling in the morning sun. "I'm sure many people did. I was young then and lived in a village on the very outskirts of the kingdom. We pretty much kept to ourselves." She seemed uncomfortable that she was now talking about her past and, desperate to move the conversation along, she quickly added, "So where were you when the Bloodthorn Wall went up?" Almost immediately, she apologized. For anyone in the kingdom it was an uneasy memory to recall. "I'm sorry," she said. "It's just that's when the kingdom really turned for the worse."

Patience had already heard Hamelin's story. Now her thoughts drifted back to that fateful night she had tried so hard to forget these past five years. She was so enwrapped in her thoughts she did not realize how far they had traveled.

"We'll rest here," Goldenhair said. "We're among friends here."

Patience temporarily shelved the dark memories and whirlwind thoughts that had preoccupied her mind as she looked ahead to see where "here" was.

"This is the village of Aishew," Elizabeth explained as they neared the collection of drab grey shacks that lined either side of a washed out, muddied road. Many of the buildings were pieced together from what seemed like parts of other buildings, painted panels of red or blue, cracked and faded, new wood hammered next to older wood.

Most of the houses were makeshift, built on short stilts and consisting of a single floor. Other buildings had collapsed or were abandoned to various stages of ruin. It seemed to Hamelin and Patience that Aishew had once been a much greater village than what stood before them. Now only the most steadfast of villagers remained, rebuilding with an overhanging sense of remorse. Discarded crushed rock from walls, broken panels of wood, and other pieces of junk piled nearby had become overgrown with weeds and was home to rats and cats that bounded from sight of the strangers.

Those few villagers who were in sight paid the group no notice, barely bothering to look their way for more than a moment before they continued with the daily chores. Not even the sight of three large bears walking through their town had warranted any attention. But Hamelin noticed something curious.

"They're all women."

"The men who were conscripted years ago never returned," answered Goldenhair as she led them uphill. Ahead was a larger building that seemed more intact than the others. "Those men who were left behind were too old or sick," she said.

"Aishew barely survived the beanstalk war," added Elizabeth as she pointed to another house further out, abandoned with half of it clearly nothing more than a burned pile of rubble. "And the queen's rat army periodically shows up in towns and removes children, just the boys really, to keep any attempt at an effective uprising to a minimum."

Hamelin was speechless, and all Patience could do was look around at the devastation and destitute state of the village with a sense of shock. Even though she had spent her time as a servant girl, she had grown up within the protective and luxurious castle walls. Only when she had traveled with Hamelin as they fled the kingdom did she see how other commoners typically lived. Seeing Aishew was seeing the worst of it. Even a little girl could see the town's former glory lying within the rubble, with pieces of ornate signs or brass fixtures now molted green from exposure, and even on the very road they walked, the mud and dirt gave way to patches of gilded worn cobblestone pushing through the cracks.

Patience moved closer to Hamelin as they walked on. The group was heading directly toward a larger building at the far end of town. It resembled the barn-like structure of an old mill. A short, dilapidated stone wall sectioned off a yard, the wall and its small simple rusted gate crumbling in disrepair.

"We're stopping here?" Hamelin asked.

For the most part, he and his traveling companion had always stuck to the trails and roads with little more than improvised lean-tos or caves as shelter on their trip back to the kingdom. It had been at least a week or more since they had left the comfort of an inn. Even this old mill would do for a respite.

"There are friends here," Goldenhair said again as she turned and gave Hamelin a tattooed wink. "But we can only stay a few moments."

Screams of delight suddenly filled the air. They were the excited cries of children, something Hamelin had not heard in a long time.

"Goldenhair!" the children shrieked with delight as they ran from the door of the large house, across the tree-lined yard toward the group. The children brought a smile to Goldenhair's face and her eyes lit up as they ran to her. In truth, seeing them was a welcome change for all of the weary travelers. Goldenhair knelt down to hug the lot of them. There were about a dozen children, mostly girls, but none was older than ten. They greeted the group with innocent enthusiasm. The children then ran to the bears and began calling out the bears names, petting and hugging them as well. The creatures, snouting the kids and licked their faces.

Hamelin looked down at Patience. "I guess they know them." He shrugged with a smile.

Elizabeth quietly explained, "We've stopped here many times. It has been a good way to get information out to the rest of the commoners throughout the kingdom. The woman that lives here is known all over the villages for her help with the children. She talks with many people about the resistance, collecting resources, and keeping the kids safe. The children are mostly orphans or they got separated from their parents who could not keep them safe from the queen's army."

One of the children picked up a stick, holding it like a sword.

"I'm General White!" she proclaimed. "And my army of dwarves will defeat you!"

Her army of dwarves were in fact two other children on their knees, waving sticks with playful menace.

The girl turned to another girl, who also brandished a stick like a wand and wore a small broken embroidering hoop as a crown.

"I'm Queen Cinder!" she shouted in mock evilness. "I will turn you into my rat army!" She waved her branch at the others with a playful smile as one of the "dwarves" got down on all fours and started to squeak.

Then a younger girl, wanting to join the fun, ran over shouting, "I'm Goldie hair! I'm Goldie hair!" Kerker the young bear bounded alongside the child in a playful manner.

"Kerker," the girl squealed, "get the Queen Cinder!" She pointed to the girl with the hoop on her head.

Kerker promptly sat down next to the small child, then laid down and rolled over on his back and stretched his paws upwards, indicating he would rather get his belly scratched than defeat the evil queen. This caused the children to erupt in a chorus of giggles. The girl with the hoop crown quickly got back into character. "Ha! I've defeated your bears, Goldenhair!"

Then another girl jumped in front of the pretend queen. The girl had pulled off her small shoe and triumphantly held it in the air. "I have the only thing that will defeat your evil, Queen Cinder! Your glass slippers!"

Then she tapped the girl with the hoop crown on her shoulder, and the girl did a pretend swoon, carefully falling down to the ground. "No! Not the glass slippers!"

Patience had quickly become uncomfortable with the children's impromptu play.

A woman appeared at the door of the house dressed in a simple grey-ish dress, wiping her hand on her apron as she leaned on her cane. Her hair was long with streaks of grey, silver, and white.

"Hello!" the old woman called out in a friendly manner to Goldenhair. "I see you have brought friends. Come in!" she said. "Come in!" She looked over as the children and the bears ran about the yard chasing each other. "Katelee! Don't pull on Kerker's ear like that, sweetie. Play nice."

"Nikko Dos esqu benal jove tu! Jove tu," Goldenhair called out to her bear. And then she turned and said reassuringly, "The bears will be fine with the children. I told them not to eat too many of them before dinner."

"I know they will be—they always have been. Ah, Mavor Goldenhair, it is good to see you." The old woman smiled and then gave her a hug full of warmth and generosity. Mavor stood tall and stately over the old woman, a vision of youth and vitality next to the fragile and aged friend that greeted her kindly.

"Your English is getting better," remarked the old woman.

"I have been away from people for a while," replied Goldenhair, "but, this language, it comes back to me. I am sorry," she apologized. "I have some supplies, but we can only spare a short visit."

Hamelin leaned over to Elizabeth as they walked toward the house. "Who is this? Is this General White?" he whispered.

Elizabeth looked at him askance and shook her head in response. "An old friend," she answered simply.

The old woman invited the others in with a wave of her hand. "I am Bertha Goosefoot. Call me Bertha." She tapped at her foot with her cane, which, though wrapped in cloth, was noticeably misshapen. "Always pleased to meet new people." She patted Hamelin on the arm as they walked through the door, her deformed foot, giving her an endearing waddle.

"There is talk that General White's army has fought with the queen's forces. Any news?"

Goldenhair replied. "I know that Snow White's army is on the move again, but not much more than that can I offer."

"I will be sure to tell the others." Bertha smiled.

Goldenhair reached into her pack and handed small wrapped packages to the old woman. "Letters, for the boys downstairs," she said, "from their parents."

Bertha hesitated as she took them. Goldenhair took her concerned look as one for revealing the secret hideaway to the newcomers. "They know. It's okay, you can trust them," she assured the old woman, nodding to Hamelin and Patience. But Goldenhair had misinterpreted the old woman's pause.

"There is, ah…seed for planting in season," Goldenhair continued, placing the pack on a large cluttered table in the middle of the dark room, and pulling out several small pouches. "Syrenka and I have made some more of the healing paste for you from the forest plants." Goldenhair continued to pull out small bundles of plants and a root, going over what each one was, how it should be prepared, and what it should be used for.

Patience noticed the woman paid little attention. She still held the packet of letters in her hands.

Hamelin and the others hovered near the doorway. "So…" whispered Hamelin to Elizabeth, "What's going on?"

Elizabeth whispered back, "Goldenhair spends a lot of her time in the forests and traveling. She has made many friends. This old mill building was the only one in Aishew that had a cellar, a place where the townspeople could hide their children. Many of the parents never came back for their children. Since the Bloodthorn Wall and Queen Cendrillon's rule, she has been helping where she can. That's how she became involved with General White's movement."

Wrapped up in her explanations, Goldenhair had not noticed that the old woman had not been paying attention. "Apples?" asked Goldenhair, looking at Elizabeth. Elizabeth smiled and unshouldered her pack. She rummaged inside and pulled out a small sack of the remaining apples which she handed to Goldenhair. "I'm sorry I couldn't bring more this time. I've had some recent things to deal with," Goldenhair said as she placed the rest of the supplies on the table. She then retied her pack and threw it back over her shoulder.

"Mavor," said the old woman with a somber, quiet tone, still holding the letters. "They came and took most of the boys about two weeks ago. They took even the younger ones this time."

Goldenhair was dumbfounded as if the wind had been sucked out of her lungs. "How?" she finally managed. "How did they find them?"

Bertha shot a glance at the others near the doors and gave a nervous laugh, trying to make a lighter tone of the subject. "Well, Charlie, the red headed one, he'd been sick that week. The children hid in the cellar, but Charlie had a terrible coughing fit. The other boys tried to keep him quiet…" Her voice trailed off, but she gave a weak smile, quickly dabbing her eyes with her apron, and composed herself. "Thank you for this," she gestured to the table. "The seeds will do much good here," she finished lamely, her eyes wet with quiet tears.

Goldenhair tightened her jaw as she scowled in sadness and frustration at the news. She muttered something in her language that no one understood exactly, but her tone said enough.

Bertha placed the letters on the table, clapped her hands together, and in a decidedly happier tone said, "Well, I'm sorry I've no broth ready today, but I must at least give you some bread for your journey." She looked at Hamelin and Patience. "Please excuse the mess," she added.

Elizabeth spoke up apologetically, "Oh," she said, "We haven't introduced you to our friends." She placed her hand on Patience's shoulder. "This is Patience."

Shyly, the girl nodded at the old grey-haired woman. "Nice to meet you," she said politely. Then Elizabeth placed her hand firmly on Hamelin's tall shoulder. "And this is Hamelin." Her hand lingered on his shoulder for a long moment.

"Thank you for your generosity. And I am sorry to hear about your loss," he said.

"Nice to meet you both. It is good to see such a young and handsome man in these parts; you'll be quite popular with the ladies."

Elizabeth smiled, then slightly embarrassed, she pulled her hand away. Bertha smiled, trying to maintain a happier tone at least in front of her new guests. She headed over to a basket near a small fireplace, ripped off four large pieces of bread, and wrapped them in cloth.

"No, it's okay really. You keep it. You have many mouths to feed," said Patience.

"Not as many as I used to," Bertha replied sadly, her eyes welling up again with tears. "It's the least I could do for you all."

Goldenhair had been quiet since hearing Bertha's news; however, her face brightened at a sudden thought. She patted the woman on her back. "Do you remember the story we used to tell the children during thunderstorms?" Goldenhair asked.

Bertha Goosefoot smiled again. "Oh, they loved that one! I just told them that one the other night, in fact." She turned and faced the others. "It's not as good as when Mavor and the children act it out in the yard, but they do love that tale!"

Patience smiled politely. It was always uncomfortable to meet new people in sad times. Patience thought it was nice to see the old woman smile. "What's the story about?" she asked.

"The story of the young servant girl who steals the glass slippers from the evil queen," said the old lady fondly, adding, "I've heard that when other people tell the story they now refer to the queen as Queen Cinder; it's caught on." She turned to Goldenhair, "If there's time, perhaps we could do a show for the children and your friends?"

Patience stood there dumbstruck. The young girl had not expected the story to be about her.

"We don't have time today. I'm afraid we must be back on the road soon," Goldenhair replied, and Elizabeth nodded in agreement.

Bertha seemed disappointed and she turned back toward Patience. "You haven't heard the story, my dear?"

"I think I *am* the story," she replied, shooting a glance at Goldenhair, who then informed Bertha that Patience was a servant at the queen's castle.

The old woman laughed politely at the coincidence, but then she began to realize what Goldenhair was implying. Turning back to look at Patience, she let out a small gasp. "My goodness child," she whispered in disbelief. "Is it true?"

For the first time since they had arrived there, Patience saw hope flicker in the kind old woman's eyes. Without pause, Patience slowly slipped her pack from her shoulder and walked to the table. She pushed aside the pouches that Goldenhair had placed there, and pulled out the small, tightly wrapped cloth. As she unrolled it, she could hear the woman gasp again, this time in wonder, saying repeatedly "it is true, it is true," as the sound of tinkling glass filled the room.

The shards lay there, broken pieces of magical crystal—the glass slippers of the queen. They sparkled in the early afternoon sun that shined through the small window in the kitchen. Patience could feel a faint warmth emanating from them. With the shards finally spread out, she looked up at the old woman. Bertha's hands clasped tightly, shaking, pressed against her lips as she drew a long breath at the presence of the glass slippers. Smaller fragments seemed to twinkle alongside the large pieces. A piece of toecap and a section of the vamp and sole were among the bigger pieces, with part of the shoe's heel counter and delicate heel were most recognizable as coming from a shoe. The glass shards, despite years of neglect, still inspired awe. Except for one part of the heel that had broken off, the glass was covered in a faint tinge of dark reddish brown stain, quite similar to that of old,

73

dried blood.

Tears streamed down the old woman's cheeks, but this time they were tears of joy. There before them were the shards of the glass slipper.

Barely able to speak the words, Bertha whispered, "Is it really true?"

Patience and Goldenhair nodded. Hamelin and Elizabeth nodded too, enthralled at the sight of Cinderella's glass slippers. Hamelin had only seen them a few times, but he had never seen such an emotional response as Bertha's. Elizabeth stepped in closer to marvel at them. There was no question about it. She had heard the stories too, but it did not sink in until she saw them with her own eyes on the table.

"Oh! Dear child, thank you!" The kind, old woman cried in happiness and hugged the young girl.

Goldenhair nodded to Patience, who quickly began to wrap up the shards. Midway through, she stopped, puzzled. Patience knew the shards very well, every shape of every shard. She had spent many hours over the past five years studying them, sometimes in wonder, other times with subdued hatred that she had been given them at all. Now, she would have sworn a piece was missing—a small triangular shaped piece of crystal with a slight jagged hook that would have been part of the left slipper.

Missing piece? Ridiculous—just a flash of paranoia, she thought. Patience dismissed her doubts and continued to wrap the shards securely in her bag.

Bertha marveled at the young servant girl for moment. "That is wonderful!" She flung her arms wide and hugged Patience again, more tightly.

Goldenhair motioned to the others as she headed to the door. "We must be on our way. Spread the word that hope has returned."

The travelers said their goodbyes and merged outside, where they found Nikko resting under the shade of a tree in the yard, while the other two bears chased the children who squealed in playful delight. A few of the children ran over to Goldenhair and the other guests.

"Goldenhair! Goldenhair! We have a song for you. Do you want to hear it? Please?" The girls begged ash excitement sparkled in their eyes.

Goldenhair paused for a moment with her mouth agape, about to tell children she would have to hear their song another time. The children pleaded as Goldenhair looked over to the others; her concern was mostly for Elizabeth, for any delay would affect her the most, but she saw Elizabeth nod her approval with a smile.

"Okay," she said her thick accent. "A quick song!"

Hamelin smirked and nudged Patience, who seemed the least excited to hear it. He opened his red and yellow coat a little and discreetly pulled out his musical pipes, giving Patience a knowing wink. She responded with a halfhearted smile. Hamelin thought it odd of her, as she had always loved his playing. He pulled his pipes out anyway and with a quick adjustment to them, music drifted pleasantly in the air.

The children squealed in delight as they set themselves in a circle, holding hands in a ring around the guests. Goldenhair smiled and laughed as Hamelin played, easily catching on to the melody of the children's song. Elizabeth and the old woman began to clap in time. The children skipped around in the circle holding hands. As they sang, they shifted their direction to circle in the opposite direction. In a moment of lightheartedness, it seemed to lift spirits and harkened back to less troubling times for the children and their guests. Yet Patience was distant. Involuntarily, she listened to the words of the song that the children had devised:

> Queen Cinder, Queen Cinder, what did you lose?
> Whatever happened to your glassy shoes?
> You threw them down and they broke in twos,
> And soon we'll win and soon you'll lose!"
> Queen Cinder, Queen Cinder, What did you say?
> Tell the servants to sweep them away!
> But all of the servants have run away
> And the shards of the glass slipper
> Will come back some day.
> Queen Cinder, Queen Cinder, with the crown on your head
> Soon we'll be free and you'll be dead!

They sang and skipped in a circle three times, and the final time the children shouted out the last line of the song they fell to the ground laughing.

The travelers laughed and applauded, all except for Patience, who managed a weak smile and urged Goldenhair to start leaving. "Mavor," said Patience in a somber tone, "shouldn't we be getting back to the road?"

"Doth et esq! Nikko, Dekker gud masa, Kerker! Noth es!" shouted Goldenhair. The bears immediately wandered over to the group as the children stood up with cries of disappointment, pleading for the visitors to stay longer. These visits were real treats for the children who otherwise led a secluded existence, but as was always the case, Goldenhair and her bears would eventually be on their way. The children reluctantly said their goodbyes, first shyly to the new strangers, Hamelin and Patience, but quite animatedly with the bears, hugging them and petting them, telling them to be good and to take care of Goldenhair, and to come back soon.

Soon, the ramshackle remnants of Aishew were behind them as the group continued along the roads, not far from their destination.

Hamelin, who had been talking with Elizabeth most of the afternoon, now walked with Patience. Elizabeth caught up to Goldenhair, Hamelin presumed to discuss the upcoming meeting.

"Quite a day we're having," he remarked with a sarcastic smirk.

Patience merely looked at him with a halfhearted smile.

"They tell stories about me, Hamelin." Her tone was less than excited. Hamelin detected that the young girl seemed a little frightened.

"I tell stories all the time." He patted the coat breast pocket where she knew he kept his pipes. "It's what I do."

"That's different," she said, turning her head away. "Those stories aren't about me."

"Well, when we get back home, maybe I will tell stories about you," Hamelin teased with a smile and a wink. It was the wrong time to tease the young girl.

"I don't want any stories about me. Ever!" She yelled back loud enough that Goldenhair and Elizabeth both stopped to look over at the companions. Even the bears stopped and looked back.

"Just leave me alone, Hamelin," she added quietly and briskly marched forward ahead of Goldenhair, Elizabeth, and the bears.

Elizabeth stepped back to talk with Hamelin, who stood there perplexed at the sudden outburst. Goldenhair gave a concerned looked to Elizabeth as she did. "I'll talk with her, but for now I'd give her some time," Goldenhair whispered in her thick accent, seeming to know what Elizabeth was thinking.

"What did I say?" he shouted, but Patience was too angry to reply.

"I don't think I've ever heard her yell like that," Hamelin said, his tone despondent and flustered. "Certainly not at me."

"It's been a long day," said Elizabeth. "She is going through a lot in a very short period of time."

"Patience was looking forward to bringing those glass slippers back and giving them a home, to finally ridding herself of them. It was all she talked about," said Hamelin.

"And she probably wasn't expecting any of this," added Elizabeth, gesturing to the bears.

"Yeah, I wasn't either," he agreed. "I'm still not entirely comfortable," Hamelin admitted, nodding towards Goldenhair. "Those bears make me nervous."

Elizabeth could not hold back a smile. "I've heard that about the bears before," she said. "I'd trust her bears more than I'd trust most people. Goldenhair has an incredible connection with not just those bears but it seems, with every animal. She is very in tune with the forests; she is unlike anyone I have ever encountered. It is not like a witch's spell, she just...is. It is hard to explain. It's because of her that I'm...more comfortable around animals." Elizabeth began to steer the conversation towards Hamelin and away from herself. "But I also think that Patience might be worried that once all of this business with the shards is over, she won't have you around anymore."

"What?" exclaimed Hamelin with an incredulous look. He had never considered that a possibility. She was much younger than he was. Hamelin laughed, despite himself. "That's not true."

"You're an older man, a protector of sorts, kind of like a big brother, right?" she continued, "The two of you have been traveling together for some time, I presume. I'm pretty sure she likes having you around. I would—I mean, if I were her."

"No," Hamelin denied. "I'm pretty sure it has to do with those glass slippers," trying to convince himself that what he said was true.

Elizabeth was smiling now. "Plus, I'm sure it hasn't helped that you've been ignoring her and talking with me all afternoon."

"Oh, you've noticed that?" asked Hamelin, with a small laugh. Nervously, he rubbed the back of his head, "So you think Patience is jealous? But she's like my little kid sister."

"I wouldn't be surprised," Elizabeth said. "And you're blushing."

As the sun began its slow journey downward, the shadows began to stretch long across the road. Elizabeth left Hamelin to consider what she had said. She walked alongside the bears, enjoying the late afternoon and taking a moment to herself. Goldenhair had gone ahead to talk with Patience, who had been quiet since her outburst.

"Young Patience," started Goldenhair, "Soon, we'll be at the meeting, and if you want you can leave the shards there and return home."

"My home was at the castle. I can't even get there to see my mother," she replied dejectedly, staring down the road. "I don't have a home to return to."

"Neither do most of those children; but they have hope, because of you."

"I don't want to be anyone else's hope," Patience replied. "I didn't ask for it," she added.

"No, but you have it now. So the question now is what are you going to do with it?"

"What do I do with it?" Patience retorted. "I give these stupid glass slippers to your friends, and then it's their problem."

"Yes, perhaps, but then what?"

"What do you mean? Then what do I do?" Patience seemed confused. "I don't know," was the only reply she could offer.

"Perhaps that it is the real problem." Goldenhair's accent could not hide the words that stung true. "Perhaps what troubles you is that once they are gone you won't have them around." Her odd inflections made what she said sound nonsensical on the surface. Patience thought Goldenhair's occasional mistranslation of the language was to blame, but then she realized she understood Goldenhair's point, and that perhaps her point was true. She was so used to having the shards that, once she was rid of them, would she know what to do with herself? She would be free in a sense, but free to do what? And where? Her home had been the castle, but for the last five years now the castle was overtaken. Her home was overtaken; and she had wandered from town to town in other kingdoms with Hamelin. Now, the very thing she sought to rid herself of seemed to be the very thing that would stand a chance of letting her return to her real home. Patience wondered if when her travels and adventure ended, could she just return home again, longing for the way things used to be. Would her friend Hamelin still be around? Or would a door close forever on that part of her life, a life she desperately wanted to stay the same? As Patience thought about Mavor's point and tried to sort out her own feelings, Goldenhair announced to the group, "We're here."

Patience looked up and saw they were walking along a bluff now, overlooking a sparkling blue ocean. Farther down on the bright beach below was the dark shape of a house. The bluff descended downward with paths cutting through the tall yellow grass.

"Well, this should be interesting," Hamelin remarked with a tinge of sarcasm.

Immediately, Elizabeth turned, her long red cloak flowing behind her in the late afternoon breeze. She announced abruptly, yet somewhat apologetically, "I have to leave," with a faint smile that did not cover the twinge of worry that had crossed her face. "I forgot something back in Aishew. I'll catch up with everyone by tomorrow." It was not a convincing reassurance.

"What?" Hamelin stammered at the sudden change of plans, shaking his head in disbelief. "We need to stick together." He gestured in the direction of the house. "We just got here." They had been together most of the day and meeting Elizabeth somehow seemed to ease the worry that Hamelin had over other events. "What if you get captured again?"

Elizabeth had already walked to Goldenhair and was talking to her, ignoring Hamelin. The talk seemed hushed and serious; both women glanced at Hamelin and Patience more than once. Then with a quickened pace and a last silent glance toward Hamelin, Elizabeth headed back toward the forest.

"I'm not going to rescue her again if she gets caught," Hamelin muttered to himself.

Goldenhair stood, thinking about the young man. "She will be back tomorrow, Hamelin," she assured him with her broken English.

Nervously, he rubbed the hair on the back of his head. "I thought we were all needed at this meeting of yours."

"Why did we have to come all this way?" Patience spoke in annoyance. Aside from the stop at Aishew, they had been walking since Hamelin woke Patience up in a nervous panic near dawn. It had been a long day of traveling and quite an emotional one for Patience. "Can we just go and get this over with?"

The trio traversed the rocky outcroppings of the bluff, navigating small rickety wooden steps that bridged gaps between the rocks. Goldenhair had sent the bears a different route, an old horse trail that wound down to the beach, but was still some distance away. Hamelin and Patience followed her cautiously down the rocky path as the sun slowly began to slip beneath the clouds. Hamelin pressed Goldenhair about Elizabeth, trying to learn more about the mysterious girl in the red cloak. Goldenhair would not reveal much, saying only, "it is best you ask Elizabeth herself."

CHAPTER 6
QUEEN CENDRILLON

The view from the castle's west tower balcony had always been spectacular. As the sun's angle began to dip and its golden light carved out the texture of the clouds, casting long shadows across the landscape, the queen's Maldame took little notice; it was more important that her tea was delivered on time. Moments later a servant woman in a tattered and stained dress delivered a smartly polished tea set. She was sent away in tears after a particularly harsh scolding by the Maldame regarding her stupidity and inconsiderate delay in arriving.

The balcony was rather large and spacious, decorated with white stone carvings and topiaries that at one time were quite grand, but now had become yellowed and overgrown. The balcony itself had been lacking in its upkeep. The white stone seemed dulled and stained; the stone chipped enough so that one could kick small flakes and pebbles of rock over the edge between the once-impressive railings. The weathered curtains that adorned the balcony doors were dirty from exposure to the rain for years, their color faded by the sun and frayed from the wind and bird droppings had caked to the stone from many years of baking in the sun.

Despite the lack of maintenance, the balcony afforded the Maldame the widest view of the kingdom, and she enjoyed lording over and looking down upon all that was hers. It was this feeling that satisfied her, not so much the view.

For now, the Maldame stood alone on the balcony sipping her tea. She was an elderly-looking woman, though she was tall and in surprisingly good physical shape. Many decades of distain and scowling had left her face gaunt and wrinkled, accentuated by the fact that her silver hair was pulled back meticulously into a tight bun. The Maldame was accustomed to the finer things in life and her dress was elegant at all times, despite some showings of wear. She adorned herself with jewelry, especially at times when she was to meet with the queen; not that it was a matter of status when in the queen's presence. She liked the comforts her station afforded her. In fact, the Maldame could care less about the queen's presence. If it were not for her, she thought, Cinderella would never have become queen.

Taking another sip of tea, she smiled with self-satisfaction as she mulled over her greatest achievement. Her witches' coven ruled the throne. Cinderella, now known as Queen Cendrillon, had turned out to be quite the Maldame's protégé.

At that moment, the queen quietly and unceremoniously arrived at the doors of the balcony. Cendrillon was tall and slender with an athletic build, and walked with a natural grace. She was fair skinned and beautiful and in her late thirties, she looked older than she was. The queen's dress flowed in the warm wind, but it was more practical than formal, richly detailed in dark textures, tightly accenting her shapely form. Her long blonde hair caught glints of the late afternoon sun as she stepped out to the balcony and greeted the Maldame.

"Stepmother," she said.

"My queen," acknowledged the Maldame. "Cendrillon."

"I've spoken with Dendroba again. He took some losses against a temple guardian at the site. However, based upon a new revelation about the resistance, I've told him to move his troops toward the coast. They should be in Aishew by sunset and the coast by midnight."

"I will send sent Gael and Jovette to help ensure Dendroba succeeds" Maldame added, taking a sip of her tea. The queen was silent for a moment.

"Send your pets? Those things that used to be your daughters? That's not necessary, Stepmother. Dendroba can take care of General White and her little dwarves."

The Maldame turned to look at Cendrillon beside her at the railing. "Yes, it is necessary. That so called resistance army of Snow White's has been annoyance enough! They must be crushed before they develop into something more that we cannot control. I want to make sure of it!"

The Maldame's voiced dropped from a sharp defiant tone to a hiss of seriousness. "The magic wanes these days. Even the Bloodthorn Wall grows unruly, harder to bend to your will. Soon it could be beyond control for good. Remember, walls built to keep others out also keep you in. You will be trapped here with just an empty fairy wand. Then the magic will diminish beyond that. We're talking about the future survival of the coven, and your ability to hold the throne from people who would usurp you." The Maldame's intense glare softened. "Did I mention that this morning the guards at your mother's grave were killed? Probably by those same rebels, I'll wager. Do not ignore the unrest; it does not ignore you." The Maldame sipped her tea and then set it on the railing in front of her.

"The unrest poses little threat to our plans," Cendrillon started to say then realized what the Maldame had said. "Mother's grave was defiled? I did not hear of that, and you did? How—why would they do that? I'll double the garrison there."

"Please, you are not the only one who gets reports on the goings on about the kingdom," the Maldame scoffed. "It is just as well. That's a part of your life that is no longer your concern, my queen."

The Maldame emphasized her last word to remind the queen of a conversation they held many a time, about how Cendrillon ought not to hold on to her commoner's past. The stepmother Maldame was very good at subtle manipulation, and it had worked better on Cinderella growing up than any spell could. "I should get such concern when I die. I raised you most of your ungrateful life, not her. You were a child went I took you in."

Cendrillon considered her stepmother's words. For as long as she had known her stepmother, she had thought her a very mean-spirited person. However, it was true that Cinderella's stepmother was there for most of her childhood. Now older and in control of the throne, Cendrillon had come to regard her stepmother as a very shrewd advisor. She knew her stepmother was also the head priestess of the witches' coven, and her experience and leadership had been guidance to the young queen through these troublesome years. The Maldame had also trained her in the ways of witches and witchcraft. Though reluctant to learn at first, the queen excelled in the dark arts. Cendrillon pulled a small silver flask from a black garter on her leg, unscrewed its cap, and took a long swallow as she looked out from the balcony.

That magic, she thought, was the kind of power she had not had since she raised the Bloodthorn Wall to surround the castle's lands. It was the last of the big magic that this land had seen. She had tasted that intoxicating level of power, and she wanted it back like a warm ache in her loins.

Cendrillon could see the dark mass of the Bloodthorn Wall from the balcony.

It snaked across the landscape like a great being and covered the ground as a blanket of death, posing grave danger to anyone who touched it. She took another drink from the flask and smiled. "Such power I had back then," she reminisced with a wicked smile. "It will not matter. With the portal found, soon the magic of that land will be harnessed for our use. Wonderland won't even know we were there, siphoning it from them....including the matter of recharging *her* old wand." Cendrillon was referring to her fairy godmother's wand, which she now possessed. "In the meantime we can maintain control of the Bloodthorn Wall once we have the lycanthrope blood, and according to Gretel, that won't be very much longer. You worry far too much."

"Always the optimist you are, from cleaning the cinders from my fireplace, 'til the very day your rule as queen ends. Your plan could very easily derail and leave us in far more dire circumstances."

The Maldame, as any witch of the land, was eternally cautious in matters of survival. Cendrillon's continual lust for magic had always frustrated the Maldame. It had taken her well over twenty years to achieve putting her coven in control of the throne, as much by planning as by circumstance. Though Cendrillon was powerful and intelligent, the Maldame considered her reckless attitude to be immature at times.

"What of the guardian Dendroba mentioned? How will we defeat that? Maldame challenged. "More rats turned into troops? We no longer have the power to act on that scale." The Maldame snatched the flask from the queen's hands and threw it over railing, sending it falling down the side of the tower. It was a long drop ending with a distant clang. "I would consider the grander schemes. We are not out of the woods yet, darling stepdaughter. Our resources are drying up." The Maldame took a sip of her tea, glaring from behind the cup, daring Cendrillon to say something about the flask.

Cendrillon ignored it. "Once Dendroba dispatches the resistance, we will travel to the temple ourselves. Perhaps we'll send your spider pets to ensure that whatever guards the temple is taken care of," the queen added with sarcastic decisiveness.

"The portal to Wonderland was closed hundreds of years ago, for good reason," Maldame cautioned as she set her teacup on the railing. "We must move cautiously. The magic that resides in Wonderland is far older and greater than anything you know of. This is not something to play with like a toy."

"All the more reason it should be ours," said Cendrillon curtly as she turned abruptly to walk away, her long hair flicked behind her as if to spite her stepmother. Then with feigned politeness, the queen delicately and purposefully tapped the cup and saucer that had rested on the railing, sending them tumbling over the side.

CHAPTER 7
A GENERAL OF WHAT ARMY?

When they reached the bottom of the bluff, Goldenhair's three bears broke away from the group and bounded toward the surf, chasing and playing in the gentle waves and warm sand. "Well at least the bears seem comfortable here," said Hamelin.

"I will have to send the bears away while we are here. Syrenka is nervous about bears," Goldenhair explained. With a short command and wave of her arms, the bears ran on further down the beach. The group made its way quickly to a small rustic cabin set back among a collection of dunes and long grass. The house was similar to those back in the village of Aishew, but in far better condition. As the travelers approached, they could see a long, wooden walkway with a crude rail. The planks extended from a modest, covered porch nearly to the water's edge. A thin trail of smoke drifted upward from a rocky chimney.

Patience looked nervously at Hamelin, who smiled as if to say everything would be all right, or at least he hoped it would be. Around the house were small sculptures made from driftwood and shells and the like, surprisingly Patience with their craftsmanship as they were quite well-done and very pretty. As they approached, Goldenhair described the person they were about to meet.

"Syrenka is friend," she said in her thick accent. "She has trouble to walk, And cannot speak…*moot*, is it?"

"Mute," Hamelin corrected. "Hopefully you haven't tried to teach her how to speak," he teased with a smile. Goldenhair frowned at his joke, muttering to herself in a different language.

"Is mute," she continued, "known to her for a long time. Is very…special woman. She keeps watches on the ocean."

Patience understood what she meant. "She's a spy for you."

As they set foot on the little porch, the door of the house burst open and a bright, smiling face greeted them. Standing in the doorway, supported by a cane, was a young woman in a simple grey dress with waist-length, stringy blonde hair. She eagerly hobbled to Goldenhair and hugged her. It was clear the two were close friends.

Then Goldenhair introduced her traveling companions. "Hamelin," Goldenhair gestured, "this is Syrenka." Syrenka looked at Goldenhair and patted her own throat. "It's okay, I told them," assured Goldenhair. Syrenka smiled apologetically and nodded a hello to Hamelin. Then she enthusiastically reached out and grabbed Hamelin's hand, giving it a firm squeeze. "And this is Patience. She is a very important and brave young girl." Syrenka's eyes flashed in friendly mock amazement as she smiled, again reaching out to squeeze Patience's hand. Patience was uncomfortable with the introduction.

"It's okay, really. I'm not that important," she said, which prompted Syrenka to burst out in a silent laugh as she invited them into the house.

"Is he still here?" asked Goldenhair as they walked into the large common room of the house. Syrenka gestured, laying her head against her one hand and closing her eyes.

"Sleeping?" Goldenhair guessed correctly.

There was a fire in the small fireplace, and soon Syrenka and Goldenhair set to making Hamelin and Patience more comfortable. It was obvious that Goldenhair knew her way around the small house. Syrenka was happy to see her friend again, and to meet new ones. Patience marveled at all of the books and writings that had been shoved into simple shelves in the small but accommodating dwelling. Syrenka picked up a small slate and some chalk and began to write on it, asking if anyone wanted tea and bread. Both Hamelin and Patience thankfully accepted. Goldenhair was about to explain more regarding why they were here as they settled with warm tea in simple cups when more visitors arrived.

With an unceremonial air, there was a clatter of boots on the small wooden porch. Then with a determined knock, the door swung open and the leader of the only resistance army in the kingdom entered the room accompanied by several armored dwarves.

Hamelin stared. He could not believe that this was *the* General White. Somehow Hamelin had envisioned a gruff, battle-hardened scar of a dwarven woman with a thick and wiry white beard. However, General White was certainly not a dwarf. Tall and slender, despite her somewhat bulky white armor, she had proud, beautiful features like a princess; this he did not expect from someone who was a leader of a dwarven army.

Her presence was regal and commanding, exuding confidence and seriousness at all times. Her cool, ice blue eyes shot about with deliberate attention beneath a stern and unyielding brow. Her skin was pale, and Patience wondered if it was from spending all her time with the dwarves in their mountainous mines underground. In stark contrast to her milky complexion was a frame of long straight, raven-dark hair that fell upon the thick pauldrons and gardbraces of her armor. There were signs of wear and age if one were to look closely enough.

General White's stern face had begun to show wrinkles around her eyes and chin, and a long, thin very faint scar ran down the side of her otherwise porcelain face. Her dark hair had small slivers of grey beginning to show. She wore white, plated chest armor and a white fur cloak. Her armor was dirty in the crevasses and showed signs of nicks and damage from battle. With a sense of distance and aloofness, she briefly greeted Syrenka.

"I received the message from Goldenhair about the prince," she announced as her sharp blue eyes narrowed. "It will take but a moment for me to confirm if what you say is true."

If anyone would know what to do about this General White would; after all, she was a general, Hamelin thought.

"I've dealt with him in the past," added General White. "Then there are more pressing matters to discuss."

Goldenhair looked over toward Hamelin and Patience as if to apologize for not introducing them yet. In fact, General White had not even acknowledged their presence. Patience noted that Goldenhair, who had been strong and confident since they had met, now seemed a little uncomfortable in General White's presence.

Hamelin could see the stark contrasts between the two women, and he now figured the two to be oil and water. Goldenhair was dressed in warm brown and earthen tones, very much a spiritual person who interacted with nature, literally, he thought. But General White, he observed in the short span of time he had seen her, was very different. Her armor and weapons stood out as cold and calculated.

As a manufactured, protective shell, the armor seemed more of a barrier that kept everyone away. Snow White seemed to Hamelin to be far more serious than Goldenhair in matters of command and order. In contrast, Mavor had been warm and friendly as they had met, and in that moment Hamelin knew he preferred Goldenhair's company to the stiff unapproachable demeanor of Snow White.

One could see a fierce fire that simmered with intensity behind Snow White's cool blue eyes. General White had come into the small house with a whirlwind of seriousness and a commanding presence. For the general, the stakes were very high these days.

Hamelin cleared his throat deliberately and loudly. He stared intently at Snow White.

"Who is this?" she asked brusquely.

Goldenhair smiled politely and answered. "This is Hamelin. And the young girl is Patience." Her thick accent hid a degree of nervousness in addressing General White. She was about to explain more about the young girl's journey and the special contents in her pack, but General White was not interested.

"Did anybody follow you?" the general asked, studying the two newcomers as her eyes narrowed and darted back and forth between them.

"No!" replied Goldenhair sharply, shooting the general an incredulous look, like she had forgotten just who Goldenhair was.

General White offered no apology for her abruptness. "It's a question I always ask, Mavor." She was wary of meeting new people and did not care for these surprises. She always considered any stranger a potential threat at first. The general did not trust strangers, not after the poisoning attempt several years ago. She had never eaten another apple after that experience.

The general nodded an acknowledgement towards the two. Patience sensed that Goldenhair and the general were not fond of each other.

"Where is Prince Phillip?" White asked, getting back on topic.

"Asleep," Syrenka wrote quickly on her slate.

Goldenhair spoke up. "General, the young girl has brought the glass slipper shards."

But the general didn't hear.

"Shit," she whispered behind clenched teeth. The entire room, turned to look at what Snow White had focused on. Prince Phillip, using one of Syrenka's canes for support, limped into the room. He had been awakened by the noise and conversations and had listened quietly behind the door a bit before stepping inside. The prince stopped, however, at the sight of General White.

"Snow, is that really you?" His chiseled face brightened with recognition of the dark-haired woman before him, but quickly melted into a confused look.

General White rolled her eyes as if she had been caught. In a sense, she had been, and it annoyed her. She had dreaded the thought of meeting him again. He had remembered her more quickly than she had hoped.

"Hello, Phillip," she replied coolly.

Goldenhair looked at both of them in amazement. "You…know each other?" The others sensed that it was not a happy reunion. The general and the prince replied almost simultaneously.

"He's my brother," admitted Snow White, almost embarrassed. "My younger brother."

"She's my sister," explained Prince Phillip. "I can't believe you're alive!" he exclaimed, though not as happily as those in the room might have expected. "I haven't seen you since you ran away, what, twenty years ago? My God, the king's guards searched everywhere." Prince Phillip raised his arms to greet his older sister with a hug, but General White made no motion to embrace him.

"Thirty years now, give or take. I was fourteen and you were barely twelve," she answered curtly, her past boiling back into memory like an unwatched kettle. "I got as far away from this kingdom as I could. I hated having to deal with all the bureaucratic nonsense and the expectations, and the fancy balls and dresses. The royal family lived in luxury while their loyal subjects wallowed in destitution. So I left. But you—" White's eyes focused on the prince with less than loving attention. "You seemed to embrace the royal aspects all too well, Prince...Charming!" She sneered before continuing. "You charmed your way into bed with every princess you could find, playing the politics of every royal ball. Oh, I kept tabs little brother. You would have charmed your way on to the throne if—"

"How dare you!" The prince shot back angrily. "Where were you when the queen died? Off being selfish, it sounds like! Running away from what you were given! You broke the queen's heart, you know!"

It was obvious to Hamelin that the constant bickering could only mean they were, in fact, siblings. That would mean that General White was also a princess, thus a legitimate heir to the throne, as was Prince Phillip.

"Broke the queen's heart?" Snow White retorted. "The queen's heart? You see," General White snapped back furiously, waving her hands, "that's the problem with you, Phillip. Even now, you still refer to our mother as the queen!" Snow shook her head in angry frustration.

"But don't worry about me, little brother. When I heard that Mother was ill, I came back. I was there at the funeral, along with everyone else. I stood in the back, far away from the prince who made sure everyone saw how sad he was that the queen had died." Her tone was biting. "I paid my respects to Mother later that night, just so you know. Then I left again. I took the first ship I could find, and eight years later, when I figured no one would recognize me, I came back. Then I found out you were gone. Marchenton was left in ruin; the throne, now practically run by the witches. Where were you? You should have been here, not off on a crusade to make you and father feel better, dragging the whole kingdom along with you."

There was silence as Prince Phillip reflected on Snow White's words. Years of quiet resentment from Phillip's sister echoed in the stillness of the sudden pause in conversation.

"The king and I took the army and ascended the beanstalk. It was supposed to be a show of force to protect the kingdom—something the kingdom could get behind. We thought we'd encounter one giant, not dozens. I was lucky enough to escape alive. The king—rather, our father—died too; along with many others," he said solemnly.

"It rained blood here, and the bodies of soldiers fell from the clouds for days," recalled Goldenhair. "There was no sun for an entire month, only clouds. The kingdom's people were panicked and much fighting broke out. Beanstalk War that whole terrible time was called."

"I was not in the kingdom at the time, but I found out eventually that they had recovered most of Father's body, broken and impaled in the upper branches of a tree," said Snow White.

Many of the captured men were put through grinding machines or eaten alive from what I remember, but I do not know much beyond that," Phillip said, shaking off the nightmarish recollections. "I want to make things right again,

Snow. Doesn't that mean something? Please, just give me some time to get back on my feet. I just found out what's been happening," he said. "And I just found out that my sister's alive! You realize we're the only family left now, don't you? Aren't you happy to see your brother again?" Phillip asked, then paused for a moment, a sudden sadness catching up with him. "I need to find out about my wife," he said.

Snow White started to say something, and then stopped. Secretly, she did want to tell him that she was happy to see her little brother again. But now that it was business, General White could not afford to let herself be so distracted.

"Cinderella is not the innocent waif you left," she pointed out with a softer tone. "She and her stepmother rule this land. They are running the kingdom into the ground. Queen Cinder is a witch now, just like her stepmother."

"Cinderella?" the prince whispered sadly, dropping his head in guilt.

"Well, this is quite the family reunion," mumbled Hamelin into the awkward silence.

Then another figure strode into the small wooden house. She was younger than General White, dressed in fighting leathers, with a short bob of warm, blonde hair that almost gave her the appearance of a teenage boy. Her mailed gloved hands casually gripped the hilt of her sheathed sword.

"General," said the young woman in a formal tone. "Sorry to interrupt, but you asked to be notified when the dwarves have finished securing the area. We've also sent out several scouts, as you requested."

"Thank you, Rapunzel," said White as she looked back at her lieutenant. "We should bring your mother in now. We need to start the meeting and then be on our way. The resistance has more important things to plan for." She seemed relieved at the interruption. The young woman, Rapunzel, nodded at her general's request.

"You are a general?" asked Phillip, "You're a general of *what* army, exactly?"

"Brother, you left the kingdom with very little in the way of defense when you went to war with the giants. Cinderella became not only the queen, but also one of the top witches. Absolute power corrupts absolutely, does it not? Queen Cendrillon, as your wife prefers to be called these days, created a new army, magically transforming all of the rats in the castle into royal guards. Then she surrounded the entire castle with a huge wall made of Bloodthorns. As usual little brother, there is much you don't know about the real world."

"Obviously," Prince Philip agreed.

Snow White continued. "Most of the men of the land had followed you in battle, as you realize. To ensure her control, Cinder captured and enslaved many of the children, boys and younger men that were left behind, keeping any threat of organized force in check. Eventually, it came to the women of the land to organize any sort of resistance. But we needed men and fighters, so I went to the dwarves. In short, I am now general of said resistance. The dwarves took to calling me General White, which I prefer so as not to be recognized as part of the royal family. We'll save the explanation of the dwarves' involvement for another day."

Prince Phillip could not believe that his innocent wife, Princess Cinderella, had become the wicked ruler they were suggesting; not his Ella. Impossible, he thought. This Queen Cinder was not the common house servant he married so long ago. However, much had changed. Could it be true? Prince Phillip began to think it might be.

"With that," the general stated, "we should prepare for a meeting. What I am about to say should not leave the walls of this room. There is a bigger problem. We have just returned from battle in the mountains against Dendroba's troops. It seems they have found a gateway to Wonderland, as we feared. It looks like Queen Cinder is planning to expand her rule."

"Wonderland?" Goldenhair remarked with alarm. "I thought that was just a myth. It actually exists?"

"I'm afraid so," replied General White.

"Why, what is so important about Wonderland?" asked the Prince.

"Power, Prince Phillip."

A new voice spoke out. Rapunzel's mother, Dame Gothel, entered the room and was quick to answer such an elementary question. She was, after all, a witch herself. "Wonderland magic is more powerful than anything in this kingdom," said the old woman. "And if they are trying to gain access to Wonderland, then the times are truly desperate."

"Why is that?" Patience found the courage to ask.

"It means, child," Dame Gothel croaked, "that the magic in this kingdom is all but gone—used up, undoubtedly, by Cendrillon herself."

"So," said Patience, trying to understand, "the queen is going to steal magic from Wonderland?"

"Correct," said Dame Gothel. "But *that* magic is far too powerful, and too unstable to wield in this kingdom. A long time ago, when the fairies still guarded the magic of this kingdom, a treaty between our kingdom and the ruler of Wonderland was set up and the portal to Wonderland was sealed. But if Cendrillon breaks the seal, thus violating the treaty, she will be starting a war with Wonderland."

"Well, why can't you just create a ball of fire and throw it at the army?" asked Hamelin. "Fight magic with magic?"

The witch let out a laugh. "Like a wizard? Ah, yes wizards and their fireball spells, now there's something I have not thought about in a long time. The problem is, these days, unlike in Wonderland, the magic here is finite. It will slowly wane and eventually dissipate all together, unless it can be replenished, of course. The fairies used to do that. Now they are gone. I suspect that is why Queen Cinder is anxious to find the portal to Wonderland. In the olden days when magic was plentiful, wizards abounded. Their kind died out a long time ago."

"I've never heard of any of that," said Prince Phillip. "How do you know this?"

"My dear boy," replied Dame Gothel, "many years ago, Cinderella's stepmother and I were the heads of the witches' coven. Witches are always interested in gaining more power. But even we never considered breaking the Wonderland treaty for power."

"It looks like Queen Cinder isn't playing by your rules," added General White.

* * *

Snow White leaned against a table near the wall towards the back of the room, her sharp eyes darting around the room as she listened intently to the discussions at hand. When she was not scanning the room, she was absently shifting her sword in the scabbard at her side. She folded her slender arms across her white chest armor, dirty and scuffed from years of fighting against the queen. Hamelin found out that it was custom made by the dwarves as a gift for their new leader. The white armor and cloak that matched her fair, porcelain-like skin was why the dwarves referred to her as Snow White, using that name rather than her given name, which was Snow Marchen. Incredible, Hamelin thought, that a legitimate princess preferred a rogue's life with the company of axe-wielding dwarves to one of royal gowns.

"General White?" Someone was now deferring a question to the general. Hamelin had not been paying attention to the conversation, but General White had been. She snapped quickly from her relaxed stance against the table and walked over to join the conversation.

Not much to Hamelin's surprise, the focus of the conversation that General White was called into was directed at Patience. Hamelin had not heard Patience speak at first, only realizing when young Muffet repeated herself for General White. her words sent a chill down his spine.

"I know another way into the castle," said Patience. "There is an underground river that runs beneath it and empties into this lake." She pointed to a small lake on the map laid across the table. The lake was outside the circled area that represented the Bloodthorn Wall. "The service staff had access to it through a small room in the underground tunnels. No others but the staff knew about it. We used it to throw out a lot of the food and garbage of the castle since the river moved so quickly."

The room fell quiet for a moment. There was a way into the castle!

General White weighed this news carefully. "Except there is a problem, the castle is upstream; that river would be flowing downhill and into Lake Vasilissa, which is at least a mile and a half from the castle. It would be impossible to traverse an underground river, let alone upstream. We've no idea what's between the lake and the castle," she said. Her eyes dropped again, and to Hamelin it seemed that for a moment, the general was hopeful about the news, but then faded back to a resigned weariness. The room's morale had just been deflated like a burst water bladder. Then there came the sound of fast clicking. Chalk on slate.

Syrenka quickly shoved the slate at Goldenhair which caught the general's attention.

"What is it?" she asked, nodding in Syrenka's direction. "What is she writing?"

"Syrenka writes that if she was her younger self," Goldenhair read the chalk scribbling, "she would personally swim up that underground river. I think that it was meant to be joke," added Goldenhair as an aside; perhaps not correctly interpreting her friend's writing. Syrenka shot her a glaring look. But, Goldenhair knew she was not joking. She leaned toward Syrenka, whispering, "Now would not be the time to hear such things in front of the general." Goldenhair was right. Syrenka nodded with understanding.

A couple of the dwarves chuckled, taking what the woman wrote as a joke. General White crossed her arms again. "Is our only remaining strategic option a fool's hope and a wish? Are we reduced now to wishing that magic would solve this problem? If so, then Cendrillon has won." Her gaze locked with several others about the room. "We cannot afford to rely on such whimsy. We need to consider real world tactical information."

Hamelin glanced over at Patience, expecting to see her as withdrawn as she had been since they left Aishew that afternoon. But rather than a sulking, frustrated child, he saw a fire in her eyes; he could see the wheels turning.

"Goldenhair," said the young girl, ignoring General White's remarks. "Is there any way you might be able to find out from your animals what the underground river is like?"

Goldenhair thought for a moment. "It is a possibility."

There was murmuring about the room now as the idea that, despite General White's stance on hope, maybe this would be of value.

Something deceptively simple happened next.

One of the dwarves whispered loudly to another dwarf, "Why not just turn ol' scrapefoot here," gesturing at Goldenhair, "into a fish and send her up the river?"

Several of the dwarves broke out in laughter. Most of the dwarves in the General's resistance army had little respect for Goldenhair and her animal relations.

Dame Gothel shot the laughing dwarves a scornful look. "The word scrapefoot is an old derogatory term," the old woman explained to Goldenhair, "for a cowardly woodland creature, often a fox. Pay them no mind, dear."

As everyone continued talking, Dame Gothel, the only one in the room who was an expert in magic, had considered Syrenka's remark. Though there was only a handful of people who knew the mute hermit's past, Dame Gothel, who knew the tell-tale signs of witch spells, had recognized the crippled human's true origins. Only mermaids bleed from the legs when turned into human form. The old witch had watched Syrenka very discretely wipe a trickle of blood from her ankle—twice.

"Actually, dear daughter," crackled Rapunzel's crone-like mother, "we could turn someone back into a fish."

Rapunzel looked incredulously at her mother, who slowly stood from her seat. "We could turn the mermaid…back into a mermaid." She pointed at Syrenka with her old gnarled finger.

Then General White spoke up. "This discussion can no longer continue! These are not realistic options."

Rapunzel shot her mother a burning look. "Mother!" she barked in a loud whisper.

Rapunzel's mother dismissed her daughter's protest. "If the servant girl's claims are true and she has the glass slippers, then there is more than enough magic in a single shard to revert our host back to her mermaid form—if those are indeed the shards of Cinderella's glass slippers."

"Who's a mermaid?" asked Hamelin. He looked over at Syrenka who had tears of joy flowing down her cheeks. "I thought mermaids were dead."

"That's what the stories would have you believe. If I did not want to be hunted down or found out, I would fake my own death, so I could be left alone. Isn't that right Syrenka?"

Syrenka nodded bashfully.

"Indeed." Replied Dame Gothel. "Mermaids are a clever folk."

Even General White had to ask, "Are you serious?"

"Yes," said the old witch. "And you've been hanging around these cynical old dwarves too much." With a look of slight distain, the old woman gestured with her wrinkled hand towards the several dwarves who were in the room. "That you would think even a little magic is a fool's hope." The skin on the back of General White's neck turned red from embarrassment.

"Ridiculous!" she barked. "Even if we did all of that, what would it accomplish? Even when she is turned back into a mermaid? Even *if* she got back into the castle. It's still not a viable tactical advantage."

Patience had been listening to all of this, her mind racing with possibilities now. For five years, she had carried these shards with her and wanted nothing more than to leave them in a safe place. Here now was an opportunity not just to use them for something, but also to be part of something bigger. Here she realized she could be an asset. Although she did not relish the thought of losing even a piece of the glass slippers, it was obvious by the mute woman's expression it would be a greater help to her than the young Muffet could imagine.

Patience realized she could be even more help; it seemed people were listening to her and not dismissing her comments as a child's folly. It filled her with a greater sense of purpose. "I'm the only one here who knows the inside of the castle. Well, myself and the prince, but even he doesn't know all the servant's passages," Patience pointed out. "Perhaps if the mermaid could take me, there would be something I could do to help."

Now the dwarves were joining in, murmuring a concession to the ideas. "It would be simple enough to waterproof a small barrel that the girl could survive in during the trip, General," one of the dwarves offered, thinking aloud as some of the other dwarves muttered along in agreement. "It would completely bypass the Bloodthorns, as it is doubtful they would grow that deep."

General White realized that the others were becoming excited at the prospect of the plan; she also began to consider this a more realistic possibility despite herself. It seems there was hope. And that hope had energized a plan, even if she was not convinced it was a good plan.

"I want to do it," reaffirmed Patience as Hamelin shot her a quizzical look. Dame Gothel looked squarely at her, and Patience met her stare with steely determination.

"Then it is time we see the shards, child." Her old gnarled hands slowly patted the table.

CHAPTER 8
THE SHARDS OF THE GLASS SLIPPER

As Patience pulled the shards out and unwrapped them, even General White could not suppress her curiosity at seeing the fabled artifacts. Everyone gathered closely around the table to view them, as Patience began to describe the events that transpired the night the glass slippers broke. It was a memory she would have normally pushed away, but now she let it wash over her, in all too painful clarity; she recalled the fateful day with such detail that she felt she was there again.

Patience absently placed her hand upon the shards and could feel a slight warmth pulsing through her hands from them. It brought her a sense of confidence and comfort, helping the young girl gather her memories.

* * *

"Pai! Honey, you must be back to finish the evening chores," reminded Patience's mother. She wore her hair pulled back in a nondescript bun with soft tendrils that hung about her face.

"I will, Mother!" answered the ten-year-old girl with an impish smile. The two had finished clearing the dinner plates from the table, where the queen yet again had not shown. Queen Cinderella would never appear for most meals and while it concerned the staff, at least the food was not wasted; they had been eating very well lately. In fact, most of the staff had not seen the queen much at all in recent months. Every morning, they would prepare the queen's breakfast in the dining room, and then, when the food went cold, they would remove the untouched dishes. It was the same for the afternoon meal, and then again for dinner. If nothing else, it gave the staff something to do, and routine was always good for the servant staff, keeping them occupied with a sense of purpose and order. Occasionally, the majordomo would request food to be brought to the queen's private chambers.

Patience waved to her mother as she left the dining area. Like her mom, the young child was born into a family of servants who had worked and lived in the castle for generations. From an early age, she had stayed close by her mother and was happy to help, but she was older, nearly ten now.

"Besides," her mother used to say, "even the children of the castle's staff should be allowed some time to be children."

The children knew where they were allowed to go and how to behave in the castle, and because all of the servants knew each other, everyone kept a watchful eye. The staff had their own schooling for their children and other organizational functions that allowed them all to interact and mingle. It was said by many of the kingdom that to be in service in the Marchenton castle was a better life than living as a commoner in the kingdom.

Though there were still more duties to be done, Patience's mother would often let her daughter leave early. She suspected Patience had a crush on one of the stable boys, and since she knew her daughter would never admit it, she was not going to ask. Patience's mom smiled warmly as she cleared the last remaining plates from the queen's table.

But Patience was not headed to the stables; she had no interest in childhood crushes. Instead, she had been exploring the places the servants' children were not allowed to go; and one room in particular enthralled her.

The Marchenton castle was built with a hidden maze of small servant passages that included stairways and concealed entrances into various rooms; this was designed so that the servants coming and going were not seen by visiting guests. A network of stairways and dumbwaiters were hidden just on the other side of the regal decor of the castle's walls and rooms.

In the heyday of the castle, there would have been visiting dignitaries, grand balls, and elaborate galas of spectacle; it was necessary that dirty linens, food and garbage were hidden in transport. But these servants' corridors had largely been forgotten since the death of Queen Marchen and the Beanstalk War. It was in these dark hidden passages that Patience explored the castle.

There had been times in the beginning when she had gotten lost, sometimes ending up in the castle's abandoned wine cellars; or one time, much to her horror, into the royal catacombs and the adjacent underground river, where servants would wash clothes or dump unwanted garbage that would swiftly disappear in the rushing river and the rocky darkness.

One particular day as she explored the upper levels, she came to the end of a passage and discovered a large bedroom that appeared to be untouched for many years. This had been a dressing parlor at one time with a grand view of the land far below. As Patience began to explore the room, she discovered that it had been solely dedicated to Cinderella's private belongings long abandoned and forgotten. The proper main door to the room, which led from the tower staircase, was locked and seemingly had been so for a while as the dust on the door lever indicated. The only access into the room now was the unused servant's entrance.

The room had several large closets full of ball gowns and dresses of every sort and color. Furs and hundreds of accessories were in large, ornately decorated armoires. Petite shoes of every style lined still more closets. There were displays and boxes for jewelry—rings, intricate necklaces, broaches, bracelets, tiaras, each one more dazzling than the next. On a finely carved vanity table sat brushes, powders and a variety of other fine makeup, exotic perfumes, and ornate mirrors. Now they laid there, cold and still; much of the room covered with a thin layer of dust.

The curious child knew she should not be there, and was careful as she moved about the room. Still, she could not resist picking up a small comb from a vanity table and running her fingers over the silver carvings. She marveled at the soft warmth of a fur shawl and the fine silk of a luxurious gown. Grand oil paintings in huge, decorative frames adorned the walls, depicting the prince and the princess. This room more than any other held Patience's interest, and she would continue to sneak away to spend time here whenever she could. Princess Cinderella's private collection was after all still every young girl's fantasy.

But the most prominent display in the room was Cinderella's wedding gown, made of the finest satin and silk and the most intricate lace and beading detail. The dress rested serenely behind a glass display, as if frozen forever. Cinderella's gown showed only the slightest discolorations from the passing years and the dress still seemed to sparkle like the stars in the night sky. It was breathtakingly elegant with a long train, but looked heavy, thought Patience.

Nearby was a large pedestal, on top of which were the fabled glass slippers of Cinderella, pristine and untouched since Cinderella's wedding day more than a decade ago. They seemed uncomfortable, if not impossible, to wear; one could imagine that the tall thin heel would break if stood on, or the sides would shatter if you tried at the force of one's foot. The slippers rested on the pedestal as pristine as the day they were created, with a warm glow and polished shine full of confidence. They looked almost otherworldly in their design and construction; finely etched with decorative carvings and intricate details. Patience could not imagine how anyone could have made these, but then, a princess has far more resources than a young servant child could imagine. She had heard the stories that said they were a gift from the fairies; the slippers certainly looked like they could have been. When she was younger, Patience loved to hear about such tales of fairies. But she was nearly ten, she was growing beyond such childish stories.

On this evening, after running off from her mother's work, Patience quietly made her way up the servants' stairwells yet again to the abandoned dressing room of Cinderella. She had promised her mother she would be back in time for evening chores, and left her to finish cleaning up the dining room table. *What did it matter, anyway?* she thought. *The queen never shows.*

It was darker today. The days were growing shorter as fall turned to winter, and she hoped to look through some of the dresses before the daylight faded. She did not want to risk lighting one of the oil lamps in the room for fear she would be seen or worse, set the room on fire.

It was always still and quiet in the room, which was far removed from the bustle of the rest of the castle. But tonight, the still silence was broken. Patience quietly shut the small servant door with a soft click of the latch and took several steps into the room, heading to the largest walk-in closet to explore. Then the young girl's heart jumped in her chest as she heard the muffled sounds of a conversation. She froze for a moment, unsure what to do as the voices grew louder.

If Patience were caught, the queen's wrath would surely be felt across the whole servant staff. She looked to the door to see if it was about to open, her brain telling her to run to the servants" entrance, but her curiosity telling her to delay just a moment.

Strangely, the voices were not coming from the door; there were no shadows shuffling just behind the door's cracks. But the voices were indeed getting louder, and before, the voices had sounded muffled, yet now they were growing in clarity. To Patience's surprise, a sudden bright light began to glow and manifest near the middle of the room. She barely managed to scramble in time to the large, gown-filled closet where she quickly ducked behind some of the hanging dresses. Carefully closing the door behind her, yet leaving just enough of a crack to see, her heart pounded in her chest so hard, that she was sure it could be heard.

The light flashed in the room so intensely that Patience had to look away from it, and then it quickly dissipated into trails of falling sparkles.

It was Queen Cinderella and, impossible as it seemed—A God-mother fairy with large glowing wings and a wand.

"...brought you here to remind you of the person you are, and where you came from," the God-mother fairy said, finishing her sentence in mid-teleportation.

Patience stared in shock as she realized that the voices she had heard had been the very sound of this conversation in progress.

She had never seen a God-mother fairy before. They were rare magical beings, only talked about in stories as Gods of the sylvan folks, and she had heard more often than not, that they no longer existed. This God-mother fairy looked elderly, yet still regal with an authoritative air and magical energy about her, though the glow seemed dull. The fairy was stern with the queen, but her voice was still kind and warm.

"I implore you, Cinderella. Once you stray too far from the path of goodness, you will be lost forever in the dark woods of evil unable to find your way back. Worse yet, it will be impossible for others to see to you."

"Perhaps I do not want to be good and naïve anymore, God-mother," replied in an overly harsh tone. "Perhaps I no longer want to be reminded of those times. And if it wasn't for you, maybe I wouldn't have been on this path at all!" Cinderella stabbed a finger in the God-mother fairy's direction, punctuating her accusation.

"All of this is a lie!" proclaimed Cinderella, as she gestured her hand about the room. "Actually, I'm glad you brought me here. Now I can show you..." She pointed to the glass slippers, near where Patience had been only a moment before. "Prince Phillip married this!" She pointed toward the closet where Patience hid. "It's all just a lie! All I wanted was to go to the royal ball that one night, and by the end of it all, YOU married me to the prince—into a lie; a lie that I could never live up to!"

Patience dug herself deeper into the closet, pressing tighter amongst the fancy gowns, fearing that the queen would throw open the doors and find her.

"It was an opportunity to give you a better life." the God-mother fairy started to explain.

"I never asked for it, God-mother; I only asked to go to the ball!"

"Your heart asked for it, and your tears, child. You would have preferred to stay a destitute servant girl in your own home?" The God-mother's response seemed to infuriate Cinderella more.

"Oh, how I hate when you say things like that! My heart did? My tears?'" she mocked. "I would have preferred to have had a choice, a chance to accomplish it on my own. How do you know what my heart wished for? Do you know what my heart is wishing for now?"

The God-mother shook her head slowly in shocked disbelief at how bitterly Cinderella regarded that night long ago.

"My heart is wishing that Phillip was still alive. Can you do that? Or do you just turn pumpkins into carriages?"

"The magic of the Fae doesn't work like that."

"Then you are no help to me," said Cinderella coldly. "All your magic did is bring me unhappiness in all its grandeur!"

"You were your stepmother's servant, nothing more than a cinderwench. I gave you a chance to become something that any other woman could only wish for," the God-mother explained. "Yet even now you keep your stepmother close to you. Even now you are still her servant, this time in more wicked matters. Ella, I beg of you, do not succumb to the ways of the witches."

"The Maldame is the only family I have left" Cinderella replied in a flat tone. "Phillip is dead. The queen mother? Dead. The king? Dead. My father? My mother? Everyone is gone! How many in the kingdom have died because of this lie! A true queen could have stopped the Beanstalk War!" yelled Cinderella, her voice cracking as tears began to slide down her face. "You certainly have been no help."

"The Fae cannot interfere in matters of the royal court," the God-mother started to speak.

"I know, you keep reminding me. Yet here you are telling me not to accept help from the only person that has offered it; and if it is witches' magic that would help me maintain order in the kingdom, then so be it!" Cinderella screamed angrily through the tears that rolled down her hot burning cheeks. She was yelling so loud, in fact, the godmother cautioned her to remain calm.

"If you want to help, God-mother, let me borrow your wand. I'll make everything right again if you cannot"

"You know I can't do that. Ella, I am here to warn you. Do not fall in league with the witches. They are only using you for their own gains. If you side with them, though it might seem the right thing to do, the Fae will not be able to help you in the future."

With a sudden burst of frustrated rage, Cinderella swept her arm out against the glass slipper display, sending the slippers crashing to the floor and shattering into pieces.

"That is what your answer truly means to me," she mocked the fairy.

There was a deadly silence in the room. The God-mother fairy stared in horror at the broken glass slippers. "What have you done?" she whispered. Cinderella stood like a petulant child, her back to the God-mother.

"I never wanted to be queen. It's only because I was married to him that it fell to me when there was no one left...when I was the only vestige of royalty left behind. Every kingdom must have a ruler. But if I shall to be queen now, then I cannot be the princess I was." Cinderella bent down and picked up a large piece of the broken slipper, absently running her fingers over the sharp glass edges. She held the shard up to the fairy. "This lie is no longer my life."

The God-mother stepped closer to Cinderella. "Those were a gift of the Fae, my personal gift to you." she said solemnly, stunned at the sight before her.

"Then use your magic to fix them. Use your magic to fix a broken kingdom."

The God-mother stared silently at the broken glass on the floor, shaking her head. "Even fixed," the fairy said, "Some things cannot be remade. I am disappointed in you, Cinderella."

"Fix them," Cinderella challenged again. "Just show me you're willing to do something."

The God-mother fairy shook her head slowly again. "No," She said.

"The laws of Fae magic won't let you, is that so?" asked Cinderella pointedly.

"It is not that," the God-mother replied. "Now...now you do not deserve them," she answered, her tone deep with a resounding note of final disappointment. The fairy looked into Cinderella's eyes one last time, and then could bear no more. It was the realization of a betrayal of trust, it was the turning point of a friendship that had been close, but would now be cast aside, remaining broken forever. "Cinderella, you no longer deserve the grace of the Fae."

Her words stung Cinderella deeply. She turned away from the God-mother's damning gaze, tears welling in the young queen's eyes. Despite everything, to hear the pain of disappointment in those words was devastating. Cinderella knew in her heart that she had greatly offended and hurt the fairy God-mother. She was even more upset, because she knew it was by her own hand and that she could not stop herself. The young queen was terribly sad in that moment, because even though a part of her felt she should apologize and that the God-mother was right, her anger and frustration forbade it. She wanted to turn and hug the God-mother fairy, begging her forgiveness. And yet the very fact that such feelings welled within her seemed to push Cinderella in the opposite direction. Her sadness turned to anger. She became furious that the God-mother fairy could still expose such vulnerabilities in her. She became enraged so blindly and quickly that, despite herself, she could not stop what happened next. Cinderella cried not for what she had done, but what she realized she was about to do.

"There's a silent rage in you, Ella. I can sense the confusion of anger and frustration," said the God-mother.

Cinderella shook her head slowly, "No. I never wanted it to end like this. I am glad my mother is dead so she will not see what I must do. What her daughter must become."

"You don't have to do it this way."

"I have no choice." Driven by the fear of not being the person she always wanted to be, but of instead becoming something she loathed, the young queen gripped the broken shard tightly in her hand, she was oblivious to the pain as the razor sharp edge of glass dug into her own palm. With the jagged broken point, Cinderella whirled around and plunged the broken glass slipper deep into the chest of her fairy God-mother.

Patience watched from the closet, covering her mouth with her hands, horrified at the attack as Cinderella plunged the jagged piece of glass over and over into the God-mother. The fairy made no sound, and the broken glass slipper seemed to slide silently in and out of her God-mother's flesh with sickening ease. The only voice heard was Cinderella's sobbing, as she watched her own arm drive the sharp glass into the God-mother's heart again and again.

Finally, Cinderella stopped and pulled out the shard for the last time, throwing it to the ground among the other broken pieces. As she did, the God-mother collapsed where she stood, a vacant expression of disbelief on her face. The glow of the fairy faltered and diminished until it was no more.

It all happened in but a single moment. And for a brief second, Patience caught sight of Cinderella's face. It was wet with tears and blood, but also such despair and resignation; not anger, but remorse. Cinderella knelt beside the fairy's body and pulled the wand from her hand.

"I'm sorry," she whispered. "I need this to fix a broken kingdom."

Rising, Cinderella wiped the tears from her face with her palm. Then with the fairy's wand in hand, she opened the door to the main stairs and left, locking the door behind her.

For what seemed like an eternity, Patience remained frozen in the closet, unsure if she was even breathing, unsure if anyone would return.

Her eyes locked on the body that lay on the floor before her. The God-mother fairy lay motionless near the shattered glass slippers. It was beyond anything the horrified young girl could imagine: the queen, Cinderella, had murdered the last Fae; her own fairy God-mother. It was impossible to believe, yet it had just happened. Tonight had been the first time she had seen these mythic beings, only to see one murdered before her disbelieving eyes. Patience did not know how long she remained hidden, but she felt like she had to do something. The scared young girl feared that at any moment the queen would return.

Patience had witnessed a most unspeakable act, and though the young girl could not know at the time, the ramifications of what had transpired were great and terrible. If the queen did return to find Patience in the room, or if she learned that Patience had been there and had seen the murder, she would no doubt make sure that the girl would be silenced, forever.

Then, to her surprise, Patience caught just the slightest movement of the God-mother fairy lying in her own pooling blood. She was still alive! Most children would have run at the first opportunity to get away, but Patience quietly emerged from the closet, fearing not for her own safety at this point, but for the dying fairy. She grabbed a fur shawl from the closet and quickly crossed over to the mortally wounded fairy.

"God-mother?" whispered Patience softly.

"There isn't much time for me," the fairy whispered, struggling to speak as Patience covered the her with the shawl. The fairy's blood instantly stained and darkened the fur.

"I could get someone to help," offered the young girl. A sudden rumble of thunder underscored the tragedy.

"You were," the God-mother coughed, trying to catch her thinning breath, "here all this time?"

"Yes, before you came. I hid in the closet," replied Patience honestly.

The fairy smiled weakly. Thunder rumbled low again, accompanied by a flash of lightning. "What is your name, child?"

"Patience Muffet. I work in the castle with my mother."

With the young girl's help, the God-mother managed to prop herself up against the stone pillar where the glass slippers had been displayed. The fairy's face and clothing were drenched in blood; her grey hair was matted and clung to her neck and cheeks.

"Gather those shards, child, hurry," the Fae told Patience, offering up a weak smile of encouragement; knowing she had little time left.

Diligently, the young servant girl grabbed a velvet throw from one of the chairs and hurriedly collected all the pieces from the broken slippers. Then she folded up the corners to make a pouch.

"Good." The fairy nodded weakly.

"Let me get my mother. She can help." Patience went to hand the pouch to the God-mother fairy.

Lightning flashed brightly, illuminating the room. The fairy shook her head and pushed the pouch back towards the servant girl. Then a large crack of thunder resounded, as heavy rain began to hit the window.

"No. There is no time. You, Patience Muffet, must keep them safe now. And you must leave right away."

"Leave?" asked the young girl. "The castle? But I can't, my mother..."

"Things will only become worse now," the God-mother explained as blood trickled from her mouth. She closed her eyes and rested her head against the cool stone pillar for a moment.

"Evil grows now, more than you can understand. Take the glass slippers and keep them far from Cinderella. You must leave the castle now, or all hope of happiness for ever after will be lost to the kingdom."

Tears crept from the servant girl's eyes as she watched the doomed fairy.

"Thank you for your kindness and bravery, dear child. It shall be remembered. I will send you on your way. Then you must do the rest. You will know when it is safe to return." Weakly, she reached out and touched the pouch containing the shards, casting magic over the broken glass slippers in the cloth. Then she touched Patience's hand. The God-mother's wrinkled old skin felt cold and dull.

"Go," the dying fairy whispered weakly. "Protect the glass slippers." Then the God-mother fairy's head slid to the side, motionless.

Another brilliant flash of lightning lit the sky, followed several seconds later by a breaking growl of thunder.

"God-mother?" Patience called out. "God-mother?"

Patience watched as the Fairy's body began to glow brightly. Her hand seemed warm and tingling as it still rested on Patience's arm. Then the fairy's body gentle faded away.

There was another bright flash of light, so bright that the young girl turned away, bracing for the loud clap of thunder. But there was no thunder this time. The light had come from the fairy as she disappeared.

Suddenly, Patience found herself outside in the cold, wet night. The Fae's last dying act had been to send the young girl away from the castle. She stood in the road of a small village that resided close to the castle walls.

But Patience was not entirely out of danger yet. The sudden teleporting into the night was disorienting, and as she began to realize what was happening she was aware of screaming all around her.

Crowds of people were running in panic. There were shouts of terror and pain, people calling out names and shouting, "Bloodthorns!"

Then a man was picking her up. It was so sudden, that it frightened her and she let out a scream.

"This is the last one!" he said. "Not a good time to be standing around, kid," the tall man remarked, slightly out of breath as he scooped her up and continued running. Patience snapped into the reality of her surroundings. She could make out the castle walls in the distance.

"No! Wait! We should be running to the castle! Stop!"

Then Patience saw what was happening and why people were running away in the rain. Erupting from the ground all around them were great vines, twisting and rolling, stretching out towards the running crowds. Bloodthorns. The very place where she had stood a moment ago was now covered in thick, thorny vines. The screams were coming from people who were entangled in the thorns, the vines constricting, attracted to the warmth of blood. Lightning flashed again; Bloodthorns covered everything, reaching up into the very sky itself like a giant wall. For only a second when the lightning illuminated the night, Patience could see the remains of people dead or hopelessly entangled; struggling in vain as the giant thorny briar continued to blanket its doomed victims. Angry thunder cracked with a deafening roar.

The tall man carried Patience in a hurried fashion as he ran toward a rickety old covered wagon and tossed her into the back, scrambling in behind her. "Move! Move!" he yelled,

"Hurry Hamelin!" one of them screamed at the tall man. Hamelin crawled over a dozen other children to the front of the wagon. He quickly grabbed the reins of the waiting horses, and then with a crack the wagon jolted into motion. Patience looked around at the scared, frightened faces of the other children.

She found an empty knapsack stuffed under the feet of a crude, rickety bench in the wagon and carefully placed the velvet wrapped remains of the glass slippers in there as the wagon raced toward Marchenton's border. The tall man who had helped her into the wagon looked back over his shoulder to check on her, giving the frightened young girl a reassuring smile and a wink.

* * *

The room was silent as Patience finished her tale.

Dame Gothel had paid little attention to the story. Rather she had been preparing to make the potion, studying the glass slipper fragments, intently looking them over to pick the best one. Patience watched her nervously, still unsure that she was making the right choice by agreeing to this.

She was also sure that she had dropped a piece of the shards. She had opened the wrap more these past few days than she had in months. Somewhere, she had lost one of the smaller pieces. Had it been the night she and Hamelin camped by the road? Or was it at the willow tree? If it was the tree, then at least she had somewhat accomplished her goal. This thought did not make Patience feel any better.

"This one," Dame Gothel said. The witch held up a sliver of the magical glass.

"How do you know this will work?" asked General White.

"Fairy magic," the witch replied. She dropped the shard into a small stone grinding mortar and began grinding it into a powder. "Witchcraft came from emulating fairy magic, but over time, witches learned to twist that magic for their own purposes. Fairy magic is essentially the purest and most potent of magic, but witchcraft is handled and dispensed differently. It is a weaker form, diluted so that humans who lust for power and magic can use it; one does not have to be a fairy to control it. Now—a God-mother of the fairies created these glass slippers; in their very essence, they should contain fairy magic. This is a rare thing these days. Without the Faes' magic around these past few years, the witches' magic becomes more difficult to achieve. Eventually, I would imagine, it would be used up entirely."

The old witch worked with speed only decades of experience could produce. She added more components to the bowl, speaking in a strange, dark language as she gestured over it. "But there is another type of magic. Now, if it is true that Queen Cinder has discovered Wonderland, she is looking for it. And she will have access to a wholly different kind. Wonderland magic is the most ancient source of magic; more powerful, and more dangerous," she cautioned. "It permeates that land, contorting everything that grows and lives there. I'll tell you this much, the magic that created the beanstalk that started the war ten years ago, that wasn't fairy magic, or witchcraft. To make a beanstalk grow so tall in such a short amount of time, that is Wonderland magic at work. The question is- where did those beans really come from?" The witch turned and dumped the bowl of ground mix into a small kettle hanging over the fire, adding some leaves to the boiling broth.

"How do you know all this?" General White asked bluntly.

"Many decades ago, I was part of the coven's inner circle; there were a few surviving ancient tomes that mentioned Wonderland. There was enough written about Wonderland to know that even the coven would not risk exploring that magic. Instead, we plotted to take over the throne; even before Cinderella's birth. We could never challenge the throne directly, so we planned to steal the child that would become the next ruler. "That was my job," Dame Gothel continued to stir the boiling potion. "But what we didn't know at the time was that there would be twins. My spell was designed to affect only the boy, and it did, but not in the way we had thought. The presence of a second child in the womb had disrupted the spell. We did not even consider there would be twins. Nor did I realize the spell had gone awry. We stole the boy at birth to raise him to become king. Something had indeed gone wrong with the spell and had left the boy hideously deformed. We had faith in our prophecy. Too much we relied on it. The coven never questioned the fact that this child was not born of royalty to begin with. Instead, it followed the prophecy blindly. What we did not know was that the next ruler our prophecy foretold was actually going to be a queen. The coven raised the boy and it was many years until we realized there was an error. For my mistake, I was banished from the coven. I gave up witchcraft and tried my hand at raising a child of my own." She glanced at Rapunzel

Dame Gothel continued to explain as she put the final additions into the potion. "Maldame, who now sits with Queen Cinder, was successful in finally giving the throne to the witches; she and two other witches kept influence over young Cinderella by convincing her widowed father to remarry; Maldame became her stepmother and two other witches lived as her stepsisters. As foretold, Cinderella married into royalty. When the queen died and the Beanstalk War was imminent, both the king and Cinderella's prince were feared dead and Cinderella had to take the throne, she turned to the only person she had left as family, her stepmother. Now with royal resources and influences at hand, it was easy to maneuver the shattered Cinderella into joining the coven. By turning the queen into a witch, the witches have complete control over the throne. Their prophecy had came to fruition."

Dame Gothel held up the potion in a small glass vial.

"Let us begin," she said.

CHAPTER 9
A TRANSFORMATION

The packed room abruptly hushed as the front door burst open with a loud bang striking the wall; the cool night wind blew in the room in a dramatic entrance, swirling papers off the table. A hard breathing dwarf appeared in the doorway, dressed in battle leathers and brandished a sword. In between rushed breaths, he called out for General White.

"There is an orange glow to the southwest!" Dirty and sweating, the dwarf pointed down the beach. "A huge fire burns in the distance, visible from the top of the cliff! Our scouts have returned with news, the queen's army is upon us!" The dwarf's eyes begged for direction, his faced flushed and his brow furrowed under his thick hair and grimy armor.

Hamelin's mind raced. *What in the southwest would burn? The forest?*

"Aishew," he said in softly in realization. The small town was burning; it had to be the town. Hamelin's stomach tightened painfully. *Elizabeth.* His eyes grew wide as he remembered that Elizabeth had said she was going back to Aishew tonight. He wondered if Elizabeth was there. He did not deny to himself that although they had just met that day, he had hoped to spend a lot more time with the mysterious red-cloaked woman. A feeling of helplessness began to grow into a knot in Hamelin's gut and he did not like it. Hamelin bit his nails; he was concerned for Elizabeth but he could not bring himself to ask the dwarf more about the town.

Everyone had been listening to the dwarf, but Goldenhair had heard Hamelin as well. There was a moment of grim pause on Goldenhair's tattooed face. She knew that Elizabeth was not going back to Aishew, and would have confided this to ease Hamelin's fears, but the dwarf's news was more of a concern for Goldenhair. Her thoughts turned toward her friend Bertha and her children.

"General," the dwarf added. "Dendroba's troops are not above torching towns; we've seen it before. The rest of the dwarves have started defensive maneuvers to give you more time to retreat."

General White had other duties before her now, duties to protect the shards of the glass slipper and to keep a young girl safe; to protect the prince until he could regain his throne and stop the madness of Cendrillon. She gave a frustrated sigh; there was much that rested upon her weary shoulders. Without further pause, General White slipped effortlessly back into her role as commander, the place where she felt most comfortable. She pulled her long dark hair into a ponytail to give herself a quick moment to gather her thoughts. The general knew they would have to act fast.

"Gather your things," she commanded to the crowd in the room. "We're leaving now." Snow White stepped toward the door with the dwarf. Rapunzel jumped up, ready for action by her general's side, but Snow White had different plans for her lieutenant.

"Rapunzel, get this group to safety...bring them to the safe house near Hubbard's Ridge. If I have not caught up with you by the time you get there, try their plan. Get the dwarves to waterproof a barrel and then take the girl, Syrenka, and the potion to that lake. Whether I like it or not, it doesn't matter. Right now it is the only plan we've got."

"Any of the dwarves could get the rest of the group to Hubbard's Ridge...." Rapunzel had begun to protest. She knew she should be fighting next to the general.

General White's cool steel gaze clearly meant this was not a time to discuss. "I have to assess the field. I will fall back with the dwarves. Get these people to safety, especially that girl. And..." Snow White added reluctantly, "I guess keep Phillip hidden as well." And then General White hurried through the door and disappeared into the darkness.

From inside the house, the group could hear the shouts of the dwarves barking orders in the darkness and running past the house, down the beach. The shouting seemed to be getting louder and more intense.

Rapunzel looked frustrated for a moment. She did not want to be a babysitter. She wanted to be in the fight. The resistance had traveled here with only a small group of dwarves, and the general would need every skilled fighter she could get. Then quietly, Rapunzel's mother stepped up beside her.

"What should we do, Rapunzel?" asked Dame Gothel, attempting to hide her fear behind a calm facade.

Rapunzel's anger melted as her mother spoke, and she answered with resolve, "We leave. Now."

As the rest of the dwarves in the room quickly stuffed maps and papers into satchels, Rapunzel ordered to bring her horse. Goldenhair pushed through the dwarves and touched Rapunzel on her shoulder. There was real concern in her voice. "Are there any other horses? We are not able to take everybody. Syrenka cannot walk fast, nor can your mother, Rapunzel."

Rapunzel thought quickly. She had ridden her horse this afternoon with her mother. Goldenhair was right. She would only be able to ride with one. Her mind raced. She could put both of them on Rampion, her horse, but she would have to lead on foot, guiding Rampion by the reins, essentially slowing them all down. Goldenhair and her friends had come on foot. Goldenhair mentioned they could meet her bears at the top of the bluff, though it would take some time to summon them.

Several dwarves headed off into the night while a few others remained as escorts, awaiting orders from Rapunzel. Then Patience made her way to Rapunzel and Goldenhair. She was packed and ready, but in her heart, she was terrified. Hamelin came up behind her. Sensing his friend's fright, he put a comforting hand on her shoulder. "Don't worry, girl. We'll get out of this." Hamelin tried to push his own worries aside. "Bremensport can wait a little while," he whispered. It was his way of apologizing and comforting his young friend. Patience patted his hand, appreciating his comforting gesture. In comforting Patience, Hamelin felt like he was trying to comfort himself as well.

"Has anyone seen Syrenka?" Dame Gothel asked, puzzled suddenly by the confusion of the sudden evacuation.

The prince brushed by her politely and replied, "She is probably gathering a few things, why?"

"The potion we made from the one shard is gone," answered the witch mother.

Goldenhair snapped around at Dame Gothel's words and looked at the old witch, then broke away and searched the rooms quickly. Syrenka was not in the

house. She found Syrenka's chalk and slate with a simple message written on it.
I will return. I promise.

"She took the potion," Goldenhair guessed. She knew her friend well, and realized what she was planning. In the confusion, Syrenka had grabbed the potion and left the house unnoticed. Instantly, Goldenhair was out the door and into the night.

Everyone followed her out onto beach, where there was pandemonium as the dwarves ran and fires were set to light the beachfront. Hamelin looked over and realized that in fact, the dwarves were already engaged in fighting the queen's army, not more than fifty yards from the house. The army had been right on top them.

"How did they know we were even here?" Hamelin wondered in surprise. With the glow from the fire and the bright full moon that hung in the star-filled night, it became a little easier to see. This had been the only advantage the dwarves had in detecting the surprise attack. Had it been a cloudy night the queen's army would have sneaked right up to them.

"At least the full moon is in our favor," Hamelin said aloud to himself.

On the rough boardwalk from the house to the edge of the ocean, silhouetted against the fires the dwarves had lit along the beach they saw a figure shuffling hurriedly to the water. Hunched over and gripping the thin railing, the figure was trying to run with a limping gait.

"Syrenka!" Goldenhair yelled, and darted from the porch onto the sand, running after her. Rapunzel and the prince ran after Goldenhair. The prince was no stranger to the battlefield, however, and he heard the dwarves shout "Arrows!" he tackled Rapunzel to the sand.

"What are you doing!" Rapunzel shouted, fighting to shove him off her, not realizing the prince was shielding her with his body. Meanwhile, he called out down the beach, "Goldenhair! Get down! Take cover!"

Watching from the porch of the house, Hamelin and Patience did not understand what the prince was saying. Patience heard screams from the dwarves and then sounds of quick multiple thuds as the arrows hit. These had come silently and near invisible, the blackened arrows blended with the night as they flew. Several dwarves were taken by surprise, and silently slain where they stood. Black arrows rained down upon the dwarven lines, landing even farther behind the battle line and hitting the boardwalk with loud cracks, digging into the sand and even the roof and side of the house. The arrows struck the steps of the small porch in front of Hamelin as he stumbled backwards just in time.

Patience watched in horror as the figure on the boardwalk dropped instantly, her back arching as she collapsed. "No!" Patience silently screamed in disbelief. She sprinted to the boardwalk as well.

Most on the battlefield shifted focus to the second barrage of arrows. It seemed at first that the stars were glowing, the night sky depriving all of any accuracy in judging distance. The hundreds of lights in the sky seemed merely to grow brighter, hiding their deadly trajectories until it was almost too late. Fiery arrows came down in a flaming rain from the sky. More thuds sounded about the house, and Hamelin watched the arrows land all around. He froze in horror, unable to move as Patience ran up past him and toward the boardwalk.

The flaming arrows dotted the beach and the boardwalk, and the wooden boards of the walkway began to burn in places. Patience was still running, and he could see now both the prince and Rapunzel were scrambling to their feet. Goldenhair had arrived at the fallen figure on the boardwalk. As Hamelin watched, he became conscious of a wood burning smell and thick smoke around him. The house they were in had caught fire from the flaming arrows, and the fire was spreading quickly.

"We've got to move, madam." Hamelin tapped Dame Gothel on the shoulder, directing her attention to the burning part of the house. Hamelin could see she was terribly frightened, but she calmly nodded in agreement, gathering her cloak as Hamelin quickly began to help her navigate the few steps to the sand. As they walked around to the side keeping the house between them and the fire and Dendroba's army, Hamelin and the elderly Gothel nearly collided with the dwarf returning with Rapunzel's horse. The dwarf fumbled with Rampion's reins and struggled to get his sword unsheathed.

"Damn yer whiskers boy, watch where yer goin'," the dwarf growled. "I would have gutted you thinking yer part of the rat army." The dwarf threw the leather reins hard into Hamelin's chest in annoyance. "I hope you know how to drive one of these things; I sure don't."

Hamelin paused at the dwarf's words. A spark of an idea glistened in his eyes. "Rat army? Of course!" Hamelin quickly turned to the dwarf. "Can you take the old woman back to your safe house on this horse?" He tossed the reins back at the stout warrior.

"I would prefer to get into the battle," replied the dwarf flatly, throwing the reins defiantly back at the tall thin man.

"Please! There is not a lot of time. I might be able to stop this battle."

"You still aren't selling me, boy," said the dwarf, preferring to go fight with his clan brethren instead of leading an old woman on a horse in the dark. Dame Gothel gave Hamelin a puzzled looked.

"Please!" implored Hamelin again. The dwarf finally relented, slumping his shoulders and extending his hand, flicking his fingers quickly for Hamelin to give the reins back.

"It's probably better this way, you two would get lost, and she's the one worth savin'."

"Thank you, dwarf," said Dame Gothel.

"I meant the horse," grumbled the dwarf as he helped the old woman up into the saddle.

"Hamelin," said the Dame as she steadied herself in Rampion's saddle, "whatever your plan is, be careful."

"I can't believe I'm going to try this," Hamelin replied, more to himself than to her. Then he turned, reaching into his jacket, and jogged off down the beach.

Goldenhair had reached Syrenka before the others. Even in the moonlight, she could see Syrenka laying there close to the water's edge, legs glistening with blood, but not from any arrow wound. Her legs bled horribly from the running until the pain was so great that she could do nothing but crawl. But Syrenka continued onward, crawling toward the sea, gritting her teeth in agony and anger; cursing the crippled life of isolation she had let herself live these past years.

Determined now to leave it behind her, with every struggling effort, Syrenka used one hand to pull herself along the planks of the piecemealed boardwalk. Her other hand clutched the bottle Rapunzel's witch mother had filled with the elixir from the small glass slipper shard. She could feel the pounding boom of the surf, even the sound of the sand hissing as foam and water sifted upon the beach. She could see the moonlit outline of the waves curling about and smell the sharp scent of the salt and seaweed.

Syrenka was so close. She had not run to the water in an act of selfishness.

She did not steal the potion out of greed. Syrenka knew if she could do this, she could help her friends now.

Goldenhair knelt down next to Syrenka as she tried to crawl along the wooden boards. The wet sand and lapping waves were only a few boards from her. Rambling and upset, Goldenhair spoke quickly in a mixture of several languages.

"What are you doing?" she cried.

Syrenka looked up at Goldenhair with tears streaming down her flushed cheeks. Dirty and matted hair clung to her face from blood sweat and sheer exhaustion. She was mouthing something, but without her slate and chalk, the mute woman could not speak the words she so desperately wanted to say.

Behind them, Rapunzel had struggled to her feet, throwing off the prince's efforts; despite the barrage of arrows, he had selflessly risked himself for her.

"I do not need your help, Phillip!" She angrily refused to call him by his title. As far as she was concerned he had not been the prince for the last five years. There had been no prince of Marchenton.

"It's too dangerous out here for you, Rapunzel," he stated again. Rapunzel was furious and frustrated, growling at the well-intentioned man. Angrily, she spun around and continued toward Goldenhair and the others. Rapunzel was General White's second in command; she had survived well enough on her own, she thought. The only reason they were in this situation they were in now, was because of him.

"He should have stayed where he was; we could have handled this without him," Rapunzel fumed under her breath, making herself angrier. "Men run off and we're left to clean up the mess," she scoffed. "And now *he* is back for not even a week's time and already he's getting in the way."

Rapunzel had been on her own for many years since her adoptive mother had forced her out of the tower. She had been quite successful at her independence, and she belligerently refused to involve herself with any more men. The last time was quite enough. She cursed the memory of being pregnant and homeless. "I don't need any man's help," Rapunzel hissed.

Patience and Rapunzel arrived together at the boardwalk.

"Is she okay?" Rapunzel asked. "It's not safe out here. We have to leave."

"We should get her back," the prince added, wincing in pain from his shipwreck wound, his injuries further aggravated by his attempt to protect

Rapunzel. Prince Phillip did not want to point out that if their mute friend was too wounded, they would have to abandon her there if there was any hope to avoid capture. Already he seemed unpopular with this group.

"Well, whatever we left in the house is probably on fire now," Patience remarked, looking back at the small wooden house ablaze on the beach. She had her backpack and the shards securely on her shoulders.

Goldenhair did not even acknowledge their comments. She was trying desperately to figure out what the crippled mute was trying to say. Through her tears, Syrenka was trying to talk. Goldenhair threw her hand up to silence everyone behind her. "I don't understand what you are saying" Goldenhair stammered, shaking her back and forth.

"We have to get you back. You have to come with us." Patience pleaded, reaching out to help Goldenhair. She had been sure that Syrenka was struck by an arrow, but she could not see any arrow.

"Dendroba is in the fight!" The shouts from the dwarves echoed in the night.

Rapunzel's face lost its color. "General Dendroba is on the field!" She turned quickly to the prince, attempting to explain the direness of the news. "We must retreat." Rapunzel feared for the dwarves and for General White, who was somewhere in the battle. She feared that this would be the end of everything they had fought for; and Rapunzel was not fighting next to her general.

"Who is General Dendroba?" the prince asked amidst the chaos.

Goldenhair was still trying to help Syrenka, who had refused to stay still any longer and had now crawled to the edge of the boardwalk, looking over the dark waters and foam-topped waves. Goldenhair grabbed her shoulder again,

"You'll drown!" She said. "Syrenka, you know you can't do that. Not anymore."

Syrenka looked at Goldenhair again. Then Goldenhair realized something. Syrenka had been crying, but not from the familiar crippling pain that shot through her legs. They had been tears of joy. Goldenhair looked at the small bottle Syrenka held in her hand, the bottle that contained the potion Dame Gothel had made for her. It was empty.

"Get your friends off the beach. I can help you." It came as a whisper of music—from Syrenka; somewhere from the back of her throat, she had spoken. The sound seemed disconnected, like someone who was parched with thirst. It was the first time Syrenka had been able to speak in decades; and though it was a soft and dry voice, it had a lyrical beauty unlike any other.

Goldenhair stared incredulously at Syrenka, who smiled back as her tears of happiness ran freely. She nodded assuredly. It was true! The potion was working. Goldenhair's eyes welled with tears, and she smiled and hugged her dear friend.

"Get everyone away from the beach," Syrenka whispered again. Goldenhair turned quickly to the others behind her, wiping her tears away.

"Rapunzel get everyone off the beach. Hurry, please!" Rapunzel nodded and sprang from the boardwalk to give the order to the dwarves.

Grabbing Patience's hand, Phillip pulled the young girl away. He would take the girl to join the others. This was no place for a child. The prince had not even considered the fact that he was holding a servant's hand.

"What's going on?" Patience asked over her shoulder.

"The fish that had turned to a girl, now again becomes a fish," replied Goldenhair smiling as tears ran down her tattooed face.

Syrenka's transformation back into a mermaid had begun.

CHAPTER 10
A MERMAID'S KISS

Rapunzel raced up the beach toward the battle, scanning the area for General White. As she came closer to the clashing forces, Rapunzel drew her sword, avoiding the dwarven fires and the hastily dug ditches they had prepared to slow their aggressors' advance. To some degree, the dwarven defenses were working against the rat army. The dwarves were outnumbered, though; it was only a matter of time until they would be overrun. Fighting in a battle was where Rapunzel had wanted to be anyway. She followed her dwarven allies and hopped quickly over the fallen bodies, still looking for General White.

Darting swiftly around, Rapunzel rushed past the melees, striking out randomly at any of the queen's soldiers within reach, almost as an afterthought, as she continued searching for General White in the surrounding confusion. A huge towering form appeared in front of her. Rapunzel dug her heels into the sand and slid to a stop as the enemy stood before her. General Dendroba.

A look of recognition crossed the disfigured face of the general as he stared at General White's second-in-command. Rapunzel readied to defend herself against the towering general, but a nearby dwarven fighter had seen his lieutenant, Rapunzel, steeling herself for the fight. Quickly he dispatched his opponent and then rushed in to attack Dendroba, distracting him before he could engage Rapunzel.

"I'll help you with that one, miss!" the dwarf yelled, shouldering Rapunzel protectively out of the way as he roared in his charge against the queen's general.

Dwarves were unusually strong for their size but Dendroba was far stronger. The general parried the dwarf's attack with little effort. Then with a quick side step, Dendroba grabbed the dwarf by the face with his bare right hand. Rapunzel had expected the general to follow through with his sword on the hapless dwarf.

When she saw the general grab the dwarf single-handedly, she realized that the stories she had heard about the Lord Dendroba were true. "Fear the right hand of Dendroba!" was a phrase her resistance fighters knew all too well.

He palmed the dwarf by the face with his right hand, picked him up as the dwarf struggled futilely, and tossed him backward past Rapunzel. She caught a glimpse of Dendroba's hand and deformed right arm. Rapunzel suddenly understood why many would retreat rather than face the general on the battlefield. In previous skirmishes, she had only seen the queen's general from a distance; he was known to wear a large leather glove on his right hand. Now Rapunzel was close and could see his bare hand clearly in the surrounding light of the dwarven fires. His right arm was thinner than his other arm and longer, with elongated fingers that ended in bulbous tips. The hand was amphibious, colored bright yellow with vibrant blue splotches and large black spots. The color traveled up his forearm, his skin glistening in the firelight. As for the dwarf, he was dead before his body landed crumpled and motionless on the sand.

The dwarf's face was covered with slime where the general had come in contact with it. Much like certain types of frogs that lived in the jungles and were deadly to the touch, Dendroba's frog-like deformity of his right hand was just as deadly. The slime was, in fact, a toxic poison that killed instantaneously with a mere touch.

Rapunzel shifted her weight in the sand and readied her sword for the fight as the general confidently strode toward her, his heavy sword poised by his side. Rapunzel was never one to back away from any fight.

Dendroba moved quickly, faster than Rapunzel had expected, bringing his swing from the hip into a devastating arc. Out of gut reaction, Rapunzel raised her sword to block his swing, wincing in expectation of the mighty blow. She felt her response was late and knew her defense was not adequate; the general was lightning quick. There was a loud clang as swords crashed together, but Rapunzel did not feel Dendroba's attack; her sword never had the opportunity to defend against the blow.

General White appeared from out of the chaos of battle to block the attack.

"What are you doing here?" General White barked angrily. "Get back with the others!"

Dendroba welcomed the chance to meet General White face to face. He took advantage of the rebel leader's momentary distraction with a powerful kick from his incredibly strong legs, and shoved his heavy boot into the chest of General White, stunning her momentarily and sending her tumbling backwards a few yards from Rapunzel. Dendroba quickly slid the large black leather glove back onto his deformed right hand. He would engage General White in battle honorably at the least. Dendroba only used his right hand on those he did not respect, preferring to win by skill in battle rather than use something as easy and underhanded as poison.

Lord Dendroba now loomed over Rapunzel. He would dispatch this one quickly, he thought, so that he could focus all of his attention on General White.

"Protect White! Save the General!" Sudden yells came from the smoke and the darkness as a dozen dwarves rallied to General White's defense.

Rapunzel rushed over to Snow White. Lord Dendroba's powerful kick had knocked the wind from her, and she winced in pain as she rose to her feet, clutching her side. A couple of broken ribs, she thought. Nothing she had not dealt with before.

"General…" Rapunzel started helping the dark-haired leader steady herself as she got her feet, but Snow White threw her off.

"What are you doing here?" Snow asked again. "Why aren't you with the others?"

"There's been a change in plans." Rapunzel began to explain quickly. "We have to pull our troops off the beach now. Something is going to happen."

Lord Dendroba was battling several dwarves keeping him too focused on the fighting at hand to even take his glove off. Eventually he fought off the dwarves, but lost sight of both General White and Rapunzel in the confusion. Much to his frustration, he would not get the chance to square off with the leader of the rebellion tonight.

* * *

The pain was beyond measure as Syrenka contorted and writhed in agony. Her cries of pain were hoarse. Everyone had stepped away from her, no longer able to hold her down. Patience could not imagine what kind of agony she was feeling, yet, she knew this was what Syrenka had wanted. Somewhat naively, Patience had expected her transformation back into a mermaid to be filled with glowing sparkles. She began to understand what Dame Gothel had explained; this was witch magic at work, not fairy magic.

They could hear dull, wet popping sounds as Syrenka's bones began to change. She curled into a fetal ball, clutching her stomach. Sand clung to her wet, tear-stained face. She drew her legs in tight, and when she swung them out again they moved as one. Syrenka kicked uncontrollably, her legs now fused tightly together, as they began to transform. The flesh between them merged, now looking like someone had wrapped the lower half of her body in a wet stocking. Skin stuck to skin. Then, all over her body, Syrenka's skin began to flake off. She arched her back as if someone were stabbing it with fiery knives. Her hands contorted in agony as the webbing between her fingers expanded, and her mouth froze in pain as she desperately drew air into her transforming lungs. Gill slits ripped open along the sides of her neck. Then she was on her stomach crawling feverishly, her elbows digging into the cool wet sand toward the water.

"Syrenka!" Patience called out.

Goldenhair put her hand on the young girl's shoulder.

"We should go," she said. "The mermaid has returned to the sea."

As the first wave rolled over Syrenka's changing body, Patience thought she could make out the shape of a tail emerging from Syrenka's feet. Then as the next wave crashed, Syrenka was gone.

Prince Phillip, Goldenhair, and Patience had been so focused on Syrenka's transformation that they had forgotten their surroundings.

Now Hamelin was running toward them, pointing down the beach and yelling something they could not hear. Since the mermaid was back in the water, they had to get off the beach. Prince Phillip wondered what Syrenka meant about helping them, but as he looked at the tall man in the colored coat running toward them, his attention turned to more immediate concerns.

"—coming!" They barely heard Hamelin yell with the surf and wind behind them.

The prince looked down the beach where Hamelin was pointing and saw a large group of the queen's rat soldiers heading toward them. A section of the army spotted the small group and was close to overtaking them, pinning them against the water and blocking their escape route off the beach.

Hamelin ran directly toward his friends, trying to warn them even as he risked being trapped along side them.

"Come on!" Goldenhair shouted, grabbing Patience's hand. She waved at Hamelin to join them and started to run along the surf, away from the approaching soldiers and in the direction that Hamelin had been pointing.

Hamelin came upon them out of breath from his . "I was trying to warn you!"

The prince threw out his good arm in front of everyone, stopping them.

Hamelin caught his breath enough to finish. "I was trying to warn you not to go this way."

Patience clutched her backpack straps tightly. "Yes, but you pointed to go this way," she said.

"Actually," The prince broke in "I think Hamelin was pointing at." He motioned further down the darkened beach.

It was another contingent of the queen's army moving in from up the beach. General Dendroba had only engaged half his troops up near the house. He had sent the other half of his army further down the shore to trap them. The prince thought they were outnumbered before; now he knew they did not stand a chance.

The group could hear a single dwarven horn sounding up the beach near where the dwarves were fighting.

Goldenhair turned her head slightly. "That's General White's horn. They are signaling a retreat," she said.

"What do we do?" Patience asked. "We won't be able to make it back to the bluff, will we?"

Prince Phillip looked about the beach for a piece of wood, something nearby that he could use to fight, but there were only seaweed and shells.

The horn sounded again. Rapunzel had gotten to General White, thought Hamelin. He took a deep breath, remembering his plan.

The horn sounded a third time as the group started to run up the beach toward the bluff, difficult as it was in the deep sand.

Then Hamelin stopped abruptly, causing the others to stop along with him.

"Come on Hamelin. Don't give up," Patience said, though she, too, was exhausted from the effort in the sand.

"Let them work for our capture," added the prince.

Hamelin reached into his coat with purpose this time. "Mavor?" he began to ask, fishing around inside his jacket. "You said this army was created from rats?"

The prince gave a puzzled look. "Rats?" he asked. "Not actual rats?"

"Yes, rats," confirmed Goldenhair. "Why?"

"Are you sure?" Hamelin asked again, nervously.

"Yes. The army was created from all of the rats that lived in the castle. The soldiers are mostly rats with some human traits. Why?"

Patience saw that Hamelin had pulled out the pipes he kept in his jacket.

"Are you going to play them a song when they capture us? Or when they kill us? What are you doing?" she shouted, panic stricken. "There's not a lot of time."

Hamelin now had a wicked smile, reassured his plan could work as he twisted his musical pipes together. "Get to the bluffs. I just might be able to hold them off."

"Don't be ridiculous!" said Patience, fear in her voice.

But Prince Phillip was not going to argue with a fool. Angry at the waste of time, he began to pull Patience away with him. "Come on. We're losing our chance."

"Go, Patience. I'll catch up, don't worry. And take care of those glass slippers," said Hamelin pointing confidently at the young girl to reassure her. He gave a broad smile and the flash of a wink, and then turned and headed toward the advancing enemy ranks.

"No! Hamelin!" Patience cried. Prince Phillip and Goldenhair were already pulling her toward the bluff.

"I hope this works," Hamelin said nervously to himself.

He began to play as he ran back toward the water's edge and the approaching force of Dendroba's soldiers. As he played, he watched for any reaction from the army. Hamelin frowned. They were still advancing. Nervously, he twisted his pipes around and adjusted the notes.

The flanking groups of Dendroba's army were closing in fast; there would be no chance for him to make it to the bluffs in time. Hamelin continued to play, twisting and adjusting his songs. Come on, he thought to himself, you are all just a bunch of rats. Hamelin felt his hand start to shake in fear. What if he was wrong? He added on another section of pipe while keeping his eyes trained on the approaching men—still no response. Now he could hear them yelling, "Take him alive!"

Hamelin focused more intently as they approached. He closed his eyes tightly and continued to play. Then while he played, he looked again. This time, the queen's guards were frozen in pain. They had dropped their weapons and shields in a desperate attempt to cover their ears from the shrill and paralyzing sounds. It had worked! He had brought an army to its knees. He continued to play as General Dendroba's rat soldiers writhed in agony. To the human ear, the pipe playing sounded like nothing more than a regular tune, but depending on the configuration of the keys and added parts of his special pipes, the sound to the affected creature was incredibly painful; it was a secret that Hamelin had kept closely guarded, even from Patience.

Just as he felt pleased with the effect, something happened that Hamelin was not expecting.

"Kill him! Anything to make the sound stop!" the order came. Still wincing and doubled over in pain, the soldiers struggled to overtake the playing of the pied piper. This had never happened with the small vermin he would normally use his pipes to trap and eliminate. Yet the near crippling pain from Hamelin's music was hindering the troops' advance. With nowhere else to go, Hamelin began to move farther down the beach toward the water. He would try and drown them, their armor weighing them down, the music luring them into deeper water. The army followed him slowly, contorting in pain, wincing and holding their heads, indeed ready to kill him for the horrendous noise that only they could hear. Meanwhile, Hamelin continued backpedaling across the wet sand.

Focused on keeping the army at bay, Hamelin did not see the slow build of a large, silent wave that was pulling the water from the shore and rising up into the star-filled night sky. This mysterious wave rose higher and higher above the beach, threatening to drown everyone, including Hamelin and his painfully enthralled audience.

From further up along the rocks of the bluff, Patience and the prince saw the huge wave building as it headed toward the beach. Was this the help Syrenka had mentioned? The prince pulled the young girl away.

"Let's get to higher ground quickly," he urged as he saw the approaching wave slicing across the starry sky.

Goldenhair climbed swiftly up among the boulders; she could see that dwarves were also scrambling up the rocky bluff. She saw no sign of General White or her lieutenant.

"What about Hamelin?" Patience whispered with concern as the prince guided the young girl up the rocks.

"Your friend is buying us time to escape," he said. "He's a very brave man. Keep climbing."

"Yes, but that's not like him," replied Patience as she climbed up the rocks.

"Maybe there's more to your friend than you know," Prince Phillip replied. "Keep climbing," he added again.

The giant wave of water slid silently toward the shoreline, barely visible in the night sky, growing even greater, as it loomed high above the beach. General Dendroba noticed the wave also. With his powerful legs, he bounded to the bluff wall and easily began to ascend it, all the while shouting the order to retreat to higher grounds. Those of his army that could hear him began to scramble for the higher rocks as well. As the huge wave began to crest, many others on the beach realized what was happening, but by then it was too late to escape back up the bluff. In moments, the huge wave would cover everything up to the bluff wall with a deadly, pounding surf.

Hamelin continued to play oblivious to what was behind him as he moved backward into its path. He led the army further away from the beach cliffs and his friends, away from the beach, now walking on ground that he had not realized had been submerged just moments earlier. Still, the rat army followed him out onto the exposed floor of the bay.

The water must be around here somewhere. The beach didn't look this wide. Hamelin wondered if he had been walking backwards the wrong way. Then he heard the hiss of the sand as the water was pulled behind him toward the towering crest. The piper realized far too late that he had been walking out into the path of a giant wave that had drawn the water off the very floor of the bay. Now the crest was about to roll in and break.

Cold water swelled around him, quickly lifting Hamelin off his feet and pulling the surprised piper fifty feet toward the top of the wave. The giant wave rolled in. He had stopped playing his pipe and struggled to hold on to it. He could hear the roar now as the wave began to crest and crash. The piper could see the army he had lured toward the water now running back to the beach in a scattered, fruitless attempt to escape their impending doom.

Hamelin was above them now, at least a hundred feet in the air, pushed helplessly along the top by the great force of tons of water. The cresting wave began to curl and drop over him. Hamelin sensed both panic and helplessness, but he also felt a sense of peace. He was able to help his friends get away from the queen's army, and he was able to take out many of them who followed him down to the water. He had helped Patience; and maybe those glass slippers were important, he thought. He hoped that they were. *What are the chances that such a large wave would crash on the beach right when I go do something stupid like try to be a hero,* Hamelin thought.

He felt the force of the mighty wave abruptly drop as it began to slam onto the beach. Hamelin looked up at the bright full moon one last time, anticipating the wave crushing his body with the rest of General Dendroba's panicked army on the beach below. Hamelin was suddenly aware of his own impending demise—if he was not outright crushed by the force of the towering wave as it fell upon the beach, then he might be slammed against the rocks of the far bluff wall. Either way he hoped it would be quick. Hamelin took a last breath of air, laughing silently at this last futile act, and closed his eyes...*Here it comes*, he thought.

Then from within the great wave, two strong arms reached out and grabbed him, in the moment just before the wave broke upon the beach in foaming chaos. The hands pulled the surprised Hamelin into the very wave itself, under the water. The force of the water rolled over Hamelin and he flailed his arms and legs under the wave. As the water cleared, Hamelin was amazed to see there was a woman smiling in front of him.

Is this what it is like to die? With the bright moonlight glowing under the water, he could see that a large fish-like tail made up her lower half. It was a mermaid that had saved Hamelin. He instantly recognized the hermit woman from the beach house. It was Syrenka, beautiful in her true form. Hamelin's wide-eyed look of surprise turned to panic as the quick gulp of air he managed to take before he was pulled under was running out.

She pulled him close to her and gently kissed his mouth, holding him with her as she swam along with the waves. *Amazing*, he thought. It was like breathing the sweetest air; it was magical.

"It's okay, Hamelin," said Syrenka, able to speak. "You are safe with me," the mermaid reassured him. Her voice carried sweetly through the water, seemingly surrounding him from every direction. Then she continued to kiss him warmly to give him air. They were floating underwater now, far from shore as the wave had passed over them and crashed with devastating force upon the beach; though underwater it was heard as little more than a distant, muffled boom. Then, the sea was calm.

Syrenka spoke, happy to be able to talk again, as Hamelin could only listen. She would pause in her explanations to kiss Hamelin so that he would have air. Then she held the hapless piper close as they spiraled slowly up toward the surface. Syrenka explained about how she came to live on the beach, and about her legs and the sea witch, and the prince who broke her heart.

She continued as they swam, kissing Hamelin warmly again when he needed air. She told Hamelin that the potion made from the glass slipper shard worked and had transformed her back into a mermaid. And she had created the giant wave as a way to contribute something of measure to General White's resistance.

"Now I finally get to return home. I haven't been back in over a hundred years, Hamelin," Syrenka said, her voice choking as she became overwhelmed with emotion.

As they broke the surface of the water, Hamelin quickly located the outline of the breakers near the beach and decided they were not too far away.

"Please tell Goldenhair, that I will forever be grateful for all of her help over the years. If the sea can be of any more help to you, I will be here." The light of the full moon illuminated the beautiful mermaid's face, proud and smiling. "I fear that my actions have compromised the plan of the underground river that was discussed. But if I did not act quickly and summon the wave, all would have been lost tonight. The glass slipper shards made all of this possible. I am eternally grateful for this. I hope you understand. Please give General White my apologies. I do hope she can find another way."

"Syrenka—" Hamelin started to speak, but the mermaid leaned in and kissed him again. Hamelin closed his eyes. The warm kiss seemed endless and dizzying, perhaps even magical. For Hamelin, tired and weightless in the water, being kissed by a magical mermaid, he surrendered to exhaustion. This was not a kiss to give him air to breathe, but a mermaid's kiss that rendered the piper unconscious.

* * *

Hamelin lay on a grass hill, near the bluff that overlooked the beach the crash of the surf still audible in the distance. Something was sniffing him, nuzzling his face. Half asleep, he lazily brushed away a warm, furry muzzle. "Stop it. Stupid bear," he mumbled.

Then the warm, furry muzzle began to lick his face excitedly. With a groan, Hamelin opened his eyes. The last he remembered, he was kissing a mermaid. Now what?

The animal stepped back as Hamelin shifted and then froze. It was still night, the moon sat low in the sky. In the moonlight, staring at him with large intelligent eyes was a black wolf. Unmistakable—a wolf; Hamelin's heart began to race. If he ran, the wolf would think he was prey and chase him. *Should I play dead?* Hamelin thought. It seemed like a dream to the piper. He could feel his pipe secure in his jacket but was too frightened to move.

The wolf stretched out alongside, laying its full body comfortably next to him and paying little mind to the panicked man in the long wet coat who was lying absolutely still. The wolf let out a large yawn, its big head and sharp teeth close to the piper's face. Hamelin stayed where he was, trying not to agitate the wolf as it settled in comfortably next to him. Surprisingly, he was not as afraid of the wolf as he felt he ought to be. Tentatively, Hamelin reached out his hand and, despite rational judgment, began to stroke the wolf's soft warm fur. After all, the animal was content to lay next to him, Hamelin realized. He also thought that he was rather cold, and the wolf's fur and body were warm next to him.

Hamelin placed his head up on his arm and marveled at the majestic creature beside him. He thought it odd that out of nowhere this animal would lie next to him. How strange, he thought. But these days strange seemed to be the norm. He wondered where everyone else was, if they had made it to safety as well. And, what would they think if they came across him and the wolf? *Goldenhair would certainly be impressed*, he joked to himself. Comforted by the warm fur, he quickly found himself falling back to sleep.

The comfort was short-lived. No sooner did Hamelin drift back to sleep when the wolf released a low, steady growl. It shot its head up, intently looking off in a specific direction. Something moved in the trees. Hamelin, initially nervous that the wolf was growling at him, heard the shifting of the tree branches but dismissed it, figured it was just some small animal that a wolf would growl at anyway. Quickly, the wolf was to its feet. Though, the piper was almost relieved that there was something other than himself that had aggravated the wolf.

Then from the darkness of the branches, something huge in form leaped into the clearing. A gigantic spider, easily the size of a horse cart, now stood in front of Hamelin. Reactively, he cried out several curse words in fright and surprise. The huge spider was frightening to behold. The wolf growled ferociously as the giant arachnid circled, eyeing its potential next meal with its eight black eyes.

Then Hamelin heard the spider talk. At first, he thought it might have been someone else nearby by, but by the sound and the movement of its great mandibles, it was indeed talking.

"Weeeee ssssserve the queeeen," it hissed.

The wolf tensed, and then sprung with a vicious growl, attacking the giant spider by leaping upon its hairy abdomen.

The wolf snapped at the writhing spider's legs, digging its claws into its back as the creature twisted and hissed horrible sounds.

"We?" Hamelin questioned. But it was too late to react when Hamelin detected something moving stealthily behind him. It was another large spider. In an instant, it lashed out, baring its great fangs and plunging them deep into Hamelin's leg. He cried out in terrible pain, clutching his thigh as he fell over, the spider's venom working quickly to paralyze him.

The wolf paused when it heard Hamelin cry out. The other spider, though wounded, took the opportunity to shove the wolf off, flinging it into the trees with a yelp.

The first spider shuffled over to its companion, who was now tying up Hamelin in thick sticky webbing. "The queen would be interesssted in meeting you," it hissed with sinister satisfaction. "And you can exxxxplain how you ssssingle handedly ssssstopped her army." The two spiders had seen Hamelin's act of heroism down on the beach. "Come, Gael," the spider hissed again, "let ussss return home to greet mother."

Then quickly, the huge spiders were crawling up through the trees, wrapping the paralyzed piper in webbing and dragging him with them.

The wolf recovered and burst out into the clearing. It quickly sniffed the area where the spiders had been and then bolted down the trail. With a determined run, the wolf tried to follow the tree branches, keeping its head up as it sniffed in the air, and whimpering with concern as it watched the trees. The wolf ran quickly to keep up with its eight-legged prey.

Then somewhere along the trail in the pre-dawn morning, the ground gave way underneath the frantic wolf's feet. It tumbled into earthen darkness with a thud and the loud smack of a heavy wooden gate, as the leaves and twigs settled in the hole. It was a wolf trap.

* * *

The shivering woke Elizabeth up in the cold dawn. A covering of dirt and leaves provided little warmth. Her head pounded as she slowly opened her eyes. Her thoughts were fuzzy and her naked body ached.

There was always a moment of panic when Elizabeth did not recognize where she was when waking up after these nights. It was extremely disorienting and frightening. Today she realized she had awakened in very bad place. Quickly, despair and frustration set in and her green eyes welled with tears of sadness.

"I couldn't save him," she whispered. It was more a great feeling of loss, than a coherent thought. "Oh, Hamelin, I'm so sorry." She was in a cage; a wooden cage that had been set in an earthen pit and covered with leaves and brush. The top of the cage had closed and locked on a trigger when she fell in the night. "I can't believe I fell for a trap like this again," she muttered, grabbing a handful of dirt and throwing it against the opposite wall of the pit. "Stupid," Elizabeth chastised herself. "Mavor will be disappointed; I need to control myself better," Elizabeth reprimanded herself. She thought she did have better control over it, but in fact, her transformations were growing worse. She tried to push open the top of the cage but the lock had closed and bolted the moment she fell in. The cage was not high enough for her to stand up in, but she could sit up, so she pulled her legs against her naked breasts, sinking into depression. Elizabeth rested her head against her knees and cried as she hopelessly waited for her captors; and she knew exactly who they would be.

The sun had climbed into the morning sky and was beginning to cloud over when she heard the creaking of a wagon and the familiar sounds of horses. Elizabeth hoped it was someone who had stumbled across the trap and was coming to help. As she heard the approaching footsteps and the rustling of leaves, the caged girl's hope sank.

"Well, well, well," came a familiar voice as Hansel peered over the edge of the pit. Immediately, Elizabeth stiffened, covering herself with her arms as best as she could to hide from Hansel's sneering gaze. "How is it we keep finding you in our wolf traps?" asked Hansel knowingly as he attached a rope to the cage. Gretel leaned over the hole, and tossed the captured girl an old worn blanket. Elizabeth quickly wrapped herself, for warmth of course, but also to cover her naked body from Hansel's stare. "The queen will pay good money for your blood. Seems werewolf blood is very popular these days—a full coffer bounty. And a werewolf pelt fetches a fortune on the trader markets."

Elizabeth did not attempt to fight from the cage. In times past, it only made matters worse. She said nothing to the two of them as Hansel threw the rope over a tree limb above the hole and tied it to a horse, pulling the cage from the hole and onto the wagon. Elizabeth retreated into quiet, sullen despair as Gretel and Hansel headed off with her in the wagon. She felt there would be no rescue for her this time. Instead, she thought of Hamelin, and hoped he and her friends were faring better.

CHAPTER 11
AN END WORLD AWAKENS

General Dendroba had only caught a parting glimpse of the interior of the temple before his quick departure. The gargantuan form of the temple guardian blocked the massive temple wall. It was later that day when the same wall began to shimmer and glow again, casting a faint illumination inside the temple's great hall. The shadows of old statues and carved reliefs stretched and danced as if welcoming the lonely event. The wall, which was dozens of feet wide and that much taller, seemed to change from stone to mirrored glass; for a moment it was transparent, and on the other side of it, a great field and blue skies could be seen for a moment. The wall began to undulate, and a shadowy figure pushed its way through. The disturbance sent waves and more ripples resonating across the huge wall, as if someone had cast a stone into a giant vertical pond. And then almost instantly, it solidified again.

A low set of carved stone steps led up to the top platform area where it met the portal wall. There the figure stood, hands on waist, surveying the room in its darkened state. Before the figure loomed gigantic statues lined up in a row that rose from floor to ceiling, their ancient forms hidden in shadow. Halfway down the steps on the right wall, in between the two closest statues, a small doorway opened to a side antechamber. Faint green light shimmered through the open doorway.

The figure moved quickly through the doorway and into the antechamber. It was a small room with a fireplace on the left side, and a faint green glow emanated on the right, from a wall of glowing rune carvings.

"This will not do," the figure said aloud in the dim light. "We will need more light." He made his way to the faintly glowing runes, and after a quick survey, he touched one.

The antechamber as well as the rest of the temple began to brighten, awash in a pale light from dozens of large white orbs that hung suspended from the ceiling, warmly illuminating the temple's ancient grandeur. Great murals and carvings that adorned the vaulted ceiling of the temple, hidden for centuries in the darkness, now revealed their silent stories again. The sudden whoosh of fire could be heard back in the main temple room as dust-laden braziers self-ignited their long dormant coals. Runes that were sparked to life with magic, traced a soft glowing path upward like ivy along the walls, pillars, and statues.

The temple of An End World was alive again. In the full light, the interior of the temple seemed even more immense. Huge vaulted ceilings rose a hundred feet high. Great stone pillars stood majestically with carvings and reliefs. Faded murals and mosaics depicted countless scenes and stories common to their land beyond. But, time had taken its toll, and parts of the temple had broken away, with sections of wall having collapsed into piles of rubble. There were alcoves filled with rocks, statues smashed by pieces of ceiling that had fallen. Other statues had simply fallen and now lay crumbled near their bases.

Standing in the small antechamber was a man-sized bipedal humanoid rabbit. He stood well over six feet tall, with short white fur covering a thin, yet muscular body. He wore a tight-fitting grey fencing vest. A slender gold chain draped from the button of the vest to a small side pocket.

The White Rabbit instantly recognized the body of the heavyset man in brown robes slumped against the wall of runes. The body had drained of color and was quite cold to the touch of the rabbit's paw-like hand.

The rabbit squatted down, placing his hand on the dead man's shoulder, patting it briefly.

"You poor genius of a fool," the rabbit spoke in a clean soft voice. "Great architect of all of Wonderland's structures. Dear Carpenter, to die such a common death is the worst of crimes." He stood up again with purpose.

"Still," the Rabbit spoke aloud, "your death is as much of a just cause for a declaration of war under the articles of the Fae-Wonderland treaty as anything I could imagine—which is the reason I am here, dear dead friend, among some other unfinished business."

He glanced over at the mantle of the small fireplace across the room. It was barren, and the rabbit knew that it should not be.

"He's taken that too?" whispered the White Rabbit to himself, shaking his head in sad disbelief.

A low rumbling from the main temple hall caught the rabbit's attention; absently ending his one-sided discussion with the body of the Carpenter, the White Rabbit said, "And now to find a man called Jack." He stood and watched the doorway for a moment, his long ears twitching as he listened to the rumbling again, his pink-colored eyes darting back and forth. Quickly he snapped back from the distraction, pulled the chained pocket watch from his fencing vest pocket, and gave a slight frown. "And if I'm to do that," he said, "I should get started. Or I will be late."

The tall rabbit turned and pressed another sequence of runes on the wall, then walked back into the main hall. The large wall that had transformed into the portal that the rabbit had walked through was now mirrored glass again, but this time it featured the enormous visage of a blonde haired woman.

"Rabbit," the visage spoke, booming with echoes through the ruined temple. "What is going on?" The voice asked simply, "Is it what we've feared?"

"My queen," Rabbit acknowledged, changing his tone, bending a haunch quickly to rest on one knee, and bowing gracefully. "Indeed, the Carpenter has been murdered in our own temple. Our guardian has been awakened..."

Another low rumbling echoed now, it seemed, from outside the temple. The White Rabbit rose to his feet. "And to further dig them a hole," said Rabbit, "the Looking Glass has been removed...and there's the desecration of official ground and property, trespassing, etcetera, if you needed any more to add to the list of treaty violations."

The visage of the blonde woman spoke again. "And what of Jack?"

"Not here, from what I can tell," the rabbit replied coolly.

The woman's face seemed disappointed. Rabbit was quick to refocus the matter at hand.

"I had hoped to remedy this situation diplomatically with the Fae," he said. "Yet they ignored my request to speak to them." It had been hundreds of years since the Fae and Wonderland had any dealings, but the White Rabbit thought it best not to mention such minor details. Rabbit's gazed stiffened in determination. "However, these blatant violations have gone too far and will require a presence of force. It is my recommendation to prepare an army to travel here. The sovereignty of Wonderland shall not be compromised."

"Invasion? Rabbit, are you sure this is necessary?"

"Necessary? your Highness," Rabbit responded, quite offended at the very question. "Of course it is necessary. Oh, my dear girl, despite your crown, you still hold onto your childlike naivety. It is one of your endearing charms. These transgressions must not go unchallenged. All of Wonderland is watching how you handle this situation. It will speak volumes to your subjects."

"I'm not so sure that they would care, Rabbit," the queen replied, sounding unconvinced. "I have ruled for more than three hundred years, and I've done so as one who has brought peace and order to Wonderland."

"That is all the more reason this invasion is important," Rabbit quickly interjected. "We've discussed this at length already. You have demonstrated you can rule with a velvet glove, my queen, and I would cut off the head of anyone who would dare contest that. But here is an opportunity to show that when confronted with an injustice, you can rise up and defend the land." Rabbit added, "We've not had need to do so since you took the throne. It is good we have this opportunity to remind your subjects that they can be protected."

"I suppose you have a point, Rabbit," the queen admitted reluctantly. "After all, you've served the throne since long before I came to Wonderland."

Rabbit smiled. "Ah, those were the days! It is a marvel to see how you have grown from a curious little girl into the proud ruler that you are. I am honored to have been a part of Wonderland's most prosperous times," Rabbit added with an almost exaggerated fondness. He went on to offer another point. "Think of this as more of a military exercise, if you will. Yes, the treaty has been violated, but Wonderland's army has not had much to do aside from painting the royal roses. Honestly, our forces are far superior to any in the known realms. I doubt there would be much resistance to our occupation. It would be blatantly foolish for any to oppose our ranks. It would be more of a show of force than any real outbreak of war; safe enough for the queen herself to stand among her warriors. That would certainly impress all in your army and your subjects."

"I do not need to impress anyone, Rabbit," the queen reminded her advisor. "But I understand what you mean. Perhaps a military force would also be helpful to find Jack."

"Perhaps that as well, my queen," Rabbit concurred, though his tone was less enthused. This went unnoticed by the queen.

"Very well, Rabbit. I will have Wonderland's army prepare to mobilize. I shall send workers to prepare for my arrival there. As you are there already, Rabbit, I would like you to act as a diplomatic ambassador to discuss matters of that land's surrender and our upcoming occupation with whatever local ruling body is in place. Do some scouting along the way. Find out what you can about Jack."

Rabbit bowed his white furred head. "As you wish, Queen Alice." The giant wall faded to glass and quickly shifted back to its normal stone state. Rabbit then turned and hopped down the rubble-strewn steps and back into the side room. He squatted below the empty mantle of the small fireplace and, reaching inside the cold stone of the chute, began to feel around. "Ah, there it is!" said Rabbit as his paw came across the hilt of a hidden sword. "Still there." He took out the sword from its simple sheath. It was dirty and very dusty from the grime of the fireplace. White Rabbit pulled the sword from its sheath for a quick inspection. It made a high metallic ring as he did. The blade was sharp and unflawed. He rubbed his thumb over a small inscription on the sword's guard—"W. Rabbit."

With a faint smile of memories from long ago, Rabbit sheathed the sword and quickly attached its scabbard to his belt, where it hung smartly in place with his tapered grey fencing vest.

He started back toward the door, but stopped short. With a sigh, Rabbit looked down where his sword hung. Rolling his pink eyes with annoyance, he immediately began to wipe the soot stain the scabbard had just left on his clean white fur. "Furs and whiskers!" exclaimed Rabbit, rubbing at his leg furiously, "That's going to take forever to come out!" He looked around the room, and then using a piece of ripped cloth from the dead carpenter's robe, wiped the scabbard clean.

The White Rabbit briskly made his way past the fiery braziers, back into the main hall, and down the rock-strewn steps. He walked past the huge statues of odd creatures, queens, kings, and knights. Ahead, Rabbit could see the grand entranceway. It reminded him of a time when the temple was bright and pristine, full of wonderful smells, music, and all manner of creatures as festive occasions brought two worlds together. Now it was cold, dusty, dark, and ruined.

A landslide, partially crushed and mostly impassable, had at one time blocked the entranceway but there was now a large hole that was freshly dug out. Rabbit passed through, stepping quickly through the rocks and boulders as he emerged into the sunlight of the outside world. He sniffed the crisp mountain air. "Stale," he remarked in distaste.

He scrambled down the rocky collapse to the floor of an immense crater. The shadow of the surrounding cliffs made it dark and cool; he could see sunlight and blue sky brightening the far crater wall. "It seems our temple has collapsed into quite a sinkhole since last we were here," he said aloud to himself. Scaffolding hung from the wall, broken in pieces. "Guess I'll need to find another way out."

Scattered on the floor of the crater were various boulders and piles of rocks, as well as thousands of rock-like oyster shells. Then the White Rabbit noticed the bodies that littered the crater floor. His reaction was nothing more than observational as he surveyed the scene, expertly taking in the details. Mostly human laborers, young men and boys; judging by some of the crude shovels, wheelbarrows, picks, and smashed wooden ramps, they must have been part of some excavation team.

"Digging out our temple?" Rabbit mused. "After we hid it so well, so long ago."

There were bodies of dwarves as well, with better armor and better-crafted weapons than the humans. "Were dwarves defending our temple? Stopping them from digging here? Or did they have other motives?"

Rabbit was trying to make sense of the scene when he noticed several more bodies. These were larger than the dwarves and most of them were human bodies. They too wore armor and carried weapons, but they were disfigured and mutated; there were far less of these rat-like bodies than the others, but they were distinctive.

Rabbit knelt beside one to study the species more closely. Their faces were more misshapen; some had tufts of hair and whisker-like beards. Their hands were more like clawed paws on most, while others had longer teeth or furred skin. They looked like rats. "Rat men in armor?" puzzled Rabbit. "How absurd!" One thing he did notice about all of these "Rat men" was that they, unlike the dwarves, were in fact, uniformed. Each body wore a herald's mark of royalty, a symbol of their king or queen. "Could these be royal guards?" Rabbit certainly did not expect a royal army to look like these creatures.

"Curiouser, and curiouser," he said aloud. "Now, I don't know what to make of this at all."

A great figured loomed above, blocking the sun and casting a heavy shadow over Rabbit. It was a huge mass, well over forty feet high. Its large potato-shaped body shuffled along the ground on large flippers, undulating its mass along, pushing bodies and rocks away, or crushing them with its great weight. The guardian of the temple had returned.

The White Rabbit was not worried. As the large creature dropped its brown misshapen head, it recognized the White Rabbit as a friend. Sniffing Rabbit with large, wet nostrils, the whiskers around its large, bulbous maw twitched in recognition. From its mouth protruded two giant saber-like tusks, cracked and yellow, but very formidable. It gave a loud huff through its whiskered mouth, shaking its head up and down.

The guardian of the temple was an enormous walrus. Rabbit patted the immense creature on the side of its head.

"Hello, big guy," reassured the rabbit with a tone much like one would use to talk to a pet. "Are you sad you lost your carpenter friend? I see he fed you oysters," he said, referring to the carpet of crushed oyster shells that covered the ground.

The White Rabbit noticed small cuts and slices along its muscular flippers and belly. The ugly creature had taken blows from the battle here, Rabbit concluded. But the cuts were of no real consequence to the giant walrus's thick skin and protective blubber. "What a sight you must have been!" murmured Rabbit. He was confident that when the guardian emerged from the temple, it sent all manner of men fleeing. Or, Rabbit imagined, the battle they were engaged in was interrupted by the sudden arrival of the guardian, and then both friend and foe fought side by side against this new common enemy in vain self-defense. From the look of the bodies, the great walrus crushed many that did not flee.

Rabbit instructed, "Guard the temple until more of our Wonderland friends arrive." With another pat on the walrus's thick, calloused skin, the rabbit headed back inside. The crater wall would be difficult and time consuming for him to navigate. He recalled that there was supposed to be a hidden stairway exit in the small antechamber with the fireplace, and he headed back into the temple to see about that exit.

CHAPTER 12
ALAS, ALAS FOR HAMELIN

The sound of a distant metallic clank brought Hamelin back to a groggy consciousness. The smell of earthy mold, dank rock, and vomit drifted into his dull awareness and a throbbing headache in his temples made him wince. Hamelin lay on the ground where he had been dropped, his eyes fluttering open finally. He was not dead. *If I were dead*, he wondered, *would I be stuck for all eternity with this whopping headache?*

Humor always worked for Hamelin. His mouth was dry and his hands felt numb. When at last he tried to move, a searing pain shot through his thigh. He slowly rolled over onto his back.

A door of iron bars filled an arched doorway. He was in a small stone cell that was barely longer than he was. There was wet hay scattered about the floor and some white limestone powder that did little to hide the stink of urine and blood, along with the faint smell of wine. Torches that lined the corridor provided some light but little warmth.

Gingerly, Hamelin pulled his knee up and examined his wound. Most of his body was still covered in wispy bits of webbing but, he was more concerned that the spider's fangs had left a large tear in his left pant leg, and a large wound in his thigh that itched and burned quite painfully. He coughed and wiped away blood and phlegm from his mouth.

The memory of his attack flooded back now—the royal army ambush and the huge wave that crashed on the beach, being grabbed and pulled under the water, the cliff and the strange wolf that woke him and tried to fight off one of those large spiders. The other spider had attacked him, its hairy fangs that digging into his leg—the excruciating pain and the venom, the suffocating webbing. Hamelin shuddered in fear as he recalled those last few moments of terror.

He barely remembered passing out from the paralyzing venom. It was all so very strange, he thought, and it had happened so fast that it felt unreal. Hamelin's memory echoed another vague recollection of a hissing, muffled voice through the cocoon of webbing, *The queen would be interested in meeting you.*

He had been captured! Hamelin closed his eyes and groaned. He realized that he did not have his long coat, nor the special pipes he kept inside. he thought of Patience and the others, praying that they got away; and hoping that somehow Elizabeth was alive somewhere. How he wished he could see her again. Moaning in frustration, Hamelin sank into despair; captured and he had failed his friends, both old and new.

Suddenly, he heard the creak of a distant iron door, and pairs of footsteps echoed down the hallway. Nervously, Hamelin began to bite his fingernails, but the bitter taste of spider webbing made him spit.

A shadow fell over him as he lay on the cold stone floor. "I am told you have quite an impressive musical talent," a soft female voice said in an almost complimentary tone. A faint, sweet smell of exotic perfume drifted towards Hamelin and he opened his eyes slightly.

"Enough to compromise a sizeable amount of my force—tell me how it works."

Standing on the other side of the cell door was none other than Queen Cendrillon herself, holding his piper flute.

Oddly, Elizabeth popped into Hamelin's thoughts, and he feared more than ever that he would never see her again.

Hamelin said nothing, choosing to stare up at the ceiling and not moving save for a sudden hard swallow. He knew that by not answering, he was only going to make it worse for himself and he could feel his heart pounding with fright.

"I just asked you a question." Queen Cendrillon's tone was almost pleasant. "I am not a bad person," continued the queen, "but don't force me to do bad things for something as simple as getting an answer to question. Is it worth it?" After a pause, the queen asked again. "How do your pipes work?"

Hamelin continued to stare at the ceiling. He kept repeating over in his head, *Don't tell her anything.* He began to think of Patience and the glass slippers, hoping they were safe. "Don't let them get anything out of you," he told himself, "for Patience's sake."

The queen's tone changed. "Bravado seems so heroic before pain is involved."

He closed his eyes, squeezing a tear out that ran hotly down his temple and into his ear. He swallowed hard again.

Two of the queen's guards opened the door and stepped into the cell. They were large and muscular, dressed in black leather armor; Hamelin could smell their rat-like body odor.

"We'll get him to talk," one guard growled, as they circled their unmoving prisoner, nudging him with their muddied boots, we'll break a couple of fingers—"

"No!" barked Queen Cendrillon loudly. Hamelin noticed that the guards actually seemed surprised. Then she composed herself. "He is a fine musician. It would not be right to do that to one so gifted. I would like for him to play a song for us later."

"Wait!" Hamelin cried out. "I could sing a song for you now."

Queen Cendrillon gave a smug smirk. She raised her hand, indicating to the guards to wait a moment. "Let's hear your song, piper. Hopefully it will be something I will enjoy."

Again Hamelin closed his eyes, enjoying that he was able to delay his beating for a brief moment longer. He knew, however, this would only make the beating worse for him, but it would be worth it. These were the people that burned down Aishew, he reminded himself. Hamelin began the song he heard from the children that lived there.

> *Queen Cinder, Queen Cinder, why do me harmin'?*
> *Whatever happened to your prince charmin'?*
> *I guess he left when you became a witch*
> *Or maybe he left 'cuz you're such a bitch!*
> *Queen Cinder, Queen Cinder, with the crown on your head*
> *Soon we'll be free and you will be dead!*

"Bring him to me when you're through," the queen said flatly, glaring at Hamelin. Then she turned and walked out down the jail passageway. Even as the guards kicked and punched him, he continued to sing the whole nursery rhyme that he had learned from the children, interrupting only to scream out in pain from the brutal blows. He had started loudly so that the queen would hear him from down the hall, but was interrupted by the guards punching him hard in the gut and knocking the wind from his lungs. Yet as soon as he could recover his breath, Hamelin would continue to sing. Toward the end, as he lay in a crumpled bloodied heap, he could barely whisper it. Still he mouthed the words to the song in short breaths, tears streaming down his bruised and bloodied face as he whispered the song repeatedly, until two guards picked him up by his arms and dragged him out of the cell and down the hall. This song of defiance was now the only thing that kept the frightened and beaten piper from lapsing into unconsciousness.

The burly guards dragged him to a room somewhere else in the dungeon and strapped him to an almost vertical table. They belted his legs and arms at each corner. Another strap pulled his head back tightly, cranking the table back to a more reclined position. This forced the dazed piper to momentarily pause in his singing as he glanced about the stone room. it was small but warm and lit by many large candles carved with weird symbols, all arranged in pentagram designs. In the darker corners of the room, he could make out the shapes of small old cages and piles of what he recognized as cage traps for rats. He saw shelves lined with books and jars and other objects. He could hear the sound of boiling water and the crackling of a fireplace behind him. The air was warm and humid, tinged in smells of earthy spice and sharp incense. However, for Hamelin none of this was inviting; there was something evil about this room. Nervously, he started to whisper the song to himself again.

"Queen Cinder, Queen Cinder, What did you say?"

A door opened somewhere behind him, then Queen Cendrillon stood in front of him again. This time, she was covered in a dark hooded robe. Hamelin sensed there were others in the room, though he could not see from his binding on the table. This time, though, the queen did not acknowledge Hamelin. She was quietly chanting something. It was difficult for Hamlin to understand. As she chanted, the queen pulled a long-bladed dagger from her robes.

I'm going to be a sacrifice! Hamelin thought. Now even more frightened at the sight of the dagger, he began to sing louder and faster, almost like he was singing along with the chanting.

"Soon we'll be free and soon you'll be dead!"

He moved against his restraints to see what was happening. Ignoring Hamelin, Queen Cendrillon took the dagger and cut open his dirtied and bloodied shirt, drawing out a small thin line of blood down his chest. Hamelin was now quite scared. His brown eyes widened in fright and he whispered the song even faster.

The queen turned as another cloaked figure came forward holding a large white goose with its beak and wings strapped. They laid the bird in the middle of a group of candles on a small velvet cloth that covered a table. The goose seemed asleep, or at least resigned to its doom. The cloaked figures chanted and splashed the goose with powders and liquids from cups. Then Queen Cendrillon took the dagger and plunged it deep into the goose's chest.

I'm next! Hamelin thought. He struggled in vain against his bonds.

Queen Cendrillon drained the dead goose's blood into a chalice and mixed it with a brown boiling liquid and other ingredients that Hamelin was sure would not taste good as a tea. The queen stopped reciting the strange chants, turned and faced Hamelin again. Hamelin watched as another cloaked figure brought a small bowl. The queen held the chalice in her left hand, dipped her right hand into the brackish, paste that filled bowl. Then she reached up and traced a symbol on Hamelin's face. The paste was cold and foul smelling, making Hamelin choke just from the stench of it. It was so overpowering that he could no longer continue to sing without gagging. She traced more symbols along his chest. Hamelin's skin began to itch, and he felt clammy and flushed.

The chanting seemed to grow louder and Hamelin fought to focus on the song he had been singing, but the chanting was too loud and it was all Hamelin could hear. The queen nodded to one of her rat guards who walked over to the table and with a loud thump, pulled the table back to an even more reclined angle. The rat guard forcefully shoved his dirty, gloved hand into Hamelin's mouth and held it open. Queen Cendrillon began to chant loudly and, reaching up with the chalice, poured the hot, putrid liquid into Hamelin's mouth. Before Hamelin could react, the heavily muscled guard shoved Hamelin's mouth shut and his jaw up and before Hamelin knew it, he had swallowed the foul concoction. Hamelin choked and coughed with the harsh liquid. He tried to focus his thoughts on Patience now, but was having trouble focusing on anything as he coughed. He knew that what he had been forced to drink could already feel it starting to have an effect on him. He felt tired now, fuzzy. His vision began to blur. Finally, the coughing stopped. Hamelin could not tell if the restraining straps were removed. They felt like they had. He felt detached. He just wanted to sleep.

Fight this! he said to himself in desperate thoughts. *Don't let them do this to you!* he screamed in his thoughts.

The chanting seemed distant now, more like singing. Queen Cendrillon was whispering closely in his ear. He could not make out what she was saying, but she had a very attractive voice.

No! No! No! Hamelin heard in his thoughts. *Don't tell her anything!*

Now Hamelin could hear what sounded like someone else in the room talking and answering questions; it sounded like his own voice. Still he felt like he could just close his eyes and sleep.

She gave you a potion—she drugged you! She is making you her slave against your will. Fight it! Hamelin felt like his ears were clogged, like they were full of water, but he could clearly hear the queen talking to him.

Too tired, came another thought. *Just want close my eyes and rest a little.* As his thoughts drifted off, he heard the chanting...now it sounded like a choir of angels, singing about the glory of the great Queen Cendrillon of Marchenton. It was a nice song, Hamelin thought. Then he heard a wonderful melody that sounded like a piper flute.

"See," he heard a female voice say. "I told you he'd be playing us a song later."

It was the lovely female voice of Queen Cendrillon that he heard again, asking him all manner of questions. Hamelin felt it was perfectly fine to answer them. Ever so often, he heard another voice saying from somewhere in his head, *don't tell her anything.* It was so distant now that he could barely make it out.

Hamelin told Queen Cendrillon about his piper flute, how the different configurations and different keys could affect different kinds of animals, including rats. Like the rats that were transformed into her army; that was how he was able to lead them out to drown. He apologized for that, of course.

"Could it be used against other animals like bears or wolves for example, or people?" asked the queen.

"Of course," he replied. "But it only works on animals; it can't affect people."

The queen then asked what he knew about General White and her army. He told her everything he could think of, how they had a witch named Dame Gothel that was Rapunzel's mother. "She was helping them," he said. Queen Cendrillon seemed very interested to know that Prince Phillip was alive and working with General White.

"Oh," Hamelin said warmly. "I have a friend. her name is Patience. She used to work here in the castle. Did you know she actually has your glass slippers? She saved them! Can you believe that?"

"Really?" asked Queen Cendrillon with genuine surprise in her voice.

Hamelin then told her about how she got them and that Dame Gothel could use the fairy magic from them and how they might be used to kill the queen.

The queen was of course grateful for this information, and Hamelin was proud of himself for being able to help. He told her that they knew of her plans to enter Wonderland, and about the mirror.

"Whom do you serve, Hamelin?" asked Cendrillon.

"I serve you, my queen," replied Hamelin, with a smile as if that was an obvious answer.

"Play another song on your pipes for me."

"My pleasure, my queen." Hamelin put the pipes to his lips and began to play.

Somewhere, he thought he heard someone scream, *No!*

CHAPTER 13
A SAFE HOUSE

Patience awoke to a loose bang of a nearby wooden door slamming shut. It was daylight now. She had no idea how long she had slept, or how she had gotten to sleep with a scratchy, burlap blanket. She had been completely exhausted, and despite everything, it had been the best night of rest she had in a long time. The young girl was curled up on a pile of hay in an old, weathered shack next to a large abandoned barn. Patience sleepily began to recall what had happened the previous night. She had escaped from the queen's army as the tremendous wave crashed upon the beach and wiped out all that remained there. Then she rushed through the dark, running with dwarves, fending off any remains of the queen's army. Moving swiftly through the woods, General White had led them to a safe house. The prince had carried Patience on his back. Tired and scared, she had cried herself to sleep at some point during the journey.

As she had done every morning for the past five years, the young girl reached out and made sure her backpack, and its valuable contents, were near. Relieved, she found it lying undisturbed next to her. Patience stood, picked up her pack, brushed the hay from her servant's dress, and opened the shack's makeshift door. Outside, she found one of General White's dwarves standing guard over the shack where she had slept. Startled by the guard, as no one had ever guarded her before, Patience let out a yelp, but quickly gathered her wits. She smiled politely and offered a good morning as she passed by the armored dwarf, who barely gave a nod in return. As she headed to the barn, the armored dwarf quietly accompanied her, opening the barn door politely and escorting her in.

Inside the barn, planks of gray wood on the wall were broken and sections of the ceiling had given way between its rafters. The floor was covered in odd lines and shapes of shadows cast by dusty shafts of morning sunlight.

Patience had heard talking from within the barn; it sounded like a heated, hushed conversation. There seemed to be a general buzz in the air. Patience sensed a level of energy and excitement, though she did not know why exactly. She looked around for Prince Phillip and Goldenhair but did not see them in the barn. She swung the old slatted door closed.

General White, Rapunzel, and her mother were talking with another man Patience had never seen before. She recognized the outfit of the stranger as that of the royal army. Her father had worn something similar when he left with the king's army, many years ago. It was the same style of battle leathers she saw the rat army wearing when they attacked Hamelin and her.

Was this someone from the queen's army? Perhaps General White had captured a prisoner. The stranger was disheveled in his appearance—unshaven, with a mop of unkempt dirty blonde hair, like he had just awakened. Patience did not like this new stranger. Had he been a spy for the queen?

General White paused in her conversation with the strange man as Patience entered. Turning back to him, she commented with a nod towards Patience, "This is the girl with the glass slippers." The mysterious man looked briefly at the girl, then turned back and spoke with General White in hushed tones.

With a quick motion to a couple of nearby dwarves standing by a tall rectangular object, General White ordered them to cover it with a dirty burlap blanket. The dwarves carried the heavy object closer and leaned it up against a post. The stranger pulled the general to the side to speak with her more discreetly. Patience walked over to Rapunzel, who was sitting on a stack of hay bales with her mother.

"What's happening? Who is that person talking to the general?"

"That's Jack. He arrived late last night," Rapunzel whispered. "Finally some good news. Jack says he's found the magic mirror."

It took a second for Patience to realize…"Jack? Not *the* Jack from the Beanstalk War? He's not dead?"

"I guess the prince wasn't the only one to survive. Jack did too, and he brought the magic mirror back. First the glass slippers and now this!" exclaimed Rapunzel. "General White is trying to convince Jack to let my mother look at the magic mirror." Rapunzel paused for a moment. "How do you know about Jack?"

Patience stiffened, her eyes darted around for any sign of the prince.

151

"Rapunzel, there might be a problem," said Patience. Leaning closer, she whispered, "Does Prince Phillip know Jack is here?"

"I don't think so. He is on the other side of the compound getting some horses ready to travel. Why? Is something wrong?"

Patience hesitated, mulling over what she and many of the castle staff knew. An ugly and ignored truth had remained within the castle's walls. "Jack and Princess Cinderella were...lovers. before the Beanstalk War started, while Cinderella was married to the prince. It was just an affair, but everyone in the castle knew about it—except the prince," Patience whispered to Rapunzel.

Rapunzel paused at the revelation. Her eyes fixed on Jack. Then a crooked smile came over Rapunzel's face. "Really? That, I did not know." Rapunzel could appreciate why Cinderella would be attracted to him. "I don't think Jack knows the prince is here, either," she said. The conversation abruptly ended as General White and Jack had come to an agreement.

"Dame Gothel." General White motioned the old witch over.

The general pulled the burlap blanket off, revealing a seven-foot tall mirror. Slightly stained and smeared with grime, it otherwise looked like a perfectly ordinary mirror. Its frame, though horribly tarnished, was ornately carved in silver and covered in faded gold leaf; cracked and worn from years of neglect.

General White threw an unsettled look at Jack. "Magic mirrors," she grumbled aloud. *Soldiers*, General White thought to herself. *That is something that I could count on.* Swords, she could wield effectively in her hand. Strategies, she could work. Snow White could understand these tangible things. But now magic?

"Mirror, mirror, on the wall," the general spoke; rolling her eyes that she was even saying the words. "Who is the fairest of them all?" General White spoke skeptically at the mirror. "That's the line, right? Something like that?"

"The magic mirror is, like the glass slippers, stuff of legend." Rapunzel explained to Patience, "Everyone has heard of them in some fashion through stories and tales. And the magic mirror, if it could be used, would be the perfect device to spy on the unsuspecting queen, anytime, anywhere—very useful to General White."

Rapunzel continued. "This plan had taken place before the existence of the surviving glass slipper shards was known. Jack had convinced the general days ago that he had found it 'in his travels,' and that he could use its magic. Ultimately, it would be an advantage for the resistance. General White reluctantly agreed on the off chance it might work. They were at the site to retrieve it when they discovered General Dendroba's army was there as well."

Despite Snow White's attempts at activating the magic mirror, the object remained as it was. "See," Snow White said. "Nothing happened. It doesn't work, Jack. Let Dame Gothel take a look. It is just a mirror. I can't waste any more time on this," she sighed. "Magic mirrors and glass slippers will not save this kingdom."

"Yet it was a magical beanstalk and a power hungry witch queen that got us into this," countered Rapunzel's mother, "so why shouldn't magic be a solution? After all, magic was the problem from the beginning."

Jack gave Dame Gothel a scathing look. As far as he was concerned, witches could not, should not be trusted, despite assurances from both the general and the general's second in command, who also happened to be the witch's daughter.

Dame Gothel hobbled over to inspect the carved frame more closely. What had looked like mere decorative carvings to General White was of far more interest to the old crone.

"Well?" General White raised an eyebrow, slightly impatient. This was starting to take longer than she preferred, and she wanted to get on with the day's planning.

Dame Gothel stared intently at the mirror, running her wizened fingers over the frame and tracing its details. She ran her hand down the smooth cool glass of the mirror, leaving a streak in the dusty grime. Then she began to laugh, almost cackling. Snow White and Jack looked at each other, puzzled. The crone cackled more, like someone who had not laughed in many years.

Rapunzel and Patience hopped from the hay bale and walked closer. "Mother," said Rapunzel, "What is so funny?"

"So it *is* the magic mirror?" said Jack, with unease, trying to understand what the old witch found humorous. "I figured it would be."

"You are all a bunch of fools," Dame Gothel said, regaining her composure.

"Mind your tongue, witch," Jack spoke harshly to the old woman.

"Mind *your* tongue, Jack!" Rapunzel shot back defensively. "Don't you dare speak to my mother like that!" she warned.

Snow White held up her hand. "Calm down," she ordered.

"I'm sorry," Jack responded, making his amends quickly. His apology was surprisingly humble despite his somewhat agitated state this morning.

Then Snow White turned back to Dame Gothel and the mirror. "Is this the magic mirror or not, Dame Gothel?"

"No," the old woman answered with a smile. "It is not the fabled magic mirror."

There was a murmur of surprise and disappointment. General White looked toward the ceiling, shaking her head slowly. "I don't believe this," she said in a frustrated groan.

"What are you trying to pull on us, Jack?" Rapunzel growled. "You told us this was the magic mirror, or were you just trying to save your skin?"

Jack was stunned. "What?" He was sure this was a magic mirror.

"Never mind," Snow said more calmly. "It doesn't—"

Dame Gothel interrupted as she continued to stare back at the carvings and run her fingers down the frame in amazement. "It's better," she said. Awe and excitement crept into the old witch's voice, like the wrinkles around the old crone's eyes when she smiled at the thought of what stood before them now.

"This is the Looking Glass."

"What did you say?" asked Jack, a sudden tone of despair etched worriedly in his voice.

Rapunzel shook her head. "Isn't 'looking glass' just another term for a mirror?"

"Not a looking glass, child, *the* Looking Glass. What you thought was the magic mirror, is actually the Looking Glass of Wonderland. The magic mirror was known as just a spying device—powerful, yes, but the Looking Glass," she took a moment to grasp the realization of what stood so unassumingly before her, "is a portable gateway back to Wonderland. Of course 'Mirror, mirror, on the wall' wouldn't work," Dame Gothel mocked snidely.

The news drew everyone's attention to Dame Gothel, except for Patience, who had noticed that the stranger Jack had a terrified look on his face. Patience thought it an odd reaction to the news. Then Dame Gothel said something else that made Jack's face turn ashen with terror.

"The Looking Glass is a direct portal into Wonderland," the old witch said. "The fact that we now have the Looking Glass has made Cendrillon's chance of invading Wonderland much less likely." Dame Gothel proudly exclaimed, with acknowledgement to Snow White, "Which is good for your purposes, General! However, Wonderland would be quite upset if they found out it was removed, and they will probably come looking for it."

Jack was right—it was a magical mirror, but it was a terrible mistake. He whispered wide eyed with terror, "I took the wrong one. I never should have taken it." He backed away from the mirror, quietly repeating, "No. No."

General White looked at Jack. "What's wrong?" Jack was visibly shaken. In fact, he was terrified.

"I've been there, to Wonderland," Jack stammered. "It's an evil place." He backed towards the door. "Not Wonderland. Not again." Jack reached blindly behind him to find the door "I...I have to get some air. Excuse me." Quickly he left the barn.

"I'll go talk to him," Rapunzel offered to the General.

"Yes," Snow White agreed, "do that." Everyone was still staring at the door Jack had just gone through, trying to understand what had him so panicked that he would react in such a way.

"I thought he was in battle at the Beanstalk War?" General White recalled. "How was he in Wonderland?"

Rapunzel found Jack sitting by a pile of rotted firewood, neatly stacked and overgrown with grass. He looked despondent, and was drinking from a small silver flask.

"What's going on, Jack?" Rapunzel asked as she approached, hesitantly at first.

"I was stupid. I never should have brought that mirror back. I didn't realize—" Jack started to sob, his voice shaking; he took another swig from the flask.

"General White will work it out," Rapunzel started to say, but Jack was too distraught.

"You don't understand. I've doomed everything. Everything. It's my fault there was ever a beanstalk in the first place, my fault that the Beanstalk War even started. I was a stupid kid then, and I made a dumb decision. And the more I try to fix it, the worse it gets. Now, now Wonderland will be at war with us."

Jack dropped his head into his hand, digging his fingers into his forehead. "I just want to go back home, to the farm," Jack sobbed, "whatever is left of it."

Rapunzel walked up to him and put a comforting arm around his broad shoulders.

"Then your knowledge of Wonderland can help us. It is a tactical advantage we would not have had at all if it weren't for you. Besides, you don't know that they will invade for sure."

"My knowledge of Wonderland?" Jack started, pulling away from Rapunzel. "You are right; I do know Wonderland—that's why I know that we have no chance against their army. There are things in that land that you would swear does not make any logical sense. Yet they stand before you as real as anything. Wonderland is madness, and madness has an army you cannot imagine. It wouldn't even be a fight."

Rapunzel looked at Jack with a mix of sympathy for the poor man. Pauper Jack, who rose to fame and fortune now sits tormented and in despair, she thought. Rapunzel could only wonder what horrors the haunted man had seen. Then Jack said something that stunned Rapunzel beyond words.

"I was to be king of Wonderland," he said absently. His voice was lower and lost in memory. Rapunzel waited for some odd punch line, but Jack was not kidding. "Our army was decimated in the giant lands. Many were killed, the rest—imprisoned to be eaten later. I escaped and went looking for some other way back home. How does one escape the land of the giants when there is no longer a beanstalk? I wandered aimlessly and almost gave up. That is when I found a rabbit hole that led me to Wonderland. I was an offlander, like their queen. I lived there for many years and caught the fancy of the queen. We were to be married. But I didn't love her as much as I loved the queen back home."

"Queen Cinder—I mean, Cinderella?" Rapunzel politely corrected herself.

He laughed half-heartedly. "Things have changed here as well." Then Jack changed the topic to more immediate concerns. "It's best that I don't help your army, Rapunzel." He stood up. "I'm just going to go home," he said with resignation. "You will be better off without me. I promised your general and her dwarves a mirror, and I have fulfilled that promise. I'm sorry, but there's nothing I can do. I'm leaving."

"You are just going to stick your head in a hole somewhere? Seems cowardly to me."

"Yes, it is," replied Jack. "I've spent the past five years trying to be a hero and have lost everything because of it. I could do with a little cowardice for a change."

"Then you're not going to do anything until Wonderland comes knocking on your door?" Rapunzel asked.

"Maybe, or I'll be off somewhere." Jack shuffled his feet in the dirt, watching the pebbles scatter into the grass. "Bremensport or someplace else far, far away—leagues from here."

"I don't believe you are just going to give up and run away. What about the mirror?" Rapunzel asked, practically pleading. "Take it with you back to Wonderland—make amends. Wouldn't that stop them from invading?"

"I am not running away. I am doing you a favor by staying away. There's a difference. I would destroy that mirror rather than return it. Tell your general this—you would be saving many lives by not challenging Wonderland's army. Stopping the invasion is not that simple. There are those in Wonderland who want me dead and want an invasion. It's complicated," he explained. Rapunzel still could not wrap her head around the tales that this common boy turned hero was telling. "There are those in Wonderland who will ensure an invasion happens. I doubt they really care about the mirror at all. There are those in Wonderland who would simply use it as an excuse. The courts of Wonderland cannot directly challenge the queen. And the throne of Wonderland cannot be ruled by anyone native to Wonderland; some old standing law they have there. Wonderland's queen is being set up to be assassinated, and the invasion will provide that cover up and an opportunity to bring an offlander to rule. I found out about the plot to kill the queen of Wonderland, and was barely able to escape. That is how I ended up back here, trying to get home. I took the mirror to buy some time, I thought all of the Looking Glasses were kept in Wonderland. What were the chances that was an actual Looking Glass? I am sorry; that part is because of me. Nothing can stop this now."

Rapunzel was speechless. Her mind raced as she tried to understand all of what Jack had explained. Rapunzel saw in Jack's eyes a weary knowledge and a sad look of helplessness. Jack stood. "I'm leaving. Don't think about stopping me," he said as he began to walk toward the distant tree line. "If I were General White, I'd start trying to evacuate the kingdom."

* * *

Dame Gothel took little notice of Jack's departure from the barn, finding this ancient magical artifact to be of more immediate interest. "The gateway to Wonderland to and from here was sealed. It resided, as far as the coven could figure, at a place called An End World. That is what Cendrillon is looking for," Dame Gothel explained as she continued to inspect the Looking Glass. "The gateway was sealed on Wonderland's side. Where did Jack say he found the mirror?"

Snow White had to think a moment to recall the brief meeting she had with Jack when the dwarves had captured him. "We were up in the mountains. A dwarven scout party had found him and thought he was part of the rat army, based on his armor," the general explained. "The dwarves would have killed him, but he pleaded for his life, offering to take them to a magic mirror hidden away in a cave if they spared him. Then the dwarves brought him to me. He didn't mention Wonderland." She added, "I didn't even believe he was *that* Jack at first."

"He mentioned a cave, not a temple?" said Gothel curiously.

"The dwarves escorted him back to a cave, definitely a cave," said Snow White. "Jack went into a cave to get the mirror." Snow White recited from memory. "There was a temple discovered nearby," she added, "being unearthed by Dendroba's troops. Those dwarves who escorted Jack were the first to spot the queen's army excavating some of the temple. Then we sent our forces to disrupt their work."

"Interesting," the witch mused. "Perhaps the cave and temple were connected. That could explain how Jack got to the Looking Glass."

"But if Jack did visit Wonderland, wouldn't he know about the Looking Glass?" asked Patience.

"Doubtful the Looking Glass was in the temple, and the temple was sealed off from Wonderland for hundreds of years. But if Wonderland did find out that we have something of theirs, I assume they would come for it—like waking a sleeping dragon by taking its gold."

Dame Gothel read General White's thoughts from her expression. "It would be better they thought it lost forever than to even try to return it to them. It would only remind them of what they lost in the first place."

"Well then, let's make sure that dragon stays asleep," General White said, offering a faint smile. She then thought about something else the old witch said.

"Hundreds of years, huh? Wonderland is that old?"

"More like thousands. Ancient," replied Dame Gothel. "But there are other lands and other portals. The question is how did Jack get back here after the Beanstalk War—through a Wonderland gateway? How did the prince, for that matter? Ah! Here it is!" Dame Gothel had been searching the mirror as she spoke and found a small inscription on the dull side of it. Squinting, the old witch began to translate the inscribed words.

"T'was brillig," began the line as she read aloud. "and the slithy toves..." She strained to read the next word. "...outgrave? Outgabe!"

"What is that, some sort of spell?" General White asked.

Instantly the mirror began to glow and hum warmly. The reflective surface of the mirror began to shimmer.

"All mimsy were the—It's the code to activate the portal. It is Wonderlandian, an ancient language I happen to know a little bit about from my time at the coven."

"What!" General White exclaimed, with alarm.

"Borogoves..."

"Stop!" General White commanded, "Stop now!" Quickly, Snow White shot her hand out, shoving Dame Gothel back away from the Looking Glass.

The old witch stopped reading, and the glowing mirror slowly faded back to its inert state. "Well, it appears to work just fine. How interesting! You know General, if Cendrillon finds out you have this, it would be ringing the dinner bell. She would send her whole army after it, I'm sure."

"Believe me, I'm well aware of that possibility, Dame Gothel," Snow White replied, slightly overwhelmed at the notion. Her small resistance army could easily become a high profile target for not one, but two, more powerful and dangerous forces.

She motioned to the dwarves who had moved the mirror earlier. "Cover it up," General White ordered. "Then hide it for now."

General White, Patience, and Dame Gothel then stepped out from inside the barn and into the mid-morning light. The yard in front of the barn was active with dwarves carrying bags of supplies and moving barrels of water and all manner of equipment. Every dwarf was focused on whatever task he were performing.

Rapunzel quickly told her general the news about Jack. "Now he claims he's

159

a king?" White replied off-handedly. "And you believed his fantasies?" General White scoffed, dismissing Rapunzel's recounting. "Don't be so gullible! Jack was probably using the mirror as an excuse to get out of being killed by my dwarves or to shirk any further involvement with our resistance army. Let him leave. I doubt that boy knows anything about Wonderland or cares what happens." Snow White stopped for a second and rubbed the back of her neck. She gazed up at the bright blue sky. "I'm tired of all of this talk of magic, Rapunzel. It is distracting and destructive nonsense. Don't be so quick to buy into it, okay?" It was one of the rare moments when Rapunzel had seen her Snow White step outside of her role as commander to speak more as a friend. Then General White was summoned back to her duties for another round of updates from her dwarves.

Rapunzel was caught off guard by Snow White's disregard of Jack's accounts, and she did not entirely agree with her. Maybe this sudden interest in magic was ill considered, but perhaps there was something to it. Maybe Snow White was right about Jack. Maybe it was all an act, Rapunzel began to wonder. It was true that Jack did not seem to care, choosing to turn his back on everything. With all that was going on, Rapunzel decided not to pursue the discussion for now.

* * *

Prince Phillip was trying to adjust the saddle of Rapunzel's champagne colored horse, Rampion. Phillip tried to calm the agitated horse by talking to it and petting it, but the spirited animal only calmed down when Rapunzel approached. She had noticed Phillip was having problems and went over, giving her horse a carrot to settle down. Still, the horse seemed skittish around the prince.

"Nice horse. What is his name again?" the Prince asked Rapunzel as she began to adjust the girthing strap of the saddle.

"Rampion is a great horse. You have the bridle too tight on the left side," said Rapunzel, interjecting a critique of Prince Phillip's tacking skills. "I've had *her* since I was a teenager. Growing up, I always wished I could ride a horse, but I was never allowed to leave my house. So the first thing I did when I finally did leave home was learn how to ride. Rampion was my first horse." She patted Rampion affectionately on the side of her neck.

"Listen, Phillip. I was a little short with you last night. I apologize," Rapunzel said. "There have been many things going on."

"No apology is needed. A lot has happened since I left for the Beanstalk War.

160

It's pretty overwhelming for me as well," Phillip replied. "What troubles me is that your general doesn't seem to have a plan."

Rapunzel stiffened defensively, "General White has a plan. Your sister—has a plan." Rapunzel shot back curtly.

"Then what is it?" Prince Phillip challenged. Rapunzel hesitated—what was the plan now? Rapunzel found herself wondering. Still she defended her friend and leader. "The glass slippers have changed things, Phillip. Snow has worked too hard fighting against the queen to be without a plan. That's all you need to know."

"I am the Prince of Marchenton, Rapunzel. I will be returning to the throne when all of this madness is over. I do need to know."

General White interrupted with a shout, calling Rapunzel over. The two began to walk toward her, but Snow White quickly indicated that she only wanted to speak with Rapunzel. Rapunzel gave a smirk. "I guess you don't need to know this," she quipped as she walked over to General White. The prince, though annoyed, complied and walked back to Rampion, continuing to brush the horse's coat as he thought.

* * *

Patience's thoughts were about Hamelin. With everything that had happened so quickly, the young girl suddenly felt alone and helpless. "Despite having these legendary glass slippers," Patience mumbled to herself.

Patience had watched Rapunzel and the prince talking. She considered asking the prince if she could pet the horse, but he seemed troubled and Patience did not want to bother him. General White was surrounded by dwarves, which she guessed was typical at these meetings—dwarves giving her reports and asking for her orders on one thing or the other. Several yards away near a large tree, she saw Goldenhair in a similar meeting, except that several birds and other animals surrounded her. Patience watched Goldenhair for a moment. It seemed the whole tree was full of chattering birds. On the ground near the trunk, squirrels, rabbits and many other woodland animals scurried around, coming and going as Goldenhair directed. Birds flew from the tree in various directions, immediately replaced by others. Patience wandered to the only other person who did not seem involved in matters at hand.

"What's going on?" Patience asked.

"War," Gothel said. "Here, dearie, have something to eat." The old witch offered a small bowl of curded mix and whey. It was not much of a breakfast, and Patience was not hungry.

Rapunzel walked over to her mother. "Something to eat, I heard?" She joked as she arrived, but then her tone turned more serious. "Goldenhair has heard that there is another army massing in the mountains. Not Queen Cinder's army, either."

"Another army?" Dame Gothel repeated. "And where do you suppose another army would come from?" the witch asked in feigned innocence.

"Goldenhair's scout didn't elaborate much, being that it was a bird," Rapunzel added with sarcasm.

She glanced over at the raven-haired general in white armor who was busy going over maps with some of the dwarves. Then Rapunzel leaned into to tell her mother the rest of the news. "General White is concerned. If there is an outside army on the move, she is not sure what kind of defense the queen's army could make. Dwarven scouts went back to the beach at first light. They say it looked more like the drowned rat army, bodies of the queen's army everywhere. Our mermaid friend may have done her job too well. They took heavy losses."

"Perhaps too heavy?"

"Exactly. Any other time prior to today it would have been great news. However, this is not great timing."

"For us perhaps," said Dame Gothel, "but great news for the other army."

"Whose farm is this?" asked Patience, looking around to find some other topic to discuss. She had grown more worried about things since she had returned with the slippers and desperately wished to talk of lighthearted matters again. Hamelin had been good at cheering the young Patience into better spirits with a story and some music. She wished he were here right now to play a song.

"It's a safe house," the lieutenant explained. "Since the Beanstalk War, many farms were abandoned either because of damage or because many of the survivors just couldn't keep up. Certainly, Queen Cinder's army did not help the kingdom recover. There are abandoned and ruined houses all over the kingdom."

Patience recalled how much of Aishew was left to ruin, and now, Aishew may have been burned to the ground.

Rapunzel was pouring a small bowl of curds and whey for herself. "So from time to time the resistance uses these places. Some of the places, like this one, have hidden stockpiles of supplies." Rapunzel shoved a large spoonful of curds into her mouth. The milky liquid dribbled down her chin. Despite her mouthful of breakfast, Rapunzel added that they would not be staying too long here, possibly leaving again tonight. They would travel further inland toward the mountains and the secret dwarven caves that served as the resistance's main base.

Patience looked around at the hustle and bustle of the barn's paddock; she found one thing was still missing—Hamelin. "Has any one seen Hamelin? Since the beach last night? I hope he is okay."

Both Rapunzel and Dame Gothel shrugged. "The retreat last night was chaotic," said the old witch. "He must have gotten separated."

"True," Rapunzel agreed, "There are still dwarves coming in as well. It's early in the morning, still." Rapunzel could see Patience's worried look.

"It's just that Hamelin and I have traveled together for a few years now. We've never really been apart," explained Patience.

"If your friend isn't back by this afternoon, we'll see if General White can spare some of the scouts. Give him time." Rapunzel placed a hand on the young girl's shoulder, trying to reassure her not to worry just yet. Dame Gothel nodded towards Goldenhair's direction. "Or you could go and ask her," she suggested.

Patience looked over at Goldenhair, who was now playing with her three bears, running across the large empty patch of field as the bears were playfully bounding after her, catching up and wrestling with her. They could easily have crushed her if they wanted, but the bears seemed genuinely happy to engage her in playing. Goldenhair would jump and roll, occasionally laugh and yell out in her bear language, grappling and riding on Nikko, the largest of the three bears. On more than one occasion during Goldenhair's loud laughter or the bears growling replies, General White looked up from her business with dwarves and maps, a scowl of disapproval on her face.

"Maybe I'll ask her later," said Patience as she watched wistfully how unaffected Goldenhair was by the whole situation. Just before, Goldenhair was coordinating information with the animals, and now, she and her bears were playing in a carefree manner as though nothing had transpired.

* * *

There was a brief moment when General White found herself with a bit of a lull in her coordinating efforts. Rapunzel had walked back toward the barn, and Prince Phillip thought he could have a quick heart-to-heart talk with his sister. As he approached, Phillip was surprised that Snow White began the conversation; it was deliberate and rehearsed.

"Phillip, I want you to know that even though you are my brother and we have not spoken in many years, seeing you again at this time is a distraction I cannot afford. As a prince you are high profile target, which is another liability to my resistance army. Now that you are back, you are a threat to her throne, Queen Cinder is sure to double her efforts to destroy us if she finds out you are alive. So, I am not happy to see you. I am not overjoyed that you are back."

"And good morning to you to," Prince Phillip replied with a sarcastic smile.

"It sounds harsh, but it is not meant to be. I'm just stating a fact. Maybe if the timing of everything were better, I would be happy to see you again," Snow White tried to explain.

"Then let's fix this kingdom so the timing can be better," replied Phillip. "Don't look at me as the little brother you used to have, the younger brother you have to watch out for and protect. Think of me as the brother you will have from now on; someone to help you, so you don't have to do it all alone."

"I lead the resistance. I am responsible for the lives of these dwarves. I'm trying to restore the kingdom. Added to that, I have to worry about magical glass slippers and a little girl. Now to top it off, my brother is alive. I had my hands full with an army of dwarves. There is too much at stake now. Something is going to slip up and it will be bad. And when it happens, it's on my own shoulders because I lead the resistance."

"I've been thinking," Phillip replied. "Perhaps it would be better if I took over the dwarven army, Snow."

General White answered decisively, "Absolutely not."

"Think about it. I am a recognizable member of the royal family. Being the king's son, I do have training in military organization, and I would certainly keep you on as an advisor. I am, after all, the prince. I have a claim to the throne and that gives me certain rights in situations like this…"

"And you and Father led the entire army to ruin, Phillip. I cannot even believe I am having this conversation. You expect, after the whole Beanstalk War fiasco, that you'll come back here ten years later and I will hand over control of my army to you just because you are a prince? Did you sustain some sort of a head injury along the way? Well, since we're pulling ranks, let me remind you that I am your older sister, and—"

"Did you think of what you would do if your army of dwarves actually did take out Ella? What would you do, Snow? You already ran away from the throne once. Afraid to handle the pressures of the crown like I had been raised to? But you are technically just a princess, so it's not like it's expected," Phillip added.

"Like Ella was just a princess? Certainly, she did not expect to take control of throne when she married you. So, don't start pulling that crap again, Phillip!" White was enraged now. "It's exactly that 'more royal than thou' chauvinistic mentality I hate! I would rather be a general of dwarves than a princess! I have spent a lifetime getting as far away from being a princess as I can and I have spent the past few years risking everything to get to this point, giving everything I had. There is no way I will hand over my dwarves to you. Ever." General White silently fumed as the prince stared back at her. Her cool blue eyes simmered with a fiery anger.

Prince Phillip was surprised by her sudden outburst and seething anger.

"It was merely an idea—an option to consider. I was simply offering to help." From what Phillip had seen, Snow White did have a very well-organized army. The dwarves proved they were a force to be reckoned with, and though small in stature and in numbers, they more than compensated for it with resourcefulness and commitment.

But Snow White's anger at the suggestion quickly subsided, and was replaced with a wash of sympathy. For General White, it was impossible to see Phillip as a prince, as she had never had to regard him in that fashion. For General White, her memories of Phillip were only those of her younger brother.

"Besides, little brother," she added with a laugh, "the dwarves would never go for it."

With that, she turned and went to speak to some more of the dwarves. It had already been evident to Prince Phillip that the dwarves were fiercely loyal to General White. More than once today, Phillip had noticed a dwarf giving him a scornful look.

Then General White returned a moment later. "I'm having the dwarves ready the rest of the horses. I'm going to go show you your castle."

She motioned a dwarf over. "Phillip and I are going to ride to see the castle. We will need Rapunzel to bring the girl as well. She and those glass slipper shards do not leave my presence. Everyone else stays here until we get back." The dwarf hurried toward the barn to fetch Rapunzel as ordered. "Prepare to depart at dusk," General White announced to the dwarves. "It is safer traveling at night."

Then the dwarf who had gone to fetch Rapunzel ran back to the general, "M'lady! 'Punzel needs to see you in the barn immediately!"

Both Snow White and Prince Phillip looked at each other with alarm. Then they briskly walked with the dwarf over to the barn. As they neared the door, they could hear shouts.

"Don't touch it! Watch it!"

"It's over here now! Get it! What is that?"

As they opened the barn's door, Dame Gothel proclaimed "Got'cha!" Both Rapunzel and Patience stood around the old woman as they quickly placed a small old wooden chicken cage on a hay bale. The three gathered around to look at what was inside, not noticing that the general and the prince had arrived.

"What's going on?" General White inquired in her typical authoritative tone. Dame Gothel and the others looked up to see the general and the prince walking towards them.

"It appears, General, that the army amassing in the mountains," the old witch began to explain. General White shot a disapproving glance towards Rapunzel. That had been confidential information. "—is indeed from Wonderland. That temple portal is already active. This is certainly a creature from Wonderland."

With that, Dame Gothel and Rapunzel stepped back to show Snow White what they had caught.

Inside the wooden chicken cage was a curious thing, the size of a bat. It paced timidly in its enclosure, occasionally fluttering its wings in annoyance.

Insect-like, it had long, stick-like legs and overall resembled a butterfly, only much larger. Its body was long, arched, and brown, resembling, in an odd sort of way, the crusted edge of a slice of bread. The white tufts of hair along its underside emphasized its bread-like appearance, similar to bread that has had its crust pulled away. Its head was block-shaped and white, almost crystalline and granular in texture, like a cube of sugar. It did not appear to have any eyes or mouth. The creature's wings fluttered in agitation; they were large, about hand-sized and square shaped. The edges of the wings resembled the breaded crust-like body, and the wings themselves were covered in short, textured white hair. Each of the wings had a large shiny yellow square in the center. They reminded General White of two slices of buttered bread. It was an odd little creature indeed.

"This is from Wonderland?" Prince Phillip marveled at the odd creature, from a safe distance of course.

"It could be a spy," said General White. "A long range scout?"

"Or," Patience suggested, "maybe it just got lost."

"Either way, destroy it," General White ordered flatly.

CHAPTER 14
WHITE RABBIT IN THE HALL OF THE QUEEN

The travel from the mountain temple of An End World was expeditious and relatively uneventful, for which Rabbit was grateful. He was on a tight schedule. There had been trails and tracks left by what he figured was the retreating army he had found evidence of at the temple. The royal army had fought there, defending it, perhaps from the dwarves, he guessed. The White Rabbit prided himself on his abilities as a tracker, a swordsman, a herald, and a very good chef.

He had hoped to question some of the locals to try to gain some information about the kingdom and perhaps about Jack. He arrived at his destination with very little of the local lore obtained, but the rabbit was observant in his travels. What was not there was just as telling as what was there. The scattered farmhouses were all abandoned. He met not a single person as he walked the overgrown trails and ran along the unkempt roads.

White Rabbit would need to sort the facts out with the local ruler. After all, there were diplomatic procedures to which one must adhere. "If there is a local ruler," he wondered aloud.

Several times in the distance, as he traveled along the hills, the White Rabbit could see the castle through breaks in the tree line. By midafternoon, however, the skies had grayed, bringing a cool drizzle and low misty clouds that obscured much of the landscape. The rabbit was close and he knew the road he now walked along would take him to the castle's main gate. It was lined on both sides with large, evenly spaced pine trees, typically indicating what was known as the King's Road. Yet, here too, Rabbit noticed that it was not as kept as other such kingly roads he had encountered, nor did it show much in the way of recent tracks. The King's Road did not appear to be traveled these days. This, thought the rabbit, was quite odd. He did not know what had transpired, but as he traveled, it was becoming more obvious that something was amiss. Adding to everything, the rain had soaked through his hooded cloak, and now Rabbit was wet. He hated being wet. The road began to wind uphill and around a long bend. There the rabbit stopped, coming upon an entirely new problem.

"Bloodthorns," he noted. "Interesting."

Before him stood a tall rise of dense Bloodthorns, easily twenty feet high, that had grown across the road and into the forest as far as the eye could see. They were entangled in the brush and undergrowth of the forest and wrapped around the trunks of trees, spanning across the branches, and tangling and choking the limbs.

"Well, that explains why nobody uses this road much," he mused quietly. *Was this the problem of the land, the castle cut off from its kingdom by a wall of Bloodthorns?* He stood a moment in uffish thought, the heavy drizzle beating on the hood of his cloak.

The White Rabbit knew well that what he was about to do was a breach of protocol. Using Wonderland magic outside of his world was a blatant violation of the treaty. *Not that anyone is around to enforce it,* Rabbit thought. It seemed to him that it was his only choice. To circumvent this wall of thorns on the off chance he would find a way to the castle would take too much time. At that thought, he pulled out his pocket watch and checked the time. He did not want to be late.

With a sigh, the White Rabbit resigned himself to use his magic, but he would not do it on the main road. *Just in case,* he thought. He trotted a couple of yards off the road, past the pine trees and behind an old log, well out of view, muttering to himself that he couldn't believe he was about to do this. He really did not want to.

Kneeling down, he closed his eyes and reached his furred hand out, as his other hand clutched his gold pocket watch. He began to speak softly.

"'What matters it how far we go?' His scaly friend replied." The rabbit continued to recite the words as some sort of magical incantation. "'There is another shore, you know, upon the other side.'"

The leaves and pine needles that covered the ground in front of the rabbit fell away into a large hole that formed where he had placed his hand on the ground. The hole was nearly five feet wide and dark. The White Rabbit stood again, checking his watch before he placed it in his pocket. He stood before his rabbit hole, not relishing the thought of his magical transportation, though he used it many times. Often, it would leave him feeling a little nauseous and with a headache. But he knew this would take him directly to the castle's main gate, exactly where he wanted to go, because that is how rabbit holes worked. Then Rabbit stepped out and dropped down the mysterious hole.

* * *

"So what has the piper revealed?" asked the Maldame, coming out of one of the side rooms in the hallway and joining Cendrillon as she walked past her.

"Many things," Cendrillon replied absently. She was focused on her thoughts and continued walking. The Maldame strolled alongside her stepdaughter.

"That was the last of the sacrificial geese you used. Until our plans play out, what left of our magic is to be used sparingly. I hope it was worth it."

"The pledges are dismembering the rest of the animal and storing it for use in later spells; we are not completely devoid of the magic yet," Cendrillon answered, still walking with purpose. "The spell on the piper is sufficient for now. But it is weaker than I would have preferred. He should be disposed of at the first sign of it wearing off." They were in a rarely visited part of the castle now, and Cendrillon pulled a key from a chain around her neck.

Immediately the Maldame recognized the area. "What are you doing?" she asked, slightly puzzled.

"The piper told me something," said Cendrillon. She inserted the key and with a slight click unlocked the door. "I have come to see if it is true."

Inside the door was a stairway. The air was stale and dank, the floor and walls of stone covered in thin dust. Ahead, a winding stone staircase rose upwards and out of view as dull grey light illuminated the hallway through small, dirty windows.

"And what did the piper say?" asked the Maldame again as she followed the young queen up the stairs.

"News I am not happy about. Phillip, my charming prince, is still alive, and has returned to Marchenton," Cendrillon replied with sarcastic annoyance. They continued following the tall staircase upwards. "And he's working with General White, which indicates that he means to take back the throne."

"The prince survived?" the Maldame asked. Even she was surprised at this latest revelation.

Cendrillon elaborated. "Dame Gothel is helping them."

This news infuriated the Maldame. "Dame Gothel! How dare she!" The Maldame seethed at the thought of the former ally now in league with the rebels.

"Well," added Cendrillon condescendingly. "That is why you should kill people rather than exile them. That was what—how many years ago?"

"Shortly after your birth, actually," the Maldame replied.

They had reached the top of the stairs now. There was a larger landing here with a small sitting area and a large decorative glass window, crisscrossed with lead caming lines. The sitting pillow, once a deep purple, was now dust-covered and faded from the sunlight. Nearby was a second old, age-worn, wooden door.

"This is why General White is as dangerous as she is," said Cendrillon as she inserted her key into the lock. "She is a leader and can rally the people together. She is quite resourceful, if she has Dame Gothel and potentially others. She has the dwarves working with her as well." Cendrillon paused at the door. "I wish to speak with General Dendroba personally. Summon him back to the castle." Then she had another idea. "Do you remember Gretel and her brother?"

"The witch hunters?" Maldame said. "Yes, quite well."

"We should hire them to track down General White and Dame Gothel. A little outside muscle could not hurt. I was going to humor Dendroba and send them up to the excavation site to deal with something there."

"I'd rather see those two dead—or worse if possible—before we hire them again," offered the Maldame.

"We could do that too. After all, they are bringing the werewolf in, so we'll be back on schedule soon."

The Maldame folded her arms against her chest. "Bringing it here themselves?" It was not an idea she liked. They were the kingdom's most successful witch hunters back in the day, and the bane of everything the Maldame had worked for. "Many witches and comrades were slain by those two—witches rounded up like caged animals and brought in for justice." The Maldame spat the last word like poison.

"We've hired those two to bring in the werewolf. I understand they are already en route. They are useful enough. I will have Dendroba hire them. If they could find General White, it would be worth it," added the queen.

The Maldame changed the distasteful subject. "Why are you up here?" she asked. "You never come up here."

"The piper said something interesting; do you remember my glass slippers?" She turned the key and with a soft push, she the door opened with a creak. There was a flutter of wings as startled birds flew out of the room through the broken glass window. Rain splattered upon the sill, and when the wind shifted, the rain sprayed into the room, soaking the already ruined rugs. Here was Queen Cendrillon's private wedding collection, the memorabilia of another lifetime.

Here, too, was where Cinderella died and Cendrillon was born on a fateful night five years ago. Cendrillon had not been back since. There seemed a chill in the air, and the queen could not tell if it was from the broken window or her own memories. The room was now a home to birds and creeper vines that had found their way through the window and laid claim to everything inside. Cinderella's vanity table and furniture were spotted with mold, weathered and worn from exposure to the elements, dirty from the rain and covered in the droppings of birds. Fine royal gowns of pink and powder blue lay upon the ground, ripped, torn, and ruined by birds and animals seeking to make nests of the royal material. Creeping ivy covered the walls and had already claimed a chair and a desk near the window. The greedy ivy worked its way up a pillar that stood in the center of the room, the pillar that one time held the fabled glass slippers but now held only faded memories and the droppings of birds.

In here were things familiar to Cendrillon, as though from a distant time, and she found each memory more revolting than the next. There was the mirror where she would innocently brush her hair while she sang songs and where her makeup was prepared for yet another royal princess ball. The mirror was now cracked and so dirty that Cendrillon could barely see her own reflection. Silver brushes, now darkened and tarnished, lay where she had left them over half a decade ago. Cendrillon and the Maldame crossed the room to the pillar where her glass slippers had been on display. They was no sign of them. Cendrillon slowly inspected the pillar base and ivy covered floor around it.

"Such a naïve young child I was back then," Cendrillon mused absently. Then she explained more. "The piper claimed my glass slippers had been stolen. I left them broken on the floor. Indeed, it is true, they have been taken. I wanted to see for myself."

"So what if they have your glass slippers! They are merely a trinket; a souvenir from another time."

"Perhaps," replied Cendrillon, "they are planning to use them to kill me somehow. The piper told me something else."

The Maldame listened as she casually explored the room, stopping to poke with her shoe in curious disgust at a long discarded pile of pink silk chiffon on the floor.

"Well, did you not murder your God-mother fairy with your own glass slipper? Those glass shoes of yours can be pretty sharp."

"Don't mock," replied Cendrillon, "The piper told me that Dame Gothel could extract the fairy magic from the glass slipper remains. Looking back on the night of the ball, it would make sense."

The Maldame looked up from the empty pillar where the slippers had been. "Impossible," she stated. But Cendrillon was lost in her memories, remembering a happier time, now distant and painful.

"The God-mother fairy had transformed various lizards and mice, a pumpkin into a carriage, and even my dress for me during the nights of the ball. And each night at the stroke of midnight they would change back."

"Typical fairy magic," the Maldame scoffed.

"But not the glass slippers," Cendrillon recalled. "Those never changed. They were permanent, a gift of the Fae, my fairy Godmother had said. That was how the prince found me."

"Yes, I remember that day. Jovette tried to cut her own toes off to fit into that damned shoe."

"Then it is quite possible that the fairy magic remained within them."

From behind them, there was the sound of a polite clearing of the throat. Rolling her eyes with smoldering annoyance, the Maldame turned to see an elderly man, thin and in poor health standing in the doorway.

"What is it majordomo?" the Maldame sneered, annoyed at the interruption and the inevitable delay it would bring.

Despite old age and dwindling health, the majordomo of the castle kept to his duties; even his general dislike of the queen and her stepmother did not deter him from his obligation to serve the throne, no matter who sat in it.

"My queen," the majordomo said, "There is an emissary who requests a meeting with you on urgent business." His tone was stoic as usual. "He awaits an audience with you in the great room." With that, he raised his head, awaiting her response.

Queen Cendrillon glared. *Emissary? Here? Who would dare?* The Maldame, standing nearby, gave the queen a look of surprise. She had severed all diplomatic ties to ensure complete control over Cendrillon's rule. Over the past decade, there had been discouragements regarding diplomatic relations which served to increase the isolationism that was eventually, and quite literally, manifested by the creation of the Bloodthorn Wall.

The majordomo added, "He claims to represent the sovereign realm of a place he calls Wonderland."

Queen Cendrillon felt the hairs on her neck stand on end; her stomach tightened. This was bad news, and completely unexpected.

There was a pause until the Maldame stepped into the conversation. "Here?" she queried. "Make sure that he does not leave. Cendrillon and I will be there momentarily," she told the majordomo.

"Very good, madam," said the servant in a formal, yet uncaring reply.

"That will be all," the Maldame said absently and fluttered her hand to dismiss him. He lowered his head, turned, and retreated down the stairs.

As soon as the old man was away, Cendrillon expressed her apprehension. "Emissary? We should kill him," she said.

"That's your answer to everything," replied the Maldame. "We need to find out what he knows."

"They obviously know something is amiss or else they would not have sent someone." A tinge of panic now crept into the edges of the queen's voice. Would her plans to tap into Wonderland's magic be derailed before she even had a chance to start? She was so close to completing her plan. Now this, she thought. It would be too much of a coincidence. Cendrillon's sudden worry must have shown on her furrowed brow.

The Maldame scowled at the young queen. She did not approve of this sudden panic. It was a sign of weakness. "You are as inexperienced in these matters today as you were when you first sat on the throne. Such a lack of maturity can cause great disaster at these crucial times. Here is a chance to redeem the mistakes you made during the Beanstalk War." The Maldame scolded. "I already have a plan to handle this." She headed toward the door, then on a thought, she turned and faced the queen. "For the record, I said reopening the portal to Wonderland was a bad idea. Pray I am wrong, child."

Any measure of panic now left the queen quickly; she had steeled herself. Her blue eyes glared fiercely. "I am queen," said Cendrillon. "Do not dare speak to me like that."

The Maldame was not fazed. "You are queen to all...except me. Do not forget your place. Right now you are a child, scared that you are about to be caught with your hand in the cookie jar. I am the Maldame of the coven, and I made you." The Maldame's voice rose in frustrated anger. "It was fun to play princess," the Maldame gestured about the room, speaking in a voice seething with contempt. "But while we reminisce about the past, our future is quite literally knocking on our door."

"I will handle this matter!" Cendrillon burst out angrily, frustrated at her stepmother's attitude and hurt by her words. "You would do best to ready for travel to the site as planned, Stepmother." Cendrillon hissed the last word in disrespect to the Maldame's station.

But the Maldame quickly countered. "What I will do is meet the emissary in your stead. You will follow along and observe from the side. Enough of all of this," she pointed about the room. "This room should be burned. It is full of nothing but filth!" With that, she walked down the stairs to meet the emissary, leaving Cendrillon alone in her ruined chamber.

* * *

Rabbit checked his pocket watch again as he waited for the queen's arrival. It had been an hour at least since the castle's majordomo had left him there.

"Much too long a time to be gone," the White Rabbit thought. He found the castle to be very still. There was seemingly only a handful of staff and plenty of palace guards, the rabbit noted. "I hope that won't become an issue," he thought. Rabbit saw that the guards all resembled the bodies he saw at the temple. Perhaps a plague had affected them, he thought.

The guards had searched him roughly when he appeared at the front gate. They removed his sword and scabbard, and then escorted him to the castle entrance. He had spoken briefly to the majordomo, and a maid had graciously offered to take his wet cloak, and kindly starting a fire in one of the great hall's many fireplaces while he waited. The maid even brought the rabbit some warm tea. "Most accommodating," the White Rabbit acknowledged to the servant. She paused, staring at the Wonderland emissary. After a brief moment, and a sip of tea, the rabbit obliged her curious stare. The castle staff was abuzz with the news of a royal visitor; everyone was excited and a little curious.

"Yes, I am a real rabbit," he said. "No, it is not a costume."

Embarrassed, the maid bowed slightly and then quickly hurried away.

The room was long with a large multi-vaulted ceiling and arched sets that ran along either wall. The room opened into a large, theater-sized great room setting with three levels of balconies and all manner of heraldic banners of every kind and color draped along the walls. Once used for great galas, the large empty room echoed with sense of faded grandeur. Cold, unlit chandeliers hung silently near the ceiling. Below them, in the center of the great room, was a large ornately carved throne made of wood, velvet and leather. It sat on a raised dais with deep red carpet runners draping the steps on every side of the throne.

Then at last, the majordomo returned and announced the queen. "Queen Cendrillon, ruler of Marchenton." Accompanied by other palace guards, the Maldame entered with the crown upon her head. The White Rabbit studied her. She was an older woman and seemed quite wise and distinguished. He felt a little relieved that things might now progress more quickly.

As he approached the queen's throne, Rabbit observed his protocols and knelt on his furred knee. He bowed his head and, as is customary, waited for the queen to speak.

"Representing the sovereignty of Wonderland, Ambassador, uh...Rabbit," the majordomo announced.

"Rise, Rabbit, and explain this unannounced visit," the Maldame requested coolly.

"Thank you, Queen of Marchenton. I am humbled."

"So, you've come from Wonderland? How did you get here?"

White Rabbit stammered for a second. There were protocols to address, and the directness of the queen had caught him off guard.

"It is within the accords of the Fae-Wonderland treaty—"

"*How* did you get here?" the queen asked louder this time.

Perhaps this was not to be as easy as expected, thought the rabbit.

"The Gate to Wonderland," answered the White Rabbit. "It is required by the Fae-Wonderland treaty that you are to be notified of several transgressions—"

"And how did you get within the castle borders? That is not a row of hedges we keep outside," remarked the queen, referring to the Bloodthorn Wall.

"Queen of Marchenton, if I may!" started the Rabbit with an insistent tone.

The elderly woman leaned back in her throne for a moment, glaring at the rabbit in silence. She motioned her hand for him to continue.

The real queen, Cendrillon, watched her stepmother's performance from the shadows, knowing full well she relished the role.

The tall rabbit cleared his throat, tugged his vest coat to straighten it, and then began to explain.

"Some time ago, we had a trespasser from your world. Aside from the trespassing itself, he also committed several major crimes for which he must be extradited to face charges. I have brought paperwork listing what Jack has done."

He looked up at the queen who sat in silence. The rabbit handed the sealed scrolls to the majordomo, who in turn passed them to the queen. The queen quickly glanced over the scrolls and dropped them to the floor.

"We care nothing for your laws…" the Maldame started, but her performance was interrupted.

"Jack?" asked Cendrillon, stepping out from behind the pillar. Hamelin stood with her.

"Yes," answered Rabbit with some confusion as this new stranger addressed him. "He was a commoner from this kingdom. The Queen of Wonderland herself has a personal interest in his return."

The Maldame was not listening; instead, she was slyly observing Cendrillon, gauging her reaction to this news.

"How did Jack arrive in Wonderland? And what sort of personal interest?" asked Cendrillon. The news of her lover's survival distracted her from the matters at hand.

It was just a quick exchange but that, coupled with her disobedience, was enough to infuriate the Maldame. Before the conversation continued further, the Maldame reacted.

"Guards! Seize this intruder! He is now an enemy of the throne!" she ordered, pointing to the rabbit. She would imprison the rabbit and get answers that were more exacting later. After all, the rabbit never explained how he got into the castle.

Instantly, the rabbit stiffened. "This is most uncalled for!"

Four guards stepped out from behind the queen's dais, while two others approached from behind him, leveling long-poled halberds toward the rabbit. He braced into a defensive position.

Perhaps the guards were unsure of the unusual sight of the rabbit, or they did not expect such a creature to offer resistance. One of them hesitated; looking unsure, the guard's shoulders drooped slightly, and Rabbit went on the offense.

With amazing speed, Rabbit burst toward the nervous guard, quickly disarming and disabling him with a flurry of punches and devastating kicks. Rabbit's sharp claws sliced the guard's face to ribbons. The Wonderland emissary then called out— "This act of aggression will not be viewed favorably!" The White Rabbit whirled around, easily darting away from the slower attacks of the surprised guards. He expertly fired a quick sidekick and sent another guard to the ground, breaking the guard's leg awkwardly, much like a snapped twig.

"In fact, in accordance with the Fae-Wonderland treaty, I hereby notify you that Wonderland sovereignty is in full right to declare a state of war."

The rabbit continued to explain, slightly out of breath as he dropped low to the ground, picking up a halberd from one of the fallen guard's and using it to sweep two other guards off their feet. He then stomped his foot on top of their chests with such force that he broke ribs and punctured lungs.

Then in a great bound, Rabbit leaped into the air and landed on the dais in front of the Maldame, who was still sitting on the throne. It had all happened so fast that it took the Maldame completely by surprise. The other guards froze as the rabbit held the weapon at the Maldame's bosom.

"—and I am now in a position to accept your complete surrender."

More guards filed in surrounding them. With the rabbit standing on the throne, holding the Maldame at spear point, the Maldame held up her hand to keep them away. They complied, not wanting to risk the life of the queen's mother.

The Maldame glared menacingly at the rabbit. Her jaw clenched, but she remained steadfast. If she could kill the transgressor with a look, she would have. There was no fear in her eyes, just pure anger.

"Get off my throne!" she growled defiantly to the rabbit.

"You are hereby notified of Wonderland's intent to extricate Jack for crimes against the realm. Until such time as Jack is located, Wonderland will maintain an occupying army in your kingdom," continued the rabbit quickly.

"Get off my throne," the Maldame growled again, the razor sharp spear hovering over her chest.

"Detaining an official emissary only escalates the matter further."

Then the rabbit stopped. As if in great pain, he suddenly fell backward, wincing. He dropped the spear and grabbed at his ears before falling to his knees and tumbling down the dais steps.

Cendrillon stepped through the circle of guards; Hamelin stood next to her quietly playing on his magical pipes a song that only a rabbit could here. For the rabbit, it provoked paralyzing, excruciating pain.

The White Rabbit could not bear the pain. As soon as he landed, several guards rushed in, securing him as a prisoner.

The Maldame quickly stood, and then stepped briskly away from the throne toward Cendrillon.

"Yes, Maldame that was an inspired plan. Thank you for sitting in for me, I would have hated having a spear forced on me," Cendrillon remarked sarcastically. She turned to Hamelin, "Would you escort the prisoner to the dungeon? Perhaps he'd like to hear more of your song."

"I would be happy to play for him, if that is what you wish," replied Hamelin, still enthralled by the queen's spell. He followed the guards as they dragged the rabbit to the dungeon.

"The piper has his uses," Cendrillon mused.

"You are in way over your head now," the Maldame snapped. "You couldn't handle the Beanstalk War, and now Wonderland is about to march on us!"

"That does complicate things," replied Cendrillon. "Holding that rabbit is going to be dangerous."

"Complicate things!" Cendrillon's stepmother fumed. "Complicate things? Yes, it does. This was supposed to be a simple matter of opening the portal, siphoning some magic, and being done with it! You now have a war on your hands. You should thank me for capturing that rabbit, hopefully we can use it as a bargaining chip, or at least get some intelligence out of it."

"I was not the one to call for his imprisonment, but what is done is done. I will send word to General Dendroba to return immediately to the castle," Cendrillon offered.

The young queen was caught up in her own thoughts and the news that Jack was alive. Many memories and feelings that she had suppressed for years seemed more in the forefront of Cendrillon's mind. Her feelings were certainly of a different nature than when she heard the news of her husband, the prince, who was alive as well. Jack had offered her comfort, company, and pleasure in contrast to the prince, who focused solely on raising an army and the threat of attack that Jack had initially brought to his attention. Those were dark times, and Jack had been a light, whereas the prince had only added to the darkness. That was many years ago. Back then, Princess Cinderella found that she could relate more to the commoner Jack than the royal formalities Prince Phillip offered. Now Queen Cendrillon had spent a decade honing her feelings of hatred for her prince. However, the news of Jack's return was truly unexpected and the queen found herself unable to quell those old feelings for her lover, though she knew she must.

Things were different now.

"We should see to finding this girl and my glass slippers. We will need all the magic we can get our hands on. Have Jovette and Gael go back out and search for her."

Cendrillon had never sought to utilize her pets until now. She had always disdained the very thought of their existence, but the two large spiders had proved to be effective in the capturing of Hamelin, and Cendrillon had to acknowledge their usefulness. Now, desperately and reluctantly the queen called upon their service.

"Finally," whispered the Maldame aloud, "she concedes to my way of handling things."

CHAPTER 15
LITTLE MISS MUFFET

The group arrived on horseback at Hubbard's Ridge by mid-afternoon under grey skies and a thin, cool drizzle. Once they had dismounted, Rapunzel took Rampion and the other two horses to secure them nearby. Patience stood and looked solemnly at her home for the first time in years. "Closer than I've been but it still seems a lifetime away," she thought aloud.

General White turned to Prince Phillip. "Maybe now that it is before your own eyes you will realize what dire circumstances are at stake." She pointed to the valley below. "See for yourself, Phillip, all that you have missed these past years."

They stood on a small section of Hubbard's Ridge that jutted out like a peninsula from the rest of the ridge line. The ridge dropped off below them about fifty yards at a steep angle, covered with shale and loose rock, and carved with eroded gullies that disappeared in a mass of thick, dark briar. The entangling underbrush of bramble was a tight mass about waist deep, which extended further, covering everything and dominating the landscape. In the distance, the prince could see the deadly briar rising high above the rest of the valley floor. It was a huge wall of Bloodthorns piling up almost as tall as the castle's own ramparts. He could barely see the castle in the distance, as it was nearly obscured by the Bloodthorns and by the misty drizzle.

"For ten years the thought of seeing the castle again kept me alive, it's good to see home again, even from a distance." Phillip's heart filled with sadness at the reality of the sight before him. "Is that the Bloodthorn Wall you mentioned?"

"Yes," said Snow White. Then she added, "It is nearly impossible to cut or to burn, and dangerous to be around." It was almost as if she had been reading her brother's own thoughts and trying to convince him otherwise. "One scratch that draws blood, will trigger a feeding constriction from the briar, which inevitably causes more pricking and more constriction as one tries to free themselves from the surrounding thorns. It is a horrible way to die. I've seen it happen far too often."

Prince Phillip stood a moment in thought, staring out across the landscape. "If one were to be fully dressed in field plate armor, would that not protect?"

"Protection for one person, maybe two, perhaps," General White answered, "if they were lucky, but there's not enough armor like that to protect a whole army, not even for the army you led into battle. Even if they could get as far as the thorn wall, if one were to lose his balance in that kind of armor, I cannot imagine how he might regain his footing. The farther you get in, the harder it would be if a problem occurs. You'd be trapped in the middle of that." She swept her hand across the landscape before them. "We've tried a hundred ideas. The dwarves brought cutting machines that barely made it twenty feet in before they were entangled. Several dwarves died in the Bloodthorns just trying to free the machine."

The prince looked out across the deadly bramble, trying to imagine the scene as Snow White explained. "Even if you had a sizeable group survive that and get on the other side of the Bloodthorn Wall, they would still have to contend with a fully defensible castle with hardly any hope of sustaining any kind of siege. Believe me, little brother, the dwarves and I have gone over this." Snow White continued to recall the various attempts to circumvent the deadly Bloodthorns. " The use of large planks to step on top of the Bloodthorns was very unstable, slow and made for an easy target."

"But why? I cannot believe my princess would be capable of this. To what advantage is this whole Bloodthorn nonsense?" Phillip asked, genuinely puzzled.

"It has overgrown considerably from what they were five years ago. I guess it was a way to protect the castle. It works," Snow White said. "We haven't been able to mount any kind of offense. Rather than try to attack the castle directly these days, we've decided it's more effective and damaging to hit and run against Dendroba's army when they march on the outside; at least for now."

"I don't know who this General Dendroba person is. Certainly, he was not under my watch. His troops must return to the castle at some point, yes?"

"From what we can put together," she answered, "Dendroba is part of the witch's coven that rules with Cendrillon. He runs their army now, and he does it well. He is smart, and there were a few times when, if not for luck, he would have had us. I've learned some things by watching what he does." Then Snow let out a long breath, "They come and go through the Bloodthorns using magic. Dendroba has a gold orb he uses, and the magic from it creates a path. They used to do it a lot, but now the army stays away more often and for longer periods. I think they are also having trouble with the Bloodthorns now."

The prince listened. It made sense to him, but there had to be a better way. "Could the dwarves just dig a tunnel under all of this?"

Snow shook her head. "No. That was the first direct attempt on the castle. That was my big idea and one of the reasons I sought an alliance with the dwarves in the first place." Snow White shook her head back and forth as she spoke. "To dig a tunnel under the Bloodthorns would have taken a lot of time, even for dwarves. The dig site would have to be far away and safe. Some of that briar is a half-mile wide. The site had to have been heavily defended all the while. It would have been too big to hide from the royal army patrols. And escape options are very limited in a tunnel—very easy to get trapped."

With a heavy sigh, Prince Phillip tried to figure out any other method for getting past the Bloodthorns and back to his castle. He watched a hawk flying lazily in the grey sky, circling for an easy meal. "You should have allied with the birds instead of the dwarves." He nodded towards the circling hawk. "They would have no problem with the Bloodthorns."

Snow looked at the hawk. "That's probably one of Goldenhair's, keeping an eye on us," she remarked, almost annoyed at the very idea.

"Goldenhair's a strange one, isn't she? How did she do that with the animals, back at the barn—does she really talk to them?"

"Yes, actually, it seems she does. I do not really know how, but it has come in very handy for the resistance. Therefore, we tolerate her involvement. Still, I think she's too..." Snow made an uncharacteristically odd face and waved her hand, "out there."

"And the glass slippers?" said the prince. "Do you think they will matter?"

Snow looked out over the dreary, mist-covered landscape. "If someone had asked me a week ago if you were still alive, I would have said no. And I'm still not sure about that," she joked. "So the glass slippers, who knows? Maybe. Gold orbs, magic mirrors, now this Wonderland stuff. I was never one for such things. How do you plan for a war with magic as a factor? I am not someone who subscribes to magic. But even I have had to make certain concessions these days...and it makes me a little frightened. Yet, I have heard the stories about the glass slippers. Those stories give people hope. I guess in a way that is just as important. Hope is a magic I can relate to. For a moment, we had a new plan. Even the dwarves were excited. That's changed now, but it meant something to see the them get excited again."

"The old witch's potion worked. I saw it," said the prince. "I watched that girl turn into a mermaid." There was conviction in his voice. "And that was from a tiny sliver from the shards. If that was just the one piece, I can't imagine how much magic one slipper has, let alone two."

"The magic that is in them," Snow White replied, "is not something you or I know how to deal with. The best thing we can do is keep the glass slippers away from Cinderella until we can figure out what to do with them."

Snow White looked at Phillip. "You asked about a plan. The plan is to survive to fight another battle, to try and help those that have chosen to stay behind or had no choice but to stay behind; biding our time until another plan might work." She paused, reflecting on the years of struggle she had been a part of. "All we can do now is be a thorn in their side, but a thorn in the side still hurts. That is the plan. Our resources are thin these days. At best, we've got about two hundred able-bodied dwarves here and another five hundred we can depend on back in the mountains."

One last time, Prince Phillip took in the sight offered by Hubbard's Ridge; then he turned to head back to the horses. "It's good to see you again, my sister. There was always an empty hole in my life after you left. That we have some family remaining is important. Mother would be proud. In these dark times you've kept the true light of Marchenton from being extinguished."

Then with a smile, Prince Phillip added, "You know, this evil queen, Queen Cinder, is it?" laughing a little at the nickname. "She's your sister-in-law," he teased.

"Well, she's your wife. You deal with it, then," Snow teased back.

"Fine," replied the prince. "Can I borrow your army?" he asked with a smile.

"No," said Snow White flatly. Then her tone shifted. "Phillip, how did you survive the Beanstalk War?"

The question caught the prince by surprise. "I don't really remember much," he replied, quickly becoming uneasy with the topic. "It is strange. Everything that happened before Syrenka pulled me from the water is a fuzzy memory."

"You were away for ten years, and you don't remember any of it?"

"Just sort of disconnected impressions. I have a vague recollection of considerable death but otherwise, I have not been able to recall much. If you are asking me how I escaped, well, I wish I could remember that myself."

"That is strange, little brother," General White observed. She thought about Jack, who was quite obviously affected in a different way by his experience.

Prince Phillip paused to recall a childhood memory. "What was it Mother used to call you?"

"What? She used to call me a lot of things," Snow white replied, smirking just a bit.

"There was one I remember though—fairest one!"

Snow White laughed out loud. "That's right, Mother used to call me the fairest of them all. That one? You actually remember that one?"

"I remember there was one time you tried to save all of the chickens in the royal coops because it wasn't fair that we were taking their eggs," recalled the prince.

"I saved a pig once," Snow White admitted. "Snuck him out of the castle and set him free," she reminisced. "Yes, that was my battle cry growing up—'it's not fair!' You were not privy to the screaming matches mother and I had. How I railed against her sometimes. How it wasn't fair I had to take embroidery classes with the other girls while you went and out hunting with father. It wasn't fair that I had to wear a corset. It wasn't fair that we had servants. Mother and I fought all the time towards the end. I was a handful."

"Yes, you were always complaining how things weren't fair," repeated Phillip.

"Anytime I went on one of my tirades, Mother always tried to yell over me how life wasn't fair. There was one time," Snow White remembered pointedly, "she told me how if I was so concerned about what was fair and what wasn't, that I should just leave the castle; go out on crusade and change the world so it was more in line with what I considered just. That way she would not have to listen to me complain all of the time. That was our last fight. After that, I left."

"And here you are, years later, still trying to make things fair for all," Phillip observed.

"Mother was right, life isn't fair, but it's up to us to make it that way."

"You know, in all of these years, I never knew why you left. But there was always a part of me that hoped you'd sneak back into my room one night and take me with you."

Then abruptly, Snow White withdrew from anything further on the conversation. She retreated from the sudden uncomfortable childhood recollections to the safety of more immediate concerns. "Well, we'd better get back. We will be heading up to one of the dwarven strongholds in the mountains tonight. It is a long trip. We'll have to reevaluate our resources and come up with another plan. That plan with the mermaid seems short-lived."

Phillip was slightly confused at the change in conversation, but he agreed with his sister. "She did sort of take the potion and run, but she saved our lives in the process."

They turned to head back to the horses when they saw Rapunzel, who called out to them, "Have you seen Patience?"

"We were about to head back. We should find her," replied General White.

* * *

Patience had gone back to the horses. She was surprised that she had no further desire to see the castle. She knew seeing the castle would remind her of her mother, that there was no way for her to go and see her mother again, though she was so close. *If I had waved from the ridge, could Mother have seen me?* She wondered.

Patience had not eaten anything today and decided to eat while she waited for the prince and the others to return. She found the skin that contained the whey and curds she had politely turned down earlier, and poured it quickly into a small bowl she used for meals while traveling with Hamelin. She took a spoon from her pack and walked over to the nearby tree line to get out of the cold drizzle. Just inside the trees, it was drier as the overhanging branches provided some cover from the light drizzle. She found a small mound of dirt and grass near a fallen tree. Though it was nice to sit down, she was hoping they would leave soon and head back to the safe house. She wanted to get back, hoping that somehow Hamelin would be there waiting for her.

Patience noticed that the prince and General White had been getting along better today. When Rapunzel was not working with General White, she was spending time with her mother. Patience missed her mother and then realized how much she missed Hamelin's company. Then there was the matter of Elizabeth.

186

Patience knew Elizabeth was closer to Hamelin's age. She knew that even though they had just met the two instantly liked each other. She began to feel even more alone, and was surprised that her sadness was turning to tears.

She had no idea that nearby something large was watching her with eight evil eyes. Hidden above in the large overhanging branches, a giant spider watched. Gael. The Maldame had ordered her and her arachnid sister to capture the young girl who now sat, unsuspecting, below her. The spider slowly and silently began her descent, lowering herself on an impossibly thin strand of silk, working it from her spinnerets.

Gael had not always been a spider. Her arachnid form was intended as a temporary punishment. The two sisters were the daughters of the Maldame. They were very competent witches in the coven and well-suited to contribute to the Maldame's plot to subvert Cinderella before she could marry into the royal family. Even though they had failed at the initial attempt to break Cinderella and gain control of her before her marriage, the full scope of the prophecy soon revealed itself when Cinderella brought her step-family into the castle to help her oversee tragic times after the Beanstalk War. Inadvertently, she had all but delivered the witches to the throne they sought, though it was not in the way they had initially considered. While the Maldame worked her influences on the queen in her emotionally fragile state, Gael and Jovette set to work on clearing the way for further coven control.

Silently, the hideous spider slid effortlessly to the forest floor, well behind the unsuspecting Muffet. Her spinnerets disconnected the line of silk. Gael could feel her spidery poison glands contract, and her fangs swelled with her deadly fluid. Just a scratch would leave her victim paralyzed. Gael and her sister Jovette were ordered to bring the girl with the glass slippers back alive.

The sisters had dedicated themselves to servicing the coven, but once they were living in the castle with opportunity to experience the newfound wealth and extravagances of the royal family, the witches lost focus on their plan. Distracted by fine clothing, jewels, and decadent galas full of exotic foods, they embraced their newfound royalty with lustful abandon. Such distractions angered their mother, the Maldame, and after failing one too many times to show up for a coven meeting, the Maldame tracked the two girls to one of the royal family's chateaus.

Infuriated at the two witches' indiscretions, the Maldame turned the girls into large, hideous spiders. However, they retained their humanity and awareness within. They were to remain like this for one month. If they proved their loyalty to her, the Maldame would change them back, but throughout the kingdom, magic was beginning to weaken. The witches overused magic once they had direct influence on the throne. Witches throughout the coven were using magic indiscriminately. A month later, after the sisters had shown their devotions and begged forgiveness, the Maldame was not able to change them back. Their only hope was to help the Maldame secure enough magic to turn them back to their human form. Since then, the two large spider sisters became excellent agents for the Maldame's other duties. They were scouts, spies and assassins for the Maldame, doing her dirty work in the hope that someday they could be changed back into human form.

"Patience," Rapunzel called out, looking for the girl. "We're heading back."

Then Rapunzel turned toward the tree line and froze.

She spotted the young girl sitting among the trees, but Rapunzel also saw something else, something large, moving through the trees toward the unsuspecting girl.

Patience did not notice what was behind her, nor did she see Rapunzel begin to sprint towards her. She had dropped some whey on her dress and, annoyed, bent down to wipe it away, hoping it would not stain. As she shifted to inspect her skirt, something caught her attention. It was a huge hairy spider well over five feet wide and at least three feet tall.

Terrified at a sight so hideous and unexpected, Patience let out a shrill scream, and then threw her bowl of curded cheese and liquid whey at the monstrous spider. The creature did not flinch as the bowl struck across its head. Patience turned and ran. The spider darted forth, but its great size made maneuvering through the trees difficult. Patience scrambled and started to sprint across the clearing toward Rapunzel.

Another huge spider, Jovette, erupted from the trees in a great leap, its eight legs stretched wide as it flew towards the terrified Patience. It landed deftly in the young girl's path, blocking her way, and sending Rapunzel sliding in the mud to avoid the surprise attack.

General White and Prince Phillip had rushed forward at the first sign of trouble, but quickly skidded to a stop at the sight of the second giant spider.

Without a moment's hesitation, the spider spun its hairy abdomen around at Patience, launching a spray of webbing behind it to ensnare the frightened girl. With a shriek of surprise and horror, Patience turned and ran to her right, barely dodging the webbing. Rapunzel reacted quickly; her hand flew from her belt side. A flash of metal streaked through the air as a slender dagger sunk into the spider's eye cluster. The spider let out a horrific squeal, its body wincing in agony, as it turned quickly from left to right, trying to see with what was left of its eyes. It no longer pursued the girl. Now the eight-legged monster cautiously moved towards Rapunzel, hissing angrily.

Snow White pulled a knife from her belt, cursing that she had left her sword in the scabbard tied to her horse.

"I think you made it angry, 'Punzel," White muttered. She pushed her brother behind her protectively.

"There's not much room to back up, Snow," the Prince informed the general. The spider was between them and the tree line, blocking them from the road where their horses stood. Behind them was the ridge, with nothing but a drop to the Bloodthorns below. They were trapped.

Then the first spider, Gael, emerged from the tree line and darted directly toward Patience, its eight legs pumping to drive its massive body forward.

Patience sprinted along the tree line, heading back to the road and toward the tethered horses. The horses were spooked by the presence of the giant spiders. They began to rear up, kicking and pulling at their reins, wide-eyed in panic to get away. Patience hoped she might be able to climb onto one of them and outrun the spider, who had gained ground and was nearly on top of her.

"Give ussssss the glasssss ssssssslippers, girl," Gael demanded in a hissing growl.

With a dull crack, the horses broke down the wooden branch they were tied to. Then with a final rearing, all the gear that had been loosened on the saddles fell as the three horses raced away. Patience's hope of escaping on horseback was now running away from her.

Then Patience saw the pile of gear from the horses, and the hilt of General White's sword. Half stumbling forward as she dove at the hilt, the young girl grabbed the general's sword awkwardly, pulling it from its scabbard. She struggled to face the spider that was bearing down on her. Patience did not realize how close the spider had been behind her, as she hefted the heavy sword in front to protect herself.

"We will take the glasssss sssslippers from you!" Gael hissed again.

"No!" Patience heard herself scream. In that last moment, she shoved the sword forward and Gael ran full force upon it, unable to stop herself. The spider's great size and momentum drove her onto the blade, stabbing it through her fanged mouth and directly into her head. The spider gurgled and flailed in pain, almost tearing the sword from Patience's terrified grip.

Gael pulled herself backward off the blade of the sword. As the dying spider desperately grabbed at its wounded maw with its long front legs, Patience found herself doing something she never thought possible. Like in a dream, she rose to her feet. She leaped towards the spider, the general's sword in hand, and landed on top of the hairy abdomen.

With two hands, Patience Muffet drove the sword straight down into the massive spider's head, killing it. She stabbed it repeatedly, fear and pent up frustration giving way to a liberating anger over everything she had seen in these past five years. She was not aware that she was screaming or that tears had welled up in her eyes and spilled down her face. Her anger at the glass slippers she had been forced to carry, Hamelin's disappearance, the Bloodthorn Wall, the queen, the war, even at Elizabeth for wresting Hamelin's interest away. With every driving stab of the sword into the spider, Patience's childhood naïveté melted away, which was perhaps what infuriated her the most. Today, her childhood innocence was slain like the dead spider she crouched upon.

There was still another spider to contend with. Jovette.

Rapunzel slowly backed up until she, too, stood next to General White at the edge of the cliff.

"There's no chance for us to out run that thing." said Rapunzel.

It hissed again, more malevolently if that was possible, and somewhere behind its fangs, it spoke, much to the surprise of General White. "Sssister isss dead. For that you will all die!" Though half blinded from Rapunzel's dagger, the creature tensed, preparing to pounce.

"Maybe not for us," General White replied. Then she looked over at Patience, who sat dazed upon the dead body of the other spider. "Patience! Run!" screamed the general as loud as she could.

Snow White saw more movement in the trees where Patience had been. She did not know if it was another spider or something else. Then, she had heard the familiar "thunk" of a crossbow firing and almost instantly felt her shoulder explode in a spray of blood and fiery pain. A crossbow bolt drove itself deep into her flesh. The force of it spun her, knocking her off her feet.

She did not see the half blinded spider leap at Rapunzel, as the young lieutenant screamed, "No!" and tried to run over to her fallen General. Phillip rushed over to Rapunzel, pushing her out of the way as the spider slammed full force on top of the prince instead, its momentum sending both the Prince and Jovette tumbling over the ridge down toward the Bloodthorns.

As General White lay bleeding in the mud, she only saw Patience turn and run across the trail darting into the forest on the opposite side as some of General Dendroba's men emerged from the woods near the ridge, giving chase.

"Run, Patience," Snow White whispered, closing her eyes from the pain of the crossbow quarrel.

Prince Phillip found himself tumbling down the fifty-foot embankment of the ravine, sliding uncontrollably toward the Bloodthorn bramble that waited at the bottom. Jovette struggled to gain a foothold to right herself as her hairy, segmented legs flailed against the rocky slope. The prince then tried desperately to grab at anything to stop his fall; dust and gravel were blinding him as they stung his eyes and covered his face. He braced himself for a fatal collision with the Bloodthorns.

The great spider had more momentum and slammed into the Bloodthorns first. Following behind, the prince landed feet first on top of the flailing spider, its great hairy body providing a barrier against the deadly bramble.

Phillip regained his bearings after a moment. He quickly realized his precarious position would not last as the spider tried to pull itself away from the Bloodthorns. Panicked, he looked down at the struggling arachnid, expecting to see Bloodthorns enveloping the creature. But this was not so. The spider was temporarily entangled, but nothing more. Unfortunately Phillip realized, the spider's blood did not trigger any response from the thorns. The prince did not want to hang around; he had a feeling that if he fell upon the Bloodthorns, his fate would be far worse. It seemed the thorns only reacted to certain kinds of blood, warm and red, Phillip quickly surmised.

As he looked down, he saw Rapunzel's dagger still lodged in the spider's head. Quickly he reached down desperately trying to grab the hilt as the spider writhed. After a few close attempts Phillip was able to grab the hilt and pull it free. Jovette shrieked in agony, and as she shifted from the pain, she slid further down the embankment and deeper into the Bloodthorns. Phillip quickly drove the dagger into the loose gravel of the ridge wall before he could fall into the deadly briar. The dagger held fast as an anchor to which Phillip desperately clung. Though strong, he could feel the wound in his shoulder burn as he began to pull himself back up the steep rocky slope, away from the spider and the Bloodthorns.

Seconds after Phillip pulled himself further up the slope, the spider pulled free of the thorns. The prince breathed a sigh of relief when he realized she was not giving pursuit. Instead, the badly wounded Jovette crawled away across the bramble, heading in the direction of the distant castle.

When Phillip was positive the arachnid was not going to pursue him, he focused his energy on climbing up the slope. Digging his feet into the loose gravel for support, he drove the dagger in again, and pulled himself up. Now he could feel a terrible pain in his shoulder. A dark wet stain of blood welled from the wound Syrenka had bandaged just a few days prior. If Phillip were to slip now and fall into the deadly briar, they would surely receive a feast from his reopened wound.

Not wanting to be a meal for the Bloodthorns or the spider, Prince Phillip quickly and with tremendous, painful effort pulled himself toward the top of the ridge.

Much to his surprise as he crawled over the top, several soldiers from the queen's rat army were waiting for him there. An even greater surprise was that they did not appear to recognize him as the prince. *All the better*, Phillip thought to himself as a measure of relief. *If I am recognized, it would surely be a detriment to the others.*

There was no chance of avoiding capture and Prince Phillip knew it. He had nowhere to hide or run. As he saw the guards peer over the ledge, look down, and exclaim that they had found another one, Phillip slumped, disheartened, and lowered his head with a defeated sigh. But before anyone could notice, he deftly palmed Rapunzel's dagger out of sight of the guards as he began to climb back over the ridge, hoping they would not fully search him.

As Phillip surrendered, the soldiers grabbed him and lifted him to his feet;

others kept their swords drawn on him. He considered engaging the guards in a fight, but thought better of it. The prince counted a small group of guards, perhaps a dozen. He saw both Rapunzel and his wounded sister bound and being led to a horse-drawn wagon with a large cage in the back. He could see others in the cage, as well.

Nearby was the general of the queen's army, Phillip guessed correctly—General Dendroba. The broad shouldered general stood above his troops with a commanding presence. Caught up in other matters, Dendroba had his back turned and was talking to two others, a woman and another man, both dressed in hunter's gear. The woman held a crossbow. Phillip had recognized Gretel and her brother from their time as the royal witch hunters. Perhaps if Dendroba and the others had looked at his last prisoner they might have recognized Prince Phillip. Instead, they had turned away. The prince's hands were shackled behind him as he was led to the wagon's cage still within in earshot to overhear their conversation.

"Upon arriving at the castle, payments will be arranged for you and Hansel. Your tracking skills have served the queen well, yet again," Dendroba said. "Of course you'll be paid handsomely."

Gretel smiled. "Excellent. It is a good thing we were in the area to help. Now, what about the wolf girl? Her bounty is still worth twenty-thousand?"

Dendroba sighed, "Yes, it was very convenient you were here, like so many other times," he said with a tinge of sarcasm. "You'll be paid for the werewolf, but only after she turns. Then she is to be skinned and bled completely. The blood is the important part, and more potent if it is captured in wolf form. Once that is delivered to the queen, you'll receive that payment," assured the general, his patience now waning at Gretel's conversation. Every time they had dealings together, it seemed to Dendroba that Gretel's only concern was money and compensation. He understood, of course, but to the general such discussion quickly turned boring.

"If the court is so inclined," Gretel added, "for an extra five thousand in compensation, Hansel and I will provide you with the wolf's bones and teeth. But we retain the pelt."

Dendroba wanted to get his small group of surviving guards back to the castle, and dismissed Gretel and Hansel, "Of course, yes, yes. We will work the rest of the details out when we get to the castle. Have we not always paid you generously for your efforts in the past? Let's get going."

Dendroba hated dealing with contracts. He pointed to a group of guards, trying to end the conversation with Hansel and Gretel. Dendroba barked another order. "Find that girl! Search every tree if you have to."

Phillip was handled roughly into the wagon's cage, which took up the cargo space of the wagon but was only four feet in height. He saw Rapunzel tending to Snow White's wounded shoulder. Much to his surprise, Rapunzel's mother and another girl, her hands tied with dirty rope and wearing only an old blanket, rounded out the list of occupants. Phillip's expression of confusion was clear, and Dame Gothel explained. "They arrived shortly after you left and took the safe house by surprise. They killed every dwarf they could before the rest of them got away; I was captured by Hansel and his sister. Lucky me." She gestured to her bruised face.

Snow looked over. "Mirror?" she asked quietly, obviously in pain.

"It's safe," replied Gothel, "still hidden—they won't find it."

Snow White nodded with a wince. "They beat you up pretty bad, Gothel."

"I'll live. I've known more witches that have had it far worse at the hands of Hansel and Gretel."

"Well, if I get a chance I'll show them what payback means," grumbled Rapunzel. "You do not practice anymore, Mother. They should not be beating up old women. I can't believe Hansel and Gretel tracked us down. What traitors they are. What sell-outs. Sell-outs! Cowards!" Rapunzel yelled out, kicking the bar of the small cramped cell in frustration.

"Snow, are you okay?" Phillip asked as he shuffled over to his sister.

"Oh, now you are concerned?" White replied. It was an attempt at teasing, but Phillip's facial expression of hurt and confusion told her he was seriously concerned.

"I'm fine," she assured him. "It looks worse than it is." She smiled through the wincing pain. Snow White desperately wanted to take the uncomfortable attention off her.

"Elizabeth, this is...you know who," Snow White said with a wink, not wanting to bring attention to the fact he was the lost prince.

"She works with you?" Phillip asked, surprised that such a disheveled mess of a girl was part of White's resistance army.

"Not exactly. She works with Goldenhair," Rapunzel started to explain. Dame Gothel interrupted. "Oh!" the old witch gasped in recognition, studying Elizabeth. "She's a lycanthrope—a werewolf. They are not native to the kingdom though. You have wandered quite far, haven't you? That she has been captured and is being brought to the castle is very interesting."

Elizabeth looked shocked. "What?"

Rapunzel misinterpreted Elizabeth's reaction and offered a brief explanation. "My mother is good at being able to blurt out these sorts of things," she said apologetically.

That was little comfort for Elizabeth. Glancing around, she could tell her companions were uneasy about being caged with a werewolf. Despite that, Elizabeth found herself intrigued by the old woman's statement.

"What do you mean?" Elizabeth pressed, hoping the explanation would overshadow the revelation of the secret she kept.

"If Queen Cendrillon is capturing werewolves, that means she is really losing power to control the Bloodthorns. These Bloodthorns do not like certain kinds of blood, and were-blood especially. The transformation properties of werewolf blood are deadly to the Bloodthorns. I have seen the briar retreat away from werewolf blood. In theory, this girl could walk right through the entire wall unscathed." The old witch added, "Cinderella will probably drain your blood when you turn."

Elizabeth's face went ashen.

"Well I hope they get us out of this cage before you change into a wolf," the prince smiled half-jokingly, trying to ease the growing tension in the small cramped cage. He did not help.

"Me, too," replied Elizabeth in a more somber tone. She had no idea what would happen. She had been captured by Hansel and Gretel on more than one occasion, but this time it seemed different. This time, Elizabeth felt there would be no rescue.

General Dendroba barked some orders and climbed heavily onto Hansel's wagon and then the wagon gave a lurch and began to pull away. Every bump jolted the prisoners as they headed in the direction of the castle.

They had not been moving for more than a few moments when, amidst a sudden commotion, the wagon stopped abruptly, the horses rearing up. From the cage, the prisoners could not see very well.

But they had heard it, the distinctive roar of a huge bear, three bears, in fact. Goldenhair!

The captured companions could hear the yell of the guards and the screams as the bears tore through them. They heard Goldenhair speaking quickly in her mysterious language, commanding the bears.

Finally, Elizabeth and the others could see Goldenhair; she was fighting off several of Dendroba's soldiers with a long wooden staff. It was almost a dance as Mavor Goldenhair moved expertly around, easily landing blows and knocking down the brutish soldiers.

Inspired by their rescuer, Prince Phillip shifted around in the cramped cage and tried to kick open the door. The force of his efforts made the wagon rock with every kick.

Seeing an opportunity as one of the distracted guards drew near the cage trying to back away from an approaching bear, Rapunzel's arms shot out quickly through two bars, pulling him back hard against the cage. She wrapped her arms over the guard's head and used her shackles to choke the guard until he collapsed.

Then without warning, the wagon rocked violently to the side, tossing all the prisoners hard against the cage bars.

The largest bear, Nikko, rose in front of the cage like a wall of brown fur. Towering against the side of the cage, his massive front paws braced against it, he began pushing the wagon, attempting to topple it.

Gretel and Hansel were both thrown from their seats, landing hard along the road.

General Dendroba leaped down easily and drew his sword. "I do not have time for this," he growled. His soldiers were no match for the other two bears that chased after them with monstrous roars and swatted them down with the razor sharp claws that lined their huge feet.

The situation was quickly turning against him, but General Dendroba was determined to regain control. He would take out the bear's leader.

Goldenhair landed another blow on a guard, sending him unconscious to the ground. Then she saw General Dendroba approach and quickly spun around into a defensive posture.

Nikko swatted the lock with his powerful claws as Phillip kicked hard at the door, but the lock was too strong and the cage too small and crowded for him to get any real advantage. The others watched helplessly as Goldenhair squared off against the queen's general.

Dendroba held his sword with his muscular left arm, holding his skinnier right arm and gloved hand back to counterbalance.

Goldenhair and Dendroba circled for a moment, sizing each other up,

The blonde-haired warrior twirled her staff in a deceptively lazy manner.

Then quickly she struck out with it. Dendroba blocked and countered with incredible speed. In a fluid motion, he brought his deadly sword down at Goldenhair, who could only pull her staff back in front to block. Again, he brought the sword down with great strength and speed that surprised Goldenhair as she reeled back to block the general's devastating swing. Her staff shattered in two, like dead wood against Dendroba's powerful strike.

Concern grew across Goldenhair's face, a realization that as strong as she was, Dendroba was stronger. As nimble as she was, he was surprisingly just as agile.

Goldenhair had been involved in many fights and could hold her own quite well. But now there came a dreadful fear—that she was fighting an opponent who easily outmatched her.

With her staff shattered, leaving her weaponless, Goldenhair scrambled to keep out of the general's reach. The style of her fighting had changed from confident to struggling desperation. Quickly, Goldenhair looked around for some other weapon or something with which to defend herself.

The huge general feigned another swing, forcing Goldenhair to shift away. Dendroba's swing suddenly changed direction at the last moment and caught the golden-haired warrior squarely across her head with the flat of the blade sending her to the ground, blasting the air from her lungs with a startled cry as she fell hard on her back. Dendroba's attack still drew blood; her blonde locks smattered with crimson. The blow had left her dazed, and her ears were ringing. She lay stunned, trying to catch her breath.

Then, a large shadow covered the fallen Goldenhair. The shadow fell upon Dendroba as well, though he unaware of what was behind him. There came an angry and deafening roar as Nikko, the largest of Goldenhair's bears, ran from the wagon to protect Goldenhair. The bear rose menacingly on his hind legs. Sensing an attack from behind, Dendroba whirled around and was now dwarfed by the great grizzly bear. The bear bellowed another intimidating roar, and then attacked with such ferocity Dendroba could not defend against it.

With his great arms, Nikko swatted Dendroba to the ground with ease. Then the bear ripped through the general's thick leather armor like paper with his razor sharp claws.

In an instant, the bear was on top of Dendroba as the general struggled to avoid the claws and deadly teeth. The struggle was over quickly as the bear pinned the General down with its crushing weight. Nikko's head drove forward, its huge gaping mouth poised to kill. Dendroba instinctively threw his arm up to defend himself.

As Nikko dug his teeth into Dendroba's arm, Dendroba let out an agonizing scream. The bear's iron-like jaws crushed down hard. Then the bear shook his head violently side to side, and with a sickening popping sound, ripped the General's arm from its socket.

As quickly as the enraged bear had attacked, Nikko backed away in an almost submissive manner, suddenly disinterested in continuing the attack.

Dropping the General's bloodied arm onto the ground, the bear staggered away, shaking its great head and making short grunts. The bear only took several steps, and then collapsed.

"NO!" Goldenhair cried in such heartbreaking anguish that the very forest seemed to pause. She scrambled to her feet with sudden disregard for anything else. She ran to Nikko now laying on his side, his breathing shallow and labored.

Still on the ground where he fell, Dendroba groaned as he grabbed the mauled remains of his right arm. Much like some amphibians might lose a limb or a tail to a predator only to have it grow back, so did Dendroba lose his arm. The poisonous right hand of Dendroba was gone, for now. Nikko unknowingly had bitten down on the poisonous appendage, getting a fatal mouthful of Dendroba's deadly contact toxin when he ripped off the arm.

Dendroba rolled over and rose to his feet; clawed and bloodied, his left hand covering the stump where his right arm used to be. He hobbled back toward the wagon.

"Let's move out! Now!"

Not the way he would have preferred to have taken care of things, he thought, but there was a schedule to consider. Glancing back only once, Dendroba saw Goldenhair sobbing deeply and hugging the limp body of the bear as it lay in the middle of the road.

"What?" replied Gretel. "Kill her!"

"No. We have to get going," Dendroba grumbled. "Leave her. She's no longer a threat."

Gretel studied Dendroba's face a moment as he pulled himself up onto the seat of the wagon. "You, you don't actually feel bad about her bear? Do you?" Gretel hissed incredulously. "Is that it, some sort of compassion?"

"Do not question me on this," Dendroba replied coolly. "We've neutralized the attack. Our main priority is to get to the castle by nightfall. There's no time for this now."

Gretel cursed under her breath and grabbed her crossbow, quickly loading it.

"Leave it alone, Gretel," General Dendroba warned.

Gretel ignored Dendroba's remark, pulled her crossbow to her shoulder and settled in to aim a fatal shot at the unsuspecting Goldenhair as she sobbed over her dead bear.

Hansel looked at his sister, "Gretel, there will be another chance," he said with a diplomatic tone. "We have to go—" But before anyone realized it, Gretel had aimed and fired. Dendroba grabbed the crossbow stock to stop her, but Hansel's sister had gotten off the shot.

Gretel glared at Dendroba. How dare he grab her crossbow or try to misdirect her shot, her icy look seemed to say. Then the glare turned to smug satisfaction that he had been too late.

Gretel looked over, expecting to see Goldenhair slumped over the body of her dead bear.

Knots tied in Gretel's stomach and the blood drained from her face when she saw Goldenhair standing next to the bear's body, holding the crossbow bolt meant to kill her. Goldenhair, despite her sorrow, had caught Gretel's killing shot out of the air, and it brought a chill down Gretel's spine. The indescribable glare that she saw on Goldenhair's face gave even the steel-hearted Gretel pause. Perhaps, Gretel thought, that this time she had made a grave mistake. It unnerved her, and she remained silent for a long time afterwards.

Hansel cracked the reins, and the wagon jolted quickly into motion again, moving away from the scene of the ill-fated ambush.

CHAPTER 16
BLOODTHORNS

Lord Dendroba seemed unusually introspective as his group traveled on toward the castle. It was obvious to Gretel that the bear's death had affected the queen's general, but she did not know or care why.

Dendroba found himself recalling a time from his childhood, a time he had not thought of in many years that had now resurfaced after his confrontation with Goldenhair. Quietly, he mulled over his recollections.

* * *

Early winter snow dusted the road as twilight gave way to dusk and then to a chilled night. Crisp, white clouds sliced across a rising moon. Standing at the side near a stone bridge stood a young boy. The lad fussed as an older woman adjusted the buttons on his overcoat and pulled his hood over his deformed face.

"Phyllo Dendroba—stand still! You are too excited," the woman scolded. "How are you to go and learn the ways of the throne? You will do so with properly buttoned clothes."

Young Phyllo paid little attention as he could see the bouncing lights and hear the horses of the approaching carriage.

"Is that the king? He's here!" he said excitedly, pulling away from the woman. "Maldame, he's here!"

The carriage came to a stop just before the bridge. The door opened and a well-dressed and regal-looking man stepped out into the cold mud.

"Are you the king?" Phyllo blurted out instantly.

The man laughed politely. "I am certainly not King Cole, young man. But I will take you to meet him." He turned his attention to the Maldame. "I trust payment is in order."

Maldame handed the man a large sack of coins. "We are grateful to King Cole for this opportunity. It is important that Phyllo can spend some time with a true king before he takes his own throne. Stewards and advisors are no substitute for the insight of royalty."

"His Highness is more than happy to oblige, madam. The payment is nothing more than a token to our driver." He tossed the sack to a man sitting atop the carriage. "We shall return the lad to you in the spring." Then quietly the man added, "With this, my debt to the coven is to be considered paid."

The Maldame nodded. "Agreed."

Then she turned to the boy. "Phyllo, learn much. Take notes, for you will be a king one day as well." The young boy adjusted a large leather glove on his right hand and picked up a knapsack. He hobbled excitedly to the man and climbed inside the richly decorated carriage. The man followed and sat across from him. His gaze turned sour for but an instant at the sight of the young boy's deformities up close, he knocked on the dark mahogany wall, signaling the driver to leave.

The witch's coven had, in accordance with their prophecy, kidnapped Phyllo at birth and done their best to teach the boy to rule as the future King of Marchenton. The coven taught and trained him in everything they could in preparation for taking over the throne. They had books on war tactics and heraldry, old records of laws, and of course, when was older they would teach him witchcraft. Phyllo would become the direct link between the witches and their rule over the kingdom. The Maldame felt it was not enough though, and a unique opportunity to mentor the young Dendroba with a real king in a neighboring land was too good to pass up. She wanted to make sure that they would have someone on the throne who not only served the witches' interests but also could effectively rule. It did not serve them any purpose in the long term to put a helpless, unprepared puppet on the throne, only for him to ruin everything because of a lack of experience. It was worth the effort the Maldame had decided, if it meant also having an effective ally. This would guarantee the witches' control over the kingdom for a longer and more beneficial time. The witches were cunning, able to gain a contact in the neighboring court to secure Phyllo as a page to King Cole himself.

Phyllo's time in King Cole's court consisted of some of his happiest childhood memories. He spent days learning heraldry and warring tactics, wines and music. There was always pipe music playing and fiddlers who played the most uplifting reels and jigs. The warm smells of food wafted through the grand halls. Phyllo would explore and study all manner of art in great libraries. He slept in a grand room on an elegant bed and dressed in princely attire for all manner of lessons. The king took to Phyllo as if he were one of his sons, ignoring his deformities with jovial confidence, and encouraging Phyllo in all of the lad's questions.

Phyllo learned much in the short time he was there, and he was sad to have to return to the coven.

To cheer the boy up, King Cole gave the young Dendroba a gift. It was a champagne colored wolfhound puppy. At the sight of the young dog, Phyllo's eyes had lit up. He had never had any pet at the coven. As the dog licked the young boy's face, Phyllo named the dog "Cole," which brought a warm smile to the face of the generous King.

Phyllo spent his final days at the castle playing and learning how to train the puppy. His gross deformities tended to isolate the young boy from having many friends and going to social activities, but with his new pet he had a companion who never judged or ridiculed him for his looks; the two were the best of friends.

The day came when Phyllo had to return to the coven. The carriage left the boy and his dog back at the very same stone bridge he had been picked up at. Strangely, there was no one there waiting for him. Phyllo and Cole waited in the grey drizzle, the boy growing concerned and disappointed. Eventually, the pair made their way to the back coven sanctuary. Phyllo pounded forcefully on the entry door, confused as to why he had not been greeted in a far more welcoming manner. A young warlock Phyllo had not seen before finally opened the door, though he did not move to let the boy in.

"Where is the Maldame?" Dendroba demanded, "Where are Jovette and Gael? Where is Dame Gothel? Can I at least come in?"

"So the Prince of Frogs has returned!" The warlock said in a sarcastic and unwelcoming tone. Phyllo disregarded the all too familiar insult.

"Let me in!" Phyllo ordered again. The warlock blocked the doorway.

"Gothel?" The warlock sneered, "Gothel was exiled months ago for her failure to decipher the prophecy correctly. Oh, you did not hear the news?" he said with biting sarcasm. "That's right...you were away, too busy learning how to be royalty. Seems the Prince of Frogs is not going to be king after all. The Maldame herself and her daughters are now overseeing the true heir to Marchenton's throne—a girl named Ella. I guess she'd be your twin sister, but it's clear who got the looks, frog-boy."

"What do you mean; I am not to be the king?" Phyllo asked, stunned at the news that diminished what he had been raised all of his life to believe. That he was to be king had been the driving purpose behind everything in his life. The witch's prophecy had told them this is what would be. Now it was wrong? Adding to it all was how quickly he was to be discarded. "This all happened while I was away?" Phyllo started to push through the door, but the warlock shoved him back hard and Phyllo fell back into the mud. Cole stood by Phyllo and barked at the warlock.

"Your free ride is over, frog-boy. They put your stuff in the stables. If you want to remain part of the coven, you best be mucking stalls in the morning." The warlock slammed the door and with a large clunk barred it from the inside.

"Come on, Cole," Dendroba said, disheartened as he got up and wiped the cold mud off his pants. "We can stay in the barn. At least it is dry there. Then we can figure this out in the morning."

With his head down, the dog obediently followed Dendroba inside. Phyllo made a pile of hay and found a lantern that provided some light and heat. There was a dirt-stained blanket covering some barn tools that Phyllo took to wrap himself with for warmth. It was a far cry from the royal bedroom he had stayed in over these past months. Cole had found a piece of frayed rope and tried to get the boy to play a game of tug with him. Phyllo obliged half-heartedly, but exhaustion quickly overtook young Dendroba. He made sure Cole had water to drink from a small bucket and gave his dog some of the dried venison he had remaining from his trip. Cole curled up quietly next to Phyllo as the lad softly cried himself to sleep.

It was just before dawn when Phyllo woke up from his deep slumber. Something was wrong. Cole was missing. Dendroba quickly looked around the dim stillness of the barn, but did not see anything. Then Dendroba noticed something else was wrong. His large leather glove was missing, exposing his frog-like deformed hand; the poisonous, moist skin was covered in dust and hay. He always slept with the glove on in his bed at the castle and the dog was only allowed to sleep outside the door to Phyllo's bedchamber.

"Cole," Phyllo began to panic. "Cole! Come here buddy!" the young boy called out with alarm. Phyllo franticly got to his feet and called out again as he searched for his glove and his dog, beginning to fear something terrible had happened.

Then he saw Cole behind a nearby hay bale. The dog lay motionless, his eyes dull and still. Saliva and foam covered his muzzle and the ground around his mouth. Next to the dog was Dendroba's glove—the cuff obviously chewed on. Phyllo's puppy was dead, poisoned from the glove that the deformed boy wore on his toxic right hand.

Phyllo knelt down and cuddled his dead dog, wondering if he had absently removed the glove during the night or if Cole had managed to pull the glove off for something to play with.

"I'm so sorry. I'm so sorry," Phyllo whispered as he cried, petting the dog's soft brown fur with his left hand. the boy's only friend was gone, and he was responsible. Tears streamed down the left side of Phyllo's cheek, as he could not cry from the right side of his deformed face. He did not know how long he stayed there sobbing with the dead dog in his lap.

Among the tools in the barn was an old shovel. The young boy cried as he gently laid Cole's body in a freshly dug hole in the barn, placing the small piece of rope in the grave.

The next thing Dendroba remembered was pain. One of the tools he had found with the shovel was a small axe dull with rust. Furious and distraught, Phyllo blamed himself for his dog's death. The boy had resented his deformities before today, but now he truly loathed them. With the axe held tightly in his left hand, he placed his right arm on a worn cutting block, used to split firewood. He raised the axe high above his head. "I hate you!" he yelled at his right hand, choking through tears. Then he took a deep and angry breath and brought the axe down hard on his own right arm, severing it below the elbow.

Weeks later and much to the boy's dismay, his right arm had re-grown to its frog-like semblance and toxic nature.

Phyllo stayed at the coven sanctuary, working almost as a slave, but still he studied and learned what he could from the witches. He never ventured into that barn again.

Dendroba had not thought about that incident in a very long time.

* * *

As the cart moved along, a somber silence encapsulated the cell. Rapunzel sat next to her mother. Elizabeth pulled her legs to her body, wrapped her arms around them, and rested her head. There were stained blankets and odd traps that partially covered the top of the cage and provided at least some shade of privacy.

General White had little to say. Phillip sat next to her and checked the wound, ripping part of his shirt to use as a bandage. "It isn't much," he said, "but it's something. You are still bleeding, though." Phillip remembered how Syrenka had expertly tended to his wound. It was healing well in a very short time, despite its recent reopening.

After a time, the old witch, sensing despair was setting in, spoke quietly.

"At least the young girl is out there and not in here with us." She said.

Rapunzel lifted her head. "True. And Patience still has the glass slippers," she added.

Snow White shook her head. "Yes, but the only one who could actually do anything with them is sitting in here with us," she nodded in the witch's direction. "So what good are those shards now?" General White gave a frustrated scowl. "Welcome home, Phillip."

Phillip looked at the disillusioned group.

"Hope," replied Phillip.

"What?"

"Hope," he said again. "Even you said it, Snow, that the story of the glass slippers still gives people hope. The dwarves had hope back in the house at the beach. Right now, as long as that little girl has those glass slippers—we still have hope."

"Quiet in there! No talking!" a gravelly voice from outside the cage shouted. A guard riding a skittish horse banged the cage with his sword. "Prisoners don't get to talk!" he ordered as he began to maneuver his horse behind the cart, following closely.

Snow White gave a small, sarcastic laugh. "Well I guess it's just us that have a fool's hope."

Somewhat absently, Elizabeth, who sat listening to the conversation, began to sing to herself. It was the song she had heard the children in Aishew sing.

Queen Cinder, Queen Cinder, what did you lose?
Whatever happened to your glassy shoes?
You threw them down and they broke in twos
And soon we'll win and soon you'll lose!

Rapunzel listened. "I've heard that song. All of the children in the kingdom sing it."

"Really?" replied Elizabeth, "I thought it was just made up by some local children I met."

"Not at all," replied Rapunzel. "In every town we visit there are always children who sing that. Then, at the end they all fall down in a circle, right?"

Rapunzel smiled, trying to remember the next verse.

Queen Cinder, Queen Cinder, What did you say?
Tell the servants to sweep them away!
But all of the servants have run away
And the shards of the glass slipper
will come back some day.

The guard shouted again, "I said no talking!"

But the two women ignored him, and then they both sang together to finish the song.

Queen Cinder, Queen Cinder, with the crown on your head
Soon we'll be free and you'll be dead!

They sang it again louder this time as Dame Gothel, and then the prince joined in. The guard shouted again, smacking the bars with his sword.

The prisoners sang it a third time. Spirits lifted in the satisfaction of rebelliousness and that their outburst was unsettling the guards. This time even General White joined in.

Queen Cinder, Queen Cinder, what did you lose?

Whatever happened to your glassy shoes?
You threw them down and they broke in twos
And soon we'll win and soon you'll lose!
Queen Cinder, Queen Cinder, What did you say?
Tell the servants to sweep them away!
But all of the servants have run away
And the shards of the glass slipper
will come back some day.
Queen Cinder, Queen Cinder, with the crown on your head
Soon we'll be free and you'll be dead!

With an abrupt lurch, the wagon stopped moving.

"Why have we stopped?" asked the prince, straining to see.

"I guess we're making too much noise," Rapunzel joked.

The guard smacked the bar again with a loud clang. "Knock it off!" Now the guard sounded more nervous than angry.

Prince Phillip looked around, recognizing the area.

"This is the Kings Road," he said with surprise. He remembered the tall rows of pine trees lining the sides of the road. He had not realized the bumpy trail they had been traveling on had smoothed out. Then Phillip looked at Snow White with a sudden realization.

As if speaking what the prince thought, General Dendroba's voice boomed from atop the wagon. "These are the Bloodthorns!"

The prisoners could not see Dendroba as he bellowed his orders to soldiers. "Those of you who wish to remain behind, return to camp. Those who choose to travel in the Bloodthorns, keep a tight formation as we go through. Watch your heads! And keep up! This is going to be a tight trip. Once the path closes, we won't be able to reopen it until the witches have replenished the magic."

Only a scant few of Dendroba's remaining soldiers mustered to the wagon. The rear guard moved his horse closer to the cage, nervously looking around. The guard's horse seemed more on edge now, hoofing the ground and pulling at the bit.

Snow strained to look through the bars of the cage. Was this how they were able to get through? She hoped to see for herself. The answer came soon enough, as General Dendroba began to chant. Out of the view of the prisoners, Dendroba pulled out his small gold sphere and held it up at the tall impenetrable wall of Bloodthorns.

"Magic," whispered Dame Gothel. She listened to the words, "He's parting the Bloodthorns. I'm surprised there's enough magic left to do something like this."

"This is probably the thinnest part here," General White speculated, taking a mental note should the information prove useful at a later time. She looked at Phillip who seemed to be studying the guard.

As Dendroba repeated the incantation, the Bloodthorns began to part. The branches and bramble creaked and groaned as it reluctantly gave pass. One could almost feel the begrudged movement that came from the thorns as they opened to reveal a path. The thorns loomed overhead, so dense they seemed to block out sunlight. It was a tight passage, and as the wagon moved along the path, the thorns menacingly pulled back into place behind them.

"Stay away from the bars," Snow White said. She winced in pain from her wound as she shifted towards the middle. "I've seen what Bloodthorns can do." The group watched with a mixture of amazement and trepidation as the handful of guards led the way; followed at the end by their wagon. They slowly made their way into the Bloodthorns. Everyone in the cramped cage moved more tightly together to get just a little farther away from the bars; everyone except the prince.

As soon as they were fully surrounded in the Bloodthorn passage, Phillip burst into action. He had not been watching the guard as Snow White had thought. He had been watching the cage door from his first attempts at kicking, and more so from the bear's attack, quietly realizing that the lock had been damaged. As the cart continued through the thorny briar, Phillip had watched as the lock slowly continue to dislodge itself further with every bump.

With renewed effort, Phillip began to kick at the lock again.

"This is not the best time to try to escape," said General White in a hushed voice. "What are you thinking?"

"This is the perfect time," he replied with a heavy grunt.

"In the middle of the Bloodthorns?" Rapunzel asked incredulously. "We'd never survive!"

Phillip kicked again, the lock bending even further. He had an idea. There was one guard riding behind them. The distracted guard had been concerned more about traveling through the Bloodthorns, but now realized the prisoner was trying to escape. "Hey! Settle down in there!" he barked loudly. Again, the prince kicked, and again the lock strained closer to breaking. "We're not escaping," he grunted with every jab of his feet against the lock. "She is," he nodded at Elizabeth.

The guard smacked the bars with the sword trying to jab it through the bars. "I mean it! Knock it off!" the guard ordered.

"That's—"

Kick.

"What—"

Kick.

"I'm trying—"

Kick.

"to do!"

With one last desperate kick, the damaged lock finally gave way and the cage door swung wide. The guard's horse, spooked first by the Bloodthorns and now by the violent opening of the cage door, suddenly reared up and sent the surprised guard tumbling from the saddle and into the Bloodthorn bramble, which he became immediately entangled in. Everyone in the cage watched as the guard struggled to get up. The thorny vines caught on his clothes and armor, and as he tried to pull them off, he quickly became even more entangled. The Bloodthorns began to constrict around him. Soon, he began shouting for help, flailing and trying to pull free. His skin tore on the sharp thorns, and as more and more Bloodthorns drew blood, even still the briar tightened.

The doomed guard was hopelessly trapped now, and the deadly thorns drove endlessly into his skin. The bramble completely covered him—now he was a moving lump on the briar-covered path yelling and crying as the wagon moved further along toward the castle. It was a slow and painful death. The guard's horse was nowhere to be seen.

"We cannot stop!" Dendroba yelled, hearing the screams behind them. "Anyone lost in the Bloodthorns is dead. We move forward."

They could hear Hansel and Gretel discussing matters of money with Dendroba, they were not paying any attention to the prisoners.

"Phillip!" said Snow White. "What are you doing?"

"Keep your voices down," he replied. "I've got a plan." The prince pulled

Rapunzel's knife from his boot, the one he had carefully tucked away as he climbed up the ravine. Then he shuffled over to Elizabeth and awkwardly cut through her rope bindings with his own bound hands. As soon as Elizabeth's hands were free, she went to help loosen Phillip's bindings, but he pulled away, slipping the knife back into his boot.

"Not enough time," he said. "Hurry! We could be out of the Bloodthorns any second. Elizabeth, you have to jump!"

"Phillip!" General White growled in a hushed yell. "What's going on?"

Phillip explained in hushed tones as quickly as he could. "Rapunzel's mother said the Bloodthorns won't touch her because she's a werewolf. It did not occur to me until I actually saw the Bloodthorns make a path. Elizabeth can escape and walk right out of here. We cannot. The guards are distracted; they're more worried about the thorns than us," Phillip said. "They have not noticed yet but they could any second. Elizabeth has to jump now!"

Snow White and Rapunzel looked at each other for a second, then at Dame Gothel.

The old witch affirmed the prince's plan. "It could work," she said. "The sun is getting low—it will be dusk soon."

Elizabeth had not expected any of this. "But what if it doesn't work?" she said, hesitantly crawling toward the open cage door.

"Prisoner of Queen Cinder or the Bloodthorns. You would be dead either way, my dear." Dame Gothel reminded her.

"But without Elizabeth's precious werewolf blood, there's no controlling the Bloodthorns. Which means we, along with Queen Cinder would be trapped!" General White began to understand Phillip's plan.

"What about the rest of you?" Elizabeth asked.

"We can't escape now. We would be dead for sure in these Bloodthorns. But you will be okay, Elizabeth. You need to jump—now, before anyone realizes what is going on. It's the only way...trust me," Prince Phillip pleaded. "We'll play prisoner for now. You go find Patience and those glass slippers."

Elizabeth nodded, though frightened at the prospect of it all. She looked at General White, who nodded her support. Elizabeth then turned and looked at the bramble that closed behind them. She closed her eyes and took a deep breath.

"Here goes," she muttered, and then jumped from the back of the moving wagon and into the path of the closing Bloodthorns.

Elizabeth hit ground and rolled, kicking up a dusty cloud. The wagon and its guards continued on their way.

Not one Bloodthorn touched her.

Cautiously, she got to her feet, turned, and saw the wagon and her friends in the cage disappear into the thick tangle of the Bloodthorns ahead.

For many years, Elizabeth hated, feared and resented her curse. As she reached out her hand, seeing the thorns retreat from her touch, she finally felt a sense of empowerment. She marveled as the Bloodthorns pulled back away from her at every step. As she started to walk back through them, the briar parting to give her a wide birth, she began to sing softly.

Queen Cinder, Queen Cinder, what did you lose?
Whatever happened to your glassy shoes?
You threw them down and they broke in twos
And soon we'll win and soon you'll lose!
Queen Cinder, Queen Cinder, What did you say?
Tell the servants to sweep them away!
But all of the servants have run away
And the shards of the glass slipper
will come back some day.
Queen Cinder, Queen Cinder, with the crown on your head
Soon we'll be free and you'll be dead!

For the first time Elizabeth could recall, she was looking forward to her transformation into a wolf tonight.

* * *

The wagon continued to move along as quickly as the reluctant Bloodthorns drew away from the road. More than once, General Dendroba, held out his magical gold sphere from atop the carriage, ducking reflexively as the withdrawing briar gave up its precious space. The deadly bramble, once waist level at the start, thickened and built up as it got closer to the castle and now towered above them like shallow canyon walls, closing quickly behind them in a tight, entangling mass.

211

Hansel drove the nervous horses forward in an uneasy trot, slouching down in his seat to avoid the looming briar as well.

Traveling like this took more time, and Gretel was frustrated that she was unable to gauge any real distance. At most, the Bloodthorns were half a mile thick, but to her it felt like they had traveled five times that distance.

Aside from the moaning and snapping as the Bloodthorns retreated, the nervous heavy trotting of the horses, and the wooden creaks in the wagon, the rest of the area was quiet and still. Not a single bird sang their song. No one dared make a noise, for fear of breaking Dendroba's concentration on the spell When Dendroba suddenly spoke, it startled Gretel and her brother.

"We need the horses to move faster," he announced grimly. "The magic will fade before we reach the other side."

Gretel gave Dendroba a nervous look. "I'd guess it's too late to turn back."

"There is no turning back. We have traveled in too far," Dendroba explained, as he had journeyed this route many times before. "I will use the last of the magic I have to force the path through, and then we only have until the Bloodthorns are able to close back. If we stay at this pace we won't make it."

Hansel gripped the reins tensely and then exhaled. "Alright, General. Ready when you are."

Gretel considered the options. "If you don't have enough magic now, we'll be trapped in the castle. That will cost you."

"That's what the queen needs the werewolf for," Dendroba answered, annoyed. "Tonight is the last night of a full moon, and it will be the last night she'll turn for another month. The werewolf's blood will be enough to get the Bloodthorns under control again. You can leave first thing in the morning. I'll happily hold the door for you to do so."

Gretel seethed at Dendroba, "If we are trapped in the castle, we'll be charging the throne a per diem."

"Gretel!" Hansel glared at his sister from the other side of Dendroba, who began working the magic from his golden orb. "Can we worry about that at some other point, please? Let's just get out of the frying pan and then we can deal with the fire."

Gretel instantly began a condescending reply. "It is better if it's agreed to ahead of—"

"Enough!" Dendroba bellowed angrily. "We do not have time for this."

Then with a loud yell, he shoved the small golden orb forward with his one hand and a large shockwave of energy boomed forth, pushing the Bloodthorns further to the sides of the path. A few hundred yards ahead, they saw a clearing and part of the castle wall.

"Go!" Dendroba bellowed at Hansel, and Hansel wasted no time. He snapped the reins and sent the horses into a frenzied gallop. It was an all-or-nothing, last-chance dash.

Dendroba yelled to those of his soldiers who remained, "Keep up with us or die in the Bloodthorns!"

As quickly as the path cleared, the Bloodthorns began to return to their impenetrable form. Brambles laced across the road in front of the wagon. There was still quite some distance to cover as the deadly bramble began to intertwine above them. Hansel focused on driving the horses as fast as they would go. He hoped that speed and momentum might help them avoid the deadly entanglement. Dendroba honestly did not know if they were close enough to castle to make it through.

The speeding wagon was still a hundred yards from the end of the magically created path as the Bloodthorns began to collapse around the far exit. There was a great lurch and a heavy cracking sound that rocked the wagon from underneath.

The wagon's right rear dropped with a jarring bounce, nearly rolling onto its side as the panicked horses dragged it along. Gretel was almost thrown from her seat. As she looked back, she could see the wagon's wheel and broken axle tightly wrapped with the Bloodthorns. They had become so caught up and entangled in bramble that the wheel was ripped from the undercarriage. Further back in the enclosing briar, she could hear screams from several of Dendroba's soldiers who could not keep up.

They were still fifty yards away from the clearing. The horses slowed from the dead weight of the wagon and soon began to whinny and became spooked as they pulled along. The bloodlusting bramble was taller and thicker now, scraping sharply at the draft horses' legs.

Dendroba and the others could see the wall of the castle clearly now. Only twenty yards to the clearing. The horses pulled on, kicking and bucking as the Bloodthorns threatened to wrap around their legs.

Another great lurch and a crashing drop came as the other rear wagon wheel broke off. It was all the prisoners could do to hold on to the cage bars tightly, so as to not fall out of the open door. The sound spooked the already frightened horses further, sending them pulling even harder.

With that last great effort, the wagon, its riders, and their prisoners, all battered and scraped, barely made the passage through the Bloodthorns. The deadly briar wall closed tightly behind the wagon, with no other rider emerging.

After a moment of stunned silence, Gretel turned toward Dendroba from the now lop-sided wagon seat.

"I expect you will pay for our wagon," she said sternly.

CHAPTER 17
FAE GAIA

"Run!"

General White's order still echoed in Patience's thoughts. She had quickly weighed the idea of hiding, but felt she would be found too easily. She committed to running, and she franticly scrambled to secure her backpack. She had the shards. She could not be caught like the others. If she were, there would be no more hope.

The sun was setting quickly now. The day turned into orange and red skies, and then dimmed to night as Patience ran. Dendroba's soldiers were persistent, and the lead Patience had gained was diminishing. Now it was getting harder. She could not see the forest path very well in the darkness. She could hear the soldiers close behind her, their heavy footsteps shuffling in the leaves of the forest floor. Her heart was pounding in her chest. Was that their heavy, rhythmic breathing or her own?

Patience managed to dodge a low branch, but in doing so, she was scraped in the face by another branch. She barely noticed the sting. When she ran to the left of a large tree, she heard her pursuers shout, "That way! She went left!"

Now Patience knew she would be captured if she stopped to hide. They were yelling at her, too. She blocked them out, trying to focus instead on her pounding heart. She knew they were not saying anything she wanted to hear.

Patience was scared, but she knew she had a few advantages. She had youth on her side, she was smaller, and she could navigate through the woods more quickly. Finally, she had several yards of distance on them—not enough to safely hide and lose them, but certainly more than an arm's length. She could not keep this pace up much longer though. Her hips burned and her legs felt like jelly.

She turned her head and looked back to see how much ground they had gained, and in doing so, did not see the stump that jutted out of the ground in the darkness. Blinding pain shot through her foot. Then with a grunt, Patience went down hard on the ground. Something sharp and hard scraped her hands. She tasted leaves, dirt, and blood. She lay there stunned for only a brief moment, despite the air knocked from her lungs, and then she was back up, scrambling to her feet, not registering the pain in her hand and foot. She hunched, ducking and darting though some brush, still too scared to stop and try to catch her breath. *Keep moving,* she thought. Her running was reduced to limping in long strides and she could feel warm, wet tears flowing down her face.

Patience heard leaves rustling behind her. The queen's guards were still hunting her. She ran more slowly this time and to her right, changing her direction once again. She was crying in earnest now as she began to feel the sharp pains from her fall. Maybe it would be better if she just hid somewhere. Maybe they wouldn't find her. Maybe she would be safe until the morning. Patience had no idea how long or how far she was chased and no concept of where she was. The only thing she knew was that she was scared, as she had never been before.

She heard the guards, but this time their cries were not vulgar, terrifying remarks of what they would do when they caught her. The queen's guards had slowed to look for her. They had lost sight of her when she fell!

Patience held her breath. Quickly, she scrambled behind the trunk of a large tree. Standing perfectly still, she tried to listen past her thumping heartbeat. The forest at night seemed especially dark and still now, though the breezes rustled the treetops above. As Patience focused, she heard the sounds of acorns occasionally falling through the leaves and branches like skipping stones and landing on the ground with a soft plop. Insects chirped, and owls quietly chortled as they watched the ground for prey.

For now, the guards were not chasing her, but they were still searching. As she stood there, Patience slowly realized something else. Careful not to make a sound or any sudden movement, she reached behind her and hefted the bottom of her backpack. It seemed unusually light; as her hand pushed the canvas easily. Something was not right. She knelt quickly where she stood and pulled the backpack off her shoulders. It came away too easily, like crumpled cloth.

The glass slippers! She thought. "No. No. No," she whispered quietly. Quickly, she untied the flap and shoved her hand into the opening. Empty.

No! The glass slippers were missing.

Frantically, she felt around the inside and then felt her fingers slip out of a frayed hole on the side. The pack had torn open. There was a long, ragged gash, and the pouch that held the glass slippers had fallen out.

The pouch was lying , somewhere on the forest floor, most likely where she had fallen. *Wherever that is*, she thought in despair. The forest was easily disorienting in the daytime, but far worse in the pitch of night. Patience felt her stomach drop, then tie itself into knots. Her eyes welled with tears once again. She had lost the shards. Even worse, the guards who were looking for her might discover them.

Then she heard the crunching of the leaves as men approached. More twigs snapped underfoot in the darkness. Patience drew a sharp breath. She had a heavy, unmistakable feeling that she was not alone. The sound of another twig snapping was very close, and Patience froze.

From behind the dark mass of a tree, a figure moved, jumping out almost in front of her. One of the queen's guards had found her.

"Over here!" the guard shouted loudly. He had almost walked right into her. Patience had not been paying attention, distracted by her loss of the shards.

"Hello, girly," the guard chuckled deeply. "You gave us quite a chase."

Patience was about to turn and run, but the guard grabbed her quickly by her arm.

Then from the corner of her eye, she saw the darkness move. Something big and silent was traveling quickly as it leaped onto the guard with a flash of white teeth and yellow eyes.

Patience barely managed to get out of the way as the darkness gave a primal growl, taking the startled guard to the ground.

It was a very large, black wolf. The guard's screams were gut wrenching. Patience scrambled to her feet and ran, praying the wolf would be too busy with the guard to give chase.

In a blind panic, she ran as fast she could, afraid that the wolf would be after her next. Hearing the grisly, muffled screams fading behind her, Patience was glad it was dark so that she did not have to see the effect of the attack.

The girl fled into the night, indifferent to the branches that slashed at her face and cut her arms and legs. She hopped over broken logs and rocks as best she could, aware of them only enough to avoid stumbling. Her legs burned with pain.

Her breathing was hard and shallow. Frightened and panicked, she did not even realize that the forest floor had dropped from beneath her feet, and she found herself tumbling in the darkness down a steep slope. Rolling uncontrollably through the leaves, she bounced painfully off several small tree trunks in the darkness. Branches and rocks jabbed at her sides as she continued to fall in the darkness. The ground seemed to open up as her momentum sent her tumbling off the bottom of the hill and into a tall thicket of reeds. Finally, Patience came to rest in the dank, leaf-covered mud that pooled up around her legs. She lay hidden among the tall reeds and stayed motionless out of fear, exhaustion and despair. Her eyes searched the hill, watching for any signs that she was followed by the guards or the wolf, but nothing moved except the wind in the trees. There was no other sound but her own breathing and the gentle rustle of the reeds.

Patience recalled what Goldenhair had said as she listened to the growing sound of the wind. *The winds of destinies press many a tree, a branch, and even a single leaf into action.* Strange, she thought, that she would remember that at such a time.

Patience continued to listen to the wind flow through the reeds, and it eventually calmed her. The girl stayed there listening and watching, for how long she did not know. The night had grown still. She was exhausted and the pain from her fall throbbed with a dull presence, but still she did not move from the reeds. Again, she allowed herself to cry. She had lost everyone. She had lost the glass slippers, and she had lost herself. She had failed General White, and everything the resistance had fought for.

She thought of Hamelin, who had been missing since the fight on the beach. What if Hamelin was dead? Her mouth quivered as she fought to control it. The tears were uncontrollable now. It was her fault that they were here in the first place. *If it was not for me,* she thought, *and my stupid idea to bring the glass slippers back, everyone would have been okay. Why did I do this?* She could not understand her own insistence on returning with the shards. Everyone had believed in her— Goldenhair, General White, even the prince. She shook her head as the tears burned her cold cheeks. Now she had let them all down. She deserved to lay here in the mud, she thought.

Eventually, Patience realized it was getting brighter. There was a light glowing nearby, casting long shadows in the reeds that swayed back and forth. She thought that it may have been the sun rising, but it was something different. A very soft light shone behind her, different from any torchlight or lantern she had ever seen. She did not get the feeling that this was a light held by anyone, or anything, looking for her. The light was something else. It was like moonlight, but warmer.

It had been a long time since Patience had seen the guards or the wolf, and she decided it was safe to move. She wanted to find out more about the light, and strangely, she was not afraid. Slowly, Patience crawled out of the mud. Her feet were frozen and her body was stiff, sore from the running and the fall, and aching, as if complaining about having to move again. Once through the reeds, she rose to her feet, brushed the leaves and dirt from her clothing, and looked for the source of the light.

Her surroundings seemed familiar. Then Patience realized that she *had* been here before. It looked different in the dark, but she had somehow stumbled back to the grave site of Cinderella's mother. Here was the pond, and the glowing light softly illuminated the willow tree from within its shroud of leaves. Despite her hardships, Patience could not help but laugh a little at the irony of coming full circle. Curious about the light, she began to limp slowly to the tree. She wondered if anyone else would see this light and come looking. As she drew closer, Patience had a strange feeling that, as bright as it seemed to her, somehow no one else would notice.

A warm inviting glow came from behind the curtain of willow leaves, the swaying branches caused shafts of light to dance beautifully about. Patience hesitated for a moment before she drew back the willow branches. Exhaling a deep breath as she prepared herself, she parted the branches and stepped inside.

It was far brighter here. Sparkles of light darted about, full of energy and warmth, as wisps of ethereal mist swirled. Instantly, Patience could feel the presence of what could only be called real magic.

Then she paused, seeing a figure enveloped in the light. It appeared to be a woman kneeling on one knee. Her head was down and her hair fell about her shoulders, concealing her face. A cloth wrapping, as from a burial shroud, covered her body.

Patience considered quietly stepping back, but then she heard a voice. It was warm and soothing, almost like a song, and somewhat motherly.

"Why are you sad, young Patience?"

The figure stood, tall and slender, and as she arched her shoulders backwards, a huge pair of translucent butterfly-like wings seemed to erupt from behind her. The wings were immense, quietly unfurling in a burst of sparkles and energy.

At first, Patience thought, that this was the God-mother fairy she had helped that night five years ago, the one that had lain dying from Cinderella's strike. Yet the figure that stood in front of her was much younger, she realized. But how?

"Are you Cinderella's fairy God-mother?" Patience asked. The mysterious glowing woman smelled like warmed hazelnuts.

The woman smiled with recognition. "In a way I am. I have those memories." Then she added, "And Ella was also my daughter. The fairy magic now inhabits the body that is buried here. You may call me Fae Gaia." The woman looked around the tree, familiarizing herself to the area. "The piece of the broken glass slipper you placed on the tree has brought me here."

I knew there was a piece missing, Patience thought. A wash of relief fell over her.

"The magic of the Fae coaxed you to this task of bringing the shards to this burial place." Fae Gaia walked over to Patience, and with the soft touch of her hand wiped the dirt and tears from the young girl's face. "You have been brave, little one. Do not cry."

Sadly, in an apologetic whisper, Patience said, "I'm sorry. I lost your glass slippers."

Again, Fae Gaia smiled reassuringly. "They are not lost, little one. It seems you have a friend who has brought them to us."

A look of confusion crossed the young girl's face. With a gesture, Fae Gaia parted the willow branches behind Patience, and to the young girl's surprise, a large black wolf walked slowly inside to join them. Frightened, Patience stepped backward, but Fae Gaia placed her hand on the girl's shoulder to calm her. The wolf carried a familiar rolled pouch in its mouth as it would its own cub. Gently, it placed the pouch at Patience's feet. They were the glass slipper shards. Then the wolf slowly backed up and stood there waiting. "Thank you for finding this for us, Elizabeth," said Fae Gaia.

"Elizabeth?" questioned Patience. "Why did you call it Elizabeth?"

"That is Elizabeth, your friend. She is a lycanthrope. During the week of a full moon, she takes on a wolf form at night," Fae Gaia explained calmly.

How did she know? Was that the magic of the fairies? Patience wondered, her thoughts dizzied from everything that had happened. She looked at the wolf again and the wolf looked at her, seeming to nod in confirmation. Finally, Patience understood.

It was Elizabeth who had attacked the guards to save her. With her keen sense of smell, the wolf had found the glass slippers where Patience had dropped them and tracked her to the willow tree.

"Thank you," she smiled at the wolf, extending her hand. The wolf cautiously leaned over and began licking her hand. Patience reached over to pet the soft, thick fur. Elizabeth was a werewolf. She wondered if Hamelin knew, and tried to imagine what his reaction would be when he found out. Poor Hamelin, thought Patience, remembering that she did not know if he was alive or dead.

Then, Fae Gaia swooned for a moment, throwing her hand out to catch herself against the trunk of the willow tree.

"The magic stored in the slippers is great. All of the magical energy that remained in the land was put into them when they were given to you, as well as the essence of the last God-mother fairy. Still, even working with the magic stored in the slippers, it will take some time for me to be at full strength." The Fae shook off the weak feeling. "There will be time to rest later."

As if she had heard the young girl's thoughts, Fae Gaia spoke. "It seems my summoning has come at a time of great sorrow and trouble," she said, perhaps sensing it from the very air. "While I recover my strength, young Patience, you must tell me all that has transpired. Then I shall take all of us to where we are needed most."

Fae Gaia paused to sense the night wind. When she spoke next, her voice was of crystal, yet her tone was of steel.

"What wickedness has befallen my daughter?"

CHAPTER 18
WITCH'S HONOR

The Marchenton castle had no dungeon. It was a surprise to Prince Phillip that he was about to be imprisoned in one. The prince could not help but look around at the deterioration of his beloved castle. The rooms and hallways he was familiar with as a child now sat in gross neglect.

What has happened since I left? How did it come to this? he wondered, as he was silently led with the others into the dungeon to be locked away.

How long until someone realized who he was? Did any of the staff recognize him? He could see the castle servants scurrying out of the way like frightened mice as the guards escorted their prisoners. If any of the servants did recognize him, he thought, would they even care at this point? The prince understood that most people in Marchenton thought he was dead and blamed him for abandoning the kingdom to pursue a costly crusade.

"Maybe the kingdom would be better off if I just rotted in the dungeon," he muttered quietly. Keeping his head low, he dared the occasional glance to see how far his beloved castle had fallen and soon recognized where the dungeon was.

"The wine cellar," Phillip said. His fellow prisoners did not acknowledge his observation. Defeat had begun to fester amongst the group. They wore it heavily like the shackles about their arms.

The huge alcoves of the castle's wine cellars had been converted into rather crude cells. Bars lined the arched openings. Each alcove was divided into two holding cells with a wall of bars separating each cell. The wine cellar was dimly lit by candles dripping from enormous wooden chandeliers that hung from the high vaulted ceiling of the hallway. They provided little light, keeping the recessed corners of the cells hidden in dark shadows. General White, the prince, and the others and were shoved roughly into one of the cell, the door locked solidly with a resounding metal clang.

"She converted the wine cellar into a dungeon?" was all the prince could say in hushed disbelief. "Did it have to be the royal wine cellar?"

"Welcome home," General White said with cool sarcasm.

"Same to you, dear sister," replied the prince, reminding Snow White of the lineage she sought to forget. General White was in too much pain, however, to continue the exchange. Instead, she leaned up against the cool rock wall and slid down onto the hay-strewn floor.

"What do we do now?" asked Rapunzel as she tested the thick solid bars and the crude metal chains and shackles restricting her arms. The prince slid down the wall, sitting next to his sister.

"Your wound is bleeding again," Phillip said quietly as he inspected her shoulder.

"Let it," she answered gruffly.

Sensing Snow to be in a foul mood, he changed the topic to something more optimistic. "The soldiers here seem to be sloppy when it comes to handling prisoners." He checked the small dagger he had managed to hide in his boot back at Hubbard's Ridge, the same one he had used to free Elizabeth. "This might be useful."

But Snow White's explanation rang with undeniable logic.

"The only reason they didn't bother to check us thoroughly is because they don't care. We are not going to be here long. They are probably preparing the gallows for us right now."

"All the better to fight then." Rapunzel grumbled as she paced, trying to keep her mind off Snow White's morbid observation and the claustrophobic similarities between the cell and the tower in which she had grown up. Then something outside the cell caught her eye.

"Hamelin?" Rapunzel asked with surprise.

The tall, lanky piper had been walking quickly down the main hall of the dungeon, putting his pipes away into his yellow and red patchwork coat. He stopped suddenly, surprised to see his friends.

"Hamelin!" Rapunzel whispered loudly as she rushed to the door. Hamelin turned to see them. Everyone looked up, happy to see the piper was still alive.

"What are you all doing here?" he asked excitedly.

Rapunzel replied quickly in hushed tones, "Hamelin, you have to find a way to get us out of here."

Hamelin paused suddenly. His demeanor stiffened; something was wrong. "I don't think that would be a good idea," he said in a dazed monotone voice.

Rapunzel looked at him. "What do you mean?" she asked flatly. She noticed that even though Hamelin had sounded happy to see them, his face was oddly unemotional.

"My queen would not approve," he said dully. Then quickly his tone was cheerful again. "She asked me to come down here and play music for one of our guests. I've been playing for a while until he fell asleep."

Dame Gothel had gotten to her feet and now stood by Rapunzel, studying Hamelin intensely.

"Daughter," she said, "he's under Cendrillon's spell."

"I'll go and tell my queen that you are down here. I am sure she would be happy to meet my friends finally. I've told her all about you." His tone was cheerful as he smiled, but there was dullness behind his eyes. Then he turned and disappeared into the shadows, heading toward the dungeon's exit.

Rapunzel was stunned.

"Told her all about us?" repeated General White. "That can't be good." She looked over at her brother. Until now, no one outside of this small group had known about his return. Concern grew at the thought of what might happen if or when Cendrillon found out about the prince.

Rapunzel rested her head on the bars and stared down at her feet. "Yeah," she mumbled with a disheartened sigh. "I'm sure the queen would love to meet us."

Gothel consoled her daughter by patting her softly on the shoulder as she turned to go sit back against the wall. They sat in silence for a while, deflated fully by their capture and despairing for their friend Hamelin.

"What guest was he talking about?" the prince asked, but before anyone could reply, the door opened. A group of soldiers stepped in front of the prisoners' cells, parting to reveal the unmistakable form of General Dendroba.

"Open it," he ordered sharply. The guard opened the cell door and several of his soldiers rushed inside, holding General White and the others at sword point. Suddenly, the reality of their situation became sharper as Dendroba stood there, watching his orders being executed.

Gothel quickly hid her face with the blanket, hoping Dendroba would not recognize her. It had been many years, and Dendroba was only a child when Gothel was in the coven, but she did not want to risk anything more. Dendroba took no notice of the old woman.

"Now that you have us trapped in your cell, are you going to finish us yourself, Dendroba, like killing fish in a barrel? I honestly thought you were a little better than that." Snow White struggled to her feet; she would stand before her enemy, rather than sit upon the floor, but a guard shoved her back down. Everyone shifted, bracing for the situation to turn to blows. General White started to stand again. The guards moved to again subdue her.

"Enough! Let her stand," Dendroba ordered in a deep voice. "I'm not here to execute anyone."

General White rose to her feet unsteadily and faced Dendroba through the bars. "Yet." She finished his sentence mockingly, adding with cold sarcasm, "The night's still young." Dendroba ignored her. With a quick wave of his hand, he gestured to another set of guards and they hurried into the cell. They brought buckets of water with drinking ladles, clean, fresh rags, warm, wrapped bread and fruits, and some blankets.

"Provisions to clean your wounds, and some food. I assure you none of the fruit is poisoned. The rest of the accommodations aren't much, I'm afraid."

General White was quiet. Her jaw clenched. She did not expect such a gesture from the leader of the queen's army, and did not want to trust it.

"Keep it," she growled. The soldiers retreated from the cell, locking the door again. But Snow White was alone in her defiance.

Tired and defeated, the others accepted the provisions. Rapunzel hesitantly took some of the fruit, sharing it with her mother. Then she handed the old woman a blanket to stave off the chill from the cold, wet stone floor. "Snow, let it go for now. Save it for another time," Phillip pleaded as he moved toward the water and took a sip from the ladle.

Dendroba ordered the soldiers to return to their posts. The disfigured general was about to turn and leave. He had done what he felt he should have, even if the queen's Maldame would not approve or if his prisoners did not appreciate it.

"What is the point, Dendroba? We will be executed regardless." Snow White's tone changed to a more civil discussion with an undercurrent of defeat in her voice.

"You've been a worthy opponent, Miss White. I would be remiss if I did not acknowledge you as such. So consider this a gesture of professional courtesy, general to general."

Snow White was humbled. For the past several years, she had considered Dendroba to be nothing more than a brutish commander, but she could recall many instances when she had been suitably impressed with his strategies and tactics when their forces had clashed.

"Thank you. That is kind of you, General," Snow White said, despite herself; and how sincere it really sounded had surprised her even more.

Dendroba paused. He had been trained since birth to rule as king, but never more did he feel like one then he did now. To rule his army of common grunts who only responded to fear and aggression, Dendroba had buried much of his leadership and diplomatic training—things he had enjoyed far more than barking orders. He had been far too complacent in playing up the monster in favor of the man. This one small gesture had been a rare opportunity to display his civility. He relished it, perhaps even more than his recipients did. White was someone he could actually relate to, someone he considered a peer, rather than the common soldiers who surrounded him on a daily basis. He would never admit this aloud, but secretly he longed to have someone he could converse with in common interest. If there were a way he could sit and just talk to the rebel general, he would welcome it.

"You are welcome," Dendroba replied. Then, abruptly and without another word, he left their holding cell.

"I thought we were dead," Rapunzel said, breathing a sigh of relief after Dendroba was out of earshot.

"We're not out of the woods yet," General White, reminded them. "Far from it," she added as she watched Dendroba leave the dungeon.

Phillip began to prepare strips of cloth to help Snow change the dressing from her arrow wound. He then took a moment to check his own wound. "Whatever Syrenka packed into this wound, it has healed remarkably fast," Phillip observed.

The old witch wrapped the blanket around her shoulders. She offered an apple to General White, who absently waved it away with her hand. "No, thank you, Dame Gothel," she replied.

"Take it, General. You need to eat something." And she placed it in Snow White's hand. Then a weak voice whispered from the shadows of an adjacent cell. A form shuffled in the darkness, his face hidden in shadow, covered by an old hooded cloak.

"Perhaps one could spare some fruit for a fellow prisoner?" the haggard voice strained. Everyone was startled by the presence of someone in the other cell; even Snow White looked over with surprise. The prince took notice as well, and he momentarily stopped redressing his wound with the water and cloth Dendroba had provided. General White tossed the apple to the prisoner in the adjoining cell.

"Have an apple," she said. The mysterious prisoner extended his hand and caught the apple, exposing his white furred paw. The stranger took the fruit with a gracious "thank you" and quickly devoured it in passionate bites.

"Any prisoner of the queen is our ally," replied Rapunzel, and offered the stranger some of the water Dendroba had given them.

"Your generosity is appreciated." With a furred hand, the stranger took the ladle, emptying it in a few desperate swallows. The hood of the cloak fell away as the stranger drank, revealing the form of a huge white rabbit, his furred face dirty and matted with dried blood.

This was quite an unusual sight for Rapunzel and the others. Their surprise at the stranger's appearance must have shown on their faces, as the rabbit immediately began to offer an introduction.

"I am liaison to the Sovereign Realm of Wonderland, imprisoned here despite diplomatic intentions. You may call me Rabbit, as I don't think anyone here will contest the fact."

Prince Phillip suddenly spoke up, his voice sincere and regal, "As a royal son of Marchenton, I apologize for the harsh treatment you have received. You've visited at...an awkward time."

"I fear it is too late for apologies, Son of Marchenton, from you or those responsible for such transgressions." Rabbit shifted around more, revealing the heavily bundled stump of a severed leg. "Son of Marchenton, some who sit on your throne felt it necessary to remove my foot, among other less graphic transgressions, as if they thought it would bring them better luck than it apparently was doing for me. I'm guessing by the fact that you are imprisoned down here, you are not in league with the present ruler."

"That would be a correct presumption, Rabbit."

"You are from Wonderland," repeated Dame Gothel. "So the portal has been opened? It is true? Cendrillon has succeeded."

"This Queen Cendrillon, your ruler? No. The portal had already been opened prior to her involvement. By a man named Jack. He used it to travel from Wonderland back to here. The portal use alone is a capital violation of a treaty that has long been upheld. Unfortunately, Cendrillon has further aggravated the problem. And, I will share with you that my queen, Alice, will be sending an army of soldiers to remove your queen and any other threat from this side of the portal."

"Jack's alive?" asked the prince in astonishment. He knew of only one person named Jack, and that was the only person he was hoping did not survive the war. "Beanstalk Jack? The farming lad—Spriggins?"

Rabbit nodded. "I believe so."

"Wonderland's army is invading?" General White interrupted.

"Yes, as an occupying force. I would offer you advice in appreciation for the courtesy you have shown. Should you escape this place, run. Get as far from your land as possible. I can tell you that your kingdom's forces are significantly outnumbered and inadequately equipped from what I have seen. Wonderland's army is a force to be reckoned with."

"Is there any way we can negotiate a truce, perhaps to call off the attack?" asked the prince.

"I am afraid it's not so simple." Rabbit paused. "Think of it as a game of chess. You play chess here, don't you? Most places do," Rabbit said, not waiting to hear a reply. "Once the pawns have moved, the battle is to be waged until there are only three options, a victory, a stalemate, or surrender. Against Wonderland's army, I would wager defeat or surrender are your only options, especially now that our queen is in play."

The moment was cut short by a loud noise from the hallway.

"We'll speak more, my friends," Rabbit said in hushed tones. Then, pulling his cloak about his head and shoulders, he shuffled back toward the shadows of his cell.

"I should cut off the other arm, the one that doesn't grow back, for your failure." The gravelly voice of the Maldame echoed down the hallway. "Gretel," she spat with contempt, "is demanding we let her and her brother Hansel leave. It seems when she found out we were no longer able to provide a path through the Bloodthorns, she was very," the Maldame paused to choose her words, "unruly. I really do not cherish the idea of being hostess to these witch hunters."

Dendroba had returned, this time followed by the Maldame. She turned to him, "but now we are all trapped here at the castle, and the Bloodthorns have outgrown our magic because you let the werewolf escape," the Maldame scolded, not caring who was listening.

"This situation has become intolerable. My stepdaughter's plan has been nothing but failure after failure. I will be taking matters into my own hands to get us back on track; even if that means removing that Cinderwench from the throne permanently. The coven did not waste years of effort to have control of the throne, only to be rendered trapped and useless by some bushes and this Wonderland nonsense. We are the ones who should be invading Wonderland, Dendroba."

General White and the others had overheard the conversation, including Rabbit. They glanced at each other with looks of concern. From the darkness, several other guards emerged, dragging Hansel and Gretel. Both were unconscious and severely beaten. The guards had not held back in trying to restrain the two mercenaries, even someone as large and muscular as Hansel. General Dendroba had accompanied the Maldame back into the dungeon. He gave a quick glance at General White in the cell.

The soldiers deposited the unconscious siblings in the cell across from White and the others.

"Frankly, I don't know why I bothered to keep them alive." She walked over to Dendroba. "Or why I should keep you alive." Then something caught the Maldame's attention and her smoldering anger paused.

"What's this?" she asked with deceptive pleasantry. "Since when do enemies of the queen get fruit?"

General Dendroba stood motionless, his jaw clenched in anger. It was true, prisoners intended to be executed were not allowed anything in the cell, and in every other instance it was a rule he abided by.

"Answer me, General. Since when do enemies of the throne deserve the queen's fruit? Did you order your men to do this?"

The Maldame fumed. Of course, there was no answer to her question.

Dendroba said nothing. He could barely remain still. He trembled with rage at the Maldame's constant baiting and humiliating remarks.

"I thought I had trained you better than this, Phyllo. Maybe you should go back to mucking stalls. You are dismissed, General. We'll talk about this when we meet with Cendrillon later," she said.

"As you wish, Maldame." Dendroba replied. Turning curtly, he quickly left the dungeon, loudly slamming the door shut in anger.

"Open the cell! Guards!" the Maldame barked again. The soldiers rushed in, swords pointed at the prisoners to keep them at bay. She pushed past Dendroba's huge frame and stepped inside.

The Maldame turned her attention to the prisoners. "I hope you've gotten your fill." She scooped up the bowl of fruit and handed it to a guard.

"And here's something to wash it down with!" She kicked over the two buckets and water washed across the cold stone floor beneath where the prisoners sat. One prisoner in particular piqued the Maldame's attention; huddling next to Rapunzel, with a blanket covering the face. As the water rushed against her legs, the prisoner shuffled, and the blanket fell away. She was trying to avoid being recognized by the Maldame, but it was too late.

"Gothel," the Maldame hissed with smug satisfaction in her discovery. "It seems exile has not been kind to you."

"What you called exile, Maldame, I called retirement," Dame Gothel quipped back defiantly. "It seems that royal gowns don't wear well on a witch."

Maldame smiled. "My most trusted sister of the coven, how far you have fallen, joining the very rabble you sought to rule. We should have killed you."

"Leave her alone," Rapunzel growled at the Maldame, straining against the guard's sword point. It was a futile show of bravado by the young lieutenant. "She's just an old woman now."

The Maldame turned to Rapunzel, bending down to more closely savor the simmering glare from her prisoner.

"Old woman? Is that how you refer to your own mother? But then, she's not really your mother, is she?" the Maldame said coolly. "Don't think we didn't keep tabs on her in her retirement, child."

Rapunzel's fiery stare remained unwavering. "Just leave her alone," she repeated.

"You do not tell me what to do!" the Maldame replied with sudden fury. "Didn't your mother teach you any manners?" Then with lightning-fast speed and surprising strength the Maldame backhanded Rapunzel across her face, sending her sprawling to the ground. The Maldame's fingernails had drawn streaks of blood across Rapunzel's cheek. "I have no reason to keep you alive, child." The Maldame took a menacing step toward Rapunzel.

The guards kept everyone in the cell at sword point; stealthily, Phillip tried to reach the small knife in his boot. He stared at General White to draw her attention to what he was doing, but when Snow White glanced back she shook her head. Not the time, she seemed to say.

"Wait!" Dame Gothel called out. She knew more than anyone how malevolent the Maldame could be. "Your issue is with me, not the girl. Let us make amends my coven sister. I can take you to the Looking Glass."

Snow White felt her stomach drop. "No," she whispered in shock. "Please don't do this," she spoke under her breath. Snow White stared at Dame Gothel, pleading silently with her eyes, but Gothel would not acknowledge her gaze. General White felt a hot fire flash across the back of her neck as she listened to Dame Gothel's betrayal. no one noticed the rabbit in the other cell was paying attention as well.

"If you want Wonderland's Looking Glass, I can show you where it is. But if there is any shred of regard for our history Mal, please do not harm the girl." Fear for Rapunzel's safety showed through the wrinkles of the old witch's face.

Maldame thought for a moment. "Very well, Gothel," she said with a pause. "If you want to play that card, fine. Your child will not be harmed."

Maldame's posture eased. "Witch's honor," she promised. "But you will tell me where the Looking Glass is, and if it's not there...she dies."

"Traitor!" General White hissed at Dame Gothel, unable to control herself.

Rapunzel shook her head at her, "Don't tell her. No!" Tears ran down her cheeks, mixing with the blood from her cut.

Dame Gothel turned her grey, tear filled eyes to Rapunzel. Then, she looked away. "The Looking Glass is buried in the hay of the barn floor of the farm house your troops attacked, southwest of Hubbard's Ridge." In a moment, the Maldame's stance stiffened, her eyes focused with resolve. Then with an unusual quickness, she pulled a small dagger from the folds of her gown. There was a flash of metal as she plunged the blade deep into Dame Gothel's chest.

"Mother!" Rapunzel screamed.

Dame Gothel tried to speak, her mouth agape, twisted in pain and surprise. She had tensed forward as the blade pierced her heart. Her eyes glanced over at Rapunzel again, then slowly dulled and fixated into space. Her body went limp against the wall as she exhaled slightly, one last time.

The Maldame stood up, pulling the dagger from the body.

"Consider the hatchet buried, dear sister."

Rapunzel lunged at the Maldame only to be overpowered by the guards, who held her firmly before she could even get close her mother's murderer.

"You're all considered outlaws to the throne, an offense punishable by execution," said the Maldame. "Something that I will be looking forward to."

Then she turned to the guards, "Get that garbage out of my dungeon before it stinks up the place any more than it already smells. Do not bother with a grave and do not waste the lime. Toss the body off the ramparts and let the Bloodthorns feed."

Rapunzel and the others were restrained as two more guards entered and dragged the body of Dame Gothel out of the cell. The only thing left behind was the worn, thin blanket she had used to cover herself.

Then the Maldame and her guards left the prisoners in their dungeon cell as Rapunzel's cries echoed through the stone corridors.

CHAPTER 19
TO MEET A PRINCE

The night air was warm with a cool breeze that tickled the torch flames on queen Cendrillon's balcony. The queen had stood at the balcony's rail for most of the evening, and the night's breezes were beginning to chill her skin. She found herself staring at the hundreds of small enemy campfires that dotted the distant horizon, wondering if she had made the same mistakes she did when she first assumed the throne. Her plans were crumbling again. The campfires belonged to another invading army, which again she was almost powerless to stop—an army so powerful that it did not bother to hide their position.

In her hand, Cendrillon held the inert wand of her Fairy Godmother, turning it over absently and rubbing her fingers along the smooth and worn surface. There was very little magic left in it. This was the wand Cendrillon had planned to recharge in Wonderland and she had selfishly kept it hidden; using it sporadically on her own spells. Over time, its powers had all but run out. Now it was her last vessel of magic. It likely had only enough power left, to kill one person. The prince, perhaps? Or herself, Cendrillon thought.

Since the night she had murdered the fairy, magic had been in steady decline. *My fault*, her guilt told her. *Too greedy*, she admitted to herself. The Fairy God-mothers were the land's source for magic, and she had murdered the last one of them. Now her ambitions were trapped behind the very Bloodthorns she had commanded to protect her, leaving her a prisoner in her own castle. Queen Cendrillon no longer had enough magic to control them, and because her only chance to regain control had been with the werewolf's blood, that was lost as well.

Now Queen Cendrillon could not even get to the very portal she had searched for in an effort to regain more magic. Had she left even one day earlier things would have been different. Cendrillon knew her kingdom was powerless to

233

defend against the invading army. What soldiers that remained were either trapped here in the castle or scattered about the kingdom. Her army was now just shattered remnants of what it was after the last skirmish on the beach, an ill-timed and costly error. Again, too greedy, she thought.

"All of it, my fault." The queen spoke aloud to no one as she gazed out across the night. These days she was not above bouts of frustration and extended fits of dark depression.

Tonight. the Maldame and General Dendroba would be meeting with her to discuss their next course of action. When the Maldame mentioned that she had recognized the prince who was in the cell among the other rebel prisoners, Cendrillon commanded a private meeting with him. She could not decide what kind of meeting would be though. Would she meet him as queen? Or as a wife? For the first time in many years, Cendrillon felt conflicted, and because of that, she began to resent him; more now that she was about to see him again, than she had over these past years There was resentment for when he distanced himself when his mother had died, resentment for leaving her alone to go start a war, and thinking for years he was dead, and resentment for marrying her so quickly, that she questioned if he ever fully loved her.

Any moment the door to her chamber would open, and her prince would come back into her life. A decade ago, Cinderella's new world was crushed, taking her prince away to a war that did more harm to the kingdom than good—a prince that Cendrillon had never really loved. Of course, she loved what he could give her—the royal galas. After all, she had just become a princess and had been handed a new life of royalty after living one of squalor and servitude. It was very easy to be taken in by such a life. Yet, in the months after the wedding, it had become apparent that the prince and princess had run out of things to talk about. The illusions of that fateful night they had met had dissipated, and when the fairy dust had settled, Cinderella and the prince had very little in common. No, she thought, she did not really love him. She could finally admit that to herself, after everything that had transpired. Maybe it had been her affair with Jack that had told her that, but at the time she did not know to listen.

Her thoughts began to focus more on the faults of Prince Phillip. It had been his royal gala; it was he who approached her to dance that night, who searched all over the kingdom to find her matching glass slipper. It was the Prince of

Marchenton who asked her to marry him. How could one say no to an offer of marriage into royalty, especially if the only other option was cleaning ash out of the fireplace? It was his fault. He raised an army and led the crusade against the giants, leaving her in charge of the kingdom. It was his fault he never returned until now. The most infuriating part of it all, she thought to herself, was that upon his return he would still only know of her as his princess, and not appreciate all that she had done while he was away (and what she had to become to do it). All of *this* was because of *him*.

Cendrillon heard a knock at her chamber door. Quickly, she placed the wand on a small table on the balcony. Her hand then brushed lightly across her leg as she adjusted the fold of her dress and checked the concealed, slender dagger secured with her garter.

She closed her eyes for a moment, feeling the night's chilled breeze on her skin and took a deep breath. *His fault*, Cendrillon thought, *not mine*.

"Enter," she commanded. Three guards entered the queen's chambers escorting the prince gruffly. He offered no resistance. Though his hands were shackled, he stood confidently.

"My queen?" one guard asked humbly, presenting the prisoner.

"Remove the bindings and wait outside in the hall. No one enters," Cendrillon ordered.

One of the guards spoke. "Is that wise, my queen? The Maldame's standing orders, given the incident with the rabbit—"

"You dare question me?" Cendrillon yelled. "I am queen, not her!"

The guards unshackled the prince as ordered and then quickly left Queen Cendrillon's private chambers.

The room itself was immense. The two stood in the sitting area with carved arched alcoves and wall hangings. Directly behind them were a set of tall glass doors that opened to a huge balcony. Next to the sitting area was a large, marble tiled area covered with an ornately detailed rug. Several small steps led up to another section of the room where the queen's opulent master bed sat, surrounded by finely crafted tables, sitting chairs and armoires. There was a whole section above them accessible by a formal staircase that lead to the queen's dressing area with mirrors and closets and sitting tables. On that level was the royal bath. Prince Phillip had been here before. This was his mother's room.

There was a long pause as the prince and former princess sized each other up—the couple that had been hailed by commoner and royal alike as the embodiment of "Happily Ever After." Now the two stood and faced each other. For the moment, neither stood as prince or queen, but two ordinary people in a broken relationship and an awkward meeting.

For Prince Phillip, this was an opportunity he had been hoping for, a chance to talk face to face with his former wife. Or, was she his wife still? There was little precedent for circumstances like this, he realized. Perhaps he could talk to her in a manner that might make sense, make her understand. He still refused to believe this was his same Cinderella who now stood before him wearing a tight black dress that revealed her shapely bosom, turned from innocent housemaid to a seductive, evil witch queen. "Queen Cinder, Queen Cinder…" The song he heard Rapunzel and the others sing echoed in his mind. A silent moment turned into an uncomfortable pause.

"Pumpkin—" Phillip started to say, using the pet name he gave her after their marriage.

Cendrillon cut him off almost immediately. "Don't be stupid, Phillip," she snapped. "I am not your little princess anymore."

"Ella, I—"

"Address me as Cendrillon," she demanded, "Queen. For that is who I am now. This is what you have made me."

The prince was taken aback. "*I* made you?"

"You left, off on your silly crusade against the giants. You left me alone to run the kingdom. Everyone thought—I thought you were dead. Your army was missing and an invasion from the giants was sure to happen any day. That was the fear you left behind in the kingdom. The beanstalk would come back any day and rip our world asunder, again."

"But Ella—Cendrillon, I am back," answered the prince trying to remain positive. "And I am alive! I thought you'd be happy at least for that." A flicker of disappointment crossed his face for a moment when his wife remained silent.

Cendrillon demeanor softened. "A part of me is, Phillip. And the rest of me now hates that one little part. You have been dead to me for ten years. Still, meeting with you here, like this, is not something I would do with anyone else, if that is any consolation to you. But—" she added quickly, "this will be our last meeting." Cendrillon had allowed herself this one last moment of compassion. "I wanted to see you once more, for closure sake." She turned away from him, finding she was unable to look at him anymore. Then she took a deep breath and gathered her resolve. "I will have to regard you as an enemy of the throne after this," said Cendrillon solemnly.

In that moment, while Cendrillon looked away, Phillip quickly ducked down. He reached into his boot and palmed the dagger, slipping it to a more accessible location.

"Ella," pleaded the prince. He stepped close to her now. "Please, there has to be another way." He was behind her now. She could feel his presence.

"The Maldame, the other witches of the coven, there are things in motion that cannot be undone," Cendrillon replied. She turned and faced the prince. There was a moment's pause as their eyes locked in close proximity.

Phillip folded his arms around and embraced her softly, taking a moment to feel her silky, blonde hair and the faint smell of her perfume. Cendrillon's head leaned against his chest in a comfortable way, almost as a memory of the first time they had danced at the gala many years before. Phillip closed his eyes, feeling the queen's body relax, if only slightly.

"We can work this out together," he said, whispering to her. Slowly he began to reach back around, pulling the knife from its hiding place. He could feel the queen shift slightly in his arms. There was not much time, he decided, resolving to commit to his plan. *Make it quick for her at least,* he thought.

"I've made a mess of things as queen," Cendrillon admitted, putting the prince even more off guard as she looked down at the floor, her soft blonde hair falling around her and hiding her face.

"I'm sorry," he started to say. Then there was a sudden, burning pain in Phillip's gut.

"Me, too," Cendrillon answered in a sudden change of cold absolution. She had driven her own dagger quickly into his abdomen, he realized, as Phillip felt the unnatural metal in his stomach, Cendrillon had stabbed him, just a moment quicker than he could do the same to her. The pain was spreading out like the blood from his wound. Phillip pulled himself back off the dagger's blade. He looked at Cendrillon with her sternly clenched fist holding the dagger firmly, her hand covered in his glistening, dark blood. Phillip shook his head in horrid disbelief. His own knife, which he had grabbed a moment before their embrace, now fell to the floor with a weak clanging sound. Looking down at his blood soaked shirt, he absently moved away from her, stumbling toward the open balcony door in some subconscious effort to get away. Phillip tried to speak. He took another step back, but his legs went weak and he staggered backwards, finding himself stumbling outside against the balcony rail. He tried to prop himself up. Then his strength gave out and he slid down onto the balcony floor.

"Wh-why?" he struggled to say as he covered his wound with his hand in a futile attempt to stop the bleeding.

"Don't play dumb, Phillip. At least go out with some dignity." She kicked his dagger away from him as she strode over. "You were going to try to kill me."

She stood over the wounded prince. "You still do not understand. I am not the same prim and proper princess, Phillip. You are the last part of a life that no longer exists for me. I cannot afford any compromising reminders. And yet you look so surprised."

Prince Phillip had closed his eyes. His breathing labored as he struggled to speak above the pain of his deep wound. "—doesn't have to be this way. Ella, I always loved you," he said weakly.

"I guess you never will understand. I loved you too, in a different life. Just not in this one. For ten years, I thought you were dead. So really this is not too much of a stretch." She waved her bloodied dagger at him. "Goodbye, my charming prince." Using his tunic to wipe the blood from the dagger, she placed a kiss on his cold forehead as she tucked the blade back into her garter and left him to die. Queen Cendrillon turned away and headed over to the table to retrieve her wand, ignoring the silent, lonely tear that trickled down her face. She did not immediately notice that the balcony began to glow a little brighter than the normal surrounding torchlight.

* * *

The majordomo of the castle had always maintained for these past five years, that no matter what happens, the servant staff still go about their daily duties—not only to honor their station but to uphold the ideals of the kingdom(and not necessarily who is on the throne). This also furthered the purpose for the staff. They felt what they were doing had a greater meaning. He also knew also that with purpose was hope, but there was another purpose and a far greater hope. It was organized by the elderly majordomo in secret, a task that rallied the servants to maintain their daily duties so as to avoid notice of anything suspicious; even if it meant setting the dinner table for the queen every night, though she never came.

While the servants went about their castle chores, they had also organized secret meetings and a plan of escape from the castle. The great wall of Bloodthorns rose up almost five years ago and shortly after that, it was apparent that the castle staff would be trapped. After three years now, their plan was finally near completion. They had dug a small tunnel under the castle and beyond the Bloodthorn Wall. The tunnel was not much, no bigger than a large crawlway, and it was kept well hidden in a section of the castle's foundation where neither the queen nor her guards had any chance of finding it. It was near a breach in the catacombs, deep beneath the castle where an underground river broke through. The servants had used the river for disposing of garbage. They also used it as a guide for where they would dig the tunnel.

There had been quiet murmurs that tonight they would finally break through far enough to clear the Bloodthorn Wall. Freedom was at hand.

But for now, ritual airs were to be maintained and cold, royal dinners needed to be cleared from the table—tonight's duty for one of the housemaids. It was hard for the housemaid to maintain her diligence when the prospect of freedom was close tonight. As she cleared the fine tableware, there was a bounce in her step and a quiet whistle as she carried the cold food back to the kitchen.

Catherine Brown's hair had fallen from its bun and she let it dangle. Tonight she was going to be part of the group that would be digging the last section of the tunnel. It was the first time in five years that she had known even a little happiness. Tonight, freedom would be realized. Catherine cleared the last bit of silver and china from the table and turned to leave when a voice froze her in her tracks. It was not the first time she had imagined hearing that voice. Catherine Brown knew that every time she would look, thinking she heard the voice, her heart would break again with disappointment. Therefore, this time when she heard the voice, she did not turn around immediately. That was the past, she thought. *Tonight I am headed toward the future,* Catherine reminded herself, trying to bury the painful memories of losing not only her beloved husband but her child as well. She continued to step toward the door. The voice spoke again.

"Mother?"

This time it sounded more real than she had ever before imagined. Catherine Brown turned to look, steeling herself for the usual disappointment. She stood silent for a moment, not believing who was standing there before her. A child stood in the doorway. Her child—and almost exactly where she had last seen her five years ago.

She dropped the plates in a loud shattering crash.

"Patience!" without hesitation, Catherine Brown rushed to hug her long missing daughter. Patience ran to meet her and hugged her tightly, tears flowing from both mother and daughter.

I thought you were dead, Pai," cried Patience's mother. "I thought I'd never see you again." Patience hugged her even tighter, saying, "Oh, I've missed you."

Her mother then looked at her from arm's length, wiping the steady stream of tears excitedly from her cheeks. "How did you get back in here?" she asked, suddenly. "Was the tunnel completed ahead of schedule?"

"Tunnel?" Patience replied with confusion. Then a smile broke across the young girl's face. "Not through a tunnel," the girl laughed. "A God-mother fairy brought me here. She is going to help us, all of us. I will explain later. Oh Mother, I have missed you. So much has happened, but I need your help first."

* * *

Rapunzel sat upon the floor of the cell holding the blanket. "For all those years I hated what she did to me growing up. I cursed her name every night; I wished she were dead. I vowed never to see her again. But I broke that vow for you Snow; she was the only witch that stood a chance to help the resistance. At least reconnecting gave us a chance to reconcile some things. She's dead because of me."

General White shook her head. "Not because of you. The Maldame killed her after your mother told her where the Looking Glass was."

"She was trying to protect me. Not everyone gets to be a long lost princess you know, with royal family reunions of long lost princes." Rapunzel glared at General White. "Some of us just have a tower in the woods and our mother. Now even that is taken from me."

"You are right, Rapunzel," Snow White said. "I'm sorry. You have been a good friend, and you deserve more. I was not around when my mother died. And

I never even had the kind of relationship that you had the chance to have since you reconnected with your mother. You broke your vow to never speak to her again for me and our cause. I am truly grateful and deeply sorry. Now, I will lose the only part of my family I have left also. If we cannot get out of here, Cendrillon is going to kill him. He went anyway. He knew she would try to kill him."

Snow White dug at the floor of the cell with the heel of her boot. She focused on that for a moment, trying to kick away at thoughts that made her lips quiver with sadness. It was either that or give in to the tears. However, as a leader, she refused to show such weak emotions, even now when she did not feel like a leader at all. "And if we don't get out of here, everything we fought for these past years is for naught. Cendrillon wins."

She could hear Gretel and Hansel in the other cell across the way. Gretel had given up yelling for the guards, with Rapunzel yelling equally as loud for them to shut up.

"Steel yourself, Rapunzel," Snow White ordered. "We need to be focused on the immediate situation. I am sorry about your mother, 'Punzel. You know I am. She was very helpful to the cause, but I need you with me, lieutenant—we need to figure out how to get out of here. Perhaps if we called for the guards to remove the blood, we can overpower—"

Then a solemn voice spoke quietly from the cell next to her. It was the rabbit.

"Pardon me, but I could not but overhear about the Looking Glass. Were you to tell me about it, I would be greatly interested in its whereabouts."

General White barely acknowledged the White Rabbit. "I'm not sure I can do that right now," she said.

"You weren't able to overpower the guards with swords pointed at your chests the last two times; and there were more of you then. I might be able to leverage more time against my people's invasion if I can return the Looking Glass to them. Is that worth something to you?"

Snow White looked at Rabbit, deliberating for a moment. "You have a point. I suppose we have no reason to hold on to it, then. However, since both you and I are locked up here, what difference does it make?"

Rabbit replied confidently, "I would just need to collect my possessions from the guards. I can take care of the rest, I assure you."

"Well, when that happens," replied Snow White, "I'll let you know. In the meantime, we are both stuck here. The Looking Glass and your possessions might as well be a million miles away as long as we're in these cells."

Rabbit thought for a moment. "I will make you a deal. You are a general? The other large man referred to you as such."

Snow White sighed. "Yes, I am a general. The army I command is far outside this cell, however."

"Even still," Rabbit continued, "you may find what I have to tell you as useful in your line of work. All I ask for is that you tell me the location of the Looking Glass in exchange."

"How about I hear what you're offering, and how you think you can escape," replied General White. "Then I'll decide."

"I would tell you about Wonderland's army. This is not so much a leak of privileged information, than an up-front attempt to dissuade and deter greater conflict. I would imagine from your perspective this information is, well, you may do with it what you wish."

"You're going to tell me about your army in exchange for the location of the Looking Glass now?"

"Yes."

General White thought a moment, looking at Rapunzel who, with a nod, gave her approval. "What have we got to lose?" Rapunzel mouthed silently.

"Well then, it's a deal, Rabbit. Tell me about Wonderland's army."

The Rabbit settled in a bit as he began to explain. It almost sounded like bragging. As she listened, she realized Wonderland's army was vastly different from her army, or even the queen's royal army.

"Are you familiar with a typical deck of cards?" Rabbit started. General White nodded, "Cards like playing cards? For poker?"

"Wonderland's army is structured like that. There are four divisions—hearts, clubs, spades, and diamonds. Each division has its own purpose on the battlefield, and each division has sub-ranks within."

"Go on," said General White, now more interested.

"The hearts are typically general infantry; they are the grunts, while the clubs division specializes in siege and heavy artillery."

"Did you say heavy artillery?" General White interjected.

"Yes. It's quite an impressive sight on the battlefield, I must say." Rabbit continued, "Spades divisions typically are archers, pikemen, and spearmen. And diamonds are aerial support."

"Aerial, as in flying?" Rapunzel questioned.

"Yes, mostly gryphons and great crows." The rabbit paused, unsettled. "And other things I won't mention—stuff of nightmares. I hope it doesn't come to that." Rabbit regained his composure after a shudder and went on to describe the sub-ranks.

General White and Rapunzel exchanged concerned looks. Perhaps Rabbit was right, they thought. General White's dwarven army could not defeat Wonderland on the battlefield.

"The sub-ranks are basically the same throughout. For example, in the hearts divisions, ranks two through five are the lower level grunts—swords, light armor, axes, and shields. The stronger, more powerful weapons and armor are for ranks six through ten. That's where you'll find the heavy cavalry, hearts six through ten."

"Heavy cavalry?" General White repeated, her mind swimming with visions of the Wonderland army the White Rabbit was describing.

Then each division has its knaves, specialized for each of their divisions, of course—non-combat support, medical, servants, smithies and the like. Then the upper command ranks viceroys or kings."

"What about queens?" asked Rapunzel. "Don't decks of cards have queens?"

"There is only one queen of Wonderland now. That's Alice," corrected Rabbit.

"And aces?" the General asked. "What are those?"

"Well, I can't really get into that," Rabbit started.

"Then no deal," said Snow White abruptly. "Either tell us all of what you offered, or you get nothing from us."

Rabbit considered the situation for a moment. "Very well," he said. "An ace isn't so much a ranking as it is its own division. There are four aces in Wonderland——unique individuals, special privileged operatives, reporting directly to the queen," explained the rabbit. "I am one of them. There is another called Hatter. And another called Cheshire."

"And the fourth?" pressed Rapunzel.

"——had been a very wise advisor to the throne, the Caterpillar," said the rabbit, hiding his true distain of the fourth ace.

"Was it an actual caterpillar, like you are a rabbit?" Rapunzel inquired.

"Yes, but nothing in Wonderland is as it seems, my dear—except death, I'm afraid. Our mutual friend Jack was going to become the next ace to the queen. She fancied Jack since he was a stranger to the world, an offlander as she had been. Then things got problematic and, well," Rabbit outstretched his arms, "now here we are." The White Rabbit forced a smile. "Is this information worth the Looking Glass to you?"

"Why would you share such tactical information?" asked General White with suspicion. "How do I know you're not lying?"

"To begin with," explained the rabbit, "You will not be able to defend against our army. That is a fact you must face, I am afraid. The knowledge will not affect the outcome of the battle. But hopefully, sharing the knowledge might convince you not to be so foolish as to meet us in battle in the first place. In that regard, sharing the knowledge in hope of avoiding pointless war is to everyone's advantage. As for trust, everything I have just told you is true, including the part about your inability to stand against our army. Why would I lie? The real matter of trust here resides on whether I can trust you to tell me the actual location of the Looking Glass. As you are a general, my trust resides in the understanding that such tactical information is enough for a general to do the honorable thing."

"How many in your army, Rabbit?" asked General White. "That is information that is worth something to me."

"Which division?" Rabbit replied.

"All of them."

The rabbit paused and thought a moment. "I would guess over ten thousand."

Just then, there was a slight commotion out of sight of the prisoners, toward the cellar's doorway entrance and further up the hall. Though no one could see what was happening, it was loud enough to give Rabbit a sudden jump.

"Quickly then. I've held up my end of the bargain. Tell me what the old woman said before she died. Tell me the location of the Looking Glass!"

"Wait a moment," said Snow White. "I think there's something going on." She nodded in the direction of the guarded door.

"No visitors!" the guard barked.

"But we're not visiting. We're just delivering the evening meal to the prisoners."

Another female voice, this one older than the first voice, spoke up. "I understand your confusion. We do not have prisoners in the dungeons very often these days, but I assure you, this is proper procedure direct from the queen. If you want some you can try some," the voice offered.

Then there was a yell from the guard followed by a large growl and a quick metallic bang.

General White stood up quickly and rushed over to the bars along with Rapunzel, trying to see what was happening down the hallway. They heard the jingle of keys approaching in the darkness.

"What's going on?" Gretel said in a loud whisper.

"Shut up!" Rapunzel whispered back.

Then Patience was at the cell door, hastily fumbling with the keys to unlock it.

"Patience!" both General White and Rapunzel yelled in unison.

"I have to get you out of here, and we have to hurry. She has a plan," the young girl said quickly and somewhat out of breath. "General White, this is my mother." Patience added the introduction quickly, and the two of them exchanged quick nods of acknowledgement.

With a click, the heavy cell door swung wide open. Rapunzel bent to hug Patience.

"Thank you, Patience," she whispered with relief. "But how did you get here?"

"Who has a plan?" General White asked, stepping into the dungeon hallway.

"Fae Gaia, the God-mother fairy," replied Patience, answering both questions. "She has returned to save us."

She stepped back to reveal a large black wolf standing quietly behind her. Patience said proudly, "And this is Elizabeth. She's a werewolf."

* * *

Rapidly, a bluish white light grew increasingly brighter behind Cendrillon. The stark shadows of rock and ivy grew and slid along the wall, following the silent movement of the bright light. Cendrillon finally noticed, and then turned to see where the strange light was coming from. Her private chambers were on one of the highest balconies of the west tower of the castle. No one could approach from outside—it was impossible to climb. Cendrillon turned and froze in her tracks at the light that was before her.

"Daughter Ella—you have disappointed us," said a stern female voice from the light. The light floated high above the balcony; it dimmed suddenly to a soft pulsing glow, revealing the form of Fae Gaia, God-mother of the Fairies. Cendrillon did not expect to see a God-mother fairy. She had killed the last one of them over five years ago with her broken glass slipper. But that was not what truly surprised the queen. The God-mother fairy that was floating down to the balcony was someone she recognized from her childhood. It shocked her to her core. Cendrillon spoke a word she had not said in over thirty years.

"Mother?"

As impossible as it seemed, her own mother floating in the air before her was a God-mother fairy. Her mother had died when Cinderella was only ten years old, but she recognized her face and her voice instantly. Her mother had been the only resounding positive force of kindness in her life. Though taken from her early, Cinderella's mother had been an influence that helped her through many years of abuse growing up with her stepmother and stepsisters.

Fae Gaia stood on the balcony with a faint glow and sparkles showering her body. Her huge fairy wings spread out behind her.

The hard armor breastplate the Fae Gaia wore and the long katana-like sword she held was a reminder that this would not be just a friendly reunion. She moved with a silent, elegant grace as she bent down to briefly inspect the slumped body of Prince Phillip, touching him gently with a small flash of glittering light. Then the God-mother fairy rose and leveled her smoldering gaze at Cinderella.

"Prince Phillip still lives," spoke Fae Gaia. "For that you are lucky. I will heal him."

"This is impossible," Cendrillon said in disbelief. "You died. Father buried you beneath the hazelnut tree. I saw it."

"Impossible only exists for the fool," replied Fae Gaia. "The magic of the Fae, stored in the remnants of your glass slippers, have summoned me. I have returned, as both your mother and the new God-mother of the Fae. The Fae are angered by what you have done. You have squandered the responsibility you were given, and now you intend to throw everything to destruction. As your mother,

Cinderella," the God-mother fairy paused, "I am very disappointed."

"Mother—I am so sorry." Standing in the presence of the towering Fae, staring into the stern gaze of her own mother, Cendrillon was overwhelmed. She was no longer a queen but a scolded child, hanging her head in shame.

"It is too late for apologies," Fae Gaia chided, drawing her long, thin sword up toward the queen. An ethereal mist rolled off the blade in evaporating licks. Cendrillon threw a quick look to the table on the balcony and saw the Fae Gaia's old wand, which she had placed there moments before. She spread out her arms and began slowly circling around to the table.

"Mother, please," Cendrillon begged with convincing deception, stalling as she moved closer to the table. The Fae Gaia followed her intently with the point of her sword.

"I've missed you," said Cendrillon. "After your death, times were hard. It was all Father could do to raise a child and deal with the loss of his wife." She inched closer now, the Fae Gaia still unsuspecting. "I've done the best I could growing up, with the responsibilities that were thrown at me. It was too much. I was so young."

Cendrillon bumped into the table hard enough to make it rock, and she then went to steady it, but all of it was deception. She quickly plucked the Fae's wand up unseen.

"The kingdom must be restored," replied the Fae Gaia. "This reign of evil tyranny must end. You have brought another war to the doorstep of this kingdom, and you must be punished."

"What are you going to do, then? Kill me in cold blood, Mother?" replied Cendrillon with icy emphasis on the last word. "It's your fault I am like this!" Cendrillon burst out in sudden rage, "If you hadn't died, you could have been there to raise me yourself!"

Then in desperation, Cendrillon pointed the old wand at the Fae Gaia.

"There may not be enough power left in this wand to correct my mistakes, but it's enough to kill you." Cendrillon waved it in a menacing fashion.

She had circled toward the edge of balcony now with Fae Gaia standing between her and the room. She saw past the God-mother fairy as the door to the room inside opened. Maldame and General Dendroba walked in to meet with the queen, and were astounded to see the God-mother fairy standing there. The

Maldame recognized her immediately. "Guards!" she yelled.

* * *

"Hello?" shouted Hansel. "Open our door. Toss us the keys," Hansel pleaded.

Patience gave an unsure look to the general. General White shook her head. "Leave them," she said. Rapunzel tapped the general on her shoulder and nodded towards the other cell.

General White held out her hand to Patience. "Let me have the keys for a moment, Patience."

"Someone is coming," said Patience's mother, who had been keeping an eye on the dungeon entrance.

General White took the keys and went to the adjacent cell. She quickly opened the door, then stepped inside and helped Rabbit stand. The grateful rabbit put his arm around the general and together they walked out of the cell.

"Thank you," said Rabbit. "Did I hear that there is a God-mother fairy in you midst?" The rabbit was distracted for a moment as he looked nervously at the large black wolf that stood solemnly by the girl's side.

"Yes," replied Patience, "she has come back to save the kingdom."

"Your name is Patience? Well, you are a brave girl, Patience," the rabbit said as he took a moment to admire her. "I would be very interested to meet your Fairy God-mother friend," he added.

"Rabbit, if we can find this Fairy God-mother—will she be able to help us stop this war? Maybe she can renegotiate the Fae Wonderland treaty?" General White asked. "Perhaps there's still a chance we can avoid this whole war?"

"Undoubtedly, a presence of the revered Fae would put a stop to it all," Rabbit replied, still musing over this latest revelation.

"Then let's get you back to Wonderland so you can tell Queen Alice!" General White helped Wonderland's emissary toward the pile of collected belongings near the dungeon's entrance. As she did so, she told the rabbit quietly where the Looking Glass was kept.

"Thank you," he said. The White Rabbit quickly picked up his sword and belt. Reaching into a small pouch on the belt, he produced a small piece of chalk. Then he drew a small circle on the floor and recited a short poem, as he had done before. The outline flashed in a sparkle of blue light and a large hole appeared on the floor where the rabbit had drawn the circle. There was a brief pause as Rabbit stood on the hole's edge, preparing to jump in. He looked at General White.

"I can't take you with me," the rabbit apologized. "It's against treaty. We don't need any more violations."

"We've business to attend to here, anyway," replied General White. "Hopefully you will be able to get back and convince your queen to not start the war."

"Thank you all, my friends. It was an honor to have met you. You serve your kingdom well," offered the rabbit. "Good luck in your travels." With that, he stepped off and dropped into the hole. The floor reverted back to normal seconds afterward.

Then a tall figure stood in the doorway, blocking the hall light from behind him.

Everyone froze at the sight of the figure. Rapunzel clenched her fists, preparing to fight.

The wolf turned and wagged its tail, recognizing Hamelin. But, as it began to walk towards him, the wolf stopped, and the hackles on its back stood up. It lowered its head and growled, sensing something was wrong.

Then Patience shrieked happily. "Hamelin!" she shouted and began to run over to hug him. She had missed her friend terribly. "I was so worried about you!" she called out happily. Rapunzel was quick to grab the excited girl by her shoulder.

Hamelin was still bewitched under Cendrillon, and though he sounded excited to see Patience, his expression was still the dull emotionless stare.

"Queen Cinder put a spell on him, Patience. He's not himself," Rapunzel whispered.

"Oh, no," replied Patience with hesitation. Still, she was glad to see that he was alive. "Can we change him back?"

"I don't know," Rapunzel replied quietly.

"I bet the God-mother fairy can change him back," she said confidently.

"My friends," Hamelin started, "I don't think my queen wanted you out of your cell. You should go back in and wait for her. Perhaps I could play some music while we wait," said the enchanted piper.

Snow White thought quickly. "Actually, Hamelin, the queen let us out. She wanted us to meet her in her private chambers. Perhaps you can show us where it is."

"She would be happy you helped do that," Rapunzel added, hoping to convince the bewitched Hamelin further.

"I have been to her private chambers—I know where they are. Since you've been released from the cell, I will take you to her."

"Just one thing," said General White. She held the cell keys up and walked over to Hansel and Gretel's cell. The large wolf followed. Gretel and Hansel watched from their cell as Snow White held the key ring up, then dropped the keys to the ground in front of the cell, certainly close enough for Hansel and Gretel to reach the keys and unlock the door if they wanted.

General White looked at the large black wolf who she knew was Elizabeth and pointed to the keys. "Stay," she ordered. "If they try to get out, kill them." General White returned to the others. The wolf sat and stared at the two prisoners, issuing a low growl as Gretel knelt down near the bars. The wolf then stood up, briefly taking a step back and then sat on its haunches again, daring its former captors to try again.

"Let's go." Rapunzel looked back one last time at the bloodied blanket where she last saw her mother alive. "You will not have died for nothing, Mother," Rapunzel promised. Then she and the group followed Hamelin through the castle, heading toward Queen Cendrillon's private chambers. General White silently hoped she was not too late to help her brother.

CHAPTER 20
THE ARRIVAL OF QUEEN ALICE

It was a short time later at the temple known as An End World when the White Rabbit appeared, eager to finalize his plans. Rabbit looked up at his tiger-sized friend, making sure he was out of earshot of temple workers and royal staff. "We've got a problem, Chesh," Rabbit said in a concerned low voice. "They have a God-mother fairy working with them."

Cheshire's large blue cat eyes widened even more with acknowledgement. "That *is* a problem. Are you sure?" spoke the cat in a calm and measured tone.

"There was a castle servant girl who mentioned that a God-mother fairy had helped them get into the castle. She was rather insistent when I asked her, but I did not see the Fae with my own eyes."

"Still," Cheshire growled, "a living Fae could stop our invasion cold if Queen Alice finds out. She would prefer to negotiate the whole war away before we had our chance at Alice. There is no slower death than by diplomacy and committees."

"Yes, and the grounds for Wonderland's occupancy are thinly veiled at best. The treaty actually says that no denizen of Wonderland is to step foot on Fae protected territory, at all. Not that these fools who rule Marchenton would know anything about the treaty. The Fae are to moderate all interactions as needed."

"Alice thinks we tried to contact the Fae, but I made sure our requests never got out of Wonderland," Cheshire Cat added with a grin.

"But as long as there is a Fae alive in this realm, Wonderland would be considered in violation of the treaty." Rabbit thought for a moment, "Chesh, you'll have to go and take down the Fae," Rabbit said. "You are the only one who can get there quicker than I can right now." He patted his bandaged stump of a leg for emphasis. "I'll have to get this looked at. Besides, Alice will want me around when she arrives."

"It must drive you mad," observed Cheshire with a mock sympathetic tone, "being around the one thing you can never have."

"If it wasn't for Jack's involvement, things would have been different," the rabbit remarked.

"It's not entirely the lad's fault," Cheshire said. "We all knew it was Alice's time to be removed. We all agreed to it. Jack just made it that much more convenient."

Rabbit growled, "Getting Jack is my only interest in this. If Jack wasn't in the picture, I'd leave Alice on the throne."

"Of course you would, Rabbit," Cheshire smiled knowingly. "Don't lie to me; you have much more interest in this then just some petty love triangle."

The cat thought quickly, and then realized what Rabbit had said.

"Did you mention a girl? Is she the offlander you have chosen to replace Alice? You have a thing for little girls," he purred. "Another child? Rabbit, must we?" Cheshire protested with mild irritation. "Seems to me the one who already has experience in running a kingdom and was able to imprison you and take your foot is far more qualified to rule Wonderland than another pretty girl. Frankly, I tire of dealing with children."

"Yes, this girl, Patience, has a touch of magic from the Fae. She would be perfect," answered Rabbit. "The Maldame, the queen. She's a loose end, Chesh. She also knows where the Looking Glass is. We might need to take her out as well, before she gets too curious about finding it. We should at least secure it before anyone else discovers it. The Maldame is far too wicked and power hungry to control. That's why it must be the child. Besides, that Maldame person did cut off my foot."

"I don't think you're being objective, Rabbit. I think, like last time, your personal preferences are again clouding your judgment from what we all are trying to accomplish. Hatter is not going to be happy with news you are doing more of the same."

"Just take out the Fae, Cheshire, and mind your own business," Rabbit shot back, annoyed at the accusation.

The temple portal began to glow again.

"Ah, but you seem to forget," the cat's body shifted and faded away, leaving only a toothy grin for a moment, "I am mostly incorporeal." The cat's body faded back in. "I'm tangibility challenged. It is not as if I can appear out of nowhere and plant a dagger in the Fae's back."

"Now who is lying to whom? You can find her easily enough, and you can kill her. I know you have your ways. Don't be such a scaredy-cat."

"Hmm," the Cheshire Cat mused aloud. "Perhaps I can kidnap the Godmother fairy back to Wonderland and dispense with her there. Nevertheless, rabbit holes connecting directly to the land are forbidden these days. It's not a big deal to create the holes when they connect within the same realm. But to go to Wonderland, if you and I open two in such a short timeframe, it will surely draw the attention of the Caterpillar. He is connected to Wonderland's magic more than anyone else. It is very easy for him to shut them down in mid-hole. You remember what happened to Mary Anne. Still, less risky than trying to sneak an offlander back through the temple."

"That half blind, obese, old fool barely knows what world he's in anymore. I'm not worried about the Caterpillar." Rabbit no longer hid his annoyance. Then he paused. "That was unfortunate what happened to Mary Anne." He shuddered, trying not to think about how he found the remains of the poor girl, pulled and stretched like taffy, barely alive as she lay draped across the land for almost a quarter of a mile, horribly disfigured, and crazed into incoherence. Mary Anne died an agonizingly slow, painful death with all of Wonderland watching. Crying and sobbing, asking if they were—*there yet? It sounds like a wonderful place, Rabbit. I would love to go.*

"I still miss her sometimes…" Rabbit said, "and I still have the nightmares to prove it."

The Cheshire Cat was only half listening. "What about Hatter? He could kill the Fae."

"Hatter remains in Wonderland, dealing with the Caterpillar. As long as he continues to delay the Caterpillar's metamorphosis, this will work. We have a short window of opportunity here to change the throne before he changes. Who knows what will happen to Wonderland when he finally does change. Besides, we are only going to do a connection once. I also know where the Looking Glass has been hidden. I will bring the child back through there. Since that's considered an official two-way portal, it shouldn't raise suspicion."

Then the glowing portal began to hum. Temple workers and royal staff began to gather in front in anticipation of their most important arrival.

"She's coming," Cheshire said, cutting the conversation short. "I will go tonight. You should get ready."

"Kidnap the Fae or kill her, whatever you want to do. Just remove her from the chessboard." Rabbit stepped back into the shadows while the Cheshire Cat melted away into the air.

First through the giant wall-sized portal came a five-foot-tall, slender green lizard with a cream colored underbelly. He was dressed in regal attire and carried a small trumpet adorned with a royal flag. He looked about nervously with quick head movements, as lizards often do. He snapped to strict attention in front of the gathering temple crowd. Then with one final lick of his eyeball with his long purple tongue, he brought the trumpet mouthpiece to his mouth and played his royal announcement music.

"Announcing the arrival of our beloved Queen Alice—benevolent ruler of her united Wonderland. Long live the queen!"

Then the lizard scurried on all fours to the side of the portal.

The gathered temple crowd shouted their response in unison, "Long live Queen Alice!" Rabbit rolled his eyes and looked in the direction of where the Cheshire Cat had last been visible. He shook his head in disgust, knowing the cat could see him.

Then Queen Alice stepped through the portal onto the sovereign ground of her temple, amid polite applause from her adoring subjects. "Thank you, Bill," she graciously acknowledged the lizard's efforts.

Alice the child had grown up into Alice the woman, the magic of Wonderland twisting time so that three hundred years was little more than thirty. Though she detested such things as war, she did enjoy dressing for the occasion, ready to lead her army into battle. She wore a rather form-fitting suit of royal plated armor, decorated in ornate detail, accented with chain mail trim and enameled with dark crimson. Donning the formal armor did give Alice a certain sense of power, more so than the crown she wore. She felt commanding in an almost sexual way as she walked down the worn stone steps from the dimming portal, tossing her silky light brown hair to the side as she waved to her adoring crowd.

No sooner had the queen stepped from the portal and onto the floor of the old temple than she was bombarded with updates from her staff. Alice held up her hand, signaling them to be silent as she was about to speak.

"Cheshire Puss," Alice called out affectionately as the staff that crowded around her parted to see to whom she was speaking. Alice stared at a seemingly dark, empty corner of the temple. "Cheshire Puss, why do you hide from me?"

Cheshire emerged from the shadows, almost complete in appearance. He was tall at the shoulder, well above four feet. The cat was tiger-like in appearance. He had a larger than normal mouth full of sharp pointed teeth with two large incisors protruding down in a pronounced fashion. His eyes were the most electric, almost unnatural blue, and his fur was a swirling milky white with unusual stripes that seemed to move slowly across his body in an ever-shifting pattern. The stripes seemed to generate from his large head and move down across his back, then down his legs and up his tail. At his best concentration, his body struggled to maintain its solidity. As with all cats, the Cheshire Cat walked with a certain amount of aloofness and arrogance.

"I was merely trying to avoid being underfoot, as you've put it."

"Is Rabbit with you? I do so wish to speak with him."

"I have not seen him," Cheshire replied coolly. "I'm sure he will be here shortly."

One of the surrounding staff nervously interrupted.

"My queen," he said with a quick nod. "My apologies, but we must prepare your transport to the main camp site. What would her majesty prefer to ride— guinea pig, dodo, or gryphon?"

Alice thought for a moment, amused at the prospect of her choices and excited to get to decide on something. She gave this seemingly minor question considerable thought before finally settling on her answer. "Guinea pig. It's a more comfortable ride."

"Might I suggest, my queen," interrupted the Cheshire Cat, "that the troops would be far more receptive to the sudden appearance of their leader on a majestic gryphon? Arrival by royal guinea pig does not have that same commanding, awe-inspiring entrance."

"I suppose you are right, Cheshire Puss," replied Alice. "It is a little more 'awww' inspiring than awe-inspiring, but they are just so cute. Very well, ready a gryphon."

Suddenly, right in front of Alice's feet, the ground seemed to fall away and for a moment a gaping hole formed. Then the ground filled and solidified, and the White Rabbit lay on the ground where the hole had disappeared. His dirty and matted fur was the first indication Rabbit had been beaten, but Alice gasped in horror when she saw the bloodied stump where the Rabbit's foot had been removed.

The Cheshire Cat thought it was an overly dramatic entrance, considering they had just been talking in secret a few yards away, but Rabbit wanted to make sure his ruse was authentic. Then Rabbit spoke—coughing at first, his appearance and demeanor vastly different from when he had left the castle, though he knew no one here would know otherwise.

"Barbaric! I was barely able escape alive," the Rabbit said weakly. Alice bent down to the Rabbit, her soft hair brushing across his bruised face.

"Poor Rabbit!" She comforted him, her delicate hand stroking his fur.

"They had no interest in a peaceful resolution, my queen. They had no regard for the treaty. My foot—" he began to cry, gesturing to the bloodied remains of his ankle. "I was left to rot in their dungeons."

"They will surely pay dearly, Rabbit," said Alice sternly. "How dare they." She hugged the Rabbit again. "I was hesitant when you suggested we occupy this land, but I see now I should have trusted you from the beginning. We are well within our rights to be here. See to your leg, dear Rabbit. I shall go and do what I do best."

In no time, the queen's gryphon mount was brought to her and quickly they were airborne. It was night, but Alice could easily see in the distance the campfires of her awaiting army.

"Gryphon," Alice shouted over the flapping of the beast's great, feathered wings, "when we land, I want you to bring me one of our jabber wranglers."

"Yes, m'lady," the gryphon replied as he glided down toward a small stage surrounded by a sea of soldiers and other personnel. As they flew down quickly over the heads of the expectant crowd, the gryphon screeched loudly, announcing the arrival of the queen. Great applause erupted from the crowd. The gryphon landed between two large, flaming braziers that marked the edge of the stage. Alice dismounted with the help of two diligent, large bipedal mice dressed in worker's leathers.

Queen Alice waved to the crowd, smiling, motioning with her hand to settle down. After several moments, she began her speech.

"We are not here as invaders," Alice started. "We are here to protect the sovereignty of our wondrous land and our way of life as a Unified Wonderland. We are here because this world could not respect the very laws they helped forge. We are here to repair their disrespect and arrogance, and remind them that there is no action without due consequence."

The crowd was fully engaged, shouts of agreement sprung up readily. Alice continued, "We are here to fight, for they have not listened to any of our more noble efforts. So they will hear, instead, our victory through steel. We shall stay in this land until they learn wholly their mistake and beg us for forgiveness. We are not here as marauders or barbarian savages. We shall do what we must. Wonderland fights with honor and does so with a measure of integrity that will blind our foes. We shall set examples to our enemies of how they should behave in battle, and shame them in surrender without even lifting a sword."

At that, some of the crowd booed in jest. followed by a general eruption of laughter, even from Alice as she continued with her speech. "But if it comes to battle, we will decimate them. We will fight as we did at the Battle of Cards when the mighty Red Queen fell before us. Our fight will be just and we shall wave our flags in victory as we did after the battle of Bishop Falls during the Chess Pieces War, when the White King fell to his knees and begged to surrender."

More cheers broke out, and Alice had to pause for a moment after trying to yell over the enthusiastic crowd.

"There is nothing this world can offer that we do not already enjoy in the comfort of our land. Do not pillage. Do not burn. Treat non-combatants with respect, though they are inferior. We would impress them with our manners so that they would rise up against their own army to defend us. We are not just soldiers. We are teachers. We will we teach our enemy how to surrender. We will be tested— and by the measure of the tiniest dormouse to the noblest of the duchesses to even the great Caterpillar himself, we will own the day. In the morning, we strike camp and march toward battle. Tonight, honor yourselves, the greatest warriors of Wonderland. Be noble, be fierce. Show mercy and show no mercy!"

Now the soldiers began to clap and cheer, yelling their approval as the crowd became even more energized.

"If it comes to battle, we will own the battlefield," Alice shouted above the noise, "right down to the very last words that our fallen enemies will hear in their bloodied ears. To those who threaten us, what do we say?"

"Off with their heads!" the crowd shouted as Alice yelled over them, riling them even further.

"To those who choose a doomed path of opposition, what shall be the last words they hear?"

"Off with their heads!"

"And when we strike fear into their misguided hearts as our steel strikes the killing blow, what are the final words they shall hear?"

"OFF WITH THEIR HEADS!"

Hundreds of soldiers from Wonderland's army yelled and cheered, continuing to chant "Off with their heads!" as Alice left her rough encampment stage. It was hard to imagine such a speech could come from an otherwise soft-spoken queen. However, Alice had been queen for a long time and knew the importance of a well-rehearsed rally.

As requested, the gryphon met the queen afterwards with a small, lanky man dressed in a leather apron. The apron was embossed with a symbol indicating he was a Knave of Diamonds.

"The Jabbers are having a hard time adjusting to the new environment. They are exceptionally cranky, m'lady," said the man.

"Let one loose, wrangler, and instruct him east toward the castle. Those creatures are smart enough to know what to do after they've arrived. Give this little kingdom a taste of what they will be up against. Let them know their transgression will be paid back a hundredfold," Alice ordered the knave. "Let them know Wonderland is coming. Release the Jabberwock!"

CHAPTER 21
STEPMOTHERS AND GOD-MOTHERS

The queen's guards were a little unsure about how to handle the glowing, sword-wielding God-mother fairy known as Fae Gaia. The three guards who had come to the Maldame's call approached the glowing intruder warily with their weapons drawn.

The Fae made short work of them, however, demonstrating how dangerous and powerful a vengeful Fae can be when cornered.

One of the bravest of the group of castle guards rushed forward with his sword. Effortlessly, the God-mother fairy parried the attack single handedly with her glowing blade. There was an elegant flow to her motion and great strength in her parry, and she easily disarmed her opponent, sending his weapon to the ground and stopping him in his tracks. Then she brought her other hand up with determined grace, and a flash of sparkling light erupted silently from her fingers. The surprised guard caught the full burst of the Fae magic in his face. Instantly, the guard became distorted and began to shrink, reverting to a small black rat, his original form. The Fae had undone Cendrillon's dark magic. The rat scampered back out the door, running past the Maldame's feet.

It was the first time the Maldame had actually seen the raw magical power of the Fae. She knew that, despite all her years of studying witchcraft, she would prove to be no match for the innate magical ability of the Fairy God-mother. The Maldame also knew the Fae could be eliminated by more conventional means, as she had already met her demise from a broken glass slipper.

The next guard hesitated, startled by the unexpected transformation. The Fae's movements were fluid. With a sweeping arc, she brought her blade down, slicing across the chest of the attacker. Then with a flash, there was a small brown rat where the guard had stood. The Fae had returned another of the queen's rat army to its true form.

Such power! Even the Maldame could not help but marvel at the display, envious to be able to wield such magic a witch could never truly attain. As she watched and studied the Fae Gaia's attack, she then noticed something. As the Fae dispatched the second guard with her magic, she saw the glow of the God-mother fairy dim slightly. There was a slump in her stance but she steadied herself quickly. It was the slightest of correction that the average onlooker would not have noticed, but the Maldame was a keen observer. The God-mother fairy, who stood so proudly, had shown the slightest suggestion of weakness. The Maldame saw that as powerful as the Fae was, expending her magic as she did on the guards was making her weak. The Maldame never expected the guards to be able to take down the Fairy God-mother, but it gave her time to study the Fae, and it had paid off. As the final guard began to engage the Fairy God-mother, the Maldame turned to her general.

"Keep the Fae busy, Dendroba," the Maldame commanded.

Dendroba nodded. He, too, was studying the Fae as she fought with the guards. He also noticed the Fae hiding her weakened state. With his one hand, he had already drawn a throwing dagger from his belt as the last guard stepped in to distract the Fairy God-mother.

"She is still weak. Her power is finite," the Maldame whispered to Dendroba. The stepmother continued her thought in her own mind as she plotted. *Once she deals with Dendroba, she will be even weaker.* The Maldame had an idea.

The last guard was behind the God-mother fairy now and swung in earnest with a wide arc. Sensing the attack, the Fae crouched at the last moment and spun. The guard's swing cut the air above her. The Fae shot a burst of magical energy at the last guard, and the force hurled him backward and down to the floor. The ethereal tendrils of the Fae's magic returned the ugly hybrid guard to his original state. However, this guard's transformation had been different; not a rat this time. Instead, a small mouse scurried and disappeared along the wall. To the Fae's surprise, there was also a small child—a boy of no more than ten years old was lying on the ground, startled and dazed by his own transformation.

The God-mother fairy stopped.

"Children, Ella? Disgraceful. You captured children and transformed them to do your malicious bidding," the Fae accused angrily, staring in disbelief at the young boy. "You have taken the children from the kingdom to serve you, your desperate witchcraft bonding them with rodents because your magic is not powerful enough. How could you have fallen so low?" The energy around the Fae seemed to sharpen and bristle as Fae Gaia grew angrier with the queen.

The child panicked as he came to his senses. Unaware of what had happened and where he was, he quickly scrambled to his feet and ran out of the room in a frightened panic.

Cendrillon did not know what to do, The return of her mother as the Fae Gaia stripped all sense of her royalty, and her plans melted away. She stood dumbstruck, watching everything fall apart around her as her thoughts scrambled to make sense of it all. Her mind raced to sort out who she was and the life she had led. In a sense, she was frozen, unsure how to act in the slightest. Only when the Fae Gaia spoke her name again did Cendrillon finally focus on the reality of the situation.

With the Fae's attention on Cendrillon, the Maldame sought to act, "Now is your chance, Dendroba. Get her!" the Maldame hissed.

The God-mother fairy whirled back around, sensing another attack. A dagger whizzed by, slicing through the great glowing wing of the Fae, causing her to wince with pain, though the wing was ethereal and not physically damaged. The deadly dagger had missed its mark and dug deeply into a wooden desk at the far end of the room.

The God-mother fairy had no time to prepare herself for Dendroba's next attack. As quickly as he had thrown his dagger, Dendroba leaped across the room in one powerful jump. As the God-mother fairy turned, Dendroba's huge body plowed into her with such force that it slammed her to the ground. Dendroba pulled another small dagger and raised it high to plunge into the Fairy God-mother.

The Maldame had not expected Dendroba's attack to be that successful. She had expected him to be taken out by the Fae's magic which could very well still could happen.

The Fae Gaia looked intently at Dendroba. Just as he was about to bring his dagger down, she stopped the general cold with nothing more than a few simple words. "Do you think I would not recognize you as my own child, my own son?"

Dendroba was stunned. He had known about his relation to Queen

Cendrillon as a brother. Yet somehow, it never seemed real to him—just another story told by the witches. He had learned about the circumstances of his birth and the tragic disfigurement from the witches' miscast spell. However, being confronted with the truth that this was his birth mother had given him an unexpected jolt. He was about to kill his own mother.

"What did you say?" he asked, lowering the dagger from its deadly position.

Dendroba had stopped long enough for Fae Gaia to act. She brought her glowing sword up quickly and seemed to cut right through Dendroba's thick chest in a single swing. The Fae's sword was magical, however. The blade was ethereal and passed through him like a ghost.

Dendroba reacted. Scrambling to his feet, he backed away from the Fairy God-mother. He realized he had been struck as he felt the warm power of the Fae's magic wrap around him. "That's...that's my real mother," Cendrillon stammered in disbelief.

"I'm confused—I...don't know what to do, Maldame."

"Get out of my way, you little cinderwench!" the Maldame yelled at Cendrillon. The Maldame growled in frustration. She then rushed Cendrillon through the balcony doorway and summoned her plan. Jovette.

The Maldame's last surviving spider assassin always lurked nearby to protect the Maldame. When Gael was killed, Jovette had retreated through the Bloodthorns back to the castle. Now she was called upon again.

"The cheap magic of witchcraft is nothing to me," said Fae Gaia, as she began to stand. "It is a perverse abomination of the true magic of the Fae—nothing more than a cheater's parlor trick, a cowardly attempt at power from greedy people undeserving of true magic," the God-mother fairy spoke as she slowly got to her feet, wearily using her sword to steady herself.

"There is nothing your witchcraft can create that I cannot undo."

Dendroba felt the Fae's energy wash over him. He felt a tingling sensation under the bandages where his right arm was removed earlier that day. His legs and the right side of his body seemed on fire. He looked to the God-mother fairy as she spoke. Almost immediately, he realized his right arm had grown completely back in a matter of seconds, and it felt different. General Dendroba held up his right hand and saw to his stunned disbelief a perfectly normal human hand. No longer was it a long, thin arm covered in shiny and brightly- colored skin.

Whenever he had attempted to cut off his hand in the past, it had grown back the same, long yellow and blue fingers with large bulbous tips—toxic and deadly to anyone he touched. Now his arm was no longer poisonous or frog-like.

All other concerns left Dendroba instantly. Total shock had given way to a growing realization of his change. The transformed general reached up and touched the right side of his face with his right hand. Where there had been bumps of calloused skin and deformities, there was now normal, smooth human skin. Dendroba quickly looked around and spotted a dressing mirror. He raced to it, barely realizing his awkward gait and limp were gone, as well.

Phyllo Dendroba grabbed the mirror, turned it and looked at himself, his frog-like disfigurements fading away before his own eyes. He looked like a normal person for the first time in his life. Dendroba was speechless, forgetting all of what was going on around him. The last bit of Fairy magic faded away as he looked at himself in the mirror and watched his new head of hair fall neatly into place. He had hair! Gone were all his deformities; it had been a childhood wish that had finally come true.

The Prince of Frogs was now finally, blessedly, a normal human. Dendroba was overcome with the sudden unleashing of emotions—anger at the witches for their stupidity and for their inability to fix their own mistake that had deformed him so. Now his mother had done in an instant what the witches could never do. Dendroba marveled at this. Quickly, the excitement for this new turn of events gave way to fear. Fear of change and the unknown. He was accustomed to his deformities. They gave him a certain sense of power. Dendroba had relied on that fear and mystery to command. No longer would he be the feared general he once was. For the first time in his life, Dendroba felt a wet tear roll from his right eye onto his warm right cheek

The Maldame frowned as she watched Dendroba's transformation. She doubted he would continue to fight the God-mother fairy after this turn of events. Regardless, the wicked stepmother thought, her plan had still been successful. The Fae's power was diminishing, and it seemed the fairy was oblivious to the deliberate exploitation of her weakness.

"It is time to stop these foolish attempts at true magic," the Fae Gaia demanded, raising her sword at Cendrillon. "It is time, Ella, to put you in your place."

Cendrillon stepped back further out the balcony as the God-mother fairy pressed forward with her sword. Focused on her daughter, she ignored the Maldame, who began to step away from balcony and move toward the door. Nor did the fairy take notice that the Maldame had quietly picked up the fallen guard's sword. "There will be one last attempt, troublesome Fae," muttered Maldame.

The Fae followed Cendrillon toward the balcony.

"No, Mother, please," Cendrillon pleaded, holding her hands out in front of her, begging. "There must be some other way."

As the Fae stepped closer to Cendrillon, something huge erupted from the balcony doorway, jumping in front of the queen and pushing the God-mother fairy backwards.

With gargantuan legs outstretched, Jovette attacked with incredible speed and surprise. The huge arachnid seemed to fill the room as it leaped at the unsuspecting fairy, knocking her down and smothering her with its massive and hairy body. Jovette's front legs battled to pin the fairy down for a fatal fanged strike. It seemed the spider would make quick work of the Fae, crushing the fairy beneath its deadly bite.

But then, Jovette stopped. There was no sign of the God-mother fairy beneath the great spider's body. The great spider was still for an instant. Then the blue ethereal blade of the Fae Gaia, thrust upwards through the spider's midsection as the Fae rose triumphantly from its body and hovered in the air above. Jovette shrieked, flipped to the side and collided with Dendroba as she crashed into the furniture.

The huge spider flailed about on its back and the Fae Magic was again at work, transforming the giant spider and undoing the witchcraft that had changed her form. In a flash of light, Jovette the girl now lay naked and unconscious on the floor.

"No!" yelled the Maldame in disbelief, enraged at how easily her plan was defeated.

Fae Gaia had become very weak from expending her magic before fully recovering from her reappearance. She was not prepared to handle such great feats so quickly. Her glow was very dim, and the Fae was breathed heavily as she slowly rose to stand, staying on one knee for a moment, and then leaning on her sword for support.

"Using too much magic," the Fae whispered. Across the room, Cendrillon stood very still, too conflicted to either flee or fight. She could only watch.

The stepmother was hesitant to engage the fairy in straight on fight, even considering the Fae's weakened state. It was too foolish a risk, she thought. Her sharp eyes darted to the door, gauging how quickly she could make her escape.

During the commotion, the prince had regained his strength, thanks in great part, to the Fae's healing. Phillip was awake, and feigned unconsciousness while he waited for an opportunity to act. He reached over, grabbed his knife from the floor, and rose quietly to his feet. Then he rushed the queen from behind to take her by surprise. Phillip stood behind Cendrillon now, one arm wrapped strongly around her arms, pinning them to her chest. His other hand held the knife to the queen's delicate throat.

"That's enough!" commanded the prince. "Cinderella's rule as queen ends. It is over." He grabbed her leg and searched quickly; pulling the knife she had stabbed him with from its hidden sheath. Then he tossed the blade over the balcony and into the night air. Cendrillon shifted and struggled in silent anger, unable to break free of the prince's hold.

Just then, the Maldame's luck turned. An opportunity had quite literally burst in. The door flew open wide, catching everyone's attention. Standing in the doorway was Snow White. Rapunzel stood behind her, with a firm hold restraining Hamelin, who was still under Cendrillon's spell. When Patience spotted the God-mother fairy in the room, she quickly scrambled from her mother's side, slipped between the others and raced over to her.

"Patience! No! Stay back," her mother screamed, trying desperately to grab at her child as she rushed through the doorway. Patience had seen the prince holding the queen and thought it was safe, but had not noticed the Maldame standing close by. The Maldame snatched her as she passed, grabbing the girl high on her thin arm and pulling her in. The Maldame then quickly put the sharp sword's blade to Patience's neck.

"Back away!" the Maldame yelled, holding her hostage tightly. "Release the queen or the child dies," she ordered. No one risked attacking the Maldame with her sword digging into the young girl's flesh.

Patience's mother shrank away from the crowded doorway and disappeared down the hallway unnoticed as the others focused on the treacherous stepmother and her young hostage.

The God-mother fairy was standing now, watching young Patience struggle against the stepmother's surprisingly iron-like grip.

The Maldame barked again, "Release the queen." She looked at the God-mother fairy. "This is not some witch's spell you can reverse. This is a real blade and a real throat. I know fairies like you cannot take a life, but I can. Now release the queen!" To emphasize her point, the stepmother dug the blade deeper into Patience's neck, causing the girl to cry out.

Prince Phillip pulled the knife away from Cendrillon and let her go. He could not risk the life of a child, especially not the life of the brave young girl who had helped them so much.

"Very well," Phillip said with a sullen mix of frustration and resignation.

As soon as the prince eased his grip, Cendrillon spun and punched him squarely in the face, sending him reeling backwards, bracing himself against the balcony rail. In a moment, Cendrillon was on top of him; she disarmed him and now held his own knife up to his neck, the point drawing blood underneath the soft flesh of his bottom jaw. The blood trailed down his neck in a thin red line and dripped off into the darkness below.

General White dropped her sword to the ground. "Okay—you win. Just don't harm them. Let the girl go at least."

From the wall behind the Maldame, a small panel door opened silently. The Maldame did not notice until a dinner knife was pressing into her neck.

"Let my child go," Catherine said sternly. She had come back to the room through one of the many hidden servant passages.

The Maldame relaxed her grip on the girl, allowing Patience to run free. Patience quickly ran to Rapunzel, who wrapped her arms around the terrified girl.

But the Maldame was desperate. In an angry burst, she grabbed the surprised servant's wrist and forced her to drop the knife, painfully twisting Catherine's arm, and causing the woman to scream out. Untrained in combat or deception, Catherine was no match for the wicked stepmother; then with a quick motion, the Maldame drove her sword forcefully up into the servant's stomach, letting the woman fall to the floor.

"Insolent wench," the Maldame hissed.

With Patience away from the Maldame, there was a sudden flash of metal through the air, heading directly at the Maldame's head. The Maldame, seeing the movement at the last possible second, instinctively ducked out of the way, narrowly avoiding the thrown blade. The dagger clanged hard against the stone wall, shooting sparks from the force of the strike.

At the far side of the room stood Dendroba, his muscular right arm still extended from the throw. Then Dendroba charged. The Maldame watched in disbelief as Dendroba, who had served her with decades of sworn loyalty, now had the traitorous audacity to rise up against her. At the last moment, realizing the huge hulking general was almost upon her, the old witch yelled with rage and lifted the sword. But not quickly enough, as Dendroba batted the attack away and plowed full on into the Maldame. With brute force, he tackled her to the ground, the blow knocking the wind from the old stepmother. As she hit the ground hard, it rendered her unconscious.

Patience struggled free from Rapunzel's protective hold and ran to her fallen mother, tears falling free from her cheeks as she sobbed. Her mother managed a weak smile. "Patience, I am so proud of you. Your father would have been so proud." She started to lift her hand to touch her daughter's face. "So happy to know you are alive—"

Her mother's eyes fixed and dulled, and her head went slack. Her bloodied hand that tried to caress her daughter's cheek fell away limply. One final breath left her body, and Patience's mother lay still. Patience cried deeply, her words lost in a guttural sobbing, her face frozen in anguish.

Queen Cendrillon, with the knife poised at Phillip's throat, looked over her shoulder to see the commotion. The Fae had regained enough of her magical strength for one last burst of magic. As soon as the Maldame was incapacitated, Fae Gaia acted. The God-mother fairy leaped into the air. "This ends now, Ella! For good!" She threw her sword at the surprised queen. Cendrillon had no time to move, and the flying ethereal blade impaled her with a powerful blow. The sword disappeared in a flash of fairy sparkle as it struck the queen, but the force of the blow sent her rolling over the balcony's railing. The God-mother fairy paused in shock as she watched her daughter disappear over the side of the tower's balcony.

Prince Phillip was quick to react. He twisted and shot his hand out, managing to grab Cinderella's arm and catch her from plummeting hundreds of feet to her death, though the momentum of her fall nearly pulled him over the edge himself. She was unconscious from Fae Gaia's strike, and was dead weight on the prince's already wounded shoulder. Wincing from the pain, he fought to hold onto Cinderella as she dangled precariously from the high balcony. His wounds from the shipwreck raged anew at the shock and strain of holding on. Phillip fought through the pain and struggled to pull Cinderella's limp body back over the railing. Snow White quickly realized what was happening and rushed to his side, helping her brother. With one final lurch, the three collapsed on the floor of the balcony. Cinderella was alive, but unconscious.

His chest heaving from the exertion and pain, Phillip looked at his sister. "Despite everything, I couldn't just let her fall."

"Don't worry. I wasn't going to let her die and get off that easily, little brother," she replied, still winded.

At the same instant, Hamelin abruptly shook his head, "What's going on?" asked the puzzled man. "Why are you holding me?" he asked Rapunzel. The spell that had been cast on him seemed to have ended abruptly when Queen Cendrillon was struck by the Fairy's sword. Rapunzel let him go and shoved him away from her.

"You've been under Cendrillon's spell," she said matter-of-factly. "And you've been a jerk." Rapunzel could tell that whatever spell had been cast on the poor piper was now broken. The light in Hamelin's eyes had turned back on. She pushed past him."It's a long story." She went over to comfort Patience.

"The last thing I remember was a wolf licking me," said Hamelin in a daze. "And something about a dungeon, oh, and a giant rabbit," Hamelin added. He scrunched his face, confused by what he had just said, and rubbed the back of his head trying to sort his recollections out. Then he saw Queen Cendrillon lying on the floor. "Is that the queen?" he asked. "Is she dead?"

"Cinderella will live. I have put her in a Fae's sleep. It's a magical rest that will hopefully undo all the evil that has invaded her spirit," Fae Gaia explained, then turned to Hamelin. "You are lucky her spell has broken over you. If her magic was stronger, you would still be enchanted."

Patience pleaded with tear-filled eyes, "Please Fae Gaia, please save my mother."

The Fae Gaia looked sadly at Patience, as if her heart were wrenched in pain at the sight of the young girl. "I am truly sorry, dear child. As powerful as Fae magic is, it only affects the living. I cannot bring anyone back from the dead."

"You brought Cinderella's mother back. Fix her, Fairy God-mother. Please do something. Make my mother a fairy, too."

"There would need to be another Fae Gaia like me to inhabit your mother's body. I'm sorry, but it's not the same. Although I hold the thoughts and memories of her mother, as the Fae Gaia, I am merely borrowing this body, in a sense. The Fae can heal the living, but cannot affect those who have passed. I cannot do what you ask, Patience," she insisted. "I am deeply sorry."

Rapunzel stood by Patience without a word and, bent down, and hugged the girl as she broke down and cried.

"I'm sorry," Rapunzel whispered as she tried to console the child.

The Fae Gaia stepped away to look upon her own daughter.

"When will she wake up?" asked Phillip.

The Fae had noticed her old wand lying on the stone floor of the great balcony. She picked it up as she answered the prince's question, "That depends on how much she needs to sleep," replied Fae Gaia. The wand began to glow. "Still some energy left in this old thing. Good," the God-mother fairy remarked. "I will use this for now."

The Maldame awoke and cackled as Dendroba hefted her to her feet. "It doesn't matter if Cinderella ever wakes up. The damage is done now that Wonderland is invading. If the coven can't rule the throne, then let it be destroyed."

Snow White looked at Fae Gaia. As much as she hated to admit it, the stepmother was right.

The Fae stepped toward the Maldame, ignoring her comment even though it stung with truth. "As ruler of the witches' coven you will be held accountable for your actions and the desecration of the kingdom of Marchenton," proclaimed the Fae in a booming voice.

"What are you going to do? Execute me? You cannot. Fairy God-mothers don't kill," the Maldame yelled. "You can't even let someone else do it! It's against your Fae nature," she mocked. "So go ahead. Whatever punishment you deal, I can take!"

Then a young woman's voice from behind said, "Let me kill her." It was Jovette. She had regained consciousness after her transformation from spider to human. It had been several years since she had a human body, and she now wrapped it in a sheet from the nearby bed. She was tall, broad shouldered and olive skinned, with a mass of black hair that fell about her shoulders. Her appearance was somewhat exotic and gypsy-like, though she was not overly attractive. Jovette was unsteady on her feet; she had been used to eight legs for this past number of years, and it took a moment to get used to walking on two legs again. "She deserves death."

The God-mother fairy interrupted. "As much as I understand your thirst for vengeance, the Maldame is correct. I cannot allow a life to be intentionally taken."

"Then leave the room for a few minutes," replied Jovette as she walked over, dragging a length of sheet across the floor.

"Daughter," the Maldame cooed. "It's so good to see you again." Her voice dripped with sarcasm.

"I cannot allow that to happen," said Fae Gaia, raising her arm to hold Jovette from coming any closer. Jovette stopped at the fairy God-mother's outstretched arm. Then she snapped her head forward, sending a large glob of spit that smacked the Maldame directly in the face.

"Don't ever speak to me again," Jovette said with simmering rage at the Maldame. "For as long as you live, which if there is any justice, will not be very long."

The God-mother fairy spoke again. "Imprisonment," she said with finality.

"I can escape from any prison," the Maldame dismissed the Fae Gaia, still maintaining her airs of power. "I will be sure to make your lives a hundred times more miserable than they already are. Go ahead, lock me in a cell!"

"I did not say anything about a cell, witch," countered the Fae Gaia as she summoned the energy from her wand. "But you shall be imprisoned."

The Maldame had a momentary look of fear as she started to glow. The God-mother fairy, using her old wand, began to teleport the Maldame to her imprisonment.

Then rather unexpectedly, Rapunzel impulsively rushed forth, producing a small knife. Before anyone could stop her, she reached out and slashed the Maldame across the face with a deep stinging cut. It was not enough to kill, but it would leave her with a painful scar, one she would not forget.

"That's for killing my mother, you wicked bitch!" was the last thing the

Maldame heard. Then in a flash of light, the Fae had teleported the old stepmother Maldame to her imprisonment.

"Where did you send her?" Jovette asked, "What sort of prison?"

"An outdoor one," was all Fae Gaia replied.

* * *

The Maldame regained awareness as she materialized from the Fae's spell. It was night, cool and dark with a damp earthen smell. Her eyes adjusted to the darkness. She was outside. The Maldame could see stars in the sky and clouds that crawled away from the full moon, lighting the darkness even more. Then the old stepmother realized she was on the top of a small hill. She could see part of the castle in the distance obscured by the twisted vines and bramble of the Bloodthorns. She was surrounded in a small pocket, an open patch of dirt. It was a small space that a person could stand in, but not much else as there was hardly any space to move. It would be near impossible for her to pick through the thicket without at least scratching or pricking herself, and after that it would only be a matter of time before she would become more tangled and ensnared. The Maldame was very familiar with Bloodthorns. The old woman would suffer exposure and rain and chill at night. This was not imprisonment. It was a slow, torturous and agonizing death.

The Maldame let out a frustrated scream of anger. Then she felt something warm trickle down the side of her cheek. She reached up and wiped it with her finger, then tasted it on her lips. It was blood.

Rapunzel's knife had cut her down the side of her face. She had not even realized it had happened in the moment before the Fae Gaia had transported her. Gently, the Maldame patted the wound. More blood gushed around her fingers, dripping down the side of her face. It was a deep cut, she noticed. Then it dawned on the old witch—she was bleeding—in the middle of the Bloodthorns. She could hear the creaking of the carnivorous vines growing around her ever so slightly, sensing the warm blood. The Maldame tried to convince herself the noise that surrounded her was just branches moving from the wind, but she could feel her small claustrophobic pocket of space in the middle of the Bloodthorns constrict just a little more around her. The Bloodthorns could sense a meal was near.

* * *

Calmer now, Patience sat beside the body of her dead mother, quietly mourning the time they had spent apart, and wishing they could have spent more time together. *If only things had been different.*

Hamelin stepped over to the young girl. "The queen had me under a spell. I am sorry for anything I might have done. I am so sorry you lost your mom, Patience. All this time we have traveled together, we have talked about this day. It was supposed to be a happy day, y'know?"

Patience hugged her piper friend. "I know, Hamelin. I'm glad you didn't die."

"Me too, kid," Hamelin replied. "At least we're still alive. And you finally got rid of those glass slippers. Quite an adventure we had."

Nearby, Rapunzel eyed General Dendroba. "What about him?" she asked both Snow White and the prince. "He may have changed on the outside, but he's still the general of the queen's army."

Dendroba sat there awaiting his fate. After all these years, he thought, he no longer had to serve the coven. He was a man now, not a monster. Deep down inside, Dendroba felt happy.

"For all we know," Rapunzel growled, "he could have been aiming for the girl and missed—horribly."

"And her?" Rapunzel asking snidely, gesturing towards Jovette. The stepsister sneered back at Rapunzel.

"Don't worry about me, girl," Jovette retorted. "I'm not going to stop you." With disinterest and haughtiness in each footfall, the stepsister walked past Rapunzel to a small armoire. Its door had been broken in the preceding scuffle. Jovette began to look through some dresses, holding a few different ones up to judge their size.

"I'm not going to help you, either," Jovette added as she picked one of the queen's dresses, gathered her sheets about her, and headed towards the door. "After years of being a spider, the only thing I'm going to do right now is take a bath."

Rapunzel stood in front of the door, blocking Jovette from exiting.

"Out of my way, girl," Jovette demanded.

"Let her go 'Punzel," White said. "She's not worth bothering about. We've got bigger problems."

Rapunzel stepped aside to allow Jovette to pass, which the stepsister did, but not without flicking her hair in Rapunzel's face. "Peasant," Jovette spat with derision.

"She's not going to do anything," Snow White assured.

"You looked better as a spider," Rapunzel remarked loudly so Jovette might hear.

Snow White put her hands on her hips and considered what to do about General Dendroba. They had clashed many times as enemies, but Snow White had watched him help save Patience and give them an opportunity to stop Cinderella's stepmother. She did not forget what Dendroba had said in the dungeon about professional courtesy. Nevertheless, she knew he was still lord of the queen's guards.

General White stepped over to Rapunzel and put a hand on the younger woman's shoulder.

"Alright, Dendroba," Snow White said, "What's your story?"

Then Rapunzel stiffened. "Are you mad?" Rapunzel whispered angrily to Snow White.

"I have no queen to serve, no army to speak of, and no desire to continue this fight," Dendroba said flatly. "I am prepared to surrender and take responsibility for the actions of myself and my men."

Dendroba opened his arms wide, signaling his surrender. Snow White sensed sincerity from Dendroba. The more General White spoke with him the more she began to realize he was far more complex than she had thought, and perhaps even honorable.

"I still don't trust him," said Rapunzel.

General White was far more grounded in experience than the brash young lieutenant was. She knew Dendroba to be intelligent and he seemingly, was respectful of this new situation. Yet, General White admitted to herself that as much as she wanted to, she did not fully trust the Prince of Frogs, either.

"You will need my son's help," remarked Fae Gaia. The God-mother fairy had been tending to Prince Phillip and to her daughter Cinderella, who still lay unconscious from the fairy's magic.

"All of you," said Fae Gaia. "Will need to work together, to put aside any differences and pool your resources. There is still much to do."

The conversation was interrupted by a loud, gruff clearing of the throat coming from the chamber door. Standing stiffly at the doorway was the majordomo.

Dendroba excused himself from royal reunion, preferring to be alone in his thoughts on the balcony.

"It is good to see you again, sire," the old servant said to the prince. It was sincere, even if his tone lacked any enthusiasm. Phillip smiled, glad to see his faithful steward. The majordomo then turned to General White. "And Lady Snow, it is nice to have you back home, as well."

"Hello, Henry," replied General White politely. "It's good to see you, too."

Snow White blushed that Henry had recognized her. After all, it had been many years since Snow White had set foot in the castle.

The majordomo spoke again. "Will you need your chambers prepared?" he asked of General White.

"No, thank you, Henry," she replied. "I won't be staying long."

"My understanding of our royal laws is that with Cinderella now removed as queen, the leadership of the throne would revert to the next oldest in the family. That would be you, Lady Snow Marchen."

"What? Is that correct, Henry?" Phillip asked with surprise. "I thought it was mine—the eldest male child."

"Well, it was never an issue because Lady Snow was thought lost. So, you being the only child, that would have been a correct assumption. But your father's laws are very clear on the matter; the eldest child takes the throne."

Snow White shook her head. "News travels fast, it seems. No, if anyone should take the throne it should be Phillip."

Henry corrected the general, "Lady Snow, you are the older of the two siblings. Royal law dictates the eldest is to assume the throne. And now that you have returned, he is not the oldest eligible anymore—you are."

Snow white stammered, "But I don't want the throne. Give it to Phillip."

Henry responded. "Indeed, but that is the law. I did not want to be trapped in this castle for the last five years, yet we do not always get what we want."

Phillip could see the blood drain away from Snow White's face. "Perhaps we can sort this out a little later, Henry," Prince Phillip offered. He, too, had presumed he would take the throne when he returned, not thinking it would go to his older sister.

"Very well, sire." The majordomo appeared to back down a little. "But the kingdom must not be without a leader."

Then Rapunzel stopped, cocking her head to the side. "Wait a second," she said, slightly puzzled. "Do you hear that?" She paused again, listening intently to make sure.

"It sounds like singing!"

CHAPTER 22
JACK AND THE BEANSTALK

I might as well stand on a table in the middle of market and shout, "Does anybody want a cow?"

Trying to sell Milky-White at market had been a waste of a day, and young Jack was all but defeated. His mother's words still hung over him like chains. "Son," she had said. "It will now cost more to take care of your father's old cow than we can afford. Neither one of us has the means or desire to slaughter a cow properly. We cannot afford to hire a butcher. We simply have no money and that cow is the only thing we might be able to sell to at least survive the winter. Then in the spring, perhaps the soil will be better. I doubt you could sell it for anything more than stew bones, but if you cannot sell the cow outright, trade it for chickens. If nothing else, find out what a tanner would offer. I'd go myself, but my legs aren't what they used to be."

Jack stopped by the tanner as the market was closing for the day.

The tanner was a huge, mustached, bald-headed man. He had watched Jack wander the market with the cow all day. Before the boy could speak, the tanner gathered his things.

"I'm sorry, son. Cow's too old. Hide won't stretch right." Then he went inside his small shed. Jack shuffled dejectedly out the gates and back down the long road. The sun was setting and it would be rather dark by the time he returned home.

Market was closed.

* * *

He had one bean left. Jack rolled it around in his fingers in one hand absently as he pondered what he should do. He took another long drink from a bottle in his other hand, hoping the harsh ale would dull his memories. The bean was warm in his hand. Had he another four beans, he could plant them and make another beanstalk, he thought. Jack looked at the bean in his hand. "This is all your fault," he said with a drunken slur, as if the bean could hear him.

Wonderland was the source of the magic beans. Jack knew this tiny nondescript bean's power all too well. Plant it in the ground and it would grow up to the sky, even breaching the portals into other, far larger worlds. Here it was considered magical, but in Wonderland, this common bean did no such thing. Plant it in the ground there, and it grew like any other bean. However, in Wonderland this same bean if baked into a cake would give a growing property to the person that ingested it. If the bean was boiled and distilled into a liquid, it would have an opposite effect. Incredibly, it would cause anyone who drank it to shrink to a height of six inches.

Jack had learned many things as Alice's companion during the time he was gone from this world. He had been lost for a nearly decade. The latter part he spent living in Wonderland. As near as Jack could figure, he had stumbled across Wonderland and had stayed there for nearly two years. However, time is twisted in Wonderland, and back home almost four years had passed. It was beyond rational belief for Jack—maddening he thought. He considered eating the one bean. How easy to put it in his mouth and swallow it with another gulp from his nearly empty bottle of ale. Perhaps it would end his misery for good. Jack drank the harsh ale again as if to practice. Smirking as he did, he imagined how they would find his body, with a giant beanstalk growing out of his mouth. It would be an appropriate way to die.

* * *

"Nice night to be out walking your cow," a voice said in the dusky evening. "I saw you walking that beast toward the market this morning." A tall lanky man approached, trying poorly to smooth out his mass of unkempt hair as he presented himself to the boy with the cow. "No luck at market I'm guessing. Tough crowd there, very picky," he said. "Are things so bad that you have to sell the cow?"

"I've no money, sir, if you are trying to rob me. I just have the cow. It would be a fitting end to my day if you were to steal my cow. Then I would ask you to murder me, as I'd rather that than return home to my mother's temper."

The stranger laughed—it was deep and rather odd sounding. "I'm not trying to rob you, son. I said to myself, if I see that young boy walk back with that cow, I would do a good deed today and see if I could not help him out. I actually have need of a cow. Any cow will do."

"Oh, then good stranger, I can only offer to sell you my cow. I must bring back money so that my mother and I can buy food for winter and seeds for spring."

The stranger seemed to pause a moment with a devilish grin on his face.

"Let me offer you this, then. I have seeds, beans actually. These beans will grow enough food for you between now and first snow if you plant them tonight. I have plenty of them myself and I can spare a sack of them, if you will give me your cow. I'm sure if your mother sees you've failed and returned home with that cow she would be very upset."

The stranger held up the small sack of beans. On the side of the sack was two words that said, curiously enough, TAKE ME.

Jack was wary. "I don't know. I have never planted beans before. Seeds take a while to grow. Won't these beans take just as long? I'm really supposed to try to get some money, or chickens."

The stranger was calm and patient. "What's your name, boy?" he asked politely.

"Jack Spriggins, sir."

"Jack, I'm trying to help you out. You've spent all day at market and you weren't able to sell your cow." The stranger looked over at the dull-eyed beast. "You're lucky the cow was able to walk all this way without keeling over. A dead cow would be impossible to sell."

Jack had not considered that. Jack's mother was concerned she could not make the walk to market and considering how old his cow was, it was a very similar comparison.

The stranger continued, "These beans will grow big and fast. They are——" The stranger paused for a second. "They are fairy-dusted beans. They will give you enough food for the winter, and in the spring, you will be able to sell beans and make money from that, as well. I'll take care of the cow. You can even come and visit her, if you like."

Jack thought about it a moment. It seemed like the logical thing to do, and it was the only option left. He hoped his mother would understand.

"Very well, sir. If nothing else, we will have bean soup tonight."

Maybe they could sell the extra beans, Jack thought. People would pay a fortune for magic beans. Who know, Jack began to wonder, by next planting season they could be rich.

"Smart boy, Jack. Your mother will be proud. It's a tough decision." The stranger

offered the sack of beans to Jack as the boy handed over the walking rope for the cow.

"Her name is Milky-White. She likes to eat the tall grass and she loves clover." *Jack said as he patted the cow on the shoulder. "And your name, sir?"*

The stranger smiled as he placed the beans in Jack's hand.

"Matt. Matt Hadner. Nice to do business with you, Jack Spriggins."

* * *

"Damn beans." Jack kicked the hay around with his foot as he recalled that fateful meeting. He sat amidst the hay bales in the old barn of the safe house. A small nub of a candle was all the light he could spare in the darkness. The hulking form of the Looking Glass covered in burlap and rope stood silently in the shadows. It was night, and Jack was waiting until morning, hoping someone from General White's resistance would return. When Jack returned in the late evening, he saw the bodies of dwarves and the queen's guards scattered about, and he realized that the safe house had been compromised. He found the Looking Glass wrapped and buried in the hay. He would only wait one night, he thought. If no one came by morning, he would take the mirror to another location.

On the other hand, perhaps he would destroy it. He laughed to himself at that absurd thought. He pulled the bottle of ale to his cracked lips and drank heavily, finishing it in a few quick swallows. Cursing at the mirror. Jack spat as he glared at it. " I hate you. You're an abomination." With drunken frustration, he threw the emptied bottle at the wrapped mirror. The bottle shattered and produced a wet stain as it struck the wrapped Looking Glass. Jack shook his head in despair. "The mirror doesn't break," he said dejectedly. "I couldn't break the mirror even if I wanted to."

There was a creak as the wooden door of the dilapidated barn swung open. An all too familiar voice interrupted Jack.

"Well, well, if it isn't Jack Spriggins. I was expecting to recover the mirror tonight, but this...this is just too easy."

Jack whirled around, startled by the voice. In the dimness of the candlelight, he recognized the intruder.

"Rabbit," Jack sneered. "The last time I saw you, you were fighting off a Bandersnatch in Tulgey Wood."

"Yes, well, that would make sense as you tricked it into attacking me."

"I was merely distracting you from killing me," countered Jack.

"As you can see, it was only a momentary distraction," replied the White Rabbit as he limped into the barn. A slight glint of candlelight reflected off a metal prosthetic foot that Rabbit now wore.

"Apparently," Jack retorted, quickly sobering up with the Rabbit's presence. He found himself quickly returning to his old mannerisms in the presence of his old acquaintance. He could feel his old self starting to return, even as Rabbit drew forth his slender sword.

Jack's eyes quickly darted around. He saw his small axe lying on the ground where he had been sitting. Its blade shone warmly in the candlelight. He shuffled cautiously towards the candle, gauging the White Rabbit as he did. Jack knew how dangerous the White Rabbit was.

"I see your plan for world domination is coming along, Rabbit," Jack said, trying to stall a little bit. "You've gotten Wonderland's army to invade. All thanks to setting up a sucker with a bunch of magic beans."

Rabbit started to advance slowly on Jack. "I can't take the credit for that. That was Hatter's plan. However, there are a few details that still need to be tidied up," Rabbit implied threateningly.

"Just so we're clear, Rabbit, are you trying to kill me because I found out about your plot to overtake Wonderland, or is it because you're in love with Alice and you couldn't stand to see her marry another offlander like herself?"

Rabbit bristled, allowing Jack's words to get under his skin, but it was only for a moment.

"Officially, my dear boy, you are wanted by the court for stealing the queen's tarts."

"You mean the tarts you framed me with? Those tarts?" Jack replied.

"The sentence for which is death by beheading, I'm afraid."

Rabbit stepped closer. "If it's any consolation, the queen did order a stay of execution for you."

"Somehow that part is going to get lost in translation, isn't it?"

"I'm afraid it is," Rabbit glared. Then with a hateful, despising growl, Rabbit leaped at Jack with frightening speed. Jack was quick, though. Nimbly tumbling away from Rabbit's vicious attack, he quickly picked up his axe at the same time and quite deliberately knocked the lighted candle over. The old dry hay bales took the fire instantly in a blaze, crossing quickly over to the Looking Glass. Its alcohol stained burlap wrappings easily ignited.

Rabbit swung tightly in quick succession as Jack stumbled backwards, still feeling the effects of the ale he had been drinking. He was within his wits enough, though, to block Rabbit's attacks with the woodcutter's axe he carried.

"What's the matter, Rabbit? Still annoyed that Alice would choose me over you?" Using the thick axe handle with both hands, Jack blocked the second attack from Rabbit, pushing him off balance. This gave Jack enough time to hop to his feet.

"It's unfair, isn't it? After all, you watched her grow since she was a child, right? Isn't that what you told me in the past?"

The fire easily engulfed the hay, the old wooden timbers, and the floorboards, more quickly than even Jack had planned. The door through which Rabbit had entered only moments before was impossible to get to from the intense heat and fire that now raged. The rabbit continued to trade blows with Jack, keeping him focused on the immediate danger of his attacks.

"I made her queen!" Rabbit yelled above the din of the growing inferno. "I made her the true queen of Wonderland!"

"Yes," Jack yelled back, as Rabbit quickly parried Jack's swing. "But you're still just a rabbit. Alice could never love you any more than an owner loves her pet!" This infuriated the White Rabbit even further. His tempered discipline began to crack.

The fire was surrounding them now; the roof was rolling with flames and pieces of fiery wood fell with a loud crash. Thick black smoke filled the barn, and flames licked at the two combatants. As they struggled to fight, hot orange embers fell about, stinging Jack and singeing Rabbit's fur coat.

"It doesn't matter now, Jack!" the rabbit shouted above the blaze.

"With Queen Alice no longer on the sovereign soil of Wonderland, her rule can be challenged. Alice will never return to Wonderland!" Rabbit feigned a swing, catching Jack off guard, and landed a massive punch that sent him sprawling to the floor, his axe sliding into the hungry flames of the ever-growing fire.

"You can't take the throne, Rabbit. No native of Wonderland can rule solely. Only an offlander can rule Wonderland as one," said Jack. He knew the rules of Wonderland well from the time he spent with Queen Alice. In a place as chaotic as Wonderland, rules such as that were Alice's attempts to bring order. Now it seemed they were about to work against her. Jack winced, struggling to get up. The heat sucked his strength. Sweat stung his eyes. Smoke choked him. For a moment he had lost sight of where Rabbit was.

"I already have another offlander in mind for the job. A new Red Queen, Jack." The rabbit suddenly emerged from a wall of smoke and was standing over him now. A strong kick from his powerful legs landed squarely on Jack's shoulders, smashing Jack back down to the floorboards and knocking precious air from his lungs.

The fire was out of control now, and Rabbit realized it had grown too dangerous even for him to remain much longer. He raised his sword. "Burned alive is a terrible way to die, Jack. So I will at least make it quick for you...for Alice's sake."

There was a loud, splintering, popping noise as the roof began to collapse above them. The White Rabbit was forced to jump away or risk being crushed in the flaming debris. Rabbit crashed backwards through the fire-weakened walls of the barn, rolling on the ground away from the burning structure. He quickly got to his feet just moments before the entire barn collapsed in a fiery heap.

"So long, Jack," said the White Rabbit. In a way, Rabbit was glad he could tell Alice that Jack was lost in a fire. At least it was true. Rabbit did not have to be directly responsible for Jack's death. He felt a little relieved at this—his paws were dirty enough in the grander scheme. Rabbit watched the building's remains burn for a few moments more. He would have to wait for the fire to subside before he could approach the Looking Glass. He knew the fire would not damage it. Quickly he created a rabbit hole, one that did not lead back to Wonderland. Rabbit disappeared through it as the flames of the collapsed barn reached high into the night sky.

CHAPTER 23
A SLEEPING BEAUTY IN A GLASS COFFIN

Word spread quickly throughout the castle that the queen was no longer in power and the prince had returned. Within an hour, all the castle servants and staff had celebrated the news, everyone patting backs and shoulders, and wiping tears of happiness from their faces. Long forgotten smiles returned and then gave way to laughter as the servants stopped their work, waking others to tell them the good news. Many of the castle guards, mostly of the accursed Rat Army loyal to the queen, feared both Cendrillon's fall and retaliation by the servants. In fact, most of them quietly hid away, choosing cowardice and self-survival over attempts to oppress any uprising.

"Rapunzel, take Hamelin," Snow White ordered. "Go and see what is going on."

In a few minutes, Rapunzel and Hamelin made their way down the stairs to a walkway that overlooked a great hall. Further down was an alcove and another set of stairs that led to the crowd-filled floor of the great hall. The sound from the great hall was louder now. They could hear flutes playing, clapping and singing, guitars and drumming. Best of all, Rapunzel saw castle staff dancing everywhere. The food they had prepared night after night for a cruel and uncaring royalty was now a feast for their celebration. enthusiastically, they hoisted tankards of ale, and popped corks from royal wine bottles. There was an excited energy in the air, and it buzzed with joyous fervor.

In the middle of the great hall, a huge circle of children and servants had gathered. They were dancing to the impromptu music, jumping around and changing direction as they shouted and sang loudly.

Queen Cinder, Queen Cinder with the crown off your head! Now we are free because now you are dead!

"Is it over now?" a castle servant asked Rapunzel. "Really over? Is it true?" The smiling servant wanted desperately to believe that the torment of the last five years was at an end.

Rapunzel could not contain her smile. "Yes," she replied. "You are free from Queen Cendrillon's rule forever." Rapunzel knew there was much more to it, but tonight she thought to let castle servants celebrate. The festive merrymaking was contagious, and soon Rapunzel and Hamelin were caught up in the dancing and singing. Throughout the celebrating one could hear, "We're free!" repeated countless times.

Rapunzel thought of her mother, and she was overwhelmed with guilt for joining in the celebration. She had promised herself that the next day she would go search for her mother's body to give the old woman a proper burial. Hamelin noticed her look of sadness. Pulling off a last piece of bread and shoving it into his mouth, then quickly pushing it into his cheek to talk, he walked over to the lieutenant amidst the revelry.

"Rapunzel, is everything okay?" he asked as he swallowed the bread.

Startled, Rapunzel wiped her wet eyes with her palms. "When I was growing up, my mother would visit me, and she and I used to spend the day dancing and singing in my room. I used to love to dance. I have not really danced since. I hated my mother for many years; it has only been during these last few weeks that we have reconciled. But, I just—I miss her right now." She fought back tears. "She would have loved to have been here for this."

Hamelin extended his hand. "Then let us dance for her. Let us dance for all the sacrifices your mother and the rest of us have made," he said smiling, with a friendly wink.

Hamelin pulled out his pipes as he danced, and played a tune for Rapunzel, hopping around her until she could not help but smile. Rapunzel gave the piper an unsure look at first, but pushing back her tears and laughing along, she finally danced with Hamelin.

"I'm sorry I called you a jerk before," she said as they twirled around.

"I probably was," Hamelin admitted with a smirk. Other musicians joined in, and soon Rapunzel found herself whirling about in Hamelin's arms, enjoying the dance despite herself. The song ended with much applause, and Rapunzel placed a small kiss on Hamelin's cheek.

"Thank you for that, Hamelin. You're a good friend," Rapunzel said with a heartfelt grin. Then she quickly disappeared into the crowd as the musicians began to play another tune.

* * *

"Patience, come here please," said General White quietly from the queen's balcony.

When Patience approached, Snow White took a moment to speak privately with her.

"Your mother did the bravest thing she that any mother could do. The prince and I lost our mother when our queen died. Even Cinderella lost her mother, as did Rapunzel. We all know how you feel, and we will all help you," Snow White offered. She spoke not as the serious minded general, but more consoling, and in manner Patience had not seen before.

"You have been one of the bravest people I have known. And your loss must be very hard for you, but there is more that is going to happen before we can truly allow ourselves to grieve. You have done more than any child I have known—you protected the shards and delivered them to us. I cannot ask anything more of you. It was the only way to truly stop Cendrillon. Now, there may be a war soon and another army will try to take this castle if we cannot stop them. You know this castle and its staff better than anyone does. Better than the prince," she whispered assuredly. "I will be at the front lines being a general. But I need you for a special mission—to stay here at the castle and help the staff. You will be my special liaison to the majordomo, Henry." Snow White put her hand on the quiet girl's cheek. "Okay? I need you to be strong. I want you to be safe, and you'll be safer here than anywhere I'm going."

Patience nodded. "Are you going to be the new queen?" she asked, "You would be a good queen."

"We'll see, little one." Snow White smiled at her, then gave Patience a quick hug and kissed her on her forehead. "We will go see what Henry has in store for us in a few moments."

Patience went back to her mother, finding a sheet to cover her body as she said one last silent goodbye. She waited for Snow White and thought about what she had said. She would ask Henry to help her bury her mother by the apple orchards.

Turning away from Patience, overwhelming emotion suddenly washed over General White and her eyes filled with tears. Quickly, she wiped the tears from her face and, shaking her head, she stood up, wondering what had triggered such an unexpected emotional reaction. Perhaps it was the feeling of being back in the very castle she had left many years ago. Perhaps it was the realization that her time as leader of the resistance was now finite, that either by defeat on the battlefield or through victory, soon she would no longer need to command the dwarven armies; or had it been that people expected her to take the throne? What should she do now? Snow White cleared away her tears as to clear away her thoughts and regain focus. *It's not over yet,* she told herself.

* * *

Fae Gaia spoke to Phillip as they stood next to the body of Cinderella, "There's one last thing. To ensure the Fae sleep is not tainted, Cinderella will be quarantined."

"What!" exclaimed Prince Phillip.

"Completely sealed away—it's for her own protection while she recovers." The God-mother fairy seemed to reach into the shimmering glow that flowed around her, as one would reach into a pocket to retrieve a coin. Then with an "ah" as she found what she was looking for, she pulled out the glass slippers, now intact. Fae magic rolled off them and dispersed into misty tendrils.

"Cendrillon needs to stand trial," Snow White demanded. "She has ruined the kingdom, consorted with witches; her army has killed villagers and imprisoned children. She tried to murder the prince. The kingdom deserves to see justice exacted. She needs to be locked away, or burned at the stake."

"General White," replied Fae Gaia. "Queen Cendrillon is dead. The evil that my daughter has been exposed to over the years—this Queen Cendrillon persona—will be wiped away by this last spell I will be able to cast. When it is complete, Ella will have no memory of her time as queen. She will revert back to the person she was before you had left, Phillip. That is the only way. So in essence, Queen Cendrillon has died here tonight."

"Ella has been under a spell all along, then?" asked Prince Phillip.

"No. There was no trickery or magic involved. It would be easier to deal with if that were true; something external to blame, would have been better. Unfortunately, no spells other than the years of temptation, corruption, bitterness and grief have taken its toll and the witchcraft has driven my daughter down a darker path." Fae Gaia looked at the still body of Cinderella. "It is hard to watch, especially as part of me is also her mother. I wish I could have been there for her. In my own death, I feel that I have failed her. So I would ask of you General White, to let this mother have a chance to give her daughter another chance."

"I don't agree, fairy," Snow White answered. "However, I will respect your request. Cendrillon is dead. I will have no issue with the princess Cinderella. But, should anything happen that is reminiscent of the old Queen Cendrillon, I will not hesitate to strike her down next time." Snow White looked sternly at the Fae. She was deadly serious.

"How long will she have to be quarantined?" Phillip asked with anxiety now wavering at the edge of his voice. "Is it really necessary? Can't she just sleep it off?"

"She will sleep it off Phillip," answered the God-mother fairy, walking over to the feet of the unconscious Cinderella. "The magic will work itself through all of her and return her to a more balanced state, safe from the influence that years of black magic has had on her." The Fae Gaia lifted the delicate ankle of the sleeping queen, and effortlessly slipped one of the glass slippers on her foot. It sparkled elegantly, like polished crystal, as Cinderella lay motionless. "If that influence is not removed, she will be at risk of turning back to evil and embracing it tenfold. All your efforts would be lost."

"How long then?" Prince Phillip asked again. "The night? A couple of days in isolation? When will she wake from your magic?"

"A hundred years," answered the God-mother fairy solemnly. She lifted Cinderella's other foot and slid it into the other glass slipper.

"But we'll all be dead before she awakens! I didn't risk my life to return just to live the rest of my days watching her as she sleeps!"

The prince's concern did not dissuade Fae Gaia. She raised her wand to begin, but then paused. "There is another way. I will exclude one element of the spell I cast. Love," the Fae offered. "After the sun has set three days from now, Cinderella can only be awakened by the kiss of the man who truly loved her. Only this kiss will awaken her and complete the purging of her evil past. If not, then she will sleep for a hundred years."

"I would kiss her now," professed the Prince. "She won't remember any of this? The Cendrillon persona, the witchcraft or even when I left for the Beanstalk war?"

"Correct. She will be disoriented and frightened with all of the changes that have transpired from when she could last remember. It will be a very confusing time for her, which is why she needs to be near people who truly love her."

"Phillip, she stabbed you and left you for dead," Snow White reminded him. "I'd not be so quick with affections."

"Snow," Phillip replied defensively, "do not think that I do not love the girl I married. I have not seen Ella since I left. She was not herself when she stabbed me. If something as simple as a kiss were all that stands in the way of being reunited with the girl I knew ten years ago, then, yes, I would kiss her."

"It has to be a kiss of love, Prince Phillip." Fae Gaia reiterated. "This is not some instruction to follow or procedure to complete. You may have loved her at some point, but to truly love her now—I am not so convinced that you truly lover her now. Nor do I think my daughter has been entirely in love with you, either, as of late."

"You had that knife hidden in your boot, Phillip. You would have killed her to save the kingdom. Now you would also kiss her to save the kingdom. Do you love the kingdom, or Cinderella?" asked Snow White.

Phillip did not answer.

"You must wait at least three days. Then we shall see. This magic is strong, but it needs time to work." Then the Fae Gaia proceeded to cast her spell using the magic left in her old wand and the powerful magic of the glass slippers. Cinderella's feet began to glow and the slippers seemed to expand, growing to engulf the queen's feet and then fusing into each other, as the glass began to encase her legs. The magic crystal from the glass slippers continued to grow past the sleeping queen's waist, and then covering her breasts. In moments, the glass slippers had transformed and fully encased the queen like a transparent glass coffin, all while she slept unaware. Finally, arcane seals and runes formed across the coffin. They seemed etched in the very glass itself, but they shimmered with a faint, ghostly glow that lazily traced itself back and forth along the glass coffin. Cinderella was now completely sealed away, a sleeping beauty in a glass coffin.

"It is finished. In three days, should you wish to kiss her to end the spell, the glass will part like the receding tide—*if* your love is true."

"And you don't think it is?" the prince shot back defensively.

"It is not up to me, Phillip. It is up to you...and Cinderella."

* * *

Dendroba had stayed on the balcony, enjoying the simple pleasure of the wind blowing through his hair. He had been reflecting on the events of the night, his new physical appearance and the end of Cendrillon and the coven's rule over the throne. Then Dendroba saw something dark and alive move in the blackness of the sky. It was large and swooped silently past the balcony. He was sure he had seen something, and he stood there for a few moments watching for it. Then saw it again. Apprehension burned across the back of his neck. It was headed for the castle.

"General White! Phillip!" Dendroba shouted urgently from where he stood on the balcony. "There is something big flying toward the castle. I think the invasion is starting. Now!"

CHAPTER 24
BEWARE THE JABBERWOCK

General White and Prince Phillip rushed out to the balcony and caught a quick glimpse of a large creature as it silent began to descend behind one of the castle spires.

"That is not good," Phillip said. "We need to get downstairs to warn everyone!"

"I will stay with Cinderella and the child for now," the Fae said. "I need to regain my strength."

"Do it quickly—we might need you," Phillip shouted as the three raced out of the room, Dendroba bounded down the stairs with Snow White and Phillip racing to keep up behind him. As they quickly descended, they could hear the unsuspecting crowd still celebrating in the main hall.

"We have to warn them!" General White told the others. Then they heard a terrible sound, and laughter was replaced with cracking stone and loud crashing booms that resounded throughout the castle. The cheerful din turned to sudden screams of horror.

"Damn," Snow White cursed. She pushed past Dendroba, almost flying down the stairs to the grand hall. Chaos rained down from above as the huge vaulted ceiling exploded. The castle staff and their families scattered with terrified cries as celebration turned to chaos. With the sounds of music and revelry, they did not hear the loud crash. Only when the large chunks of rock and wooden beam fell upon them did they realize too late as some of the staff were struck by the falling ceiling and crushed outright.

Rapunzel was only inches away from being crushed as a large block of stone slammed down next to her. Several pillars shattered from the cascade of fallen rock, and the stairway collapsed. Rubble piled up across the floor of the room and huge clouds of dust covered everything.

General White arrived at the walkway banister that overlooked the great hall, but she could only watch helplessly at that moment, the sight taking her breath away. Everywhere she could hear crying, the coughs and murmurs of confusion seemed to grow louder as the dust from the collapse began to settle. Something large moved across the rubble, obscured by the dust cloud and a low, unnatural sound suddenly filled the room. It was a growl, a deep sounding gurgle.

As the cloud of dust dispersed, a huge form appeared atop the rubble. It was dragon-like, with mottled grey skin covered in thick calluses, a dangerously long whip-like tail, and lanky yet muscular arms ending in furred hands with long thin fingers and incredibly long, sharp claws. Its long legs were armed with deadly claws that scraped the broken marble and stone as it braced its footing on the pile of rock. A pair of smallish, bat-like wings, which seemed not possibly able to carry the great beast, flapped in agitation. It had a long, serpentine neck and a huge oddly-shaped head reminiscent of a fish head with its saucer-like, bulbous eyes. Two writhing tendrils adorned its head; they twisted as they sensed the air around them. Two similar tendrils draped down around its mouth like a long, thin moustache.

Its mouth held huge razor-like teeth that clicked together as it continually bleated, murmured, and uttered an almost constant low warbling. It whiffled its cheeks unsteadily in and out, snorting and blowing in small puffs as it smelled and tasted its surroundings. The creature's two large eyes seemed to reflect the nearby firelight from the torches and braziers. With another gurgling bellow, the beast lunged forth with incredible speed. It began attacking everyone in the great hall. The head darted forward like the quick, uncoiling strike of a deadly snake. Its great maw opened and jaws of flat, razor-like teeth shot out as a shark's, extending for a deadly bite and instantly cutting a hapless castle servant in half.

The crowd panicked as the creature continued its rampage. The strange monster snatched out with its sharp furred claws, raking the life out of any of those that tried to flee.

Snow White looked for any way down. She quickly darted up and down the walkway banister, but could not find any other means to exit aside from jumping thirty feet to the broken stone floor. Both the prince and Dendroba arrived on the walkway, shocked at the sight of the frightening creature. "What is that thing?"

the prince recoiled in horror. The creature seemed to be made up of the worst parts of nightmares. He had never seen anything like it before.

"The stairs are destroyed! There's no way down!" shouted General White. In the crowd, she could see Rapunzel tumbling out of a killing swipe from the monster as it shot past the trapped lieutenant. The creature slammed into the support pillars of the balcony on the far side of the room, sending more rubble collapsing down. The devastation the monster created in such a short time was astonishing and swift.

"You want to go down there?" asked Phillip incredulously. General White did not hear him. At least she pretended she did not.

Dendroba could hear the screams from the crowd as they tried to run for safety, mixed with the otherworldly noises of the horrific creature echoing loudly as it rampaged through the great hall.

"White, give me your sword," Dendroba said, reaching urgently out to Snow White. Without question, she lobbed the sword at Dendroba. He snatched it out of the air, and then the former general backed up to the stairs and ran full on toward the banister, easily clearing it.

General Dendroba had made jumps like these many times without fail.

As quickly as he had leaped over the banister, he realized he was not accustomed to being fully human yet. His wholly human legs did not provide him with his familiar power. In fact, he was so caught up in engaging the monster that Dendroba forgot he was fully human now. If not for the large table of food he landed on, he would have been seriously injured in the fall.

"We'll have to take another way around, Snow. Down to that hallway!" said the prince. He pointed across the room to a small door on the lower level. People in the crowd had rushed through and were barricading the door behind them, trapping others inside the room with the creature.

"There has to be another way." Snow White shook her head, seeing Dendroba scramble out from the mess of the broken table. "Do you know about the servant's passages, Phillip?"

The prince shook his head. "No," he said simply.

"Me neither," said Snow White, thinking quickly. "We were royalty. We never had to use them. But I know someone who would know them better than anyone else."

Without wasting another second, Snow White quickly turned and bolted back up the stairs, almost barreling into Patience who had started down the staircase. "Is something wrong?" Patience asked, "I heard screaming. The Fairy Godmother asked me to find you. I don't think she's feeling very well."

"I think the Fae Gaia can take care of herself for a little bit. Patience, is there a servant's passage down to the great hall? The stairway is blocked!" General White sounded panicked.

Patience Muffet thought for a second. "Actually there should be one around here on the stairwell." She looked around, recognizing one of the hidden doorways. "This way," she pointed.

"Phillip!" Snow White shouted. "This way, hurry!"

* * *

Dendroba recovered quickly from the fall. He could hear the servants screaming as they tried to run for the doors to escape the raging creature. The great beast seemed to tower over everything now that the general was on the ground. Its head arched upwards on its thin neck as it let out another burbling bellow. Bodies of the castle staff lay amongst the rubble, some crushed by the falling debris while others were clearly felled by the monster's attack.

But not everyone was running. Dendroba saw Rapunzel across the room gripping an unlit wall sconce as a weapon with the man he knew as the piper. The monster's massive body blocked them from escaping. The creature wreaked havoc, lashing out at anything within reach, making it dangerous to risk running past. Dendroba was sure that if the creature turned their way again, it would certainly attack them. He wondered where the castle guards were, realizing of course that many must have fled to other hiding places in the castle. Dendroba knew better than anyone that the queen's guards were cowards unless he was scaring them into action. It was one thing to bully common townspeople; it was another question of loyalty to fight off such a true monster.

Then he saw one of the castle's guards nearby, clutching his shield tightly to his chest. The guard cowered behind a pillar under one of the balconies, trying desperately not to be seen. Angrily, the general stormed over. "Get out there and fight that thing," Dendroba growled. "Your job is to protect the castle, soldier," he ordered.

The sudden appearance of the general had startled him. The terrified soldier looked at Dendroba, "You—you can't tell me what to do. I'm staying here. Save yourself!"

"What!" Dendroba bellowed, almost as a loud as the creature. The soldier shrunk back.

"I am your general, soldier, and I am ordering you to get out there and protect the throne! Now!"

"You aren't General Dendroba. My general hides his face; he is so disgusting to look at. He can kill with just the touch of his hand. I found this hiding spot first! Leave me alone!" the frightened soldier replied.

"I *am* General Dendroba!" he bellowed. Then Dendroba remembered he was not the monstrous general who had commanded the queen's army. He was a man; and it was true, his troops had only respected the fear he commanded from his disfigurement. *This complicates things,* Dendroba noted to himself.

There was no time to waste arguing, however. He punched the surprised guard hard in the face, sending him to the floor unconscious. Then, he grabbed the guard's shield and knelt over his unmoving body. General Dendroba secured Snow White's sword into his belt and took the soldier's sword in hand. When he stood back up, however, he froze. He sensed something behind him. The foul, moist warm air from a low snort confirmed his fear. He could hear the low murmur-like noises coming from the creature's throat, its teeth clicking together in annoyance.

Slowly, Dendroba turned on his heel, barely breathing, and faced the monster directly. The creature's long neck descended curiously down to the general's eye level, and its large fiery eyes stared intently at Dendroba. The beast's fleshy antennae twitched anxiously in his direction as the huge mouth slowly opened, revealing large, flat incisors covered in saliva and blood.

Very cautiously, Dendroba moved a half step backward. The monstrous head followed him. Dendroba then noticed that the guard he had knocked unconscious, who was lying between himself and the monster, was starting to come around.

"Don't move," Dendroba whispered slowly, almost mouthing the words. However, the dazed soldier was not aware of the creature near him and slowly started to get to his feet.

"Stay down, soldier," Dendroba whispered loudly, never taking his eyes off the beast. But the soldier ignored him.

"You punched me, you bast—" That was all it took. Startled, the monster's eyes widened. It pulled its long neck back, and then its head struck with incredible speed at the unsuspecting soldier. He barely had time to scream as the deadly jaws shot out, effortlessly severing the doomed man mid-chest. The bloodied remains of the midsection and both severed forearms fell limply to the ground.

Dendroba bolted across the room, his sword and shield pumping in each arm as he ran full speed toward Rapunzel. The creature instantly reacted, trying to follow, but it struggled around the pillar, having to back out instead to give chase. It bought Dendroba some time.

Rapunzel had not hesitated, either. As soon as the creature had trouble maneuvering around the confining space near the pillar, Rapunzel and Hamelin ushered some of the trapped servants towards the doorway. The creature was too big to fit within, but with its very long, serpentine neck, it could easily reach a considerable distance down the length of a hallway.

When they reached the doorway, the frantic group found the heavy wooden doors shut and locked from the other side by those who had already escaped. Everyone left in the grand hall was trapped, every entrance barricaded in or blocked by rubble. Rapunzel saw General Dendroba scrambling over the rubble heading directly towards them. The great beast rose up behind him in pursuit, bellowing loudly as it fixated on its prey.

Dendroba waved his hands at them, motioning Rapunzel and others to go through the door.

Rapunzel yelled back at him, "We can't! We're locked in!"

The beast was still barreling down on them, its tail flailing, arms waving as it bellowed and warbled. Its long neck waved back and forth chaotically as it ran, its small wings beating frumiously, seeming to give the creature even more speed.

Hamelin spoke quickly, "I think I can buy us some time!"

He reached into his pied patchwork coat and pulled out his familiar pipes. Quickly, he began to play. "Run!" he said in between his playing. "Find another way out!"

Rapunzel and the group quickly scattered back to where they were hiding as Hamelin focused on playing, trying to get beast to fall under the influence of his mysterious pipes.

Dendroba barely had a lead over the creature as he yelled at Hamelin to get away. But Hamelin played his pipes harder. Dendroba waved again, yelling at Hamelin to get out of the way. He had hoped to use the beast's momentum as it gave chase to have it slam into the doors, but Hamelin was in the way and not paying attention. As the beast bore down on top of him, Hamelin was still trying hard to make his pipes affect it.

Dendroba growled. He could not run the monster through the locked doors without hitting Hamelin. Instead, he changed direction, hoping the beast would follow by giving the monster enough time to turn as well.

But the monster broke off its pursuit of the general and continued to head straight for the doors and Hamelin.

The monster halted its pursuit as Dendroba stopped and turned to watch.

Hamelin was visibly shaking where he stood. His gaze focused down at the floor and he played as hard as he could, afraid to look up at the awesome visage of the creature now towering before him.

"It's working!" Rapunzel said as she watched from behind a rubble pile. "Hamelin is controlling it with his music!"

Even Dendroba, his barreled chest heaving from exertion, seemed to be impressed with the piper's heroic actions. The creature towered over Hamelin in suspension, transfixed to the music from the pipes.

It only lasted for a moment. The creature let out a deafening, burbling roar, and with a mighty step forward, it smacked Hamelin into the wall with its great claws. The piper never saw it coming, and when he hit the wall he dropped to the floor, unnaturally limp.

* * *

The Fae Gaia stood alone inside the queen's chambers. She picked up her wand from a nearby table and rested her other hand on the glass coffin, feeling the warmth of its magic as it pulsed through her fingers. There was a moment of clarity when the mother of Cinderella spoke rather than the Fae Gaia, though they two were fused together in essence. For a while, she was simply a mother looking over her child as she lay in the glass entombment. "Oh, Ella." Cinderella's mother spoke softly, "What mother can be mad at her child for becoming a queen? It is a dream come true. I am proud of you for that, but how far you have fallen. I do not know how long the Fae Gaia and I shall remain here, but someday I hope we can have the time to be just mother and daughter again, if for a brief moment. That would be my wish. I was taken from you too young and I could not be there to protect you, dear Ella. For that I am filled with more regret than you'll ever know."

Then the Fae Gaia sensed another presence in the room.

"So it is true. A God-mother fairy still walks this realm."

"Cheshire Cat," the Fae Gaia replied. Recognizing the voice, she turned to face the intruder, "I am surprised you still come to hunt the Fae."

"Hardly—I do not do that anymore," Cheshire replied coolly, "thanks to you. But your presence here is bothersome for us." The large, ethereal cat had appeared on the balcony and now walked softly into the room, as if gliding on air.

"I see you still bear the scars from the last time we met," the Fae Gaia observed. "I left you alive but incorporeal. You have not learned your lesson to stay away."

"Yes, that was a long time ago. I have learned to live with my intangibility issues since then. I've even made some improvement in recovery."

"Well," said the Fae Gaia, "I highly doubt this is a nostalgic visit. Your presence here is a violation of the Fae-Wonderland treaty."

"A minor detail, all things considered." The Cheshire Cat grinned and walked closer. "While there is a Fae alive in this realm, that treaty is in effect. But, and correct me if I am wrong, I do not sense the same level of magic that a true Fae would have. So I would reason you are not a full Fae anymore, thus making the treaty null and void."

The Cheshire Cat was correct. The Fae Gaia was not full Fae. She had used the body of Cinderella's mother as a vessel because her magic was limited to what was left in the slippers. The Fae bowed her head.

"That is true, Cheshire," she admitted. "But I still represent the Fae."

Cheshire waved his paw—his magic was strong—and a rabbit hole appeared in the floor behind the Fae. "You know full well the power of Wonderland magic. You can try to resist, but honestly, I am not in the mood for a long, drawn-out fight. So if we could dispense with the big climactic battle, and if you will just surrender to me, we'll be on our way."

Her magic had been all but exhausted between fighting with the guards tonight and the creation of the glass coffin. Despite that, the Fae Gaia defiantly stood her ground. "I've beaten you once, Cheshire. I will do it again." She raised her wand, pointing at the Cheshire Cat.

Then with another wave of his paw, the rabbit hole disappeared.

"Have I told you I've regained partial tangibility in my claws?" With a glint, several long razor-sharp claws popped out from the Cheshire's front paw. The Fae knew Cheshire's claws could slice through anything, as it had been the main reason they rendered him intangible. Indeed, now the claws looked very real. "Very well. I shall make this a quick fight; it is, after all, the way I prefer to do things." Cheshire approached the Fae. "Hatter has his constant planning, Rabbit has his wars, but I feel sometimes a more direct face-to-face approach works best."

With a sinister grin, the Cheshire Cat leaped at the fairy, his incorporeal body becoming a blur in the air. With both claws, he furiously raked at the Fae Gaia. The claws did not draw blood or tear flesh; rather they ripped painfully at the ethereal aura of the fairy. But it was the only opportunity the God-mother fairy had to get close to the Wonderland cat. The pain Fae Gaia endured was excruciating as the Cheshire Cat's incorporeal claws shredded about the Fae's body. She grabbed at the cat's head with one hand, barely able to push off his deadly bites, and with the other hand stabbed the wand deep into the cat's ethereal shoulder and neck. Her attacks barely fazed the Cheshire Cat. However, Fae Gaia was not without a plan. As the Fae had been stabbing the cat with her wand with every strike, the wand had been absorbing the powerful magical essence of Wonderland from its only ethereal inhabitant. Then came a quick, brilliant burst of magic from the wand that sent Cheshire scrambling backwards in pain.

The combatants paused, each taking a moment to reevaluate the situation. Fae Gaia, though badly wounded from Cheshire's initial attack, rose slowly to her feet. Ethereal essence washed about her like blood in water. But now in her hand, the Fae Gaia held her ethereal sword again, glowing brightly with renewed magic. In her other hand she held what she had been after—magical proof of Wonderland's presence in Fae territory.

The tail of the Cheshire Cat.

"My tail!" said Cheshire. The sight of his own tail in the hands of the Fae barely registered at first, but a dull pain in his hindquarters confirmed it.

"Yes, and I am going to bring this to the blue fairy—even the queen of the fairies if I have to, as proof of Wonderland's violation of the treaty. Retribution will be swift on fairy wings. Go back and tell Wonderland to prepare to surrender to the Fae."

Fae Gaia did not waste a moment. With renewed magical energy, she departed in a flash of sparkle, leaving the Cheshire Cat alone to ponder the situation.

"Damn," the Cheshire Cat muttered. The tail would grow back well enough he thought, but failing to kill the Fae and compromising Wonderland, was the real problem. He hissed in frustration and stood a moment, licking the remnants of fairy essence from his paws like a house cat would do to clean itself. He tried to work out a new plan. He could not tell Alice what had happened, as he would be implicating himself as a conspirator and traitor. He could not tell the White Rabbit that he had compromised the plan. Lying would buy him a little time. Then an idea struck the Cheshire Cat, one so devilish that it brought an ear-to-ear grin. Quickly, Cheshire waved his hand and a rabbit hole appeared. The grin lingered behind, fading last after Cheshire disappeared.

* * *

A sudden burst of motion exploded from the rubble-blocked hallway as a large black wolf squeezed through the collapsed rock and darted across the room. It stood protectively over Hamelin's body, facing the creature with its hackles bristling down its back. The creature seemed confused by the wolf for a moment, unsure what do about this latest threat. It took a step back, and then issued another bellowing roar. With a ferocious growl, the wolf leaped, snarling with a flash of white fangs and claws as it landed atop the long neck of the creature, tearing furiously with all four feet and clamping down with its jaws. The creature writhed in agony and roared in pain as the wolf attacked. It shifted its body, and with a great snap of its long neck tried to throw the wolf off. In one final swipe, the wolf was flung hard across the room, landing on the stone floor with a painful yelp, where it laid still.

Dendroba now readied his sword and approached the monster, steeling himself for a final battle. It was the only option left for him. Without any help from the castle guards, he would have to face this monster on his own.

With a loud clang, he smacked his sword against the shield, quickly getting the creature's attention as its serpentine neck whipped around to find the source of the noise.

With sword in hand, Dendroba stood in uffish thought, quickly trying to figure out how best to battle the beast. Dendroba yelled a battle roar at the monster, which answered back with a low, burbling growl. The creature lunged forward, its smallish bat-like wings in full display. Dendroba braced as the huge furred claws slammed into his shield. The great ferocity of the strike sent a shudder of pain through his arm as he ducked the wild swing. The metal shield was sliced open by the sharp claws. Dendroba pivoted like a dancer with the monster's next attack, and the majority of the force glanced off his damaged shield. The move brought him inside the creature's arm reach and close to its body.

Dendroba struck hard with the sword, landing one, then two, powerful blows in quick succession. However, the beast's hide was so thick that the sword glanced off the nearly impervious scales. The manxome creature quickly staggered back, more in surprise than injury. Its huge head struck out quickly at Dendroba in response. It was all the general could do to pull his shield over him as the huge teeth struck the metal with a loud scrape. The power of the strike knocked the general to his knees.

The creature lashed out again, its long thin neck coiling back and then shooting forward with incredible speed. With both hands, the general held his shield and deflected the strike, forcing the creature's face to the floor with a loud crunching thud. Quickly, Dendroba scrambled to his feet as the dazed creature lifted it head, shaking the stinging sensation from its face. While the creature's neck was still low, Dendroba struck out from behind his shield, swinging decisively at its huge bulbous head. But the armored scales deflected the first blow. On the second, Dendroba's sword blade shattered into pieces.

Rapunzel and the others watched as Dendroba continued to fight the creature. Rapunzel wanted to run to see if Hamelin was still alive. Then a moment later, she saw him move. Quickly, her heart sank as she realized it was the opening of the hallway door pushing against Hamelin's limp body.

Then Rapunzel yelled, "Someone's opening the door!" General White cautiously stepped into the grand hall to look around, motioning to them and any of the other survivors to hurry to the safety of the hallway. Quickly, Rapunzel led the others to the hallway entrance. Patience ran toward Hamelin as the prince pulled the motionless piper through the doors. Patience stopped for a moment where the Piper had lain. "Oh no," she whispered, picking up Hamelin's musical pipes, now broken and in pieces.

"We should do something!" Prince Phillip shouted, watching General Dendroba battle the fierce beast. Snow White looked in desperation for a weapon, realizing Dendroba had her sword. But there was not much they could do besides provide a momentary distraction as the creature's next meal.

"Dendroba, come on! Get out of there!" White yelled to the general, motioning in the direction of the hallway. But the former commander of Cendrillon's army was so engaged in battling the creature that he did not hear.

The beast rammed its head into the former queen's general, knocking the wind from Dendroba's lungs and slamming him backwards. The force of the hit drove both the broken sword and the battered shield scattering away. Without thinking, Dendroba reached out and grabbed onto the beast's long slithy neck. It reared up, pulling the general completely off the floor. The creature's skin proved too slick, however, and Dendroba quickly lost his grip; having already been lifted several feet in the air, he fell atop the main debris pile. There was a hot flash of pain in Dendroba's side as he scrambled to his feet, wincing as he did. He was used to his ability to heal quickly from wounds and thought little of this one, as well. He fumbled back quickly and pulled Snow White's sword from his belt, readying himself for the monster's next attack.

Dendroba watched as the creature coiled its head back on its long neck, preparing to attack again. Then an idea dawned on Dendroba. He recalled the wolf's attack and he realized that even though the monster's body had proved impervious to his attacks, its neck was not as protected. *How could it be so well armored,* Dendroba thought, *and still move around like that?* The general scrambled to the top of some loose rubble that had tumbled down to the floor, purposely making himself an easy target for the beast. He had a plan now, but it was all a matter of timing.

The creature threw back its head and with great ferocity, its deadly strike shot out directly for Dendroba again; it was exactly what the general was hoping for.

At the last moment, Dendroba spun away, barely dodging the creature's fast attack. This time, he swung Snow White's sword with all his might down through the creature's exposed neck. The blade cut deep with a loud snickering sound and into the tender flesh just behind the armored head. The monster let out a terrible wail as brackish red blood spurted out from the mortal wound. With fierce intensity, he quickly brought Snow White's sword down again in a vorpal strike. This time he cut completely through the doomed creature's neck. The blade sparked as it struck stone with great force with a loud "Snak!"

The creature's body reeled backwards and collapsed in a heap upon the floor of the great hall. Its long neck flailing wildly as a gush of warm blood splattered around the room from the headless beast.

Suddenly, there came a sound that General Dendroba had never heard before. It was the sound of exalted applause. "Callooh! Callay!" Servants and staff emerged from behind pillars and rubble piles, from under smashed tables and from balconies, and they all cheered and chortled in joy for the general. It was an unfamiliar feeling for the former commander of Cendrillon's army. As he realized they cheered for him, for saving their lives, a rare smile crossed his tired and blood splattered face. General White and the others spilled from the hallway door and rushed over to Dendroba.

"Nice work!" the prince cheered. As Dendroba kicked the severed head of the beast, it tumbled down to the floor with a heavy, dull thud and rolled onto its side. Its large dead eyes were glassy and stared vacantly outward and its huge mouth hung slack in its final dying breath. Then Dendroba carefully navigated his way down the tall pile of rock and wood beams.

"What was that monster?" Rapunzel asked, her face showing her repulsion at the grotesque decapitated head.

Snow White knew enough. She did not know what the creature was exactly, but she knew where it came from.

"It's a warning shot," General White explained. "Whatever it is, it came from Wonderland. Isn't that right, General Dendroba—this thing is from Wonderland?"

Dendroba heard murmurs of confusion and uncertainty ripple through the crowd. He spoke—not to Snow White, but to the frightened people around them.

"There is a war coming. An army means to destroy us. It was a fight that Cendrillon had started, but we must now finish," General Dendroba proclaimed loudly to the room. He grabbed the creature's severed head and lifted it up by its fleshy antennae.

"We, all of us, must be ready to deal with this," he said. "Queen Cendrillon is no longer in power." At that last statement, a few cheers erupted from the crowd of castle workers. More came into the room, curious about the dead creature and booming voice. "We must work together, not as a simple servant or soldier, but in a united capacity to survive," Dendroba offered in his deep voice. "This is only the beginning." He hefted the creature's head, one-handed, into the air above his head. "Tonight I set aside my old ways as the queen's enforcer. My hope is that you will trust me and work with me."

The castle staff had known of Dendroba for many years and were still leery of him. General White sensed this in the crowd and stepped forth. Everyone could hear the murmurs of recognition of the resistance leader.

Snow White stood next to Dendroba and spoke. "For those who do not know me, I am General Snow White, leader of the resistance movement against Queen Cendrillon. I stand here today as evidence that Cendrillon has fallen and the resistance has won."

Now the hall erupted with deafening cheers. Snow White waited for the cheering to subside before she continued.

"I stand here in support of General Dendroba's claims. We have set aside our years of conflict because now we are all faced with a common enemy." Snow White reached out to hold General Dendroba's right hand. There was a moment's hesitation from Dendroba, a knee jerk reaction after all, for his entire life he was not used to having his right hand touched. For the first time, Phyllo Dendroba felt the warm, soft skin of another with his right hand. Snow White then firmly clasped his hand, and they raised their arms together in unison. "Today, we must all join the fight against these invaders...as ONE!"

General White spoke over the erupting cheers. "It is also true that some may recognize me as the Princess Snow Marchen. I left the castle at a young age and I am glad to see many familiar faces among the crowd."

The crowd murmured their reaction in a collective gasp. "But there is something that you should all know, as well. Our Prince Phillip still lives, and he has returned home to lead his people to victory!"

Then the prince stepped up on the rubble and stood next to Snow White and General Dendroba. The castle servants erupted in thunderous applause for their prince.

"Together, not as servant and soldier," the prince shouted, echoing what

Dendroba had said, "but as a people united, we will overcome and we shall all be free!"

* * *

Patience sat next to Hamelin as he lay unconscious in the empty hallway. She could hear the crowds cheer, but she did not share in their enthusiasm.

"Please don't die, Hamelin. You are the closest thing to family I have left now," she pleaded through her tears. She leaned her head down to make sure he was still breathing. Then she noticed the black wolf, Elizabeth, slowly limping over towards them. The wolf looked at Patience, and then carefully settled next to Hamelin's body.

"You'll protect him won't you, Elizabeth?" Patience asked the wolf. "Because he saved you from that cage. Hamelin saved me once, too," she said. "And he saved the glass slippers."

Then Patience recalled what the Fae Gaia had told her. Fairy magic can heal the living. "Maybe it can heal Hamelin!" she said aloud. Patience looked at the wolf. "Stay with him, Elizabeth. I'll go get the Fairy God-mother."

Patience raced down the hallway with renewed hope. Nearly tripping up the stairs, she ducked into the servants' passages and quickly came out of a small door into the queen's room—the same door her mother had used to save her from the Maldame.

"Fae Gaia!" the girl called out into the room. There was no answer. "Fae Gaia, are you here?" The Fae Gaia was not in the room. Patience's hope sank. Then she heard a voice behind her.

"You are looking for the fairy, young one?" the White Rabbit asked. A rabbit hole, dark and silent lay open on the floor behind him.

"Yes. She was here before. I need her help," Patience replied but then she turned and saw it was the White Rabbit. "You are the rabbit from the dungeon," Patience recalled with sudden excitement. "Were you able to convince your queen to stop the war? Is that why you've come back?" He smelled of burnt wood and smoke, and his fur was dirty and matted.

"Uh, yes—in fact. I'm so glad I found you in time!" replied the rabbit with slight hesitation. "I need your help this time, Patience. The fairy is with my queen," he told her. "My queen has said that for her to call off Wonderland's invasion, which would save the lives of many here, including your friends I'm sure, that she

304

would not speak with a fairy or a general, but rather she would hear it from a child of the realm." The rabbit looked at Patience, trying to gauge if his lies were convincing enough. Satisfied that they were, he continued.

"There was only one child I could think of who would be brave enough. And the fairy suggested the same as me. I was honored that she sent me to find you. But we must hurry back, or we will be late. All you have to do is get in the hole."

Patience, who had looked willing to help, suddenly seemed unsure. "I don't know, Mister Rabbit. I want to help, but maybe we should talk to General White. Maybe if the Fae Gaia were—"

"Nonsense. There is nothing to be worried about. If you do this, you'll be a hero, and my queen can grant you any wish you want. All you have to do is go in the hole. It's easy."

"Can your queen bring people back to life?" Patience asked with interest, though still not entirely convinced, as the rabbit was sounding more and more urgent with his request.

"Of course! Wonderland's magic is powerful. But we must hurry back." The White Rabbit looked at his pocket watch. "We won't want to be late. Now, if you'll just step into the hole." This had been so much easier with Alice, the rabbit recalled, rolling his eyes at the memory.

Patience stepped tentatively toward the rabbit hole, still unsure, but her sheer curiosity to look down it made her move even closer. "I don't think I want to go in there," she said finally, her instincts telling her that something was not right.

With a desperate growl, Rabbit grabbed Patience by the arm. "I'm going to be late! Get in the hole!" he ordered angrily.

Patience let out a surprised shriek as the rabbit forcefully grabbed her. She reacted instantly and quickly twisted her arm out of the rabbit's grasp. "No!" she yelled, and pushed the rabbit away from her.

The White Rabbit stumbled, his metal prosthetic foot causing him to clumsily fall backward even more, and with a mixture of surprise and anger on his face, the rabbit fell backward down into his hole, which closed quickly and was gone.

CHAPTER 25
GOLDENHAIR

Goldenhair buried her face into the fur of her bear Nikko as she had done hundreds of times before. This time was different, for it was to be the last time.

She reached around and solemnly hugged the dead bear tightly around its limp neck, taking in the fur's earthy, musky smell. She pressed her face against Nikko's soft cheek and there she placed one final kiss. The bear's fur was wet from Goldenhair's tears as she pulled away, softly whispering in the language that only she, Nikko, and the forest understood. Then she stepped back from the bear, wiping her tear stained face with her forearm. She reached for the torch she had shoved upright into the ground and threw it onto the funeral pyre she had carefully constructed for her bear. Her best friend. Her protector.

The pyre was built near where the great bear had fallen, the clearing on Hubbard's Ridge where the prince and the others had been captured. The fire and smoke began to roll upwards into the night sky. The other two bears sat nearby. Their ursine heads hung low in sadness as they grieved the loss of one of their own. In the forest behind them, every manner of forest creature stood quietly. Hundreds of birds from robins and crows, to falcons and hawks filled the tree branches around them. Foxes and rabbits, deer and wolves stood together, putting aside their roles as predator and prey for a brief moment to pay respects to their chosen champion in her time of sorrow. It seemed like every animal of the forest was there.

Goldenhair took little notice of them as she watched the barrel shaped silhouette of her bear give in to the flames. Orange sparks followed the smoke into the night taking their place in the heavens, taking her bear into the heavens. The two other bears gave low, mournful growls.

Goldenhair had only distant memories of her childhood before the tragedy—the blackened, charred remains of wooden beams from a house in the woods. Standing in the ashen footprint of a room, she could still see the three beds—her father's, then the bed of her mother, and nearby, a small bed that had been hers. Goldenhair remembered crying, trying to wake her mother, calling out "Mommy!" She remembered standing there for what seemed liked hours, crying and calling for her mother and father, hoping each time she called for them, that her parents would wake up and everything would be okay. She remembered being too afraid to pull back the burned blanket covering her mother.

That was when she first saw the bears, approaching curiously, almost submissively. She was not scared. Then she heard a soft voice that did not come from the bears, but seemed to come from the very forest itself.

"Do not cry child, we will take care of you."

Now Goldenhair heard that same voice again.

"Do not cry child." The voice sounded eternally sweet, just as she had heard it as a child. Then, appearing before her was another figure, feminine and beautiful with sylvan features both ancient and young. The figure seemed to glow with the warm light of fireflies. Beneath her pale skin, a delicate pattern like the spidery veins of the most delicate leaf traced along her slender arms and thin body; similar to the mysterious patterns that also traced along Goldenhair's skin. The figure's long, dark brown hair, draped down below her waist and fell about her with the subtle pattern of wood grain, but was constantly moving as if blown by the wind. However, there was no wind, and yet there was the lightest sound of leaves shifting in a breeze. When she walked, one could hear the rustling of leaves like she was stepping along a path on an autumn's day. Then, as she reached out her hand to comfort Goldenhair, there was the most subtle creaking, as that of a tree, with each movement. When the Dryad spoke again, she spoke fluidly in the strange language to which Goldenhair was quite accustomed.

"We are all saddened by your loss."

"Mother Dryad," Goldenhair replied, speaking the same unusual language, "I am honored by your presence. You should not stray too far from the trees."

"Every tree in the forest mourns with you. You are our child. We have raised you as our own, though you are not like us. In return, you have been our guardian, our translator, and our voice in the world into which we dare not venture. Our gratitude is eternal to you. Your loss is just as much our own."

"Thank you, Mother Dryad," she said with reverent respect.

"He was a good *Bahr*. He was daylight. He was our victory and he loved you very much from that first day. We are here to be with you in your time of need."

Goldenhair took a long thoughtful look at the burning pyre. "I will miss him." Then with another thought, she spoke again, her tone more resolute and focused.

"Mother Dryad, there is a war coming to this land. My friends will need help."

"The Pines in the mountains speak upon the winds of strangers among them. Mavor Goldenhair, the dryads will not interfere in these matters. Our people will not leave the trees. Unless there is another way, we cannot help you."

"This will be a time of not only my need, Mother Dryad, but also the need of the land. I have never asked the dryads for their direct involvement, and I will not now. I know of your wishes to remain hidden. You have trusted me to protect the forests. But this time, I fear I will need more help if our land is to survive."

"We are here for you, Goldenhair. What help can we give you?"

"I will need an army."

CHAPTER 26
THE CHESHIRE CAT

It had not taken more than a few hours for the Bloodthorns to begin to ensnare the Maldame, they had snagged on her dress and caught in her hair; the Maldame pulled them gingerly away. In the beginning, she resisted the urge to struggle against the briar, but the snagging began to happen with more frequency. Soon, she had a scratch on her arm and her sleeve was caught against the briar. Now the Maldame was entangled fully around her arms and legs, a Bloodthorn twig dug painfully into the wound on her cheek from Rapunzel's cut; the painful briar ran up her face and dug into her eye. Blood and tears ran silently down her skin. Prickly, stabbing pain seemed all about her body; flinching away from the pain only added pain from somewhere else. The Maldame wondered if she would even last to see the sunrise.

Then she heard a voice.

"How are you getting on?" the voice asked. "It seems I have found you in quite the entanglement. You are the one that captured the White Rabbit, and took his foot, yes?"

Appearing from within the Bloodthorns next to the Maldame was a large incorporeal cat with a wicked grin. "And you know the location of the Looking Glass?"

"Yes," the Maldame whispered in pain.

"Excellent," replied the Cheshire Cat as he drifted about. "Then you and I have some chatting to do. I'll do most of the talking; please don't get up on my behalf."

"Bluh-Bluh-Bloodthorns." She spoke very little so as to not move too much. Still, the harsh pain on her cheek made her wince.

"Oh, these?" The cat said as it circled the Maldame. "They do not bother me in the least." He waved his ethereal paw back and forth, and the deadly briar passed through without issue.

"My name is Cheshire, and I like your gumption," he said with a flash in his eyes and a devilish grin. "It's not easy to take down the White Rabbit. I see leadership and a take charge attitude. I see someone with intelligence who isn't afraid to take risks. My colleague, the White Rabbit, wants to put another inexperienced child on the throne to rule my land. I want a new direction for Wonderland. We don't change rulers very often, and I do not want the same ol' same ol'. It's time to put a better person on the throne."

Cheshire drifted through the briar, finding a comfortable spot to rest near the entrapped Maldame. "I think you have proven yourself qualified for the position. So, I'm here to offer you an opportunity of a lifetime, which by the looks of it, will not be for much longer if you don't agree to my terms. I can save you from these Bloodthorns. I can make you the new queen of Wonderland. All I desire is the grace of the throne on matters of interest to me, and to finally put the White Rabbit in checkmate, so to speak. He's had his chance. All you have to do is say yes."

"Yes," the Maldame said without hesitation.

* * *

A dull, pinkish-grey dawn was just growing in the east, and a stillness of frost covered the field. It was a crisp, cold morning. A white, wispy mist hovered over the ground like a blanket. The barn fire had raged well into the night, but now as the sky lightened, the barn was nothing more than blackened earth and charred timbers. The stinging smell of burnt wood rose with the smoldering white smoke from the ash.

Concealed by some nearby brush, a rabbit hole silently opened up a short distance from the remains of the barn. Rabbit stumbled through the hole, the same hole he was going to bring Patience through that led back to the Looking Glass. He had arrived alone, however. Immediately, Rabbit heard voices and quickly ducked down unseen. Looking about he was stunned to see the Cheshire Cat talking with another figure he immediately recognized.

"—you would become the Red Queen," Cheshire was explaining to the Maldame, "and supreme ruler of Wonderland and of this realm, after Alice has conquered it. She will do all the work and you will reap the benefits without lifting a finger. In return I, of course, would get the Red Queen's grace on matters of interest, as I said before."

"Traitor! That back-stabbing, grinning bastard!" the rabbit hissed to himself furiously. "How dare he bring her to be the Red Queen!" It was all he could do to stay put and try to learn how far this treachery went before he jumped out to challenge someone as powerful as the Cheshire Cat. His ears twitching in anger, Rabbit strained to hear more.

"This is not Wonderland, Cheshire," the Maldame said as the rabbit hole closed behind them.

"No, Maldame, but this is where our Looking Glass is."

"Right where Gothel had said it would be." She said her thought aloud. The Maldame laughed—irony at its most rewarding. Here was the Looking Glass after all of Cendrillon's failed efforts, the evil stepmother thought to herself. All the power of Wonderland was about to be handed to her, a few scant hours after she had been sentenced to a slow death in exile. The Looking Glass stood there innocently reflecting the morning light brightly amidst the black and burnt remains.

"From here we will enter Wonderland. If you are interested in what we have discussed, that is."

"I accept your offer, Cheshire. There would have been no way for me to escape from the Bloodthorns if not for your arrival. For that, I hold a measure of gratitude to you. Truly, your magic is more extraordinary than I ever imagined."

"Step through to your new home, Maldame, I mean...my Red Queen," Cheshire grinned as he gestured his paw towards the Looking Glass. The Maldame cautiously stepped through the frame, from the kingdom of Marchenton into Wonderland. The Cheshire Cat followed, his body and a newly-grown tail fading out as it neared the mirror's face.

As the White Rabbit approached the Looking Glass, intent on confronting them on the other side, he scanned the debris quickly looking for any remains of Jack's body—a charred bone, a skull, anything. With a quick glance about the ground, the White Rabbit did not see anything to indicate a body had burned in the fire.

311

"Damn," he cursed under his breath; his thoughts raced. He stood betrayed, his own selfish plans undermined by the Cheshire Cat. Without his own favored candidate to take the Wonderland throne, Rabbit would lose any measure of royal influence; possibly he would even be imprisoned or killed by this new queen. Indeed, should they complete the coronation, the Maldame would become the new queen. But the coronation could only be complete once the previous queen was killed. It had been planned that Rabbit was to take Alice down during this invasion. For Cheshire to succeed in his plan, Alice would still need to be killed. The White Rabbit had to stop the Cheshire Cat from putting the Maldame on the throne. So it seemed he now had to keep Alice alive. But how? Then the White Rabbit realized he had an unknowing accomplice in his plan.

With his keen eyesight, he noticed footprints in the dirt and ash, footprints that were not his own, nor were they that of the woman he saw. They were a man's boot prints. Rabbit instantly knew that they were Jack's. He knelt down to study them; they were several hours old, and they led directly to the mirror, as well. Jack had survived the fire and escaped through the Looking Glass.

Jack would try to save Alice, Rabbit guessed, by stopping the Cheshire's Red Queen from taking the throne. If that happened, Rabbit would have more time for his plan to kill Alice and take control himself. Or, he surmised Jack would most likely be killed trying to stop the Red Queen's ascension. Either outcome was fine with the White Rabbit. He would return to Queen Alice's side, for now.

ABOUT ROY MAURITSEN

It was bound to happen, with pictures being worth what they are in words, that a successful creative artist would eventually entertain the idea of writing a novel. Roy's interests were somewhat atypical as a child. Aside from art and science, there were books and movies—science fiction and fantasy themed—and also role-playing games like Dungeons & Dragons, and a love of fairy tales that started at an early age with a dusty, 1941 hardcover edition of *Alice's Adventures in Wonderland*. Exploring every creative avenue available to him, Roy took every art class he could in school, and also any writing class, especially creative writing. Roy has received several awards in recognition of his artwork. But for this artist-turned-writer, the saying "a picture is worth a thousand words" wasn't enough this time. There was a story to be told, and it demanded to be written. This fairy tale epic fantasy adventure is also the inspiration for *Shards*, a concept album that Roy collaborated on and the fourth studio release by the band Gene Pool Zombie.

Roy has also somehow managed to have a successful career as a digital artist and graphic designer, and also designing book covers and TV commercials. When he's not trying to figure out how that happened, he enjoys photography, volleyball, SCUBA diving, and traveling. But most of the time, he works on 3D artwork, writing short stories for upcoming anthologies, and working on the follow up to *Shards of the Glass Slipper*. Roy lives on Long Island, New York, with his wife, Caren, and their dog, a Newfoundland mix named Coda.

CPSIA information can be obtained at www.ICGtesting.com
Printed in the USA
LVOW040931270712

291611LV00002B/46/P